The Life I Left Behind

ALSO BY COLETTE McBETH

The Precious Thing

The Life
I Left
Behind

COLETTE McBETH

MINOTAUR BOOKS
NEW YORK

THE LIFE I LEFT BEHIND. Copyright © 2015 by Colette McBeth. All rights reserved. Printed in the United States of America. For information, address St. Martin's Press, 175 Fifth Avenue, New York, N.Y. 10010.

www.minotaurbooks.com

Designed by Anna Gorovoy

Library of Congress Cataloging-in-Publication Data:

McBeth, Colette.
    The life I left behind / Colette McBeth.—First U.S. edition.
        p.cm.
    ISBN 978-1-250-04121-0 (hardcover)
    ISBN 978-1-250-04122-7 (e-book)
  1. Women detectives—Fiction.   2. Murder—Investigation—Fiction.
3. Future life—Fiction.   I. Title.
    PR6113.B48L54 2015
    823'.92—dc23

                                                    2014034048

Minotaur books may be purchased for educational, business, or promotional use. For information on bulk purchases, please contact the Macmillan Corporate and Premium Sales Department at 1-800-221-7945, extension 5442, or write to specialmarkets@macmillan.com.

Originally published in Great Britain in January 2015 by Headline Publishing Group, an Hachette UK Company.

First U.S. Edition: February 2015

10   9   8   7   6   5   4   3   2   1

The Life
I Left
Behind

Prologue

The first thing he notices is the cold. When he comes in from the garden he's always greeted by a hot blast at the door, like running into a band of warm cotton wool. Except today there's no cotton wool. This is his first disappointment. Outside. Inside. If there is a change in temperature between the two it's so minuscule it doesn't register. It's certainly not enough to thaw his fingers, which are the pink of raw meat. He inhales. Has he missed lunch? The kitchen clock tells him he has. It's gone three. What he fancies is some of his mum's chicken soup, with a hunk of that bread they baked together yesterday. He'd spread butter on it so thick he'd see teeth marks when he bites into it. Or a crispy pancake. He's fond of those too but he doesn't fancy his chances. "If you eat that rubbish you won't grow tall like your dad," she says, to which he always gives the same reply: "Fine by me," because really, he'd rather not be anything like his dad.

As it is, he can't smell anything. Not even cheese on toast bubbling under the grill. Don't tell me it's sandwiches, he thinks, clocking up his second disappointment. He's been out in the field all morning building a den with Christopher and Jamie from the house on the other side of the lane. They used a discarded wooden panel propped up against the ash tree, three old cushions from the shed and a sheet of tarpaulin he found in the back garden. A sandwich hardly seems adequate reward.

The silence strikes him as odd too. Plain weird. It's never quiet.

Not like this. Most of the time there's only two of them but they make a lot of noise. There's always a record playing on the turntable. His mum's a Doors fan, which is why he knows all the words to "Riders on the Storm," but she's partial to a bit of Abba too, a good old shimmy to "Waterloo" when the mood takes her. He likes that, the way she shakes her head down and lets her long blond hair fall about her face. Sometimes she'll relent, allow him to play "Pump Up the Volume" or Rick Astley, but only if he promises to duet with her afterward: Stevie Wonder's "I Just Called to Say I Love You." He pretends it's a chore, tut-tuts and hangs his head to one side like he's seen teenagers do, but secretly he loves it, the way they close their eyes, roll their heads about and pretend to call each other on imaginary phones. Afterward she'll try to scoop him up, surprised that she can't, because he's ten now and he's been too big to lift for years. So instead she just gives him those tickly kisses on his neck. She smells of Parma violets, which have been his favorite sweets for as long as he can remember.

He wanders into the kitchen. It's a big space with a cooker, cupboards and an unnecessarily large table at one end and a living room with a green velvet sofa and matching armchair off it. This used to be his grandmother's cottage and she had umpteen kids, which is why everything is bigger than it needs to be for just him and his mum and his dad when he graces them with his presence. Now they only come here for holidays. Opposite the sofa is a massive fire. Not one of those gas ones with fake coals plonked in the grate either. This is a real one with proper logs that snap and spit as if they're alive, and flames that cast dancing shadows across the room. Sometimes, for supper, he toasts bread on it, stabbing a slice with the big barbecue fork and waving it as close to the flames as the heat allows. He keeps it there until he feels his own face toasting and then eats it with butter, washes it down with a glass of milk.

He'd love to warm his hands on the fire now but he can see it is dead. Not even the faintest hiss or pop can be heard. One charred log sits in the grate, frosted with gray and white. "Mum!" he shouts. "I'm starving. What's for lunch?" His gaze comes to rest on the table, where he sees a glass of milk and a ham sandwich. What a letdown. Ham is only his fifth favorite sandwich but hunger doesn't allow him to be fussy. He sits at the table. He used to be able to swing his legs from the chair but they've grown too long now. "Where did my baby go?" she asks sometimes, like it's a mystery she's never managed to solve. He wolfs the sandwich down without even washing his hands and is about to take the last bite when he notices her shoes across the room poking out from the gap between the sofa and armchair. She can't have gone far if her shoes are here. It's only when he looks again that he thinks it's a bit odd that each foot points to the ceiling, like the Wicked Witch of the East when Dorothy's house fell on top of her. Only her shoes were red and shiny and his mum's are brown leather.

He goes to investigate. When there are only a few steps separating them he sees the shoes are still attached to legs. Jeans that have a rip at the knee. The jeans lead up to a stomach, clothed in a red-and-white-striped top. Around the neck is a chain. It's a gold chain with a little bird in a cage. This brings a smile to his face. She's never taken it off, not since he bought it for her birthday last year. "As long as I wear it, you'll be next to me," she told him. It's his mum's face. Her eyes are closed, although not completely, which makes him think she might be playing a trick and is ready to jump up and say "BOO!" She's like that, either joking or crying. Never a happy medium, his dad says, but he couldn't care less what his dad says. He prefers it when it's just the two of them. Joking or crying.

He stands over her, deciding against shouting "MUM!" because he thinks she's asleep and there's nothing worse than waking up with a start. Besides, she looks so peaceful, like when he creeps into her bed at night and sees her face warm and soft with dreams. He just wants to watch her for a while. When his legs begin to ache from standing, he crouches down next to her and takes her hand. She always has cold hands and feet but they're extra cold now, like ice pops from the freezer. He gives her a little shake but she doesn't open her eyes.

It's at this point it occurs to him she might be dead. He's ten years old after all, not stupid. And they have talked about this, about death. Just last night when they were saying their prayers together, blessing Granny Julia and Uncle Billy in heaven, she told him that they were watching down on them. *Just because we can't see them doesn't mean they're not next to us.* She ruffled his hair and kissed his cheek and held him really tight and said, "Sometimes people get tired, they need to rest. That's when they die. So you shouldn't be afraid of it or be sad. Even if you miss a person, they will always be with you."

He runs a muddy finger down her cheek. It looks and feels like the dough they made bread with yesterday. The red of her lips is faded, like a strawberry mivvi when he's sucked all the juice out of it.

He contemplates running to ask Mrs. Docherty across the road to come over but she has five kids and is always hassled. "What is it now?" she says with her angry face, which is actually the only face he's ever seen her wear.

So he stays put. He doesn't want to leave his mum. *Don't be scared.* He repeats her words out loud until he believes them. *Don't be scared.* What is there to be scared of? It's just the two of them. He feels the delicate links of the chain around her neck. As long as she's wearing it she won't forget him, wherever she's gone. This gives him comfort. He likes the idea of straddling two worlds: the world of green velvet sofas and ham sandwiches and another one he can't see. It makes him feel like he has special powers.

Outside, the light shrinks. It's late October, the nights are rolling in. Darkness grows in the room, shrouding it in a veil of blue and gray. He goes to fetch his He-Man duvet from his bed. He's too old for He-Man now, that's why it's in the cottage. He spreads it out, to cover his mum, and then he lies down, wraps his arms around her and closes his eyes. He sleeps until he is woken by his father's screams the next day.

Part One

One

have the dog to thank. If it wasn't for him I might still be there and none of this would have happened. That may sound strange given that the place teems with life. But it's a hurried life that doesn't veer off its chosen track: cyclists in streaks of neon, joggers chasing personal bests, harried parents tailing their offspring. Not a chance they would have spotted me twenty or so meters away, hidden in dense woodland. I was easy to miss, which was the point after all.

"It's immaterial now." This is the echo of my mum's voice from years back. She wasn't a fan of my hypothetical musings.

"You should have been here five minutes ago, I could have been kidnapped," I'd say when she rocked up to Brownies five minutes late.

"Well you weren't, were you?"

"But I could have been."

"Why do you always think the worst?" she'd ask, as if the worst could never happen.

Sunday, September 15, 2013, a shade after seven o'clock in the morning. It was a fine morning, one to snap in a picture and post on your Facebook page if you did that kind of thing, which Jim Tierney didn't. Mist rose in columns from the ground. The vast sky was tinged red. He gazed out across the park, studiously ignoring the early thrum of traffic. He liked to think that he had the world to himself in these early hours, walking through a wilderness, albeit one at the edge of the city within striking distance of a café and a cooked breakfast.

Sure, it's a bugger dragging yourself out of bed, but here's your reward, Jim boy.

By rights the dog, a red setter, should have been on a lead because it was rutting season and deer can feel threatened by dogs. I know this courtesy of a Year Six project when my class went on a field trip to Richmond Park and a park ranger told us how the large males roar and clash antlers to attract as many females as possible and we laughed at the thought of them having a shag and then laughed even more when Peter Kelly fell over and landed in a pile of deer shit. Our teacher Mr. Connolly marched us all back to school and said we were a disgrace and he would never take us anywhere ever again.

He would be surprised that I retained that fact seventeen years after the event.

So I know that from September to October dogs should either be walked outside the park or kept on a lead but I'm also thankful that Jim Tierney disregarded the rules that morning. It wasn't a blatant disregard, more of a lapse that came with the territory. At sixty-seven and having been retired for three years, the weeks and months all seemed to roll into one. As far as Jim was concerned it could still have been July. Added to that he was long-sighted and couldn't read the signs that would have alerted him to his misdemeanor. Wellington was free to roam.

Jim was well aware that Wellington was a ridiculous name for a dog.

It wasn't even his dog. His daughter left it behind when she decamped to Seattle with the family last summer. "Keep you company," she said, as if it was adequate compensation for not seeing his grandkids once a week. "That," he has told his wife more than once, "was a bum deal." To everyone he pretended the dog was "a royal pain in the arse," but he loved these walks, the purpose they gave him, and he'd grown fond of Wellington, even if there were too many syllables in its name for a man with a heart condition to pronounce repeatedly.

"WELL-ING-TON, come back here."

He was off.

"Daft dog."

It had been hard at first when Jim first took him out. The dog was lithe, too fast for him, but over time they had found their rhythm. Wellington would run ahead and then run back to Jim, who would chuck him a stick or a ball in reward.

Not today.

He was streaking ahead, his shape shrinking in the distance.

"WELL-ING-TON!" Jim shouted again, but the exertion left him breathless. He used the stick to beat his way through the long grass. Ahead he could just about see the dog, running in the direction of the park's huge iron gates. He needed to quicken his pace to stop him but he was aware of the familiar whistle of his chest.

Wellington had gone from sight now, disappeared through the gates that opened and closed at first light and dusk.

Wait till I get a hold of that dog.

Jim headed down the hill, grateful for the unusually light traffic outside the park. Wellington was daft enough to run into the road, he didn't doubt it.

When he was through the gate himself, he heard the familiar bark. Turning to his right, to the strip of common land, he saw him further down the muddy path, running into the bushes and then back out again. Thanks to an overnight downpour mud oozed and squelched underfoot as he slid along toward the dog. His hand was raised in readiness: *give it a whack, put it back on the lead.* In the event he did neither. When he reached it he simply looked and saw. Wellington's barking faded out, or at least it did for Jim, whose world stilled. He stood, hands hanging by his sides, because he had lost all power to move them. His instinct was to turn away, as if he was looking at something he had no business seeing, but his eyes remained there, transfixed. He felt the sky dip and turn, like he himself was being spun around. The context: that was what he was struggling with. He was only taking the dog for a walk and the day was too fresh and young and the sky too bright for this to happen. No, he thought managing to pull his eyes away. This has no place here.

He waited, counted to ten to allow the scene enough time to disappear. The dog started barking again.

Jim looked once more.

"Sweet Mary mother of Christ."

Minutes elapsed until he remembered there was something he needed to do. Only then did he call the police.

Two

Sunday lunch. She's been preparing it all morning, longer if you include the time spent choosing a recipe, ordering the ingredients, setting the table, selecting a wine that will complement the beef. Cooking, she knows, can take as much time as you have available, which is why she has come to like it. Time is not something Mel Pieterson is short of.

Yet the ticking clock is a source of irritation today. It is five minutes to one. She has prepared the food to be ready at one o'clock and there is no sign of her guests. By one fifteen the beef will be either overcooked or cold. Neither thought is pleasing to her. She knows all about timing and measuring to the exact milligram. She follows recipes to the letter and it has produced results. Three years ago the preparation of fish fingers would have tested her culinary expertise. She hasn't come all this way without learning that precision is everything.

"Smells good," Sam says, emerging through the door carrying the heat of the shower with him. His hair is still wet, the outline of his muscles visible beneath his blue T-shirt. For a beat it surfaces and she feels it as strong as ever: the reflex to pull him close, feel him tight against her. She's always pleasantly surprised in these instances that her muscles are still capable of spontaneity even if her mind is not.

She turns to the clock.

"It's not like Patrick to be late," she says. Patrick is habitually early, can't abide tardiness. This she remembers from their years flat-sharing. If she turned up half an hour after she'd said she'd be home, he'd be on the phone, inquiring as to her whereabouts, the same if they'd arranged to meet. He'd be texting after five minutes, saying "Where are you?" It was reassuring to have someone looking out for you in London, good to know you'd be missed if something ever happened. Not that it made that much difference in the end. She stops herself at this juncture, recognizes that this is a negative thought and works on isolating it before it sprouts and colonizes her mind completely. She knows the drill: *close it down, think of something else.* In this case the something else is the gravy, which she now gives her full attention, adding flour slowly, carefully, to ensure lumps don't form. She has an irrational fear of lumps. As a child she remembers the globules of brown matter that would appear in her potatoes when her mother had been cooking. "Just pick them off," she'd say, as if you could then go on to enjoy your meal with them congealing on the side of the plate. She stirs the gravy and, satisfied to feel it thicken to the right consistency, turns off the gas.

"Has he called to say he'll be late?" she asks Sam, who is leafing through the Sunday papers. They have the *Times* and the *Observer* delivered each week. He reads the sport, news and business sections, she reads the magazines, property and travel. A perfect division of tastes, she likes to think.

"He isn't late."

"But has he called to say he will be?"

"I haven't checked my phone."

"Can you check your phone?"

"If he's late I will," he says, turning a page in the news section.

Melody checks the calendar in case she has mixed up the time or even the date, although a mistake on her part is not a probable explanation. Her weeks are expertly planned, so too the weekends. Sam often goes kite-surfing at Camber, so the weekends he spends at home are always accounted for with lunches and dinners and lately wedding planning. There are no spare slots because if she sees a gap she will fill it. Sure enough, PATRICK LUNCH 1 P.M. is written in red capitals.

The intercom buzzes. She expels air in relief. Sam crosses the room to answer it. "What time do you call this? You're almost late," he barks into it before letting out a deep belly laugh. She smiles, rises above the sarcasm. Sam presses the button that opens the gates to the driveway and goes to meet their guests at the door.

Patrick has brought a friend with him, a woman he met at work. There has been a long run of these friends, who they no longer refer to as girlfriends because the term implies a longevity they rarely manage to achieve.

She hears their voices in the hallway, the introduction. "This is Lottie," Patrick says, followed by the sound of kisses. There's laughter too, footsteps coming toward her. "God, that smell is making me hungry," Patrick says as he enters the kitchen. "Sorry we're almost late . . . the traffic was awful on the M25, bumper to bumper." He kisses her on both cheeks. "You look lovely as usual."

"Don't try to charm your way out of it," she says, digging him in the ribs. He looks tired, overworked no doubt. Probably could have done without the drive out here, she thinks, but it's not his style to be flaky. In all the years she's known him he's let her down once and that was because he had eaten a dodgy curry the night before and had to remain within two meters of a toilet, preferably his own.

"I know by now I can never charm you," he laughs, and turning to his friend he puts his arm around her. "This is Lottie. I've told her all about your cooking."

Melody raises an eyebrow. "I wish you hadn't."

"Don't worry," he says turning to Lottie, "she's moved on from her experimental phase."

"That's one way of describing it," Sam says, handing them both a glass of Prosecco.

"There is a very average takeaway down the road where you might find yourself if you're not careful," Melody says. "Lovely to meet you, Lottie." She thinks about offering her hand but stops herself, knowing that it's too formal. The kissing comes naturally to most people but Melody has a keen sense of personal space, protects it fiercely and struggles with the forced intimacy of kissing someone she's only just met. She does it all the same.

At a guess she'd say Lottie is a few years younger than herself, rake thin, wearing skinny jeans and thong sandals and a light cotton top with little birds on it. Mel glances at her own outfit, a wrap dress Sam bought her a few years back, and feels frumpy by comparison. Lottie has blond hair which she wears down and pushes back from her face in movements that make the silver bracelets on her wrist jangle together.

Melody instructs them all to sit and puts the beef on the table, roast potatoes, roasted parsnips and carrots and onions and greens, which, she notes with consternation, are only just passable, having spent too long in the steamer.

Patrick and Sam engage in surfing talk, a new board that Patrick has bought and the waves in Cornwall when he was there a few weeks ago. From there the conversation segues into football before descending into the juvenile banter of friends who support different teams.

Sometimes, on these occasions when Patrick has brought a guest and Melody feels the chat run away from her, she allows her mind to shuttle back. Honor takes the place of Patrick's friend at the table. The years that have come between them fold in on themselves so that there is no gulf to bridge. The air rings with laughter and easy, uncomplicated chat. Melody is someone else entirely. This Melody is quick-witted, thinks nothing of opening her mouth and letting words flow out, words that entertain and draw laughter from her audience. Her voice is loud, as if it wants to be heard. She is the kind of woman who reaches for the wine bottle and tops herself up without so much as a thought to the consequences. Melody watches her old self perform this feat like she would a gymnast back-flipping across a mat. She has no idea how she does it.

"Do we have any horseradish?" Sam asks.

Melody blinks, refocuses. "Uh, yes, I think we do." She pushes her chair out and goes to retrieve it from the back of the fridge. She should speak to Lottie because Patrick and Sam are not. They are talking about the usual stuff that entertains them. What should she say? She considers this for a moment before remembering that Patrick knows her from the hospital where he works as a doctor. "What is it you do?" she asks, sitting down at the table again. When did she start to sound like her mother?

"I'm a pharmacist, been there for a couple of years. To be honest, I'm slightly bored now, it's not the most exciting job. What do you do?"

It's obvious to her now that this wasn't the ideal line of questioning to initiate. Mel does lots of things, never stops. She could produce the lists she writes every morning to prove it, the training programs to keep fit, the cooking, the planning of the wedding, but she knows this is not the answer to the question Lottie is asking. She does lots of jobs but she doesn't have a job.

"Nothing," she says and watches Lottie turn to her, beef suspended on the fork a few centimeters from her mouth, waiting for some kind of qualification, an explanation at the very least. When she realizes none is forthcoming, she returns to the beef with renewed enthusiasm.

"I am stuffed," Patrick says, pushing his chair away from the table as if his belly is so full he needs extra room to accommodate it.

"There's panna cotta for pudding," she says.

"The woman has no mercy," Patrick laughs. "I think I need a breather first if you don't mind."

"The football is just about to start," Sam says, heading into the living room.

Lottie starts clearing the plates from the table. She's gathering the serving dishes. "Leave that, I'll do it," Mel insists.

Lottie ignores her, carries on. "It'll be twice as quick this way."

Why does everyone assume saving time is a good thing?

"Your house is amazing, by the way."

"Thanks. You get a bit more for your money the further out you go," although she's minded to correct herself: *Sam got more for his money.*

"You could fit my whole flat into your kitchen."

It is true that space is not something they lack. The building was a derelict barn before Sam bought it at auction and then enlisted an architect who advised knocking it down and getting planning permission to build a new house.

She wouldn't have been brave enough to take on a project of this scale. But Sam had never been short of confidence. He even picked up the language quickly, started talking about creating something with architectural integrity and structural authenticity. She wondered where he had learned his spiel until they watched *Grand Designs* together one night and heard the presenter Kevin McCloud say the same thing. "He's obviously been listening to you," she said, although from the vacant look on Sam's face she wasn't convinced he got the joke.

The neighbors' antipathy didn't worry him either. Not even when they got up a petition against the proposed build. Mel wasn't keen on the thought of moving into hostile territory, so it fell to him to reassure her. "They'll come around," he said.

They have never come around. Not in the physical or literal sense.

"Space isn't everything," Melody tells Lottie as she wipes the endless white worktops clean. Sometimes when the sun streams through the vast glass wall at the back of the kitchen it blinds her, and in the height of summer the room gets unbearably hot. Even with the windows open.

She raised this with the architect when she saw the plans. There was too much glass. Couldn't they have a smaller, cosier area?

He gave her the strangest look, as if she had said something unintelligible. "You can never have too much light or space," he told her.

Turns out you can.

She keeps these misgivings to herself, reminds herself she should be grateful to live in a place like this. Sam would take any criticism personally because he clings to the belief that he has poured his soul into this place, that his personality is reflected in its beams and glass panels and vaulted ceilings and the paperless toilet that washes and blow-dries your arse.

Secretly she doesn't like the idea of this being a mirror of Sam's soul. No matter how hard she looks, she can't find any soul in it.

"Patrick tells me you're getting married soon." They've almost finished the tidying now. Melody puts a tablet in the dishwasher, presses start and hears the satisfying sound of the water sloshing around inside.

"Three months."

"Do you still have loads to do or are you on top of it all?" Lottie asks, sitting down at the table. Melody sighs. The fact that she is routinely asked this question by guests makes her feel indescribably lonely. She'd like to show them her wedding mood boards, the magazine cuttings. Hasn't she already blind tasted eight brands of champagne, selected red and white wine, desert wine too? Then there's the timetable she has drawn up to make sure no detail is overlooked.

"There are a few finishing touches, flowers, favors, that kind of thing to choose, but mostly it's done."

"And the dress . . . or am I not allowed to ask?"

"No, ask away. It's simple, really, more like an evening gown in champagne silk."

"Sounds gorgeous. You'll look amazing in it I'm sure."

Melody thinks of the final fitting she had last week. The way her mother started to cry when she tried it on. How she herself started to cry too, which sent Anastasia the designer into a meltdown in case the tears stained the dress.

"Come here," her mother said when she'd stepped out of the dress. In a rare show of affection she had hugged Mel.

She didn't have the heart to tell her mother she was crying because it was so tight she couldn't breathe.

Mel opens another bottle of wine. "Thanks," she says to Lottie. "Sam will love you for getting him out of tidying up," she adds, to make it look like there is a fair division of labor in the household. They go back to the living room. It is the ad break, half-time in the football. Mel is topping up Patrick's glass when Lottie nudges his elbow and sends wine splashing on to the floor.

Mel follows Lottie's finger, which is pointed at the TV screen. It's a local news bulletin, showing shots of woodland and Richmond Park and people in white forensic suits padding about inside police tape.

"I was in Richmond Park with the dog the other day," Lottie says with a theatrical shiver.

The headline tickering at the bottom of the picture: *Body found outside London park.*

"Mel!" Sam shouts. She looks down and sees she has carried on pouring the wine long after Patrick removed his glass. Dark red liquid pools at her feet. "I'll get a cloth," he says, springing from the sofa.

She stands motionless as heat rushes to her cheeks. She can feel Lottie's eyes on her now and tries to ignore them. "You OK, Mel?" Patrick asks gently. She nods and waits for Sam to come to her rescue. He returns with kitchen roll and begins soaking up the wine around her. She watches the red seep into the white paper. When he's finished, he hands her a glass, kisses her.

"This might come in handy next time, honey." Until now she's only been drinking water, but she takes the glass from him, fills it to the brim with wine and takes a gulp.

"I wonder what happened," Lottie says as Sam and Patrick settle back down to watch the second half. Perhaps they haven't heard her, Mel thinks, because they don't acknowledge her question. Mel could tell Lottie what might have happened. She could run her through a list of possibilities, each one worse than the next. Out of everyone in the room she is best placed to do this. It's her chosen subject, starter for ten. But you need air to speak and her lungs have had it sucked out of them. She moves across the room and sits on the sofa next to the window. Occasionally Patrick looks over and gives her a reassuring smile but Sam and Lottie pay her no attention, which is good, because the last thing she wants is them noting the involuntary twitch in her upper lip, the way she holds her smile, rictus-like, for too long because she knows if she lets it go her whole face will crumple. She needs to focus, so she focuses on Lottie, who is sitting closest to her, next to Patrick. The pendant she's wearing catches her eye. Is it a butterfly or a dragonfly? From this angle she can't be sure. It is silver and rises and falls gently with each breath she takes. *Why do I feel like there is no air when everyone else is breathing easy?*

A voice in her head runs through the drill like a sergeant major. SHUT IT DOWN, FOCUS ON SOMETHING ELSE, THINK POSITIVE. CATCH IT, DON'T LET IT TAKE HOLD.

Too late, she thinks. It's already snaking through her brain.

Time is a healer, so the saying goes.

The first time someone said it to her was at a support group, one she had gone to at her mother's behest. It was January, a church hall not far from her parents' house in Dorset, drafty and musty-smelling. Richard, the counselor, sat underneath a giant cross that looked like it was growing out of his head. Everyone was issued with tea or coffee. Mel had opted for tea, which actually tasted like coffee on account of the flask not being cleaned properly from the previous use. She couldn't drink it but cradled it in her hands to heat her fingers instead. Around her, a circle of woolly jumpers, nervous eyes staring out from blank faces. As far as she knew she wasn't officially depressed, but a few more sessions like this and she'd definitely be on her way.

"Time is a healer," the woman had said. She was called Tabitha or Tamara, one or the other. Not much older than Mel probably. Threads of gray ran through her hair. She fiddled with the cuff of her cardigan as she spoke.

"Honestly, it gets easier." This was directed at another man later in the session whose daughter had died in a car crash, as if time alone could erase all his pain. All he had to do was sit and wait for it to pass. Mel thought about getting up to leave, feigning a headache, but there was always someone talking and she didn't want to appear rude so she sat it out, vowing never again to listen to her mother. When Richard the counselor declared, "That's all for this week," Mel sprang from her seat. She was ready to flee when Tamara or Tabitha appeared at her shoulder.

"I know what it's like, really, but you'll feel better after these sessions," she said, nodding her head in tiny, furious movements. Her body was straight like a rod, so taut Mel was tempted to touch it to see if it would ting like a violin string. Bright eyes, shiny and manic, pinned her down.

Mel felt like she was being inducted into a cult, half expected the other woman to tell her she'd found God. She stared and waited for Mel to agree.

Just say you believe me.

If we all believe the lie we can make it come true.

"I've got to go," Mel said, guilt filling her. She couldn't give her what she wanted. She couldn't say *yes I believe you, I'm sure it does get easier.* Because she didn't believe Tabitha then and she doesn't believe her now.

Three

What can you achieve in seven minutes? You could boil the kettle and make a cup of tea, although if you wanted to do it properly, in a pot and let it brew, you'd barely have enough time to take a sip. You could go to the loo, but again, depending on the nature of your visit, you might be stretching it. You could run a mile, if you were one of those professional fit types in Richmond Park training for a marathon or a triathlon. But a man of sixty-seven with a minor heart complaint and a chest that whistled like a harmonica when he moved at pace wasn't going to get very far in seven minutes. Besides, the operator had told him to stay where he was and wait for the police to arrive. So that was what he did. Jim Tierney stood guard over my dead, semi-naked body.

Maybe if he had run away, even just a few hundred meters, put distance between himself and his discovery, he might have found life easier in the weeks that ensued. He wouldn't have had time to commit every aspect of the scene before him, the strange, gothic beauty of it, to memory. His subconscious would not have had those images to reproduce in lurid, chemical-fueled dreams. The blond hair, damp from moisture, curled in rat's tails, the dark mottling of my skin. Eyes half open, half closed, as if I was sleeping and could be revived. My left hand, open to the sky, cradling a gold chain.

By the time the sirens streamed through the air and the footsteps approached Jim, he felt like they had no place here, these intruders. He was my protector now, a sentry standing guard over me, waiting for someone to breathe life back into my airways and jump-start my stalled heart.

"We'll take over now," the DS said gently so as not to startle him.

Jim struggled with the lack of name. It was too impersonal to call me a body; such an empty word. He couldn't bring himself to say it. *Have a bit of respect,* he wanted to tell the young police officer; *so, Mr. Tierney, what time did you find the body?* The word suggested something that was unconnected to anything or anyone. A separate entity. Whereas Jim knew the threads of my life would have been woven into the fabric of my mother's, my father's, my friends." Nobody existed alone. He had a daughter so he knew this. The word was an insult to the life that had gone before, the fiery love my family would have felt for me. He would have killed for his daughter Emma. Her death would have killed him. And when he thought of me he couldn't get the image of her out of his mind. What he would have given to emerge from the police station and hold her tight in his arms, sink his face into her red curls and feel the beat of her heart. But since she had pissed off to Seattle, he had to settle for a phone call and a cuddle from his wife and the dog.

So Jim had a way of coping, if you could call it coping. He referred to me as "my girl" until he learned my name was Eve, after which he referred to me as "my Eve." In the weeks after my discovery he hoovered up every detail he could find about me and pumped them through my dead body to bring me back to life. His wife Joan thought it distasteful, this obsession, though she was careful not to mention her concern to him. When you've lived with someone for forty-four years you learn when to keep your mouth shut. If she had raised the subject Jim would have told her straight: he needed to see me as a person, to connect me to a loving family. At the very least he owed me this. And when he was satisfied I had one, he sent my mother a letter using the police as an intermediary. Among other things he told her:

I am still trying to make sense of it as I'm sure you must be. Please know that she will never be just a victim to me. I am a father too, you see, so when I think of her I try to understand what she was like as a person. I'm sure she was a fine daughter. I didn't want to leave her there but after I found her she was not alone, the police came quickly. In truth I don't think I ever will leave her. I don't think she will leave me.

He deliberated over telling her I looked peaceful before deciding against it. Jim was a man who favored the truth at all times, even when lying would have been kinder.

My fictional death, the one I often conjured up in childhood, was like an extension of life, only draped in an invisible cloak. I thought I would move around the same world, touch objects, lift a jug of milk and drop it to the floor, *smash*, just to get a reaction. I would be all-seeing, all-knowing. I would haunt Rebecca Smart for calling me a bitch every day of Year Nine, and at night (because time would still be defined) I would slip into my own bed and wait for my mum to kiss me. There would be benefits to dying, I figured, like finding my dad in heaven listening to Dire Straits and playing an air guitar.

My real death was nothing like that. There was the pain that accompanied it and there was this, the thing it had transmuted into. This pain had teeth and venomous glands. It fed off everything I saw and everything I knew had ended. When I thought of a kiss it told me there would be no more coming my way. Not a single one. Ever. It reminded me of all the hugs I had ducked as a kid, the times I squirmed away from displays of affection, and then it whipped me with the knowledge that I couldn't go back and retrieve them. It showed me an image of my mum, so clear I could almost smell her hairspray and her Miss Dior perfume, only to laugh at me because I couldn't hold her at the very time she needed me most, in those moments when every atom of her being craved me. And occasionally it mentioned the word *tomorrow*, just to taunt me with the certainty I used to attach to it. Then it left me begging for just one moment more to say all those words that didn't seem important when tomorrow still existed.

You might think it's a privilege to watch life carry on when you are gone. Trust me, it is a penance. And one, I noticed, that not everyone has to suffer. Some people who died after me passed straight through without the briefest look back whereas I found myself stuck in this limbo. It's not easy to explain how this made me feel—try thinking of the frustration of watching a diner who arrives after you but gets served first, and multiply it by a trillion and you might come close. I kept asking the question: why me? Why the fuck do I have to go through this? Can't I move on and find my dad, wherever he is, because he's not here? But if God was out there, I got the sense he wasn't amenable to answering my questions. I wondered if I should soften my tone, edit out the swearing. I thought maybe I had done something really bad in life and I was paying the price.

Not long after I died (days, weeks—I couldn't say), I was submerged in a particularly dark moment, filled with indignation about my lot, when a girl who was already here when I arrived tried to explain.

"You're here because you're not done."

"What is that supposed to mean?" I asked.

"It means there's something you've got to do."

"And how do I know what that is?"

"You just do, apparently," she said.

I thanked her because it was the polite thing to do but a few specifics wouldn't have gone amiss. This summed up my new world; nebulous and short on detail. If there was a job to do, ideally I would have got on with it then moved on. That was always my way. But no, that wasn't how it worked in this place. They laughed at my impatience. "It's not like the world you've left," said an older guy called Jonas. The dreamy, ethereal quality to his voice told me he'd been here a while. "You can't push it, Eve. It will happen when it happens."

Some of the time we talked about the lives we'd had, and there was a game we played, listing our regrets and the things we were grateful for. Mostly it wasn't the profound stuff you might expect.

People started out saying things like *I'd have allowed myself to be happier,* but when you pinned them down, you found it was the mundane preoccupations they would change. I wouldn't, for instance, have agonized for weeks over which shade of white to paint the walls in my flat. White is white, people. Remember this next time you're in B&Q and you'll thank me. I would have had more sex, been less abstemious, more open to the idea of a one-night stand or a shag on a first date. No one, according to my unscientific straw poll, wishes they'd had less fun, with the exception of a young Danish man who had so much of the wrong kind of chemical fun it killed him.

My biggest regrets were tied to the work I'd been doing in the six months before I was killed. I would be sure to make it more conclusive, tie up the loose ends. And yes, right at the top of my list I would have liked to tell everyone who killed me. But the thing you need to understand about death is that it's sneaky, it doesn't give you time to prepare, it springs up unannounced. Everyone thinks they'll get a warning. And maybe you will, if you're lucky. But talking to people here I can say that mostly this isn't the case. You are there and then you are not. It's that brutal.

On my last morning I threw on an old T-shirt, ate half a bowl of crunchy nut cornflakes and left my flat in Shepherd's Bush around nine, bursting with purpose. The morning was a glorious, sun-drenched affair, the sort that has you falling in love with life all over again. It even made Shepherd's Bush look inviting, which was as close to a miracle as you ever got this side of London.

I drove the five miles out to Richmond Park and found a space as near to Ham Gate as I could. It was still a ten-minute walk at my pace, at least fifteen minutes for your average strolling person. I was happy for it. The sky sat low, blue and clear apart from a few wispy clouds. To my right I could make out a herd of deer camouflaged in the brown summer grass. I worked up a sweat as I walked, acknowledging passers-by with a smile and a "Morning," the way I always did. If you don't do this already it's something I'd urge you to try. Even in London, a town not known for the friendliness of its inhabitants, you'd be amazed how many people return these greetings with a wave or a smile of their own, and you know, happiness breeds happiness. When I reached the gate, I slipped out of the park and on to the stretch of common land that abuts the perimeter wall. Then I went in search of a distinctive pink flower in the very place my body would be found eight days later.

I was grateful for that walk, for the stunning mental picture it granted me of my last morning. But it came at the cost of a proper coffee, a shower and a decent breakfast. Had I known what was coming, that my remaining life could be counted in hours and minutes and not years and decades, I would have treated myself to smoked salmon or eggs Benedict and a glass of champagne, a mug of coffee too. At the very least I would have made a sandwich with the bacon in the fridge that was skirting close to its sell-by date. I would most certainly have showered and lathered myself in the posh oil I thought was too posh to use. But as I said, there was no advance warning system. No dark portent in the clouds above my flat, no tinkling music that filled me with dread. It was warm. The sun trickled through me. I was buzzing with life.

I can't say this with any precision, but at a rough guess it was fifteen hours later that my life ended. Which just goes to show how rapidly your luck can change. What did I expect from those last few minutes? A montage of my best bits, like the ones they show on *The X Factor* when the contestants are being booted out? No, it wasn't the life I had lived that flashed before me, but the one I was going to have. The life I had taken for granted, in which my ambitions were acted out. *Always tomorrow.* I had all the time in the world until suddenly I didn't have any time left at all.

In the end my regret boiled down to one last living thought:

I didn't have the chance to warn her.

Four

Detective Inspector Victoria Rutter would have preferred it if the discovery of the body had been made the following day, a day when she was actually on duty and not about to take her two children aged nine and seven to see *Despicable Me 2* at the cinema. This was a treat promised in compensation for the cancelation of a Legoland visit at the end of August. Now she has two cancelations to make up for. Sometimes she hates dog walkers and their discoveries.

Her knowledge of the patch of common that lies adjacent to Richmond Park is limited to scenes of crime photographs from years back, but the park itself she knows well. It's where they come sledging in the winter, a minute's buzz downhill, then another ten to climb to the top again. Soggy gloves, cold red fingers but still the kids insist *one more time*. In a few more years, she thinks, they won't want to do anything with her, not sledging or the cinema. And here she is on a Sunday.

She sucks in air through her teeth. No matter how many times she sees one, the sight of a dead body always gets her.

A uniformed officer spots her and makes his way over. He explains that the body was found by a dog walker early this morning. "Think it might have been here a few days or more, judging by the look of it."

She turns again to study it, get the basics clear in her head: white, age at a guess late twenties though it's hard to tell, no obvious signs of flesh wounds. She notes the position in which it was found, placed as opposed to dumped, she deduces.

She stares at the body. Black knickers and a Nike *Just Do It* T-shirt, the irony of which is not lost on her.

"So who are you then?" she asks. She likes talking to the victims. Sometimes she gets more sense from them than from her team. She's learned to do it quietly, though, when no one is within earshot. Once when she was a detective constable her inspector overheard her at a murder scene. "Not answering, are they?" he laughed. She didn't tell him that they often did.

She waits, gathers her thoughts. This is the easy part, this small window of time when a body is just a body without a name or family to grieve for it. She's seen colleagues fazed by the enormity of the task ahead, or get frustrated down the line when the investigation isn't opening any doors. They want it all too easy, she always thinks. In her experience things are rarely easy. Easy makes her nervous.

She likes doors that don't open. If she's honest, it's where she gets her kicks, the reason she's out in Richmond Park when she could be eating sweet salted popcorn with her kids and watching *Despicable Me 2*.

"DI Rutter?"

A man in a white suit introduces himself as Dr. James Dukas, a Home Office pathologist.

"Any idea how she died?" she asks.

"It's likely she was strangled. This was in her hand when we found her. Probably placed there."

He passes her a plastic evidence bag. She takes it from him and holds it up in the light so she can examine its contents.

"It's a gold chain."

"I can see that," she says.

Back at the station, briefing the inquiry team, she casts her eyes around the room to take stock. How many of them were here six years ago? DS Cook certainly was. He's been around the station longer than she's been in the force. He reminds her of one of the Superking cigarettes he smokes. Thin, pale and yellow at the tips. Then there's DS Ravindra and DC Rollings. The rest she will excuse for not knowing. But not those three. You don't forget a detail like that.

They're all listening, seated, standing, perched on desks. She shows them the video of the scene, recounts what she knows, which isn't much. After assigning one officer to search through the missing persons database, she asks another to get the CCTV on the perimeter roads around Richmond Park. She waits for a groan, smiles inwardly when she doesn't get one. He must be learning. No one needs to tell her it's a shitty job; she's done it plenty of times herself. Scouring endless hours of poor-quality footage until your eyes go blurry. Once she watched twenty-three hours of it when a man's body had been found dumped in a bin in Leyton. She couldn't focus by the end, has the glasses to prove it. But she found the killer's car and they got a conviction. Nothing is ever easy.

When she's done, she takes a swig of Coke from the can beside her and brings up a slide on the projector.

"This item of jewelry was found in her hand."

She turns to study it but this is purely for show. She knew what it looked like even before Dr. Dukas described it to her. Tapping her pen against the side of the projector, she waits for a reaction.

"Isn't that the same one as . . ?"

She exhales. "Thank you, DS Ravindra. Let's bring him in for questioning."

Five

The news report could only have lasted a minute, maybe less, but it has embedded itself in Mel's mind. She's drunk too much red wine. There's a looseness in her head, a lack of self-control. She's too woozy to marshal her thoughts with the usual rigor.

As a rule she doesn't watch the news. There was a time when she couldn't pull herself away from the natural disasters, the armed robberies, the plane crashes. Every day there was a fresh tragedy that warranted her attention. Sam humored her, passing it off as a phase, an indulgence she would soon tire of, until one day he came home to find her watching a news report about the invasion of the harlequin ladybird. Seeing her puffy eyes, the dirty tears streaking her face, he took the remote control from her hand and switched the TV on to standby. Not that it mattered. She had watched it countless times by then already, committed all the relevant facts to memory. She could recite them now, if anyone asked, with the same confidence that she used to reel off the names of Henry VIII's wives and their fates: *divorced, beheaded, died, divorced, beheaded, survived.*

The harlequin ladybird arrived in Britain in the summer of 2004 and shares an ecological niche with the native two-spot ladybird, whose numbers have fallen by thirty percent since its arrival. It is advancing at one hundred kilometers a year.

She pictured the scene taking place all over Britain: the two-spot being squeezed out, consumed by its voracious alien cousin. Hiding away until it disappeared completely. This she found unbearably sad. But when she tried to explain it to Sam, it sounded ridiculous. She could see that it sounded ridiculous from the look on his face. He spent all day fixing broken people in the hospital, real emergencies next to which the plight of the ladybirds seemed insignificant.

"This has to stop, Mel."

She wished it *could* stop, all of it. She wished she could make it stop: the famines, the child neglect, global warming; and while she was at it, she wished she could save the native ladybird.

He looked at her, narrowing his eyes. Sometimes she wondered if he had the power to read her thoughts because he seemed to have a knack of knowing what she was thinking. "I mean you have to stop doing this to yourself. If these things," he nodded in the direction of the TV, "if they bother you, then why not stop reading the papers and watching the news?"

"You mean pretend none of this is happening?"

"I mean why worry about all those things you can't change. I understand where it's coming from—no one can blame you for seeing the worst in everything—but it's not helping, is it? Just try it, Mel, for me and you," he said.

She stared at his face; she couldn't understand why she hadn't seen it before. He had reached his limit, eyes lightless, begging. He couldn't do it any more, and because she loved him and couldn't bear to experience loss all over again, and because her worst fear was to be alone, she smiled and squeezed his hand and said, "OK, I'll try."

Life is about forward momentum. This is never more obvious than when you are stuck and can't move on. You walk into the room just as everyone else is leaving. You are listening to the conversation but you're not part of it. You have people's sympathy for a while, weeks, months, but it's progress they want to see. You are stuck in a groove, an endless tortuous loop, and it's boring for everyone else on their forward trajectories. So sure, take your time to mope around, lick your wounds, cry when you need to, but after that, learn how to survive.

You are a survivor. No more ladybirds. Your time is over. Slam.

This was what Sam was telling her.

The news had to go. It nearly killed her for the first few weeks. She needed to pin her dark mood on something, give it a reason for being, and without the horror stories she only had her own story. She switched to lifestyle shows, bought women's magazines to amuse herself, and she saw that the survivor stories were everywhere.

My boyfriend told me I was worthless but look at me now, under a photo of a woman dripping in bling outside a mansion.

I was sacked from my job as a waitress but now I'm a millionaire businesswoman.

Chronic asthma nearly killed me but last year I climbed Everest.

The overcoming was everywhere.

In turn she ditched the lifestyle shows and the magazines because they made her feel worse about herself. But on the nights when Sam worked late, which was pretty much every night, she still had acres of time. She needed distraction, constant, endless distraction. *Keep busy, don't stop.* Her birthday came around and her mother presented her with Delia's *How to Cook.* Not her first attempt at domestication by any means; there had been frequent missions over the years, all without result. So the book was more of a long-standing joke. "I won't cancel the restaurant just yet," her mum had laughed.

This time was different.

She applied herself to Delia and found that not only could she boil an egg, she could also make caramel, cook a joint of beef and make the gravy too. Once she had mastered these basics, she graduated to other chefs: Nigel Slater, Thomasina Miers, Marcus Wareing. She bought a different book every week. She thought Ottolenghi was a dream because each recipe demanded at least ten ingredients, most of which she had never heard of, and sourcing them took more time than the cooking.

They had never eaten so well.

This created another problem. She had never been thin, but the endless cooking and tasting had grown her waistline beyond what she considered reasonable. She enlisted the help of a personal trainer recommended by a friend of Sam's.

With Erin by her side she went out running. They took a route along the riverside and through the town, where the shops sold women's raincoats and polka-dot wellies and kitchen utensils in pastel pales: pink colanders and blue jugs. There was a time when she would have laughed at the tweeness of it all, the lack of edge, and worried that by association she was losing hers. But now she just ran without thinking. After the first few weeks, when she'd fight the urge to stop and catch her breath every five minutes, she found her legs were able to carry her along their route with ease, and when Erin suggested they turn back it was Mel who said just five more minutes. Now that she had started she didn't want to stop.

She even, after months of excuses, accepted an invitation to drink coffee with Siobhan (whose husband worked with Sam and who had therefore decided they should be new best friends). Or rather she invited her over, along with her friends. They arrived in a jam of buggies, toddlers waddling around sticky-fingering the walls. It was all fine. She could do it. Even the conversation, which was centered on the consistency of poo and what they wouldn't eat and how many times they woke up in the middle of the night, was bearable. And when the women turned to Mel to ask her what she would do, because obviously they hadn't noticed that she did not actually have a child of her own, she said, "I'd sell them on eBay." Cue outraged laughter. They thought she was hilarious.

And maybe she was. Skittering through life unburdened, so light she swore she was flying. Who was to say she couldn't be a survivor, looking forward, never behind?

It's already late when Lottie and Patrick leave, Lottie with an optimistic, "Hope to see you again." Mel likes her; it looks like Patrick does too, but she's learned that counts for nothing. If she wanted to be deep about it, she'd say he's searching for something he can't find, but she's got enough deep going on tonight as it is.

"Let's go to bed," Sam says, his arm around her, kissing her head.

Upstairs she brushes her teeth and watches in the mirror as he undresses, flinging his clothes on to the chair next to their bed. He starts his nightly ritual of stretching, arms out to his sides and then above his head. His movements are precise, practiced, like an athlete.

Did he see it too? He must have, he was sitting right in front of the television, but he hasn't even thrown a look her way. *Are you OK? Do you want to talk?* Maybe she imagined it. No. She would go along with this theory were it not for Lottie. She can distinctly recall Lottie mentioning it. Perhaps she has done such a good job at hiding it for the last four years that it's been completely wiped from their history.

Once Sam has completed his stretches he peels back the covers and flicks through his phone. Is he tweeting? What can he be saying? *Just done five star jumps and a hamstring stretch, now getting into bed.* Is that more than a hundred and forty characters?

Perhaps he's waiting for her to raise the subject. She'd like to. The words are massing in her throat. She'd like to dislodge them but she doesn't want to be accused of going back over old ground. At times it's difficult to remember what is considered a healthy topic of conversation and what is deemed to be destructive.

She gargles with mouthwash, spits it out and goes into the bedroom.

"Lottie seems nice," he says.

"Uh huh," she says.

"You didn't like her?" He rolls on to his side and plays with her hair. "She reminded me of someone," he laughs and kisses her neck.

"Stop it. She was lovely."

"What is it then?"

Tears spring up in her eyes. She shakes her head.

"Oh Mel," he says, sitting up to look at her. "Really?"

She blinks in acknowledgment.

"I thought you had missed it."

"It was right there in front of me, how could I have missed it?"

"Darling, it could be anything. It could be a dog walker who had a heart attack and keeled over. You just don't know, so why bother getting all worked up about it? Come on, don't be silly."

She's crying now, can't stop herself. Oh God, she doesn't want to cry in front of him. The last time was a day seven months ago, when it would have been strange if she hadn't cried. If you exclude that one occasion, Sam hadn't seen her cry since the day of the ladybirds. That's not to say she doesn't cry at all, because she does. There is very little in life that she hasn't shed a tear over once in a while. A burned cake (although this is a rare occurrence these days), the way her hair kicks out on one side no matter how much she tries to blow-dry it flat, the way she can never find a pair of trousers to fit her because she is only five foot one. She cries when the sky is so black she can't imagine seeing the sun again. She cries when it's brilliant blue because it makes her feel that she should be doing something to make the most of it but she has no idea what that thing might be. She cries when Sam calls to say he's working late again because of an emergency (it's always an emergency).

"Come on, Mel." He cups her face with one hand and wipes her tears with the other. "It'll be nothing, I promise you."

He's right. She *is* being silly. She can see the glimmer of fear in his eyes too: *don't take us back there.* That's why he doesn't go near the subject. It's a black hole that will suck them right down into its heart.

She remembers what it was like, the feeling that her head was populated by ants. The combined torture of always wanting to run and yet never being able to move. Delving into her mind to dissect her memories, convinced that there must be something, a clue that she had missed that would bring everything into focus.

But she could never find it.

It was Sam who told her: "If you can't make sense of your memories, you have to stop trying."

Once, she read an interview with the climber Aron Ralston, who was trapped down a canyon after a boulder fell on his arm. In order to get out and save himself he had to cut off his arm. That was how she felt. She could move on but only if she left part of herself behind.

What was it he had said? The moment when he severed the last tendon was the most beautiful, euphoric moment of his life.

It was at this point the parallels between their stories ended.

Mel had to lose part of herself to survive but there are days when she would dearly like her back.

"We've got everything to look forward to, the wedding's only a few months away," she hears Sam say. He's still trying to steer her back from the edge.

Mel lays her head on his chest. It's the part of his body she loves the most, the heat and smell of it.

"Sorry . . ." she goes to say but he puts a finger to her lips.

"You don't have to explain, Mel. I get it. You've been amazing, really, you've coped with it all so well. The baby too."

The baby. The reason for her tears seven months ago.

She has to come back from the edge. She can't go there.

She kisses him, bites his lips. She wanted to talk to him; now she wants him to stop. She needs to run as far away from it as possible.

"Would you like me to take your mind off it?"

"I thought you'd never ask," she says, attempting to make her voice sound lighter than she feels.

His hand moves down under the covers, runs from her hip bone through the dip in her stomach and downward. Mel's eyes are closed. She is conjuring a scene, trying to transport herself back there.

They steal time for each other, Melody and Sam. They rob minutes and hours from work and lie to feed their addiction. It's never enough. She has the sense that the hours they share together are simultaneously slowed down and speeded up. They can fill them with so much—talk, sex, eating, drinking, just being close to each other—and yet when it's time to leave she feels she's only just arrived.

Usually, though not always, it's the same hotel, equidistant from her place of work and his. They enter through a small reception with a different extravagant display of flowers every time they come: dahlias, lilies, ornamental cabbages. To get to their preferred room, which is nearly always free, they take the lift up two floors, turn left along the corridor through another set of doors, then follow the hallway to the end. She likes this ritual for the sense of building anticipation, but also because of the distance it puts between them and the world outside. It's the entrance to their parallel universe, where they can be excused anything.

At first these encounters would end with her saying tearfully, "We can't do this again, we mustn't," but they've dropped the act now. Any attempt at delusion seems cheap next to what they have. Which is what exactly? Neither of them has said. If they tried to put it into words, they might talk about falling hard, about having no choice: "I can't help myself," as if there is some force greater than themselves at work, and they are powerless to stop it. They might say that when they are together no one else exists, that they need each other in the same way their bodies need oxygen. Of course they believe this to be true, but it is convenient to couch it in such notions. It allows them to abdicate responsibility for their actions. It also sounds better than admitting they book a hotel by the hour to have a lunchtime fuck.

At the door they kiss. They always do this. It's a tease, an opener. They are on the threshold of consuming each other again. He's still kissing her as he puts the key card in the door and pushes it open. Pushes her inside.

He's so tight against her the heat makes her feel indistinct, like she is melting into him and she doesn't care about anything else. Nothing else matters.

He moves down to kiss her neck and she feels the pressure of his mouth on her skin. She didn't know she had so many nerve endings, millions of them concentrated in that one spot, the way he makes them sing. With a single finger he traces the line down her spine.

She can't stop this, even if she wanted to. And she doesn't want him to stop.

She commits it all to memory to sustain her when he's not here.

Her eyes are closed to provide a canvas on which to play the memory. It's always the hotel room, a younger Sam, a different Mel, the fantasy of anticipation, of wanting him. Who would have known that years later, those lunchtime fucks would still be sustaining her.

"Good night," Sam says. "Nice to know I haven't lost my touch," he laughs.

"Good night," she says.

She waits until she hears his deep, rhythmic breaths before she reaches over to her bedside cabinet and finds a little yellow pill which she takes to obliterate the day.

Wednesday is a typical day for Mel. The calendar shows that her personal trainer Erin, a gangly Australian with a big smile and a mouth packed with white teeth, will arrive at 11.30 A.M., which gives her ample time to track her imminent deliveries. There is a color-coded chopping board set designed to reduce food contamination arriving by DHL today. Although when she checks she notes that this has not even left the depot for dispatch. On the other hand, the new set of pure Egyptian supersoft bath towels in charcoal is due to be delivered around two o'clock, when Erin will be leaving. Perfect timing, she thinks.

"It's bewtiful out there," Erin says with her Aussie lilt when she arrives.

Mel sticks her head around the door and feels the touch of warm air on her face. The sky glares at her. Even though it's mid September, it still feels like summer.

"Shall we stick to the garden today?" Erin suggests. At more than an acre, it's big enough to accommodate Mel's interval training. She agrees. They start by running around the perimeter to warm up.

They chat, or rather Erin does most of the talking to give Mel her twice-weekly update on her boyfriend, or "the actor" as he is known between them with a nod to irony. In all the time Mel has known Erin, his only screen appearance has been as an extra on *Holby City*.

Today Erin has big news. He has a part in a BBC daytime drama, filmed it months ago but it airs this afternoon. Melody has never seen the actor but has collected a detailed picture of him from Erin's descriptions; dark, handsome, louche.

"It's on at one thirty; we could watch it when we finish."

"Deal." Mel would be happy to have Erin stay all day, all week if she offered.

They come to a halt. Melody knows the drill: lunges, squats, star jumps, then she rolls her body on her hips clockwise and anticlockwise. She is loose, ready to go, like a dog itching to get out of the traps.

"All set?" Erin asks. She holds the stopwatch out in front of her. Melody nods.

"Go."

It's the high-intensity interval training Mel likes best. She finds comfort in the repetition. Thirty seconds running nearly full out, then a break of sixty, then again for sixty seconds followed by a break of one minute twenty. She loses herself in the exertion of these short bursts of speed, enjoys the sensation her burning lungs give her. She pushes through it, clearing the yellow pill fog in her head. When she first started training, the lactic acid would build in her legs and drag her down. After five minutes she was unable to move let alone run. Now she barely feels it. She imagines these short bursts of activity pushing oxygen-rich blood through her body, her muscles programmed to use it more efficiently, her stride longer, more confident. Erin has taken to calling her "the machine" because she doesn't want to stop. Ever. It's the only time she is sure she's alive, aware of the forward momentum.

After the running, the sit-ups. Erin holds her legs and Melody springs up and up again, stomach muscles engaging. She never dreamed she could have a body like this, the muscle definition, the six-pack. When Erin tells her she is finished, she lies back on the grass, looks up to the sky, closes her eyes and listens out for her reward: the sound of her pumping heart, the reassurance of it.

Over lunch of carrot and lentil soup, Erin starts talking about a half marathon she thinks Melody should do.

"You're ready for it, honestly, it seems like a waste to do all this training and not compete."

"There'd be too many people around."

"But it would give you a new challenge." Even Erin wants to see progress. *Don't stop moving.* Melody thinks of the Great South Run she did with her dad when she was a teenager, the crowds; you couldn't run for tripping over people. The collective march of feet and people waving and screaming, "On yer go," at the roadside.

"I don't think so." She sees Erin look at her, searching for the thing she can't understand.

At 1:30 they turn the TV on for *Doctors*. The actor, Erin explains, is playing a cancer patient who is refusing treatment and drinking weird concoctions from a quack instead. They settle down with a cup of herbal tea. "His first appearance is three minutes in," Erin tells her. *Doctors* is not the kind of TV Melody watches so she's not familiar with the storylines. There's a shot of the waiting room, assembled patients, and Erin shouts so loudly Melody almost spills her tea: "That's him."

He is not what Melody was expecting. Small, fragile almost. She is thinking of him next to Erin's six-foot frame, the mismatch of them, when she hears her phone ring in the kitchen.

"Sorry," she mouths to Erin.

The name Polly is flashing on the screen of her mobile.

She has only ever known one Polly. Her chest tightens. Ignore it, she thinks. She has no inclination to speak to Polly. Not that it's anything personal. They got on well. Mel relied on her, wouldn't have coped without her, but it's the association she makes when-ever she calls. It's unfortunate.

Maybe she's just calling to see how I am.

This is unlikely. Polly was good at a lot of things but small talk wasn't one of them.

The ringing stops. Relief fills her. Then it starts again.

Is that part of her training too, knowing how I will react when she calls?

"Quick, he's on again, this is the best part," Erin shouts from the living room.

She swipes her finger across the screen to answer the call.

"Melody?" the voice asks for confirmation. No one uses her full name any more. Mel insists on the shortened version.

"Yes."

"It's Polly."

"I know. How are you?"

"I'm good, thanks for asking." There is a pause, both women holding back.

"I thought it would be a good idea if I came round to see you." There is no need for Mel to ask if this is a social call. Not now that she hears her "break it to her gently" tone. She leans against the island and wonders why they don't understand that she doesn't want to know. Anything. It's easier that way.

"I see. Is it important?"

"Nothing is certain, far from it, but the press have already made a few inquiries. We wanted to warn you before it hits the news."

"I don't watch the news."

"Or gets into the papers."

"I don't read them."

"It's important we follow procedures, Melody."

She wants to know but she doesn't.

"What has happened?"

"A body, Melody. We've arrested him."

Six

D ay three and they still didn't know my name. A trawl through the missing persons database brought up a few potential leads but they were quickly discounted. I'd like to think a few of my friends might have pondered my absence on social media, my lack of response to their texts, but I was a sporadic communicator at the best of times so I could hardly blame them for not reporting me missing. *She hasn't tweeted in days, there must be something wrong.*

Had I been killed a year ago, my colleagues on *APPEAL* would have raised the alarm. It was a TV program that investigated miscarriages of justice and I was a senior producer, part of a team that valued my judgment and noticed my presence or lack of it. Only *APPEAL* had been axed in a round of "efficiency savings" last year, its place in the schedule taken by a well-known presenter extolling the virtues of making cushions and candles for your home and urging viewers to rediscover the lost art of cross-stitching. I had views about this. Still do. Police make mistakes, innocent people pay for them, and smelly candles and cross-stitching aren't going to help. But the TV execs think injustice is too worthy, a step up from alfalfa sprouts and mung beans, and what people really want is to learn how to make a personalized doormat in a vintage font. I digress; the point I'm trying to make is that as a result of *APPEAL*'s demise I was a freelancer, a human plug filling gaps in rotas. No one really noticed me even when I was present. When I didn't show

THE LIFE I LEFT BEHIND 43

up, they weren't unduly alarmed, they just struck me off their list for being unreliable.

My mum's attitude to communication was far more energetic than my own. She was not the kind of person to accept prolonged silences from her only daughter. A text would not go unanswered for more than a few hours without a follow-up "You OK?" Likewise a phone call that wasn't returned the same day was eyed with deep suspicion. But the week in question was one in which the normal rules of engagement didn't apply. Her phone lay uncharged in a drawer, two thousand miles away in Greece. She was on holiday, her eighth visit to the islands in as many years, working her way through the whole archipelago (this year Zakynthos could be added to a list that included Crete, Lefkas, Samos, and Kefalonia, which remained her favorite. *It'll take a lot to top that holiday, Eve.* She was prone to these fixations, or "destination loyalty" as she liked to call it, going back to the same country year after year until a calamity ruined it for her. When our run of camping holidays in Scotland ended with the tent being swallowed up in a mudslide dad and I broke open a packet of peanut M&Ms in celebration.

On the Sunday I was found, my mum and Steve, my stepdad, had been on a Turtle Island cruise, returning, salt thick on tanned skin, to toast their last afternoon with umbrella cocktails in one of the harbor bars. The day I died, they were on Xygia Sulfur Beach marveling at the deep turquoise of the water—rumoured to contain special healing properties—while pretending not to notice the stench of rotten eggs rolling off the sulfur springs in a nearby cave.

She would never forgive herself for this, having fun while I died. Her heart was hard-wired to mine, so she thought. How could she not have heard me screaming for help thousands of miles away?

They had arrived at Stansted on the Monday, wearied by the evening flight. I was due to collect them, my mum having furnished me with all the necessary details before they left. She texted just before they took off.

Just boarded! See you soon. Love Mum Xxx

They waited in the cold for me, flimsy holiday clothes pulled tight around them. "She'll be here, Steve, it's not like Eve to let us down," my mum said when after twenty minutes he suggested they get a cab. "She's probably stuck in traffic." They tried my mobile countless times: "Hi, it's Eve, can't take your call right now, leave your number and I'll call you back."

"Eve, it's Mum. Where are you? You said you'd be here."

I did. I'm sorry.

Forty-five minutes passed before she conceded that the cab was a good idea. She sat, head turned away from Steve because she knew he was angry with me for standing them up and with her for making them wait so long.

From the window she watched the airport disappear behind them, headlights and brake lights illuminating the motorway ahead. Quickly the clear waters of Zakynthos, the fine sand and the turtles and cocktails faded to a memory. Unease grew inside her.

Oxygen, carbon and hydrogen were the biggest components in my human body, but after I died I consisted almost entirely of anger, agony and longing. The emotions were so intrinsic, I doubted if I would exist in any form without them. Maybe I was supposed to let go, be filled with forgiveness. Maybe that was what marked us out as lingerers, why we remained there when others moved on. We clung to destructive emotions. But what else was there to cling to when you'd seen what I had seen?

My mother's love for me was fierce, Teflon-coated. Whatever I threw at her—the sulks, the strops, crashing her new car, throwing parties in her pristine house when she was away, even the teenage lies, *no I am not sleeping with him*—resulted in little more than minor abrasions. Underneath there was a layer, as strong and impenetrable as the earth's mantle, that nothing could touch. This was the person I was forced to watch act on her mother's intuition. The person who had always been there for me with soup and hot lemonade, dinners of questionable quality and financial rescue packages when I was broke; the person who had bored her friends senseless with my achievements, and hung photographs detailing my history of embarrassing haircuts on the walls of her home. She had no idea where her intuition would take her. Only I could see the juggernaut careering toward her. And there was nothing I could do. Not a thing. I couldn't shout out to warn her. I couldn't save her. It was going to hit no matter what. With a force that would break her in two. All I could do was watch her shatter on impact. And afterward I didn't even get to hold her, help piece her back together.

When she woke on the Tuesday morning there was a moment, a sliver of time, when her mind was empty; a nanosecond when she was unburdened by worry. In the months and years ahead she'll wish she could stretch out that nanosecond to give her some kind of peace, a break from her head; just for a minute not to be my mother, not to have all the love without a channel for it. People say it is grief that burdens you, but that's not true. It is love. There will be days when it pins her to the bed and suffocates her with its force.

"It's not like her," she said to Steve over breakfast of toast and eggs.

"She forgot most likely. Just you wait, she'll be calling later today all apologetic for leaving us standing there."

What would he know? Mother and daughter, he could never understand.

Who should she call? Kira, my best friend, was away somewhere. The Middle East, or was it Southeast Asia? She always got the two confused. She phoned a few others. Elise said she hadn't heard from me, but then she hadn't tried to contact me either. Nat was her best bet. "I haven't heard from her for over a week," he said. She detected a trace of guilt in his voice. "I'll call a few people to see if they've heard from her. Will you let me know if you get hold of her?" he asked. My mum promised she would. Then she tried ringing my old work number but got through to the switchboard instead.

"Can you tell me if Eve Elliot is at work today?"

"I can try to put you through . . . There is no Eve Elliot listed here."

"She's freelance."

"Well we wouldn't have an extension for her. I suggest you try a mobile," the woman said as if the thought had not occurred to my mum.

She continued through her address book, scouring it for the numbers circled and marked EVE'S FRIEND. Some of them were old landlines, unobtainable mobile numbers. When a Spanish man answered one, she abandoned this particular line of investigation.

Sticking her head around the living room door, she told Steve she was out. "To the supermarket," she said. "I might be a while, there are a few jobs I need to do." He looked up from the sports section of his newspaper. "Right-o," he said. The news section had been discarded on the table.

The traffic was heavy. Twickenham to Shepherd's Bush, you could do it in twenty minutes on a good run but when did you ever get one of those? She listened to the Adele CD that I bought her for Christmas last year. That girl has got some voice, she thought as she always did when she heard her. It relaxed her for a while, warbling along. When it was finished she played it over again. There was only one other CD in the car and she wasn't feeling up to Paul Simon.

When she reached my street she had the notion that it might be best to turn around. Like she did once on a blind date, years ago, got stage fright because she didn't know how she'd manage talking to a stranger for two hours over dinner. That was in the days before mobile phones and texts. She'd imagined him waiting for her inside the restaurant before he finally realized she wasn't coming. Now she wondered what she would say if she found me. What if I was there with a man? Or sick in bed? Or had simply gone to work and forgotten about collecting them last night. My mobile could be lost, damaged. There were all kinds of possible scenarios to explain my absence and lack of communication. I'll just have a quick check and go, she told herself as she turned the key in my lock.

Food smells. Cook some fish, a bit of salmon say, and your house can stink for days even with the best extractor fan on the market (I say this without any proof because my budget never stretched to the best). Put that fish in the bin and tell yourself that you'll empty it tomorrow because tonight you're just going to have one more glass of wine and it is Saturday night and therefore OK to let your standards slip a little. Besides, you are in the middle of watching *Anchorman* for the fifth time. So you forget about the piece of fish you scraped from your plate into the bin; it was only a morsel after all. When the morning comes, you want to get out of the house as quickly as possible because your curiosity demands to be satisfied and you can't wait a moment longer.

You forget about the bin.

My mum smelt it as soon as she opened the door. The leftover fish had sat there rotting for eleven days, along with assorted vegetable peelings and fruit. My domestic hygiene standards had long been a source of disappointment to her, but she knew even I had a limit. The smell, she thought. Eve couldn't live with this.

She walked through the hallway saying my name quietly, as if to herself. The *Anchorman* DVD case was still lying on the sofa where I had left it. Moving on to my bedroom, she stood at the doorway, noted that my bed was made—I might have been slovenly in some areas but I would always make my bed in the mornings; I had even devised a system where I could make it while still lying in it—my favorite orthopedic pillow sitting on top of the duvet. She walked down the hall to the kitchen. She had her arm up, protecting her nose, but the smell cloyed, permeated everything. On the table there was a bowl, the spoon stuck to the side, what was once milk and crunchy nut cornflakes hardened and moulding. A mug next to it, pale liquid with a fuzz of blue floating on the top.

In the sink: water, dark brown, filmed with grease. The whole scene, its cumulative effect, the mess, the smell, the dust, left my mum, who could not let a moment pass without plumping a sagging cushion or banishing a stray crumb, with the impression I had not been here for years. She found herself calculating how long she had spent in Zakynthos (ten days), how long it was since she had been here, seen me in the flesh (was it really three weeks?). Had I not been here all that time? Her natural instinct was to start cleaning immediately but she stopped herself, deciding to leave everything as it was. Something was wrong and she didn't give a bugger what Steve would say, because she was calling the police.

Instinctively she bashed 999 into her phone, pausing just before she pressed dial. Her only other experience with the 999 number had been a few years ago when a group of teenagers in the street were kicking at bins and shouting loudly close to midnight. She had been told that the number was only for real emergencies. Was this a real emergency? She believed I was missing but she had no proof of it. Then again, how do you prove a person is missing? Would they measure the emergency by the number of unanswered calls or the mold growth on teacups? She put the phone down. Call the local police, that was what they told her last time. But she didn't have the number for the local police and her phone was a phone that made calls and didn't do any of those other fancy things like search the Internet that everyone told her was so important now.

She left the flat, locked it, got in the car and set off to find a police station.

The nearest one was Shepherd's Bush, but even if my mum had known where it was, which she didn't, she wouldn't have stopped there, couldn't have stopped there in fact. It's on the Green, which makes it sound leafy and pleasant when really it is a patch of grass surrounded by a traffic-clogged artery. There is nowhere to stop even if you wanted to, and the interweaving lanes of traffic constituted "London driving," which my mother avoided at all costs. She headed in the direction of her Twickenham home.

She passed through Richmond on the way and this she decided was a good place to stop. Parking was easier, and when she'd reported the unanswered calls and the dirty flat and they'd laughed at her for overreacting—maybe not to her face, but afterward when she had gone—she could nip to Waitrose, get the groceries she'd promised Steve she would collect and he would have no idea she had spent the afternoon wasting police time.

There was one person ahead of my mum, a woman wearing a hooded sweatshirt, occasionally raising her voice so it was impossible not to hear her slurred words. In normal circumstances Mum would have been tutting at the rudeness, the lack of manners, whispering to me or Steve, whoever happened to be next to her, "Three sheets to the wind, I'll bet," while making the universal hand movement for drink.

Instead she practiced what she should say. None of it sounded right. "I just know," she could say, but the police were all about evidence so she'd have to do better than that. She was still trying to formulate her words when the drunk woman shuffled away from the desk. "Waste of bloody time," she shouted as she left.

My mum moved to the counter.

"How can I help you?" the receptionist said.

"I can't seem to find my daughter," she said. Immediately she regretted her choice of words, which seemed more appropriate to describe the temporary misplacing of an object such as her keys or purse. She needed to elaborate quickly so she began the story about Zakynthos and the airport and the no-show and the mouldy plates in my flat. The receptionist raised her hand to stop the flow.

"I can take the details from you now."

The woman, who my mum quickly realized was not an actual police officer but a civilian clerk, introduced herself as Gladys and in a gentle lilting accent asked for my name.

"Eve Elliot," my mum said.

Gladys ran through the list of questions. Age—thirty; mobile phone number (for this Mum had to check her own phone). A physical description—how long did Gladys have? She wanted to tell them about the gap in my teeth that she loved and that sometimes made a whistle when I talked, or how my lips were so red that when I was a child people asked her if she had put lipstick on me. *As if.* Or my laugh, which was never hard to draw out; even when I was down and upset it always burst through, a deep and gusty cackle that reminded her of *Carry On* films. She could say my voice always bordered on the loud side of acceptable, that as a child I only had one volume setting. She'd even taken me to have my hearing tested, and sat shamefaced as the doctor told her I was a normal child who simply wanted to be heard. Even as an adult, she'd joke, I didn't need a phone to call her because she could hear me all the way from Shepherd's Bush anyway.

"Blond, shoulder-length hair, five foot four, green eyes."

"When did you last see her?" She thought back and was about to say the night before she went on holiday when she remembered calling me to cancel. "Steve can't find his passport, bloody idiot that he is, I'm having to turn the place upside down."

I was secretly relieved. I'd had a big Saturday night; I had promised myself at least two episodes of *Breaking Bad*. All I wanted to do was pull on my pajamas and settle down.

"Don't worry, I'll see you when you get back," I'd said.

"A week before I went on holiday," she told Gladys. "So three weeks last Friday." She was thinking of the passport, how they'd found it at the bottom of Steve's rucksack at five to midnight. She could have killed him then. She'd like to kill him now.

"What was her state of mind?"

Her state of mind? Were they expecting her to say I was depressed? Was that what they thought? That her daughter had just walked out of her life leaving a half-eaten bowl of cornflakes to congeal and her mother standing waiting at an airport at midnight without so much as a phone call.

"She was happy. She was always happy," she said and realized she had no idea whether this was true or not.

"That's great, Mrs. Rayworth. Would you happen to have a photograph of your daughter?" Gladys asked.

Of course she did. She always had a recent one in her wallet: "In case you forget what I look like," I used to joke.

"Here," she said. She handed her open wallet to Gladys, the photo still encased in the plastic cover.

"Is it all right if I take it out?"

My mum wanted to say no, really she would rather Gladys kept it right where it was. "Just to take a copy. I'll bring it straight back," she said, and she was gone before my mum could protest.

How long did it take to make one photocopy? She'd been sitting there a good twenty minutes, twitching in anticipation every time she heard footsteps. She wanted to leave. My mum had started something she wished she hadn't. Given the option she would rewind and make it all go away. *Just give me my photograph back and I won't bother you again.*

"I've really got to go now," she told the replacement desk clerk, an older man with a bald head that was an angry red color.

"I'm sure she'll be back in a moment."

He was right. Seconds later Gladys appeared through the automatic doors. Where was the photograph? They've lost it, she thought, the photocopier has chewed it up. She knew she should never have parted with it.

It was then that she noticed Gladys was not alone. Another woman, younger and dressed in a creased suit, was by her side. Bobbed brown hair, thick-rimmed glasses, curls licking her face. *Just the way Eve's baby curls used to.*

"Mrs. Rayworth?" the woman said. Rayworth was Steve's name.

"I'm Detective Inspector Victoria Rutter." She offered her hand. My mum's trembled as she held it out. Detective Inspector. It was all wrong. This, whatever it was, hardly merited the involvement of a detective inspector.

"I'm sorry, I'm probably wasting your time. I should go."

"I'd like to talk to you about your daughter, Mrs. Rayworth," said DI Rutter. She'd worried about them laughing at her; now she wanted to hear them laugh. She wished they would laugh her out of the building. "If you could come with me . . ." the DI said, turning back toward the automatic door.

My mum followed, aware of her insides buckling, pain splitting her head. She'd felt like this before, sea sickness on dry land, twenty-nine years ago when she was pregnant with me.

"I can't do it," she'd told my dad. But with every kick and butterfly she felt in her stomach, she knew she could. There was a life blooming inside her.

It happened quickly. Steve appeared at her side though she couldn't remember calling him herself. He held her, not knowing what to say. "It's a mistake, tell me they've got it all wrong," she wanted to scream at him. But all he did was squeeze her hand and say, "Oh love," over and over again.

She had to look. Shook her head at first; it wasn't me, couldn't be, so still there and lifeless. "Ants in your pants," she used to say because of the way I jittered and jiggled as a child, always on the move, never in one place for long. Now, staring at my face, her mind shuttered back. Holding me for the first time, warm, wriggly, red-faced, squashed, the marvel of it. Untouched skin, so soft, she'd never felt softness like it. The smell of newness from my head. Complete, that was how she felt, like she hadn't known there was something missing but now I had arrived it was obvious. "An only one," people remarked as the years went by. But she didn't see how she could love anyone else this much. Occasionally she'd read those stories, the sudden death of a child, and she'd pray to God it wouldn't touch her family. But then she'd look at me, jittering and jiggling and hollering in my big voice, and she'd think, it couldn't, could it? There couldn't be this much life and then none at all?

She touched my face, always warm, now cold, and she didn't understand how so much could be extinguished.

"What can you tell us about Eve?"

DI Rutter chose her words carefully. The parent in her would have liked to give my mum time to assimilate this new reality, but at work she wasn't a parent. She was a police officer leading an investigation. She needed information, traction. Something to go on.

My mum had always been a talker. Her conversations were a form of verbal acrobatics, flitting from one topic to another without so much as a breath. Often she'd discuss more than one subject at once, or veer off at a tangent.

Even now she wasn't short of words. There were too many. She was thinking about the question, the impossibility of it. There was so much to tell, a lifetime of information and anecdotes amassed, now forming an unruly crowd of words that surged against her temples. She needed to find a way to release them, one at a time, in order of importance and priority.

What can you tell us about Eve?

That she doesn't like cheese unless it's melted; that if you give her dinner you might think it odd that she eats all her vegetables first before starting on the meat, right down to the last pea on her plate. That she sleeps with her eyes half open, always has done since she was a baby; that she was the fastest runner in her class over 100 meters but always cheated at the egg and spoon (by holding the egg down with her finger); that she hates large ships, not just to sail on but the look of them, they give her the shivers, though we've never understood why; that when her dad died she'd sneak into my bed every night when I was asleep and when I woke she'd be holding me and I'd pretend to

*tell her off but really she was saving me from drowning. I don't think
I ever thanked her.*

*That I have just seen a body and identified it as my daughter but
really my daughter is nothing like that, so still and empty and silent.
If only you had met her, just once, you would understand that wherever she went she was surrounded by a field of energy, accompanied
by noise and chat and laughter, that you only had to be in her presence to feel revived by the life fizzing out of her.*

She looked at DI Rutter, wondered if she too was a mother, if
she would understand. How could she? No one could make you understand what this was like unless you were here. If they tried to
explain, you wouldn't believe them. There were no words.

"She's a producer. She lived in Shepherd's Bush, alone," she
started, and then more words came out and once she had started
she didn't want to stop, as if the words were her strength, her protection from everything else, because as long as she talked she could
keep me alive.

"Did she have a boyfriend?" DI Rutter asked when my mum
told her I lived alone.

"She did, but they split up in February. There hasn't been anyone since."

DI Rutter nodded. "I want to show you something." She produced
a photograph, handed it to Steve, who held it between himself and
my mum. "Do you recognize this?"

A caged bird on a gold chain.

"No," she said. "I've never seen it before."

Placed in my hand after I died.

She was weary now, bone tired. "Just one last thing. Did you ever
hear her mention a man called David Alden?"

"Never," she said with conviction.

That wasn't strictly true. I had mentioned him once a few months
ago, Sunday evening when she was watching *Downton Abbey*. I
should have known she wasn't listening.

"OK," DI Rutter said. "We'll get someone to take you home."

My mum stepped outside into the night, held up by Steve. The ground beneath her was unsteady. Around her buses streamed past, people spewed out of the station coming home from work. Tomorrow they'd do it all again. Just carry on as if nothing had happened. How could that be?

In the car she rested her head against the cool of the window and watched her breath steam the glass. Was it only last night she was traveling home from the airport wondering where in God's name I had got to? How could so much time have passed in the space of a day? She looked up at the starless sky. She'd never known dark like it.

Seven

Polly doesn't mention his name. *Him* suffices. He is their common denominator, the reason they know each other, although toward the end Mel had to remind herself of this. Polly was being paid to listen to her, so it's possible she was as bored as everyone else with the circular nature of Mel's conversations. She was just too professional to say "Let's move on, shall we, I've heard this one before."

In fairness, no one actually said those exact words, not even a close approximation of them, but it didn't matter. She knew what they were thinking. Their bodies betrayed them, a shoulder turned away, eyes seeking out someone more interesting in the room beyond her. *Not this story again.* Her first therapist said she should talk about it; "Let it all out, Melody, don't bottle it up," as if the talking itself was medicinal and would draw out the pain. So she talked. Sometimes she rarely drew breath, left no pauses or gaps in which anyone else might seize an opportunity to contribute. They were monologues, turning the same story over and over, trying to work it out. Mel could talk all right. She just didn't know how to stop.

And not even once had Polly attempted to maneuver the conversation in a different direction. Mel hoped they were paying her a lot.

In different circumstances she would have liked to see Polly again. She wouldn't be wearing those faded jogging pants for a start. Look at me now! she'd say and show her around the house and listen to her ooh and ah about all the glass: *so light!* And wait for her to squeal when she unveiled the toilet. *I have a toilet that washes and dries your arse; you see, it's true what they say, I am a survivor.*

"You OK?" Mel jumps. She's back in the living room now, startled to hear Erin's voice.

"Yes, sorry, I was miles away."

"You look a bit peaky." Erin gets up from the sofa and turns the TV off with the remote. "You missed his big moment."

"I did?" Mel rewinds events in her head, back beyond the conversation she has just had with Polly to where she was before with Erin. "The actor, shit, did he steal the show?"

"If you call three short scenes, including one where he was unconscious, stealing it, then yes." She laughs. "But it's a start, I guess. I'd better get going. Thanks for lunch." She kisses Mel and shoots her a final look before leaving. "You sure you're all right?"

"Just tired, that's all."

"Finally. She shows she is human."

When did Polly say she was coming round? Was it today or tomorrow? Mel has only just put the phone down but she's struggling to recall the finer details of the conversation. She remembers it in a broad brush stroke that colors everything else. *We're questioning him.* Hopefully it was tomorrow. Today would suggest an urgency, a rapid escalation of events. Mel's worked hard to control events, not have them control her.

It is two o'clock. Four and a half hours until Sam arrives home. She could call him and ask him to come now, but she always has trouble contacting him at work, gets the impression it is a huge hassle to everyone to track him down. *Doesn't she know not to call, is it really that urgent?*

Deciding against it, she opens the Facebook app on her phone. Mel posts her own updates now and again: *ta da, look at this cake I baked!* Or when they have friends round (Patrick mainly) she'll take a few shots—never a selfie—just to show she exists and her timeline isn't void of all activity. But mainly she's a voyeur. Not the type that derives any gratification, sexual or otherwise, from the act of looking, mind you. It's more a form of self-flagellation that leaves her feeling empty and worthless and decidedly odd. Photographs of newborn babies, toddlers taking their first steps, old friends pictured on a night out or a holiday, holding a glass of fizz up to the camera. Happy, smile-inducing moments that are out of Mel's reach. If she was more disciplined she wouldn't look at these at all because they're not the reason she's compelled to check Facebook so frequently. They're a sideshow. It's Honor who Mel is searching for. She likes to refresh her mental image of her, keep it current by noting changes to hairstyle or color. She's driven by a need to know where life is taking her former friend. Is she happy? It would appear she is, if such a thing can be deduced from status updates. Has she had children? No sign of any. She does have friends Mel doesn't recognize but who regularly appear in her photos—the last one taken in Lisbon when a group of five of them were leaning into each other drunkenly outside a bar in the Barrio Alto. *That used to be me.*

Today she notes that Honor hasn't posted anything. For five days, in fact, there's been no word from her. Disappointment solidifies in her stomach. The hurt jags at her skin. It's in these moments when she needs a friend that she feels the loss of their friendship most keenly. If Honor was here she would talk her down and reassure her. She'd probably tell her to have a shower and put on some decent clothes, suggest lunch and a bottle of wine. But she's not here. She's not even on Facebook. There is nothing to persuade Mel that they are connected by even the finest of virtual threads.

She needs to shower and change. This will kill half an hour, longer if she blow-dries her hair. Once, years back when she had a job and the days never seemed long enough to cram in everything she wanted to achieve, she began to resent drying her hair each morning so much that she went as far as to calculate the amount of time it took. The figures are still clear in her head. Fifteen minutes per day, seven days a week. Five thousand six hundred and seventy minutes a year; this almost equated to four full days a year with the hairdryer in her hand trying to tame her hair. The waste appalled her so much she had it chopped into a bob the next week. More time-effective, she reasoned. She wears it long again now.

In the shower she shaves her legs, though the hair growth, a tiny dusting of stubble, hardly merits it. She uses a salt scrub on her thighs and arms and works it into her skin in sweeping circular movements that cause patches of red to form. Maybe she could use a face mask, she thinks as she emerges from the shower, and searches for it in the drawer. There is a separate eye mask that is still in its packaging. It requires lying down, still. She doesn't do still.

Dressing first, she chooses baggy harem pants and a loose sweater from an online shop that specializes in loungewear. She gave the details to her mother last Christmas when she inquired what Mel wanted. "What in the name of God is loungewear?" her mum asked. "Why don't you just buy a pair of pajamas from Marks and Spencer like everyone else?" When Mel explained that she didn't want to wear her pajamas all day long, her mum shot her a look. *I haven't a clue what goes on inside that head of yours.*

The face mask is creamy and unctuous and sets quickly on her skin. She feels it tighten (they all say this shouldn't happen but it does). If she moves her facial muscles to talk or smile the mask will crack. But she's alone and can't foresee any reason to smile soon.

The silence is what she struggles with the most but she's learned to overcome this too by playing music. Probably the only good thing the architect did was suggest a very expensive sound system that streams the music into every room in the house. Her musical tastes are much narrower these days; she plays from a carefully curated track list, songs released in the last six years deemed safe. Previously she would dip in and out of the decades, cherry-picking her favorites to build an eclectic mix. Or did he do that for her? She can't remember which songs he introduced her to and which she discovered herself. It's easier to steer clear.

He always played music, big booming bass that pumped through the walls. Patrick couldn't stand it, would thump the wall with his fist when it got too loud. But she didn't mind. It was why they became friends, a shared love of music, wasn't it? The first time they spoke, a hot summer's day. She'd just come back from Sainsburys where everyone was stocking up on sausages and charcoal and bottles of lager. Patrick was away, the first time she'd had her new home to herself, and all she was going to do was lie in the garden reading a book in peace. She had applied suntan lotion carefully on her winter-white skin and had just sunk down on the lounger when the chat from next door's garden reached her, accompanied by the smell of barbecue smoke drifting over the fence. Someone turned the music on.

Typical.

Mel recognized the song, one from her university days in Manchester, one of the many she loved but could never remember the name of.

So she asked him, shouted over the fence, immediately self-conscious when she caught his attention and she realized she was still wearing a bikini top.

"Strings of Life," he said. ' "Rhythim Is Rhythim.' Now you're going to ask me to turn it down. Your mate always does." He was referring to Patrick. "He's not keen on my taste in music." He had a nice smile, she thought. Friendly, not her type, but good-looking all the same.

She smiled, "Unlike him I can be bought with a burger. I'm Melody, by the way, Patrick's new flatmate."

"Good luck with that." He smiled that toothy grin again. "I'm David, your next-door neighbor."

Mel jumps at the sound of the intercom. From her bedroom window she can see out across the driveway to the gates. A woman is standing, driver's door open, ready to speak into it. When no one answers, she looks up toward the house. Mel ducks down and crawls along to one end of the window, where she can peer out while using the curtain for cover. Even from this distance she notes a change in hairstyle; shorter, she thinks, and the color is darker. The way she's standing, one hand on her hip, leg turning in slightly, Mel recognizes this pose. For months it was the way she stood in her parents' kitchen, making cups of tea for the family and visitors that everyone cradled in their hands to give them something to do but no one really drank because there are only so many cups of tea a person can drink. She catches sight of herself in the mirror, curtain pulled around her, face mask crinkling on her skin. When did she become so pathetic?

Polly buzzes again. This time Mel goes downstairs to let her in, answering the door with mask still intact.

"Looking good," Polly says.

"I like to try," Mel smiles and feels the mask cracking on her skin.

Polly makes admiring noises about the house—it is a conversation starter if nothing else—about the views, which she seems to appreciate despite them being obscured by a five-foot perimeter fence. "It's like the Gaza Strip, who are you trying to keep out?" Patrick remarked on his first visit after it was erected. Of course he knew very well who they were trying to keep out.

"Do you like it out here?" Polly was standing with her back to Mel, looking out of the window to the garden. "I've always lived in the city, but you know I think I could cope with this."

"I dunno, you'd miss the sirens after a while and the takeaways are rubbish."

Mel makes tea. Polly doesn't drink coffee. She likes her tea strong, the color of teak with just a splash of milk and too much sugar. Mel is surprised by how she has retained these facts when it's been so long since they saw each other.

"The change must have been good, though." Polly comes over to the island, eyes the two mugs Mel has placed there. "Which one is mine?"

"Do you need to ask?"

"Just being polite. Two sugars?"

"I remembered." Mel pulls a face. "I don't know how you can drink it."

"Neither does my dentist, he hates me." She takes a slurp and lets out an *ahhh*. "You always did make a good cup of tea."

Ideally the conversation would continue in this vein, the comfortable, easy banter of two old friends catching up. Although comfortable might not be the best way to describe it; the comfort you feel driving along knowing there is a cliff edge ahead of you and you are going to go careering off it, which on reflection, Mel decides, isn't really comfort at all.

There's a brief lull in the chat. This is where the danger lies. More questions, Mel thinks, running through the possibilities: *How are the kids?* or did she only have one? Maybe she has two now, or even three. Thanks to the mornings she's spent with Siobhan and her mummy friends, she could sustain this line of investigation for some time. Of course she could always ask Polly about work, but she discounts this almost as soon as the idea proposes itself. She has no interest in her work. The wedding, she thinks. God, people can talk endlessly about weddings, even those (in fact particularly those) who are already married. The way they recall their own big day in forensic detail, the cut of the dress, the speeches, the quirky personal touches they added. She gets the impression that they like to talk about it because nothing since has ever fulfilled the promise and perfection of that one day. Without thinking, she holds her hand straight out in front of her to look at the diamond on her ring finger. One and a half carats, a flawless brilliant-cut diamond, Sam said when he produced it eight months ago.

"Woo," Polly says, "that's some love."

"It could be fake for all I know." Mel pulls her hand away, suddenly embarrassed by the extravagance.

Polly looks around the kitchen once more, the hangar-like space of it, and says, "I doubt that very much. When is the big day?"

"Three months." She thinks that sounds too soon, can't understand how at first it all seemed so abstract, a romantic idea too far away in the future to grasp, and now it's almost upon them. She waits for Polly to start the reminiscing. She wasn't long married when they first met, if Mel remembers correctly. But she doesn't, so Mel continues sourcing a selection of treats from the cupboard. She wishes she wouldn't call them treats; it's a habit she's inherited from her mother. *Now look, I've bought you some nice treats*, she'll say when they're on a rare visit, which immediately makes Mel feel eight years old again and deserving of a reward. *Treats:* she hates the bloody word but it's like a verbal tic she can't seem to shake. Laying them on the counter, she runs through the selection in detail as if Polly is unlikely to be tempted without knowing the individual ingredients and heritage of each.

"This is made with oats, I say it's a biscuit but Sam disagrees, he says it's a flapjack, so it's a moot point, but it's organic, and these are Florentines, glacé cherries and dark chocolate, they're really very good . . ." Shut up, she thinks. Would you listen to yourself.

"Shall I tell you what I know, then?" It takes moments for Mel who is lost in thought trying to remember where she bought the macaroons, to realize that she has just driven over the cliff edge and is now freefalling through the air.

Polly's conversation doesn't reach her in full sentences, but like some twisted game of word bingo, just individual words and their attendant images. Body, buzz, woman, buzz, strangled buzz. Gold chain.

David Alden. Buzz.

Mel thinks she's suffering from a kind of inner disturbance that in the space of minutes has shaken up everything inside her. All the images and memories she's worked hard to file and lock away come tumbling out. The neatness, the order has been replaced by internal chaos in the time it's taken for her tea to go cold.

"Are you OK?" They're sitting down at the kitchen table now and Polly reaches across it to hold Mel's hand. "I know it's a lot to take in, but he is in custody, Mel, he can't hurt you."

She contemplates this, how ludicrous it is. It's not Polly's fault. She's only doing her best by trying to reassure Mel that she is not in physical danger. But she doesn't know, because no one gets it, really gets it, that each day presents a different kind of torture: the feeling of her lungs collapsing if she's around too many people because she can't see their individual faces and doesn't know whether he is among them. Conversely being around too few people, so few you can pick out individual footsteps, sets off the noise in her head, like a microphone out of tune, and drowns out every other thought. The day after his release came the violent spasms deep in her stomach, followed by the bleeding, so much blood, the angry redness of it like nothing she'd seen before. She couldn't hold on to another life because she wasn't really alive herself. He had squeezed it out of her. As far as Mel is concerned, there is no line between physical and emotional hurt. They have blurred into one.

"We'd like you to come to the station tomorrow and give another statement," Polly says. She's still holding Mel's hand, tightly, as if she suspects that once she lets go Mel will run.

She wouldn't run, she wouldn't trust her legs to carry her. Instead she is contemplating sitting in a police station tomorrow when she should be driving down to the wedding venue to choose the wine and the flowers with Siobhan. How she's been worrying about it, wishing Sam was able to accompany her because there are too many decisions to make and the issue of the flowers and wine have become big decisions upon which the success of the day and their marriage hinges. Now they have shrunk to insignificance next to what she is being asked to do. There is no avoiding it. She'll be going back, swimming against the current of the last six years when she's devoted all her effort to going forward.

The questions; she remembers them from last time, the feeling that she was disappointing everyone because she couldn't remember enough. No, she didn't see his face; no, she doesn't know why she was walking along Uxbridge Road at 11 P.M., past the street where she lived. No, there is really nothing else she can remember that might help them.

"Were you meeting someone?" they'd asked, and all she could do was shake her head. She would have liked to have given them a straight answer, yes or no. But the memories of that night sat under a dense fog that wouldn't lift. Sometimes she thought she could make out shapes and voices but there was nothing substantive, nothing she could say that beyond all reasonable doubt was true.

"DI Rutter is leading the investigation. I should warn you that she'll be talking to the press tomorrow."

Mel can picture the headlines. They'll say it's exactly seven months since he was released, which isn't true. A glance at the kitchen clock tells her it is seven months, two days and three hours since he walked out of prison a free man. Justice: what did that even mean anyway? *The upholding of what is just*, that's what the dictionary would tell you, but in reality it was nothing of the sort. He was found guilty of grievous bodily harm with intent, which made it sound like a scuffle outside a pub at closing time. He got nine years. Which didn't mean nine years at all. More like five and a half for good behavior. Justice, they say.

It is seven months, two days and three hours since he was handed back his clothes and belongings and the doors were unlocked and he stepped out to walk under the same sky that sat over her house. Back to his Shepherd's Bush flat to play his music so loudly the bass seeped through the walls.

Her one-time friend and next-door neighbor David Alden. The man who tried to kill her.

Polly is still there when Sam returns. "I'm home," he breezes as he dumps his bag in the hall. He bursts into the kitchen. It's the smell that probably tells him something is wrong, Mel thinks. No dinner cooking, just a selection of treats almost untouched. He looks at Polly. He doesn't recognize her, Mel can see that. In Sam's world everything is still running on track. The job of derailing it falls to her.

"You remember Polly, don't you?" She sees his eyes narrow, as if trying to zoom in on her face without the disguise of her new haircut and color.

"Polly." He extends his hand in a jaunty social way. He hasn't made the connection, Mel thinks.

"Polly was our family liaison officer, Sam." She says his name slowly, with emphasis, and fixes him with a stare. *This is not a social visit.*

It happens, finally, the slackening of his jaw, the smile falling from his face. He comes over to Mel, who is standing now, and puts his arm around her as if to protect her from whatever information Polly is about to impart. *Too late. Three hours too late.*

Then he turns to Polly and she begins the story all over again.

When she's gone they say nothing, not at first. He holds her to his chest, a bear hug that is almost too tight. She likes this, the feeling of safety, the feeling that no one else can get to her when he's holding her this close. This morning's deodorant has lingered on his shirt, mixed with the smell of the hospital, reheated food: mass-produced cottage pie, she thinks, cake and lumpy custard.

She stays there until the need for air forces her to pull away. He strokes her hair, kisses the top of her head.

"You should have called me," he says.

"He's in custody, they're questioning him already. There's nothing you can do."

"I could have been here for you."

He towers over her, six foot three of him, her head level with his chest, face pressed into it. She looks up and sees his eyes worrying, the light leaving them the way it does when he's troubled.

"It's probably a mistake. Why would he . . ." Sam pauses, as if trying to work it out himself.

Something snaps inside her, a rage she wasn't aware of until the moment it bursts to the surface. "For fuck's sake stop pretending." She surprises herself with the swearing. There was a time when she swore a lot, once giving her mother a lecture on the versatility of *fucking* as an adjective. But it's not the kind of language she resorts to now.

Maybe it should be. His eyes are wide, locked on to her. He's ready to listen.

"All right, Mel, I was just trying to say that's it's early days. Even the police won't know exactly what has happened. It could all go away."

"It's never gone away, Sam." He holds her at arm's length and stares at her the way he sometimes does. As if the person before him has all the right features but somehow they don't quite add up to the Mel he knows.

"I'll make us some dinner," he says. "What do you fancy? I could do noodles, chicken katsu."

"One thing Polly forgot to tell you."

"Yes?"

"They found a chain in her hand." No one has shown her it but she knows what it will look like, she knows every detail of it.

She sees his stomach expand, air sighing out.

"This time," he says, "I hope they throw away the key."

They eat at the table. This is a rare occurrence, saved for visiting guests and family. When it's just the two of them, they eat in front of the TV, watching whatever is on, usually a property or cookery show, although the latter makes her feel like she does in a restaurant when she spies what someone else has ordered. *I'd rather be eating that than this.* Sam always has his phone by his side, flicking through e-mails or Twitter. Eat, flick, eat, flick. He's never told her what is so interesting that he can't stop for ten minutes to eat dinner.

Maybe that's why he sets the table, to give her his full attention. "Sorry it's just chicken noodles, not katsu, we didn't have any panko bread crumbs." She would have told him this if he'd asked.

Her head is an interactive inventory, like one of those supermarket systems that tells them when they need to replenish. *We are all out of panko bread crumbs.*

He dims the lights. He has a thing for lighting: uplighters, downlighters, mood lightning. When they were building the house, he enlisted the help of a light designer at considerable expense who told them there were layers of lighting—*ambient, task and accent*—and that no house was properly decorated without all three. They even have motion sensor lights in the skirting boards in the hallway. At night when she goes upstairs and the lights illuminate her path, she feels like she's on a runway, except she never manages to take flight.

They start eating. Occasionally his phone, which he has placed on the table directly in front of him, announces the arrival of a new e-mail with a ding. He's itching to look, she can tell from the way his eyes dip down toward it every time he hears the noise. It's taking all his willpower to stop him checking. Is she supposed to be grateful? He's missing the point, she thinks. Spectacularly. If he's not going to piss about on his phone for her sake then he surely should go the whole hog and actually speak to her.

She is overcome by the urge to talk. Not about the wedding or panko fucking bread crumbs or his work itinerary for the week because she already knows it will involve a lot of hours and that it will probably run into the weekend when he does the lucrative private operations. Not about problems that need fixing around the house: a dripping tap; "Can you call the plumber?" Those conversations just hang limp in the air between them, without the power to penetrate and engage. When Melody talks to Sam, to anyone, the words she really wants to say are sugared, couched in niceties or disguised as something else entirely. She's drilled herself not to tell the truth, not to show her feelings, but all she's got in return is this suffocating, oppressive loneliness that comes from being in the same room as someone but only orbiting each other, never connecting.

This time it's her phone that rings, from the living room. She gets up to answer it, grateful for the intervention.

It's Polly again. With news.

When Melody returns, she pushes the food around her plate. There is a light refracting on her fork; low-level ambient light falling on her noodles. When she prods them with her fork, they move like worms. And then there is the light that falls on Sam's face, casting a half-shadow over it. She watches him chew slowly and methodically with his mouth closed as if he is trying to impress her with his impeccable manners.

"That was Polly. They've identified the body."

Eight

Location: Richmond Police Station
Date: Thursday, September 19, 2013

DI Rutter: Yesterday we identified the body of a woman found in Ham Common Woods next to Richmond Park on Sunday as Eve Elliot, a thirty-year-old television producer from London. The investigation into her death is now a murder investigation. A postmortem has been carried out and the pathologist has concluded that the cause of her death was compression to the neck, in other words strangulation.

As a result of the findings of the postmortem we have established that her body would have lain at the site close to Richmond Park for almost a week. We are therefore keen to hear from anyone who saw any individuals acting suspiciously in the vicinity of the park, particularly around the Ham Gate entrance between September 7 and 15, when Miss Elliot's body was discovered by a member of the public walking his dog.

On Monday evening, a thirty-two-year-old local man was arrested and brought in for questioning. He is still being questioned at a London police station.

I'm happy to take a few questions. If you can tell me your name and what organization you work for. Yes, you, the man in the gray coat at the back.

Man in gray coat: Paul Tilsely, *Evening Standard.* Can you confirm the identity of the man who has been arrested?

DI Rutter: I'm unable to do that at present. The lady in the purple shirt in the second row.

Lady in purple shirt: Sunita Sharman from the *Mirror.* Is it true that you are linking the murder to a similar attack six years ago?

DI Rutter: That is correct.

Sunita Sharman: What leads you to believe it is the same person?

DI Rutter: I'm afraid I can't answer that right now. (Looks across to press officer.) I think that's all we've got time for.

Sunita Sharman: Is it true, DI Rutter, that you have arrested David Alden, the same man who was convicted for the attempted murder of Melody Pieterson?

Press officer: The detective inspector won't be taking any more questions now. We thank you for coming and will keep you updated on any developments.

Smartarse, Victoria Rutter says under her breath as she gets up to leave. There's always one, trying to catch her out. She's learning fast that you can't let your guard down, not for a second. They hunt in packs, these reporters; one sniff of blood and they're all on to you. At a guess there are forty people in the room, cameras and photographers included. Flashes in her face as she was talking. She finds it hard not to lose her train of thought, to play the professional, present the facts in the way she's been instructed. There's an art to this,

one she has yet to master: the talking but not really saying anything, the answering questions in a way that doesn't tell the jour-
nalists what they want to know. It's a dance that requires nifty
footwork. She tries to hold back; they try to coax her away from
her script.

They're looking for an angle. She is looking for the killer.

She's never been a good dancer.

She is also the least photogenic person she knows, which is some
achievement given the competition among her colleagues. "You're
beautiful but it's fair to say the camera doesn't love you," her husband Doug said once in attempting to be kind. Should she care?
She can't bring herself to worry about it. All the women (and men)
she knows have bad hair days. They don't always apply makeup
perfectly. Their noses shine under the TV lights. So what? She won't
bow to the pressure of trussing herself up a bit just to go on the
news. Or at any time for that matter. She has a job to do. Kids to
look after, a mountain of paperwork to ignore, and if all that doesn't
leave a spare moment for a manicure and a bikini wax, she's not
going to cry over it. Only once, a few months ago, shortly after her
promotion to DI, did she wish she took personal grooming more
seriously, when she spotted a bogey hanging from her nose during
a TV interview. They played it on the news all weekend. Nowa-
days she runs her finger under her nose before any press conference as a precautionary measure.

Walking out of the room she throws a final glance at Sunita Sharman, who is now engaged in chat with another reporter. Whatever
he's saying is obviously hilarious judging by the way she throws
her head back laughing. If DI Rutter was allowed to act on her instincts she'd march over there and shout in her pretty, perfectly
made-up face, "Have a bit of respect, would you? And while we're
at it, get your bloody facts right. David Alden was not convicted of
attempted murder, it was GBH with intent."

What she's not prepared to concede, not right now anyway, is
that Sunita could be excused the mistake. The reporter has been
around for a while. She will be familiar with the facts of the pre-

vious case. Enticing a woman into your car then applying so much pressure around her neck that she falls into a coma is attempted murder in most people's book, whatever label the courts might like to give it.

She surveyed him in his cell after they brought him in this morning. His pallor was not dissimilar to Eve's. Seven days dead. He kept looking around the room, to the door. Being penned in didn't suit him, she imagined. Not after five and a half years in prison. All it took was the sound of a key turning in the lock to transport him back to those long days in Pentonville, staring out of a window at a tiny scrap of sky.

Victoria had read as much of the case file as time allowed her. Enough to remind herself. David Alden had tried to kill his next-door neighbor because she rebuffed his advances, or as the prosecuting QC had put it, *he was driven to mindless violence by unrequited love*. That made it sound romantic, Shakespearean almost. She'd have put it in simpler terms: a violent thug who couldn't take no for an answer. There were forensics too, Ms. Pieterson's hair as well as fibers from her coat were found on his blue cotton jacket. There was a CCTV image of a car near the spot where Melody was found in the hours after her disappearance. An expert witness had claimed it was David's car though, as evidence goes, Victoria doesn't like to dwell too much on this.

Victoria turned back to look at him in the cell. She can't decide whether it's a blessing or a curse to find herself with. Let him stew for a bit, she thought, and went off to get herself a coffee from the machine.

When everyone was ready, DS Ravindra and DC Rollings started the interview. She watched it from another room on a live CCTV link. They would compare notes when they took a break.

She was fond of DS Ravindra. He wasn't much younger than

her and sharper than most of them in the station. She'd watched him plenty of times in interviews. His face was a picture of calm. If he was baited he didn't rise to it. Not once. Just that smile: *take as long as you want, I've got all the time in the world.*

"We are investigating the murder of Eve Elliot, whose body was found in Ham Common Woods yesterday, Sunday the fifteenth of September. We understand she was killed around seven days beforehand, on the previous weekend. What were you doing on Saturday the seventh of September?"

"I was at home with my sister and a friend for lunch and then we went to the pub."

"What pub was that?"

"The Brackenbury Arms in Hammersmith."

"And what time did you leave?"

"Around ten thirty."

"Alone."

"Yes."

"So you went home alone?"

"That's what I said."

"And you have no alibi for the rest of the evening?"

He shook his head. His face appeared to have lost its shape, like his muscles had given up the job of supporting it. Pushing himself back in the chair he looked up toward the ceiling, clamping his eyes shut. He's struggling to keep a lid on his emotion, Victoria thinks. She took note of the muscle twitching in his clenched jaw. He'd lose his temper soon, she was certain of it. Calm until he snapped. Was that when he turned on Melody? And Eve?

"I went home and went to bed. I played football the next morning. I scored a hat trick if you're interested."

"Who were you with at the pub?"

"My sister and a friend."

"They'll be able to verify your whereabouts until ten thirty, will they?"

"My sister will. But Eve won't." He rubbed his temples with both hands, covered his eyes.

"I'm sorry?" It was DC Rollings this time, straightening himself in his chair before leaning in toward David Alden. "What did you say?"

"I was with Eve most of the day until I left the pub."

"Eve Elliot?"

"Yes. She was a friend of my sister's."

"And you had lunch with her regularly."

"I wouldn't say so."

"So why that particular Saturday?"

He gave a wry laugh. "Because she had some good news for me."

Nine

EVE

There were three of us. Me, David and his sister Annie, gathered for lunch in the garden of his flat. This wasn't, as David correctly pointed out, a regular occurrence but a meeting convened by me to impart "the big news." It had been in my possession since the previous evening, burning a hole in my mind with its utter brilliance. It was the reason for my early-morning trip to Ham Gate. I was checking my facts before I told David, because you don't mess around with people like him. You have to be sure.

It took a moment after I told him for the relief to work its way through to his face. He looked like he was high. The semi-frown he always wore disappeared and his features softened to settle into a blissed-out smile. I'd got him wrong. I'd thought he was aloof but I realized then that he'd been holding part of himself back. The part that allowed him to hope. Only now when he had something concrete to grasp did his emotions spring to the surface.

We laughed and hugged and worked out a plan for the future, because for the first time David sensed there might be one. And then a few hours later it all started to go into reverse. My death would put him right back at the beginning.

Lightning doesn't strike twice, so the saying goes. But if you'd said that to David Alden as he sat in a cell, sweat blotting his T-shirt, blood roaring in his head, you might excuse him for laughing. Or

crying. Or telling you to shut up and fuck off with your empty say-
ings. Because as far as he was concerned, when lightning found you
it logged your coordinates and came back to strike you again and
again and again.

It was déjà vu, the same nightmare unfolding. Maybe it was a
different room, different faces accusing him. But it was the same,
right down to the plastic chair that made his arse sweat. He asked
himself why. Why me? But there was no answer. The first time he
was arrested he thought it was a joke. *This could never happen to
me, they'll realize their mistake soon. They'll charge someone else.*
But they kept on questioning him, telling him he had attacked her,
and then they charged him. One by one all those tenets of justice
he had believed in had fallen away. Truth wasn't enough. Not when
there was sufficient evidence to support the lies.

He could talk and talk and tell them he didn't touch me but they
wouldn't believe a word he said. Not him, a man who had already
served a jail term.

The person who had believed him, who had found evidence to
corroborate that belief, was gone. And now that I was dead, nothing else made sense.

In the same police station, in another interview room, my friend
Nat was waiting for an officer to take his statement. He'd come almost as soon as he'd heard that morning. My mum had promised
to call him when she had news of me and she kept her promises.
Or at the very least she got someone else to keep them for her. The
job of telling Nat fell to my stepdad Steve.

"I'm sorry, Nat," Steve stuttered on the phone, "but Eve's dead."

Steve never did have a way with words, but in fairness there was
no gentle way to break it. To string out the sentence, to give Nat
some warning—*Are you sitting down? Do you have anyone with
you?*—it wouldn't have been any kinder. It all came down to the
same thing. *Eve was alive and now she is dead.* Nothing could ab-
sorb the shock of those words.

Nat came almost as soon as he heard because he didn't know what else to do. And because he didn't believe it. Steve had sounded a bit moony on the phone, slurring his words, unable to provide any of the specifics Nat would require in order to verify that kind of information. He tried making himself a coffee, searched the Internet for details. He came across a few paragraphs about a body being found near Richmond Park. He tried calling me again. Steve must have been pissed, he thought. He liked a drink. Nat remembered the disapproving looks my mum shot him at barbecues and parties at their house; Steve plying everyone with booze as a cover for his own excesses. He replayed his words: *I'm sorry, Eve is dead.* What the fuck had he been drinking to say that?

Now Nat peered down at the red record button winking at him. He had dead eyes, the ones I remembered from all-night raves, taxi queues, long walks home from clubs in the cold and wind. Only this time there had been none of the preceding fun. He regretted coming. He regretted having to sit under the artificial light and inhale the body odor of the previous interviewee. He wished he had clung on to his disbelief for a few more hours. He wished Steve *had* been pissed.

"When did you last see her?" It was a young female detective taking his statement. DC Kate Chiverton. Her dark hair was cropped, with little shards of blond highlights poking out. As Nat spoke, she pulled a small silver locket back and forth on a chain around her neck.

Nat had already given her question some consideration. He had thought of little else since the phone call with Steve. "Wednesday the fourth, we met for a drink in town."

"And that was the last time you spoke to her?"

"Uh-huh." His voice wobbled. "I was in France that weekend."

"You didn't try to contact her when you came back?" I wished she wasn't so hard on him. I wanted her to go easy, crack a sympathy smile or two. But that was the problem with murder. It dragged everyone under a cloud of suspicion.

"I called her a few times, left a message."

"You didn't think it was odd when there was no response?"

Her questions prodded at his guilt and were quickly drowned out by his own. Why? Why? he asked himself. He had been filming all day Monday, editing Tuesday and on Wednesday, a day off, he slept, pretty much all day on and off. *Why didn't you know something wasn't right? How could you sleep and eat takeaway pizza for dinner when you hadn't heard from your friend in days? Because, because, in my defense, it wasn't unusual for her not to reply immediately. That's a lame excuse. What you really mean is that you didn't stop to think, isn't that right?*

Yes, that's right.

"Weren't you the tiniest bit worried?" he heard the DC ask.

"How did she seem when you last saw her?"

He closed his eyes to reproduce the image of our meeting. It came to him immediately. There I was dancing around, throwing my head back, laughing. Why was I laughing? He couldn't think. It must have been a joke he'd cracked or an anecdote. He needed to remember it, preserve it so he could tell it over and over again and keep me laughing. We were at my flat. I'd cooked a roast chicken, which we ate on our laps on the sofa. He spilled gravy on the velvet cushion. The broccoli was overcooked. "You never get your vegetables right, do you?" he said, and I promised to hide them somewhere painful.

She didn't seem like someone who was going to be murdered the following week.

Nat knew all about murders. We'd met at journalism college, mocked our peers who had drifted into PR over the years. Unlike them we stayed true to ourselves, conducting investigations, uncovering truths, exposing lies. He'd covered more than his fair share of murders, but the thing about them was they always happened to other people.

"Had she ever mentioned the name David Alden to you?"

He sighed wearily. "Yes. I know all about David Alden. She was investigating his conviction." He glanced up to DC Chiverton and saw her nod her head for him to elaborate.

"It's what she used to do at work. She was a producer on *APPEAL*, you know the program that looked into miscarriages of justice. Well, she was until they pulled it. What I'm trying to say is she knew what she was doing. Annie, David's sister, was a friend of hers. She agreed to have a look at his case for her. She didn't think it stacked up."

"Was there anything to make you think she might be worried for her own safety?" Tears bubbled up in his eyes; he wanted to explain but his words were tangled in his throat. "Nathaniel, was there something that Eve was concerned about?"

He wiped his eyes, inhaled to steady himself.

"She started to think someone might have been in her house. She said things were going missing, clothes from the line, mugs rearranged in her cupboard, an Obi-Wan Kenobi doll . . ." DC Chiverton raised her eyebrows. "Her dad had bought it for her before he died, it had special sentimental value."

She nodded, "I see."

"But there was never any proof. I just thought . . ."

"What?"

"Well, she was so focused on the investigation . . . I thought she was tired, overtired."

"You didn't believe her?"

He looked diminished, heartbroken. "No," he said.

He replayed the scene in his mind, the one that will haunt him forever now. We're in my flat and I'm crying because I think I've taken on too much, promised David Alden and his sister more than I can deliver. Nat's words are his usual mix of sarcasm, reassurance and wit, and he uses them to pick me up and give me a giant kick up the backside. "If anyone can do it, you can," he says as a final flourish. It was only a sentence, a bit of gentle encouragement from a friend who believed in me more than I believed in myself. It was exactly what I needed to hear at the time. But now he wished he could revisit the moment, erase it from our history and tell me to give up.

I'd liked to have told him it wasn't his fault.

When DC Chiverton was finished with him, she showed him to the door that led to the reception. He walked slowly, uncertain that his legs could hold his weight. "We'll be in touch," DC Chiverton said. "OK," was all he managed in response.

Beyond the station he could make out the street, people moving too quickly and with purpose. What purpose could there possibly be any more? He stopped for a moment to consider his situation. He felt like he had been sucked out of life, shown a truth that had irreversibly changed his perspective on the world, and now he was expected to go back out and walk to the same rhythm as before. He didn't think he could do it. He watched DC Chiverton fade out down the corridor, leaving him dangling. He turned slowly toward the door and his eyes caught a glimpse of blond hair. His heart exploded with relief. It was only a nightmare after all and now he was coming round. Slowly he moved toward her. She was standing with a tall man he didn't recognize and another woman, dressed in suit trousers and a shirt. Both of them blurred out at the edges of his vision. It was the woman who remained razor sharp, in focus. He was staring, trying to make sense of her features, which were so familiar but somehow not quite the same, when he heard the suited woman's voice say, "I really appreciate you coming, Melody."

It took every ounce of effort to drag his eyes away and take the remaining few steps to the door.

Ten

W hy do people have to stare? Have they always stared like this or is it a recent development? And what is it about her that invites such forensic interest? She'd like to ask the man in front of her. Either Sam hasn't noticed him staring at them (or her) or he's pretending he hasn't. But then he's good at that, the pretending.

There's a whisper in her ear. "Mel!" So he has noticed.

She hisses back to him, "He's staring at *me*," and watches him roll his eyes.

She first caught sight of him emerging into the waiting area with a woman. Mel assumed she was a police officer though she was dressed in plain clothes, hair tightly cropped around her face.

"We'll be in touch," she said to the man. Was he drunk? He was trying to stand still but his body wasn't obeying, it was swaying. One hand planted in his pocket, the other rubbing his temples.

"OK." That was all he said before he turned toward the door and brought his eyes to settle on her. They haven't left her since. Mel has the impression he's trapped in a bubble that controls the speed of his movement. He floats through the space.

Sam nudges her with his elbow. She remembers there is a woman in front of her who has proffered her hand. "I'm Detective Inspector Victoria Rutter. I really appreciate you coming, Melody."

He's almost next to her when DI Rutter says this. So close in fact that she's aware of his body giving a little jolt, like a charge of electricity shooting through him. His foot stops, suspended in mid air, and in slow motion he turns to her again, this time without narrowing his eyes. Whatever has happened he manages to bring her into focus.

There's a contraction in his face muscles, the beginning of a smile, she thinks. But then just as quickly it fades and turns into something else. What? Is he going to cry? She can't put her finger on it. Sadness. She'd say he looks sad. Washed out like he's been through the wringer. The automatic doors open, a fug of air from the street hits her. He walks out, disappearing into the crowd.

"Pleased to meet you." Sam shakes the DI's hand. Is he really pleased? She thinks not. Even someone with Sam's relentless optimism (bordering on the aggressive, Mel would say) can't be overjoyed to be here. For starters it stinks, of fetid bodies and cheese and onion crisps and general decay, and the walls, the color of stewed tea, are adorned with posters: *Terrorism, if you suspect it report it*, and her particular favorite, a drive to recruit volunteers: *Are You Special?*

Then there's the matter of Sam taking a day off work, the fact of which he hasn't mentioned yet though she's seen it hovering on his lips a few times. "Don't drive so fast, you're making me nervous." *Do you know the sacrifice I have made to be here?* That's what he'd like to say but he reins it back. His task today is to support Mel, put an arm around her shoulder, squeeze her hand occasionally and strike the right tone, encouraging but also understanding. This against the backdrop of knowing that the Royal Surrey County Hospital will be a man down today, and not just any man, but Sam Chapman, who is like ten men.

Still he shakes the DI's hand like he means it, but then he's always been an enthusiastic shaker of hands. She attributes this to his public school education. *Never give a limp handshake, it tells you a lot about a man,* he told her once, though precisely what it told you he never revealed. DI Rutter's eyes screw up a little, the point at which Melody knows her metacarpal bones are grinding together under Sam's grip.

DI Rutter explains a number of things before she asks Mel to talk about whatever she can remember, in any order: sights, smells sounds, whatever comes to mind. *Don't edit anything out, however small. You may not think it is important but it could be.*

First, though, there's the preamble, the warm-up. She retreads the ground that Polly went over. Body, tick. Park, tick. Strangled, tick tick tick.

These are the connections.

There are more.

DI Rutter passes her a photograph of a gold birdcage necklace, found in Eve Elliot's palm. She allows her time to inspect the image. "We've checked it, Mel, it's identical to the one you were holding when you were found."

Then the words: "If you are OK, Mel, I can start the tape."

She glances down at the evil red eye of the record button.

The facts:

It was six years ago. Friday, August 17, 2007. If she said she was late finishing work it would suggest she habitually left at a reasonable time, say 6 P.M., but this wasn't true so perhaps she wasn't late at all. Perhaps it was just like every other day at Fin Communications. Never-ending. It was a huge office, although it was frowned upon to call it an office. On each level were "central creative spaces" where staff collaborated (worked) at stations (desks). These were minimalist in character, lacked any form of soft furnishings or sound insulation. The constant buzz of phones ringing, colleagues talking, joking, even the overenthusiastic touch-typing of a nearby colleague were all amplified. Acoustically, it was a challenging place to work. Around the central space was a cluster of rooms each with a different name and interior. On the morning of August 17, Mel blue-skied (brainstormed) a new project for a kids' fruit snack in the Thought Pod, where the chairs were actually not chairs at all but space hoppers. The idea was that bouncing stimulated creativity. In reality the compression of air from the hoppers made it sound like everyone present was emitting a collective fart. As far as Melody was aware, no one came up with a single creative or original idea.

By 6:30, Melody (she was still known as Melody at this time) had retreated to the Womb, not because she particularly liked the red padded walls but because she couldn't hear herself think anywhere else. She had one final conversation to appease a client who had started the day threatening to pull the account after a rival software company had appeared in the *Telegraph*. She promised them that there would be much stronger coverage, hoping they didn't notice she hadn't volunteered any specifics.

As she was tidying her desk before she left for the evening, her friend Sandeep passed by to ask if she was going up to the roof for a drink. It was a chill-out zone with squashy seats, a bar and swings (swings!) because the American owners of Fin Comms wanted you to feel like this was your whole world and you never had to leave. But Mel wanted to smell air that had not been scented with banana or vanilla or whatever the scent of the day was. She wanted to take a deep gulp of London smog, bus fumes, fat frying, pizza, waffles. She wanted to see colors that weren't primary colors or shades dreamed up by interior designers on astronomical fees. In short, she had had enough. She wanted to leave. Her departing thought was that she wouldn't care if she didn't come back. Ever.

Lesson one: be careful what you wish for.

Taking the Tube, she got off at Shepherd's Bush and walked up Uxbridge Road, where Patrick was waiting in a pub with a group of friends. In mid August, at least in this part of town, families evacuated London, headed to Cornwall in their four-wheel drives or on easyJet to Puglia (the new Tuscany) or Sardinia or France. Those who were left behind were either young or skint, often both. But there were benefits to be had. The city loosened its tie and kicked off its shoes, and on rare warm days it could be found lying on the grass eating strawberries, drinking wine. Come evening, it migrated to beer gardens for cocktails or chilled bottles of rosé, which was exactly what Mel had in mind today.

Sometimes, in the heat and the rounds of after-work summer drinks, the city forgot to eat.

Lesson two: never drink wine on an empty stomach.

She peered around the back door, saw Patrick sitting with the others, five or six of them, Rory, Talia, mainly his friends but ones she had come to know well over the years. She hadn't heard from Sam and Honor, didn't know what they were up to, quashed the urge to pump Patrick for information immediately. She'd bide her time. Instead she waited at the bar, ordered a bottle of rosé, asked for a few glasses so it didn't look like she intended to drink it all herself and went outside to join them.

Patrick saw her and pulled a chair from a neighboring table over to theirs so she could sit down next to him. Mel poured two glasses of wine and handed him one, but he shook his head, pointed to the glass of Coke in front of him. "On call," he said.

"Weren't you on call last weekend?"

"Yup." He nodded. "Everyone else has pissed off to Tuscany with their kids."

She tasted the wine. It was a Côtes de Provence, strawberry and peach, chilled; she could pickle herself in the stuff in the summer months. After the day she had had at work, she felt some pickling was in order. The first glass disappeared quickly, always did. At some point she checked her phone, willing it to display a message, tucking it into the pocket of her jacket so she would feel it buzz if one came through.

"Anyone else coming tonight?" The words were out before she had time to check them.

"Not sure," he said, watching her refill her glass. "You're making me jealous."

"I'd love to drink Coke with you in sympathy but after the week I've had . . ."

"Tell me about it."

"Want to talk?" She asked. Patrick hadn't been in the best mood of late, though she knew he worked hard to cover it up. It must have been something to do with work, she imagined. Maybe he had given the wrong dose of drugs to a patient. When she'd raised the subject, delicately, in a way that wouldn't make him think she was being nosy he'd brushed it off. Tiredness, or stress, or *I'm fine*, that was all she got.

By the time she had finished her second glass it was apparent they were working on different conversational planes. She didn't mind him not drinking per se. She understood that when he was on call or training for some extreme sport event he couldn't consume a bottle of wine. It just wasn't much fun, and, maybe it was her imagination, but she always detected an air of superiority that came with the abstinence. She could swear it wasn't her who became more inebriated but Patrick who grew more sober. She slunk back in her chair, watched Patrick watching the others, cracking a smile only occasionally.

When he was in one of these moods it was best to give him a wide berth. She moved around the table to chat to Rory, a mutual friend. He had started up a new digital advertising agency and was talking about ROI and reach and engagement and content. She had enough of that at work. She gave it five minutes, asked a few pertinent questions, before going to the toilet.

When she returned, she found Patrick again. And Honor. Mel hadn't known she was coming but she was glad to see her, even more so when she helped herself to the bottle of rosé. Where was Sam? Mel inquired. Honor shrugged. "At home, maybe. I don't know," she said and took a gulp of wine.

"Anyone fancy a barbeque on Sunday?" Patrick asked. "It'll probably be pissing down by then but we could risk it."

"Maybe," Honor said. "I might be away . . ."

"Where are you going?" Mel asked but Honor had only shrugged again.

Still, they had drank and talked and laughed. Even Honor was unusually voluble that night and it wasn't down to the wine either. She had stopped at one glass, much to Mel's disappointment. "Sorry, I came straight from work, the car is round the corner," she'd said. Patrick had thawed out too. Whatever was bothering him before had worked its way out of his system. She was used to this, the dips and curves in his mood, having become attuned to them over the twelve years of their friendship. From her very first day at university Patrick had been there, his room next to hers in halls, toasting bread and sharing cheap bottles of wine at night. One night, returning from a student night called Time Tunnel with Blondie and Culture Club and Abba still ringing in their ears, they had shared a spliff and had actually kissed. A drunken, slobbery snog. She remembered him leaning in toward her and her thinking, *Well, why not? It makes a change from burning toast or trawling the room for chocolate.* There had been a series of these encounters that punctuated university life, but they didn't amount to anything more than a kiss that she recalled with a joke and an apology the next day. Patrick was a mate; more like a brother in fact. And she couldn't fancy her brother.

The thought of drunken snogs with Patrick was still present in her mind when she noticed the bottle in front of her was swaying, as if it was made of fabric not glass and could catch the breeze. Her head was full of cotton candy. She poured herself a glass of water from the jug on the table with the vain hope that it might dilute the alcohol. She'd been happy to hear Honor so upbeat and chatty but now she wanted her to stop. She needed some peace and quiet. The conversation spun around her, darted in and out, new subjects introduced, different speakers. Who was talking now? Why did she feel like she was operating at a different speed to everyone else? It was dark; overhead a canopy of lights twinkled, candles on tables sent fingers of light upward. She needed air but she was outside already.

"Are you OK?" Patrick asked.

A noise came out, something like "Uh hmm." She peeled her jacket from the back of the chair, took her bag.

"Excuse me, excuse me." She slipped through gaps between seats and tables to make her way to the toilet. She needed a pee. Yes, that was what she needed. In the cubicle she began to hover. Just this once, she thought, I'd love to sit down, because she was unsure her legs would hold the weight of her body in the squatting position. She cursed her mother for telling her never to sit on public toilets. *There is a whole proliferation of germs, Melody, millions and millions of them. NEVER DO IT.* She hovered. When she had finished, she noticed splashes of her own wee on the seat where she had been unsteady. She gave it a wipe with toilet roll before exiting the cubicle to wash her hands.

The soap foamed in her palms, tiny bubbles evaporating. There was a sign that said CAREFUL EXTREMELY HOT WATER and she wondered what she was supposed to do with this information. Not use the hot tap at all? She decided to risk it, watched tiny pearls of water bouncing off her hands. When she was done, she opted to dry her hands with a paper towel. The mirror filled the wall in front of her; it was impossible not to examine herself in the way women sometimes do, running her finger under her eyes, across her cheek. *Is this really how I look or is it a bad light? (Let it be the bad light.)* She toyed with the notion of applying more makeup. Rooted around but could only find a red lipstick orphaned from its lid and covered in the sediment that collected at the bottom of her bag. She decided against it. It's not like he's here, she reasoned. It's only Patrick and Honor.

Then what?

Did she check her phone?

She left immediately after this, dipped her head around the door that led to the garden and shouted, louder than necessary, "I'm going home." Patrick had his phone in his hand, texting perhaps. "Do you want a lift?"

"S'fine, I need some air."

"But I've only just got here," Honor shouted above the noise.

"Sorry."

Outside, her movements were slow, the traffic zipped around her.

She attempted extra large strides to create a momentum in her walk, slapped her face to wake herself and bring the path ahead of her into focus. She continued down Uxbridge Road, peering into the road. What was she looking for? A taxi? She couldn't see any. Maybe all the cab drivers had gone to Puglia too. All she saw were colored shapes flashing past leaving light trails in her vision. Why would she have needed a cab anyway? She only lived three streets away.

She wasn't going home, that was why.

It was the only feasible explanation.

What can she remember? That the night smelled of Spanish holidays, a potent combination of hot food and heat. She closed her eyes, let herself think she was on holiday, her body starfished on the sea, drifting out from the shore. The blare of a horn pierced the dream. She swayed back from the road. The Uxbridge Road was a long way from Spain.

What was she feeling? What was she thinking? A purpose propelled her forward and yet she had the sense that wherever she was headed was too far away, that her body was working against her. Weightlessness. She found it hard to plant her steps on the pavement, keep straight on the path, like an astronaut bobbing about in zero gravity.

What was her purpose? Perhaps she was hungry, heading toward the Tesco Metro to pick up a pizza? Well yes, that would have been a possibility were it not for the fact that the street was littered with so many takeaway outlets; Lebanese, Chinese, Indian, Turkish takeaways all came before the Tesco Metro. She wouldn't have bypassed them all for a frozen pizza.

Was she walking to meet someone? Had she arranged to meet David Alden? To go to the club with him?

She recalls a conversation about the club, an e-mail exchange but nothing more.

Was there anyone else she might have been meeting?

She pauses to replay the question. At one stage, not long after she emerged from the coma, it was the only question in her head, occupying so much space it squeezed out all other thoughts. Who? She knew who, or at least she knew there was only one person she would walk down Uxbridge Road late at night to see. But even in her groggy, confused state she sensed there was a reason she couldn't say his name. And when she became more lucid and the drugs wore off, she was glad she hadn't mentioned it, because on analysis it didn't stack up. He had an alibi. There was no message sent to her phone, no e-mail arranging that particular rendezvous.

"Anyone at all?" DI Rutter asks again.

Mel pauses. Victoria Rutter's eyes have locked on to hers, willing her to remember. She casts a glance at Sam. He has been staring at her too. Now he takes her hand underneath the table and squeezes it.

"Is anything coming back to you, Mel?" he says. She watches his lips move as he speaks, pink and rubbery. The flash of his front teeth, yellowing incisors. You need to cut back on the coffee, she thinks.

The doctors warned her the trauma would play havoc with her recall. Memories that had been arranged in strict chronology were jumbled up, so for instance she remembered a business lunch at the Oxo Tower on the day of the attack, but when police checked her diary it was two weeks before. Her instincts could not be trusted.

She pulls her hand away from Sam's. "No," she says sharply. Then, modulating her tone, she adds, "I'm sorry."

"Don't worry. Do you want to take a break?"

Melody shakes her head. She wants to get this over with. Closing her eyes for a second to remind herself where she was, she continues where she left off, walking down Uxbridge Road. She sees herself like a figure moving through a Google Street View. There were people around, the late-night throng, slouching bus queues, shouted conversations, air thick with halal kebabs.

Noise and people and movement.

And then they receded. Voices slipped from her earshot. Her skirt lifted in the breeze. Lights from a car coming her way. Too bright;

she blinked, felt herself dissolving. *Just walk, Melody.* Was that her voice speaking? Her heels dragged on the pavement, footsteps echoing. She stopped, no point moving forward; the pavement had turned liquid. Her name was called. A car door opened. She couldn't see the driver, out of her sight line, but the voice was friendly, familiar. She got in, thankful to have her body melt into the seat.

The forward motion of a car going beyond their destination. She didn't understand, wanted to turn back, but words were too heavy, she hadn't the strength to speak them.

"Sshh. Just close your eyes and sleep."

Her eyes obeyed.

Then, a slippage, and darkness filled her.

There's a stain on the table, darker than tea, black coffee perhaps, or Coca-Cola, although the police do not provide complimentary Coca-Cola. She runs her finger over it, feels its groove. She thinks about all the other people who have sat here before her with their stories of violence and damage that cannot be undone whatever they might like to think.

DI Rutter speaks. "Did you have a boyfriend at the time?"

"No," she says.

"Was there anyone you were seeing, more casually perhaps?" (For sex? Mel knows she'd like to add.)

There is a pause, a waiting, as if she is being subjected to a test. "No."

This is not true, much as she's tried to recast her history. But she's repeated it so many times it doesn't feel like a lie anymore.

"How old was she? Mel asks DI Rutter when she's finished remembering.

"Eve Elliot was thirty." Another parallel, Mel thinks, the same age I was when I was attacked six years ago. "I have a photograph of her here," DI Rutter says. Mel isn't sure she wants to see a photograph, but before she has time to convey this, the DI has pulled out a large picture from the file on the table next to her.

"Here," she says, handing it to her. "Her mother tells me this is recent, taken in the spring."

Eve has blond hair and green eyes. She is smiling, of course she is. That's how everyone likes to remember the dead. Who wants to dwell on the last few hours or minutes of their lives? She wouldn't have been smiling then, Mel thinks, before she swats the thought away.

Sam is watching her, DI Rutter is watching her, the DC who told her his name but which she promptly forgot is watching her.

She starts to cry.

It was easier when Eve was only a body. A body is just a physical structure of flesh and bones and organs. A body doesn't smile or wear a green fleece and a red scarf tied tightly around her neck. A body doesn't have chin dimples and blond hair that's been pulled back into a ponytail but has found its way out, streaking her face. A body doesn't look red-cheeked from exertion, elated. A body doesn't look like it's at the top of the world (although really it's just the peak of the Old Man of Coniston).

Eve is no longer a body. She is a name and a face.

A face that looks remarkably like her own.

"Are you OK, Mel?" DI Rutter asks. "Do you recognize her?"

She shakes her head. She recognizes her in the way that she recognizes herself when she looks in the mirror. The blond hair, green eyes, the tone of their skin. They could be interchangeable, Eve and Mel. Mel and Eve. All that separates them is chance. A discovery made when Melody still had a thin pulse. Their fates could have been the same.

"We understand she knew David Alden."

Mel hangs her head. A tear drips from her face and splats on to the table in front of her. She feels in her pockets for a tissue.

"I want to tell you in case you hear it from any other sources . . ." Mel looks up, sees DI Rutter's face flushed. "We understand she was trying to help him."

"Help him?" The air tightens around her. She feels it crackle with static. "What do you mean?"

"We think she might have been investigating the case against him to help him clear his name."

Mel turns to Sam but he is cradling his head in the palms of his hands.

Look at me, she wants to scream. *Look at me and tell me this is not true.*

The coffee she drank half an hour ago burns in her throat. It tastes metallic, bitter, makes her want to retch.

"We're still gathering the facts, as you can appreciate. We don't know how far she had got with this or if it is connected to her death in any way."

Mel pushes the photograph of Eve back across the table toward DI Rutter. It catches a gust from the air conditioning and is lifted up. She watches it float to the floor. The DC reaches down and picks it up.

You're not supposed to think ill of the dead, unless they are Hitler or Myra Hindley or the July 7 bombers, and Eve is none of those, but right now there are two words burning in Mel's head.

Fucking bitch.

Why was she digging around in the debris of Mel's life, trying to unpick the facts that she has spent years trying to settle in her mind? Her friend attacked her. Her friend and next-door neighbor. A man she trusted. What was it, a whim? A project? Did she have any understanding of what she was doing?

"Mel, I want to assure you that everyone here is convinced we got the right result."

Mel pulls at her top, needs to let air circulate through it. Sweat is building under her bra, down between her shoulder blades. There's an itch on her back that she tries to satisfy by scratching, but she only succeeds in displacing it. The ants are back, parading through her hair.

She has the impression she is being undone, that the contents of her head are spilling out into the room to dance before her.

Eleven

To be fair, Mel had a point. Taking on David Alden's case wasn't a whim. That would have been stupid and callous and I like to think I was neither of those things. But it may have fallen under the banner of "project." In the beginning, at least, my motives were not entirely altruistic.

That's not to say I didn't believe him. I wouldn't have gone ahead otherwise. The process is long and laborious, with obstacles every step of the way. You'd have to be crazy to do it if you weren't convinced of a person's innocence.

But he caught me at a time when I was floundering, personally and professionally. I needed a distraction and a purpose. In that respect it was as much about saving me as it was him.

Saturday morning, the first week in February, my boyfriend Mark and I were sitting at the kitchen table. Our flat was on the second floor of a four-story terrace, the height affording us a decent if narrow view of the street and a slice of skyline thrown in for good measure. A weak winter sun was straining through the window. In the distance a ridge of dark cloud sat on top of an expanse of blue, as if someone had drawn a line in the sky and shaded one half black. Rain. No rain.

We shared a paper. *The Times,* if I'm not mistaken. I was reading the magazine, or rather pondering a recipe for onglet, pickled walnuts and horseradish. It's probable I looked a little pained, like I'd sucked a lemon, which was part reaction to the idea of pickled walnut, part evidence of my annoyance at the pot of tea on the table. Although I rarely drank tea—it lacked the kick of a strong coffee—I had nothing against it or the people who did drink it. But that morning the tea in the pot, the studied manner in which Mark poured it and the sound effects that accompanied him swigging it (slurp, then an *agghh*) sent me into a spin. *He's only drinking tea. How can that possibly produce such a violent reaction? You are being unreasonable. You can't blame him for appreciating the difference between a bag dunked in a mug and a pot perfectly brewed. Can you? Can you?*

That was when I knew it was over. When your partner's habits—the sound of them swallowing food, the way they drink their tea (the way they breathe!), the whole package—begin to grate and you stop being a rational, thinking being, that's when you know your relationship isn't going anywhere.

I loved Mark because he was kind and good and because I had once been crazy about him. Because I thought he was the one. Because I wanted him to be that person. But I wasn't *in love* with him.

I hung my head and studied the onglet recipe: *trim the excess fat and sinew, lightly oil and season with salt and pepper.* Tears swelled in my eyes. Was I really going to do this? It had been brewing a lot longer than the tea. Months. The nagging sense of dissatisfaction. A growing restlessness that I needed to break out of. I had tried trawling our past to revive the old flare of excitement and work out where we had taken a wrong turn. Mark was the last person I wanted to hurt. I wanted to make it work. I recalled our first encounter, New Year's Eve 2010, countless times. We had swigged champagne from the same bottle, screamed out the last seconds of the year together with two million others. FIVE, FOUR, THREE, TWO, ONE . . . The London Eye had turned into a circle of fire, fountains of orange sparks sprayed up in the air, rockets exploded like giant dandelions in front of our eyes. We looked up to Big Ben, illuminated in a white glow. The first minute of 2011. We kissed. When had we stopped kissing?

I thought of the time we "got lost" in the New Forest and had a shag because we couldn't wait, we needed each other at that precise moment. How could that have faded into twice-monthly sex, reserved for the occasions when we got spectacularly drunk? What about the time we spent a whole month on a beach in India, eating kingfish for lunch, watching the dolphins rise and dip in the sea in front of us. Swinging in hammocks as the sun set over the horseshoe bay of Odayam Beach in Kerala and thinking that if it never rose again we'd die happy, contented with each other in the gentle night breeze. And now the thought of a long, yawning weekend had me breaking out in perspiration.

Was this it? Was this just a case of life happening to us, the same way it happened to everyone else? The couples who could quite easily go a full year without feeling the need to touch or kiss or fuck each other? Did I need to bring my expectations down a peg or two? Settle for Mark, because on paper he was everything I thought I wanted, and slurping aside, I enjoyed his company?

I had tried. Honestly I had. I'd even started wearing matching underwear again in the lame hope it would rekindle what we had.

"I can't do this any more, Mark." I blurted the words out hoping that if I said them quickly they'd hurt less. I heard the newspaper rustle. Slowly his head appeared from behind it.

He was dressed in a white T-shirt he wore for bed. A faint shadow of stubble covered his chin.

"Do what?"

I tried pointing to the table, the paper, the teapot, as if they were his answer. *No, Eve, he deserves better.*

"I'm sorry. I'm so sorry, Mark. I just don't think this is working."

He paused, gave a nervous laugh as if I had cracked a bad joke. Slowly the smile fell off his face. "I don't understand." His skin had turned the same washed-out white of his T-shirt.

I wanted to tell him that I didn't understand either. I wanted to say, "If only you knew the hours I've spent trying to make sense of it. The endless logic and reason I've struggled to apply. On paper you have everything I need, a whole list of attributes: you are funny, kind, thoughtful, you put the toilet seat down when you're finished, you cook and clean up after yourself, you love me. I hate myself for not feeling it."

"Neither do I," I said. "I just don't . . ."

"Don't what? You don't love me? Say it, if that's what you mean." His eyes were glassy with anger. "Why don't you come out and say it."

"Because it's not true. I do love you, I just . . ."

"Don't want to be with me? Fuck, Eve, spare me the clichés. That's not love. That's something else . . . friendship. It's not fucking love." He pushed himself away from the table and started prowling the kitchen. It was a small space and Mark was a tall man. He looked like a tiger penned in a tiny enclosure.

"God . . ." He cast a look over to me. "You're serious, aren't you? Did you not think to mention this, not once, you know . . . the whole time we were agonizing over Pure White or Wimborne White for the walls, or booking a summer holiday? All the plans we were making together for the future. Our future, Eve. I thought you were it. Me and you together. Jeez . . ." He grabbed fistfuls of his own hair.

"I'm sorry, Mark . . ."

"Don't say you're sorry. I don't want to hear it." He peered over at me sitting hunched at the table. He sniffed and wiped his nose with his hand. "I just don't get it. I thought we had something. God, I'm an idiot."

"Don't, Mark, please, it's not your . . ."

"If it was anyone else I would say let's try, we have something worth working for. But I know you, Eve, once you've made your mind up, that's it. You're all or nothing." We locked eyes and I could see he was begging me to correct him. My vocal cords were straining to tell him what he wanted to hear. It took all my willpower to say nothing.

"I thought as much," he said as I pulled my gaze away from his.

He walked to the door. "It's why I fell in love with you in the first place."

I broke up with Mark because I couldn't lie to him or to myself, because I wanted the big, once-in-a-lifetime love. But being dead forced me to question my decision. Would I have stayed with him if I knew I wouldn't find that love? That Mark was the last person I would wake up next to, the last person I'd ever have sex with?

In the end I always come back to the same conclusion. If I had stayed with him it would have been out of fear. And love can't thrive on fear in the same way it doesn't pay attention to reason and logic. It's not a mathematical equation. You can't draw up a list of requirements and hope to find love with the person who meets them. It's intangible, unquantifiable. It's about coming across a person who has something you didn't even know you wanted. An unknown planet colliding with your own in a moment of sheer cosmic brilliance to make you more than you could ever have been yourself. It's that knowledge that sustains you through tough times, the certainty that you will always be less without each other than you are together. And just because I will never find that love now doesn't mean I was wrong to go searching for it.

That's not to say I didn't have a few wobbles. In the weeks after Mark moved out (it was my flat, bought with a small inheritance from my dad and a huge mortgage) I was spun out wondering whether I'd made a huge mistake. I missed his friendship, noticed all the little things that he'd added to my life that hadn't registered when he was there. The music on his laptop, our chats after work over a bottle of wine, and yes, his technical know-how—who was going to fix my computer now? I missed having someone to cook for, to heat the bed. More than once I had been on the verge of calling him to beg him to come back. But I told myself my concerns were selfish, that I'd find myself in the same position again. Hold your nerve, I said.

Then the boiler broke.

It was Friday night. I was alone in the flat. A fierce cold hung over it. I'd had a crappy day at work and all I wanted to do was sink into a hot bath and drink red wine. I didn't want to find a plumber. Call a plumber. Hope he wouldn't rip me off. Stress about the price of a call-out. Whether I had enough money left on my overdraft to pay for it. I didn't want to be in the flat. Cold, alone, breathing clouds of air into the room.

Two plumbers didn't answer. The third said he could come round tomorrow; one hundred and eighty pounds for a call-out charge plus parts.

I told him I'd think about it and ring back.

I brought the duvet from my bed, a bottle of wine from the cupboard, ordered a takeaway and settled down in front of the television. Then I started to cry.

Kira called five minutes later.

"What are you doing?"

"Waiting for a takeaway," I said, cradling the phone in between my chin and shoulder.

"You've just about got time to eat it before we go out."

"I'm not going out."

"So what are you doing instead and what's the matter with your voice?"

"Nothing." I tried to make my tone high and chirpy. "I'm going to eat some food and then watch TV. I'm knackered. I can't face going out."

"Is that *EastEnders* in the background? Oh my God, you're watching *EastEnders* on a Friday night. You are watching *East-Enders* instead of coming out with me to the party."

I reached for the remote and turned the TV to standby. "I am not watching *EastEnders*."

"Don't lie, you are drawn to the misery of it, aren't you? I'll be round in half an hour in a cab." She hung up.

True to her word, Kira arrived half an hour after the phone call. In the cab she gave me a funny look before thrusting her makeup bag at me. "Lipstick might help."

"I had no time to get ready, all right." My face felt scuzzy with the remnants of makeup I'd applied for work more than twelve hours ago. I glared at her and saw her features crease into a smile.

"Anyone would think *he'd* dumped *you*."

I chose a nude color from her bag and applied it just as the cab was swinging around a corner. "Thanks," I muttered.

It was Sadie's thirtieth birthday. A party to which I had been invited but had politely declined, using erratic shift work as a cover. It was held in a pub in Notting Hill not far from Portobello Road. Its name, The W11, the same as its postcode, was written in large silver letters above the door. Outside there was a dark gray awning under which a group of smokers huddled together in the orange light of an outdoor heater. As we got out of the cab Kira said hi to one of them, a girl I didn't recognize, before we slipped inside.

The party was in a claustrophobic basement room. It looked like everyone Sadie had ever met was crammed into the room. Personal space came at a premium. I felt the bass throb in my throat. We made our way to the bar, where there were bottles of beer in huge buckets. I grabbed two, one for each of us. The music drowned out everything so each time we wanted to speak we leaned in, hand over mouth, feeding the words directly into each other's eardrums. Even then I had no idea what she was saying, just nodded along and tried to fix a smile to my face. Kira started to move with the music; she was always a good dancer. A natural. I had been known to shamelessly copy her moves when my own limited repertoire was exhausted, but my body wouldn't move as fluidly as hers. I got the sense I'd need more than one bottle of beer to get it going tonight. I shifted a bit on my feet, like a dad at a disco.

Kira nudged me.

"He's here, just over there, talking to Mark and Sadie."

He was called Fred. A friend of Sadie's with whom Kira had shared a brief encounter weeks before.

He waved in her direction, smiled a warm, toothy smile which she returned while touching her hair self-consciously. He started to make his way over toward us. She shot me a look: *don't worry,*

I won't leave you. I shouted in her ear: "Get lost. If you don't go for him, I will."

I shuffled away to give her space. The crowd at the bar had thinned out, drifted to the center of the room, where a DJ was playing in front of a makeshift dance floor. The tunes were ones I knew, late nineties dance anthems that had the crowd throwing their arms in the air, glancing at each other and nodding in recognition. A couple I recognized embraced on the dance floor and gave each other a lingering kiss. Looking around the room I saw everyone standing in groups or couples, dancing, roaring, shouting, touching. As far as I could tell there was only one other person, a man who appeared older than the rest of the crowd, who wasn't talking or dancing. I recognized the look, as if he couldn't plug himself into the energy of the night. I wasn't in the mood either. If it hadn't been for Kira I would have slipped away, but glancing over in her direction I saw she was deep in conversation with Fred, his hand lightly touching her hip as they talked. I turned to the bar and ordered a cocktail instead.

Two minutes later a woman pushed past me and knocked the glass out of my hand. The white top I was wearing was drenched with strawberry daiquiri.

I stood, head down, watching a trail of pink cut through white fabric and drip down into my cleavage so I could feel strawberry gloop on my boobs. Under normal circumstances I might have laughed. Instead I realized I was about to cry.

I felt someone push paper into my hand.

The woman who had bumped me, no doubt. I wasn't ready to look up. I wanted to disappear.

"Here, take these." It was a man's voice. "Are you OK?" He was shouting, but his voice was barely audible against the music.

"Fine," I attempted to say. I raised my head a fraction, opened my eyes. He pulled back away from me, held out one remaining paper towel. "They've run out here but I can fetch more from upstairs." He saw me about to protest. "Any excuse to get out of here for a minute."

It was the guy who had been standing on his own at the bar. I smiled. "That makes two of us," I said.

I followed him, weaving our way through the faces toward the stairs, where the noise began to recede. True to his word, he extracted a pile of paper towels from the bar, waited as I dabbed down my top. "Lost cause, I think, but thanks all the same." I pulled my coat around me to hide the stain. His face was familiar, the cut of his eyes, the line of his jaw. I glanced around awkwardly, unsure of what to do now, reluctant to go back downstairs. The pub was arranged like a living room, squashy sofas dotted around, battered armchairs, a fire. I was overcome by the desire to sit down, still my head. "Can I get you a drink?"

He hesitated. "That's probably not a good idea."

Brilliant. Now he thinks I'm trying to come on to him. I shot a look over to the door to plan an escape route. A sea of people stood in my way.

"It wasn't a come-on," I said defensively. "Just a thank-you."

"I didn't think it was, it's just . . ."

"You don't have to explain. It's fine. Thanks for the help." I went to move away.

"A pint," he said. "A pint would be lovely."

We installed ourselves in a corner of the pub, me on a sofa and him on the chair opposite. A large low coffee table was positioned between the two. I felt like I needed a loudspeaker to talk to him. He took a swig of his pint and ran his finger up and down the glass. Was he actually going to say anything? I should have cut my losses and run. Why had I felt the need to buy him a drink and prolong the evening?

"I'm sure I recognize your face from somewhere," I said when the silence grew painful.

He looked up, squinted, narrowing his eyes to take me in. "I don't think so," he replied and returned to staring at his glass.

"Are you always this talkative, or is it just me?"

He lifted his eyes and gave me something close to a smile. "Sorry."

"I'm Eve, by the way. How do you know Sadie?"

"She's a friend of my sister."

"Maybe I have seen you before. What's your sister called?"

He cleared his throat. "Annie . . . Annie Alden," he said, as if forcing the words out in defiance, before turning to the glass again to study the lines of condensation that had collected on it.

"Oh," I said before I could stop myself.

The reluctance, the studied air of detachment made sense now.

My glass was almost full, his pint too. I wouldn't get up to leave. I would finish my drink. I would talk to him until it was finished. Then I would go home.

"David," I said. "You must be David." He gave a small nod.

"You can go if you want. I won't hold it against you," he said.

"I still have a full glass of wine." I held it up to prove my point.

"Oh," he said. 'Thank you."

On the same day Mark had left our flat two weeks earlier, David Alden had walked out of Pentonville prison. His mother and his sister Annie had been outside waiting for him as the first flakes of snow fell and melted on the ground. They'd hugged, properly, without guards watching, for the first time in more than five years and led him to the car in awkward silence. In David's eyes everything appeared altered. The colors sharper, noises louder, the speed of movement of buses, people, cars accelerated. Like a ride that was going too fast for him to get on. He felt excluded, detached. On the journey back to the family home in Kent, they'd talked about the weather, about the tenant in his flat who had called to say there was a leak in the roof, about how lucky they'd been with the traffic on the way there. They arrived back at three o'clock. Too late for lunch, too early for supper. His mum produced a chocolate cake she'd baked especially, the words "Welcome Home" spidered on the top in white, leaking into the brown of the chocolate icing.

"Here's to freedom," his mum had said, raising her mug of tea. She reached out to touch his face, as if she couldn't recognize him by sight alone. "You look so different. I can't bear to . . ."

"Well it's over now," Annie jumped in, steering the conversation away from the past, the days and nights in prison, the horror of which they would never, could never understand.

David had smiled weakly, taken a bite of the cake and remarked on how good it was. His mother squeezed his hand, a light sparked in her eyes. This was what they wanted to hear, the part he would have to play.

He couldn't tell them that it wasn't over; that although he was sitting in his mum's living room, on the sofa he'd bounced on as a boy, although he could see out to the garden where the grass was lush now, not worn and brown from his childhood football games, he wasn't free. He couldn't spoil the afternoon by telling them the truth. He was still penned in a room six feet by eight feet.

"You don't need to prove anything to us, love," his mum had told him once. "I know you wouldn't have done it."

He was grateful for her love and belief when friends had faded away unsure of who he was any more. But his mum was wrong. He needed to prove it to everyone, and to Melody, who had been his friend. He needed to prove it to the police, who had charged the wrong man. Where was the person who *had* done it? He'd dreamed of him, walking the streets, inhaling fresh air, under a wide open sky. Would he do it again? Had he done it already? No, David Alden couldn't move forward by as much as an inch until he cleared his name. It wasn't the world that had altered but his place in it.

"They said I had come on to her in the car that night and when she turned me down I got so angry I attacked her. It was never like that between me and Melody. We were friends. I didn't want anything else." He stared at me across the table. "I tried to appeal, but they said there were no grounds for it. Tonight is my first night out since I was released. I can't do it. I can see people watching me and pretending they haven't seen me. I can see them whispering. Even the few who've talked to me . . . you know, the ones who say they believe me . . . I know what they're thinking. They're thinking, did he do it? No smoke without fire. That's what they're thinking." He stopped, looked across to me. "It's what you're thinking, isn't it?"

I was thinking questions, lots of them. I was looking at his face and wondering if that was the face of a man who would try to kill a friend. I was trying to glance at his eyes without being too obvious. Were they cold, or just dead and beaten?

"Yes," I said, "that is what I'm thinking."

"At least you're honest," taking a gulp of his pint. "I'll give you that. Sorry to dump this on you. I need to learn to keep my mouth shut. It's not your problem. I should never have come out because I can't do any of this right now. I can't make polite conversation because all I can think about is working out a way to clear my name, so I can get a job, have a girlfriend who doesn't worry I'm going to kill her. I'd like to be able to walk down the street and not want to disappear. No one gets it, not really. I didn't value it until it was gone. Your reputation is the most valuable thing you have. That's what they took from me. So yes, I might not be in prison any more eating shit food, but everything still tastes crap to me because it's leaked into my whole life. I need to put it right."

"Don't apologize," I said. "I wasn't exactly having the time of my life down there. I only came out because my boiler has broken and it's minus two inside my flat."

"It's going to snow this weekend."

"So I hear. I've timed it perfectly."

"I know a good plumber if you . . ." He stopped himself. "I'm sure you've got it sorted already."

"Actually," I said, "I haven't."

"I'll get Annie to text you the number. Nice to talk to you, Eve." He didn't want to ask for my number, didn't want to put me in an awkward position. I began to understand in the smallest way what he meant when he said he couldn't engage. Your reputation is social currency, the entrance fee into normal life. Without it you will always be on the outside.

He unhooked his coat from the back of the chair, gave me one last lingering look before he walked to the door and disappeared into the dark. His pint was only half finished.

When I was alive, my head was filled with the constant chatter of thoughts, endless to-do lists, meetings, deadlines, overdue bills, forgotten birthdays. I think I was fairly typical. For most of us the minutiae of life tends to crowd out the bigger picture. In that context it is easy to see how the moments that matter slip by undetected. They're unassuming, rarely announce themselves with fanfare. It's only hours, days, years later that you might look back and realize that the chance meeting with an old friend on a bus, the last-minute decision to take a trip, the choice you made to go out to a pub and not stay in watching TV changed the course of your life completely.

Death makes it easy to pinpoint my sliding-doors moments.

If my boiler hadn't broken I wouldn't have gone to the party.

If I hadn't gone to the party I wouldn't have met David.

If I hadn't met David I would still be alive.

Death makes it easier to spot other people's moments too. I had the necessary perspective, hindsight and foresight. Even as I watched Nat walk toward Melody, I knew what was about to unfold. I could predict that their conversation of two minutes, no more, would change the course of her life.

Call it fate, serendipity.

It had to happen.

Twelve

The street air is fresh and welcome after being cooped up in the police station. They step out on to a thin strip of pavement, only narrowly missing a toddler on a scooter. Mel spies the boy's mother fifty yards or so further down from the look on her face and the fact that she is shouting, "Dexter, wait there." She mouths "sorry" to them as she walks past shaking her head.

"Coffee?" Sam suggests.

"No thanks." How can he think of coffee after what they've just heard in the police station?

"Well I'm starving, wait here while I grab a sandwich." Without another word he darts into an Italian coffee shop next to the train station, leaving her standing in the middle of the pavement being bumped and jostled by shoppers. A woman carrying a Marks and Spencer Food Hall bag in each hand knocks her and glares at Mel as if she is in the wrong.

Her eyes cut over to Sam, who is now standing at the deli counter deliberating over sandwich fillings. She can feel the beat of her heart pounding through her. Quickly she walks across to the café and waits outside the door where she can see him.

Two women brush past, arms linked, chatting together. One of them says something she can't catch and they pull away from each other laughing. Dressed up, tight jeans, spike-heeled boots, chunky (architectural, she's heard it called) jewelry, red lipstick. She used to wear it; Mac Lady Danger was her shade. She felt like a right idiot asking for it at the makeup counter. And the clothes, the weekends spent in Selfridges and Liberty touching fabrics, trying them on, emerging with goods that simultaneously emptied her account for the rest of the month and made her feel like the richest woman in London.

She catches sight of her feet. What is she wearing? FitFlops that her mum bought her. Bootleg jeans that must have been in her wardrobe for more than a decade. And where has all her makeup gone? The Lady Danger red that she wouldn't leave the house without? The liquid blush that gave her instant pink cheeks.

Where has *she* gone?

She thinks of the hours spent in Julia's consulting room. Julia is her therapist. Before Julia there was Hugo, and Michael before him. Has she disappeared down a hole somewhere listening to them talk about isolating personal thoughts and representation strategies?

"What do YOU think?" Julia asks her regularly. Why doesn't Mel say what she is really thinking? Why, when she's looking at the nub of Julia's shoulder bone protruding from her clothes and the feathery hair that coats her skin, does she not say, "I'm thinking that you should eat something?"

Or "Do you actually eat anything, Julia, because it looks to me like you could be doing with a very good meal?"

Or "Did you choose the job of therapist so you could focus on other people's issues as a way of ignoring your own?"

It occurs to Mel that she has allowed herself to be reprogrammed, all her idiosyncrasies willingly ironed out. She runs on a straight line now, an even keel without modulation. No, she doesn't get so low she weeps until her eyes puff up, but then nor does she hit the highs, the moments when she loves life and wants to squeeze every last laugh out of it. When was the last time she went out without a plan, happy to go where the evening took her? The hangovers are a thing of the past, but sometimes she craves that feeling from a glass of champagne when the bubbles first hit her head.

She has become so pathetic and invisible that a woman with two bags of ready meals can bump into her and think that is OK. The old Melody with Lady Danger lips and killer clothes wouldn't have stood for that. She'd have said, "No, excuse ME," loudly, with a pointed stare, so the woman knew exactly what she thought of her.

The sky dims, like someone has flicked off the lights. Dollops of black cloud sit above her head. Sam leaves the café, a sandwich held to his mouth. Is he eating it or is it eating him? She's not certain.

"Ready?" he says, as if there's a chance she might like to stand on the street and do nothing a little longer. A spot of mayonnaise on the top of his lip moves when he speaks. She'd like to shove the sandwich down his throat.

"Ready."

At the pay machine, Sam pulls out the ticket from his wallet. Only the machine doesn't take cards, or at least the one that is in working order doesn't, and Sam doesn't have cash.

"Have you got any money?"

"No." She shakes her head without checking. She can tell by the weight of her bag that she didn't bring her purse with her. Come to think of it, why did she even bother to bring her bag? There's nothing useful in it, perhaps nothing in it at all.

"I spent my last on the sandwich." He looks mildly irritated. "Here." He thrusts the keys in to her hand. "I'll go to the cashpoint then, shall I?"

He takes off, running up the slight incline, a lolloping, gangly stride with his arms flailing at his sides. His shape shrinks then disappears entirely before it registers that he has left her on her own. Where is the car? How many levels up are they in the multistory? Two, three? She can't remember. Her eyes slide across to the stairwell. It will smell of stale urine; there will be discarded cans and crisp packets littering the entrance. Nope, she can't go that way, she'll have to use the ramp, avoid the oncoming cars. She tries to get her feet to move but they won't. They're stuck to the ground. She feels her body harden, drying out like modeling clay. If she moves, she might crack and break.

Her eyes scan the path again looking for Sam. A couple walk

toward her, holding hands, as if this is a novelty, not something they're used to. One hand in another, amazed by the simple pleasure of it. Her natural reflex is to think, *that was Sam and me once*, but this is another example of her mind appropriating memories that are not her own.

She's so focused on the young couple that she doesn't see him at first, not until he's almost upon her. When she notices him, she jumps.

He holds his hands up. "Sorry, I didn't mean to give you a fright," he says and then realizes he has seen her before. His eyes are picking over her again, the staring man from the police station.

"About before . . ." he starts. "I thought you were . . . I'm a friend of Eve Elliot's. From a distance I thought . . . well I don't know what I thought."

You thought that I was her.

A splash of rain hits her face. He looks wretched, bulging eyes ringed with dark shadows. Ideally she'd nurture the anger she felt in the station a while longer, cling on to the sense of indignation and righteousness, but it ebbs away from her in the face of the raw grief that seeps out of this stranger. There is a question flitting about in her head, something she wants to ask him, but she can't pin it down for long enough to grasp it.

His voice wavers. "You're Melody Pieterson . . . aren't you? I know your face from . . ." He can't finish the sentence, probably aware that he sounds like a stalker, she thinks. How does he know Melody's face? "I hope I didn't freak you out . . . It's just all of this . . . I don't think it can be real. I keep thinking someone is going to wake me up." The rain is coming down heavily now, like someone has turned on a tap. He is crying.

"I'm sorry." She casts a look up the approach and sees Sam heading toward her. She remembers what it is she wants to ask the man. "The police told me your friend didn't think he was guilty." She tries to keep her tone measured.

He shakes his head slowly, "I guess that's not what you need to hear."

"That's why you know my face, isn't it?" Mel doesn't wait for confirmation. "How far had she got with her . . . investigation?"

He dips his eyes. "She thought she had found something that proved David Alden couldn't have done it . . . the attack."

"Oh," she says. Sam is almost upon them now. She finds herself wishing he wasn't. Another minute, that's all it would take, two at the most, for the man to tell her why Eve thought David Alden couldn't have attacked her. But whatever opportunity she had has faded away. "I have to go," she says. "I'm so sorry about your friend."

The man fumbles in his pocket and pulls out his wallet. Sheepishly he hands her a card. "I don't expect you will, but if you wanted to . . . you can call me. I don't know a lot but . . . well . . ."

She is aware of Sam's panting breaths. Before she can turn to look she hears him ask, "Are you OK?"

"Yes," She grips the card tight in her hand.

Thirteen

What did that guy want?" Sam asks.

"Oh . . . nothing," Mel says.

They are in the car. Sam's car. It smells new, she thinks. Probably toxic, all those sealers and adhesives, not that she's complaining. She likes the scent, it reminds her of pear drops. Did Sam tell her he had a new car? How come she didn't notice? Not even on the way to the police station. She glances over to the steering wheel, sees the BMW logo. The last car was a BMW too. Maybe he hasn't changed it at all. Maybe it's her imagination, her slanted take on reality; seeing things that aren't there without noticing those things that are staring her in the face.

It's too clean. Barely a speck of dust.

"Is this a new car?"

They're still weaving through the streets of Richmond, pedestrians coming at them from all angles, so he can't turn to her and give her the full benefit of his eye roll. *You've got to be kidding me.*

"I got it last week, Mel, you knew that."

"Did I?"

"Yes, I told you." He sounds bored, tired.

"Is it the same as the last one?"

"Yes."

"So why change it?"

"It's a newer model, a better spec."

"It looks the same to me. The same color, the same model." She couldn't be less interested in cars, apart from right now when she can't get this particular car, the newness of it, out of her head.

"Do you want me to tell you where it differs from the 2010 model? I can run you through it if you want. We've got the time. I can tell you about the unique rear suspension cradle or the variable ratio steering wheel with hydraulic instead of electric boost."

Twat. "Right, I get it. I'm not stupid." They have stopped at the traffic lights next to the cinema. Under the Coming Soon banner is a poster for *Gravity*, with Sandra Bullock and George Clooney. When was the last time she and Sam went to see a film together? Have they *ever* been to see a film together? They must have, surely. You can't marry a person if you haven't even been to the movies together, can you?

The lights turn green, they start to move.

"I don't think you told me."

"Mel, for Christ's sake, I have a new car, I told you a few weeks ago. We can afford it, OK, I don't understand the problem."

The problem. Is there a problem? They (he) can afford it. Let it go, accept they have a new car. Say something appreciative, about the upholstery for instance. No, not that. It is leather. The last upholstery was leather too.

"Where were we?"

"What do you mean, where were we?"

"When you told me?"

"How am I supposed to remember? Actually, wait, I'll tell you where we were . . ." He's animated now, as if he's just remembered an answer in a pub quiz. "We were at Siobhan's house for dinner and Tim and I were talking cars and I told you I had ordered a new one."

Mel remembers the night at Siobhan's, the chatter that involved Freddie's tantrums and a potential ski holiday and how poor the service was in the new Spanish tapas restaurant in the village; *an hour before the patatas bravas arrived and I could have sworn they were reheated.* She can picture herself sitting in Siobhan's kitchen with its oak beams to give it that olde worlde feel when it was built in 1982. They ate scallops with leeks and lemon chilli butter, and lamb shanks for main. They had chocolate fondants for pudding. Siobhan smashed a glass of red wine over her dusty pink blouse. "Fuck," she said. This amused Mel in the way it would if her mum swore because it was so out of character. Mel remembers all of this right down to the wine they brought—a Chilean Pinot Noir—but she can't remember Sam telling her about the car.

"I don't think it was at Siobhan's."

Sam slams on the brake. "For fuck's sake." She thinks he is talking to her until she looks ahead and sees that an elderly woman has just marched out on to the road.

At the roundabout they turn right, heading over the Thames, an elegant stretch of the river edged with white stucco buildings on one side and houseboats on the other. If they took the left fork they would climb the hill to Richmond Park. Not that they would ever do that. She hasn't been back since she was found right next to it, although that makes it sound like she was a regular visitor in the first place, which she wasn't. The occasional picnic, a wedding once at Pembroke Lodge. It was a friend from her first job, one of those embarrassing dos where you know no one and spend the day smiling on the periphery. Then there was one winter walk through the Isabella Plantation, a separate world of color hidden away from the rest of the park. Yellows and oranges against the low sun. The four of them, Sam, Patrick, Honor and Mel out for a Sunday walk to ease the hangover.

"You could die happy in a place like this." Had she said that?

Eight months later she'd gone back, not far from the Isabella Plantation.

Almost dead.

Had he been listening?

Mel closes her eyes. It's a smooth ride, she could tell Sam that if only she hadn't got the distinct impression that the car is now a no-go area of conversation. The day has beaten her. She wants to stay awake but she can't fight sleep. The car slows, pulling up to a junction, she imagines; she hears the tick, tick, tick of the indicators. It reminds her of sleepy night-time journeys in pajamas as a child, shrouded in a blanket in the back seat of the car.

"Nearly there," her father would say.

Dropping down a gear, turning in to their street, the hum of the engine, crunch of the wheels over gravel.

She opens her eyes.

Their driveway was paved.

Gravel, she thinks. Her eyes are open, alert. The tiredness of a moment ago is stripped away. She knows where she heard the sound of gravel.

A wave of fear rushes through her. Her body stiffens. She sits up and begs her memory to release more information rather than just this tiny snippet to taunt her. But it won't, it's stubborn like that, will only ever afford her glimpses, partial views obscured by shadows so she can never be sure what it is she is seeing, if she is seeing anything real at all.

London falls away behind them. Shops thin out, patches of green stretch for longer, there are fewer people around, the housing less dense. What is it she feels? Relief? Yes, partly relief. All the reasons she once loved London are the very same ones that make her want to leave now.

Once she felt plugged in just walking the city's pavements, as if the energy was feeding up through her toes; being around so many people, all moving at speed, not wanting to waste so much as a minute or second of a day because there was so much to do and see. And the skyline drawn with Big Ben and St. Paul's, the spike of the Shard piercing the clouds; a city that offered you the chance to walk through the pages of history books while being the most modern, vibrant place she had known. At night in a taxi, or on foot, she loved nothing more than crossing one of the bridges and catching sight of the mercury snake of the Thames beneath her. The evening sky streaked raspberry red with the falling sun, interrupted by the House of Parliament. God, she loved this city. Was there any place in the world she would rather be? She'd see busloads of Japanese tourists disembarking to snap the sights with expensive cameras only to get on again two minutes later. She wanted to shout at them, order them to stop taking photographs. You couldn't capture the essence of London in a photograph. You had to breathe it, live it, immerse yourself in it.

It was three and a half months after the attack before she ventured back to London again. It was Honor's idea: Christmas shopping on Regent Street, lunch, a cocktail, just like the old days, which weren't even that old; it just felt like they were because of the chasm that had opened up between then and now. They traveled up on the train together from her parents' house in Dorset as they had done countless times. But whereas the chat had always been incessant, the easy fluid banter of old friends, now it was stilted. Sentences would end with neither woman picking up the baton of conversation. Mel found herself searching for topics that weren't emotionally loaded only to draw a blank. How is Sam? That wouldn't do. How is work? That would be a giveaway; she knew Honor hated talking about it. Even the simple matter of where they should go for lunch was fraught. Not because they disagreed but because it was Mel who had worked in town, Mel who had been tuned in to the social scene, knew where all the best bars and restaurants were. Only her mind was empty, like someone had taken her contacts book, her knowledge of London built up over six years, and deleted it with the press of a button. At this rate, she thought, we'll end up in an Aberdeen Angus Steak House.

And why did Honor, who had suggested the trip and worn Mel down with her enthusiasm, now seem like she was doing it to punish herself? As if as soon as the train pulled in and they found their seats next to each other she realized what a terrible idea it had been. Their only time together since the attack had been flying visits at first to the hospital and later to Mel's parents' house, with flowers or magazines. "Won't you stay for dinner?" her mother would ask.

"Oh Tess, I'd love to, but I can't, I've got work/e-mails/gym/I'm too tired." Delete as appropriate.

Having feigned sleep for a good hour of the journey, Mel opened her eyes as the conductor announced they were approaching Waterloo. She made a play of yawning, stretching out as if she was emerging from her slumber. Office blocks squatted at either side of the tracks, dirty gray, windows blackened from pollution. Ahead, the lines, dusted with snow, intersected like a giant macramé construction. A train sidled close by giving them a view of the carriage. A woman stared out, black hat and red lipstick. I bet she can remember the name of at least one restaurant, Mel thought.

"Ready?" Honor asked, as she waited for the doors to open on to the platform.

Mel nodded and attempted a smile. Ready was not a word she would have used to describe her feelings at that particular moment.

Had there always been this many people in London? A roiling mass that bumped and shoved her. Surely she was walking at a normal pace, a steady pace, one foot in front of the other, and everyone around her had been speeded up using some weird special effect that exempted her. The station tannoy deafened her, so much so that she pulled her hat down over her ears to deaden the sound. Birds whistled overhead under the dome of the station. Once they got outside it would ease, once she could see London, anchor herself to the familiar sights.

They crossed the road and walked over to the South Bank. Frost glittered on the pavement. Nat King Cole streamed out from the Christmas market stalls that lined Queen's Walk. They were all wooden, made to look traditionally German. She had no idea why. Did Germany have a monopoly on festive markets? On the chocolates and cheeses and plates that they sold? Beyond the market were the silver threads of the Millenium Bridge stretching over the Thames.

Honor slipped, almost lost her footing. She grabbed Mel to steady herself.

"You think they could have gritted the pavements," she remarked.

Mel was too busy concentrating to reply. One foot in front of the other, keep going, she repeated in her head as if the motion, the concentration alone, would hold her up.

Ahead, the river, the spire of St. Paul's; to her left the Houses of Parliament, Big Ben. All shades of murk, the sky and the river an identical color, one continuous sweep of gray. It was, she thought, as if someone had leached the color from the city. Around her everyone cloaked in black or brown or gray like a formidable urban army marching ahead as far as the eye could see. Only the long red trousers of a street entertainer on stilts broke it up. That and the giant white Ferris wheel of the London Eye rotating.

The ground shifted beneath her. She tumbled on to the hard, cold pavement.

It was the shoes she noticed first. All black, like cockroaches scurrying around her. So many. Too many. They were going to start crawling over her body. Stamp, stamp, stamp. The place was teeming with them. Why had she not noticed this before? Still on the ground, she moved her gaze upward, to the peak of the Shard and the Gherkin. They towered over her, dwarfed her. Was this vertigo? She corrected herself immediately. Vertigo was a fear of heights. This was its reverse, a fear of being too low down, too small next to the scale of everything around her.

"Mel! Mel!" She heard Honor's voice. "Melody, are you OK?"

Blackness descended over her.

There wasn't to be any lunch, or shopping, or cocktails. The old days had slipped from their grasp.

It wasn't long after they became official that Sam suggested they move out of London. Mel had not needed persuading. Build a new home together away from it all. Start afresh. Wipe the slate clean. He'd made it sound easy.

The day the builders left and they moved into the house with its white walls and gray floors and all that glass, she knew it had been a mistake. The thunder of traffic, sirens, the sounds of life in London had been replaced by silence. It was more deafening than anything she'd heard before.

No, she doesn't want London anymore but she doesn't want this either. People tell her it's beautiful out in the hinterlands of Surrey, all that space and peace. To her it is desolate. The nothingness of it. She feels like she's come here to die.

Home, she thinks. Where is that now?

She sees a sweep of coastline, jagged cliffs stooping over golden stretches of sand. The sea, dark and threatening, calling out to be explored. She would always run in, whatever the weather, to see how far she could get before the cold sliced into her bones. In the summer, when the water temperature rose, she'd surface-dive and kick downward for as long as her lungs would allow it. She can hear Honor's echoey voice through the water. Counting the seconds she spent below the surface . . . twenty . . . thirty . . . forty, *keep going, Melody*.

Mel rarely goes back now. Mostly when she sees her parents, they come to her. She has tried to erase it from her mind, along with a swathe of her childhood, teenage years, the memories she has lost claim to now because of what she did.

She looks at Sam, eyes fixed on the road. *Well you only have your-self to blame.*

The car slows as they drive through the village. A tractor up ahead has caused the traffic to back up. Autumn is turning the leaves red, pink and golden. They carpet the grass and pavements. Mel watches a woman and her welly-booted son trample through them, stopping occasionally to collect the best ones, the brightest colors, gather them into a white plastic bag. She used to do this herself. She'd make a collage and stick them in her bedroom so when it was winter and bleak and she'd have to drag herself out of bed on dark freezing mornings, stamping at the bus stop to heat her toes, she could re-mind herself that this would pass. That the leaves would grow on the trees again. A new season would come.

"What are you doing?" Sam has pulled in to the car park of Mama Rosa's, the local Italian. "Why have you stopped?"

"I thought we could get something to eat, save cooking."

"I'm not hungry."

"You haven't eaten."

"I'll eat later."

"Well I am."

"You just had a sandwich before we left." You've still got a bit of mayonnaise on your chin, she stops herself from adding.

"Come on, it'll take your mind off it." He has taken the keys out of the ignition and is opening the door.

"How will a pizza in a busy restaurant with kids tearing around and screaming take my mind off it? How do you even know what is on my mind? Can you read it? Is that why you don't feel the need to talk to me or ask me anything, because you've got some magi-cal power that means you just know? Sam knows what's best, Sam is always fucking right? Is that what they teach you at medical school, to know everything?" She realizes she's shouting. Sam slams the door closed again. He looks beaten, shrunken, which makes her feel guilty, which in turn makes her angry because she doesn't want to feel guilty. She wants the upper hand for once. She should have the upper hand. He deserves this.

"What is it you want me to do, Mel? Because I'm trying, I re-ally am. I've not asked you because you said you didn't want to talk about it, you wanted to make it go away. You said you were through with running it round and round in your head. YOU said that. And now it's my fault for not talking. What the hell do you want me to do?"

She'd like to scream. She could scream louder than every child in that fucking pizza restaurant, scream a scream that would snap her vocal cords. Why does he not get it? No, she didn't want to talk about it. She wanted to move on. *Let's design a dream house together* (though she knows she never dreamed of *that* house), *let's get married*, they said so she could switch her obsession from soft furnishings and color schemes to seating plans and menus and lace that doesn't catch the light in the right way, *could you find another one that does, please?* Give Mel something to do, keep her mind off it. Like a child handed a rattle. It worked, but it was only ever going to work to a point. This is obvious now. That point came yesterday in a phone call from Polly. Although really the point, if she wanted to be precise, came earlier, when Eve Elliot was murdered the week before. The same day she was choosing table settings for her wedding.

It's clear now that nothing has gone away. Those thoughts have just been lying there dormant, like little kernels of corn waiting for the moment the heat catches them and they start popping in her head.

She thought she could forget. Now she can't. She didn't want to talk. Now she does. Why is that so difficult for him to get his head around? Has she ever said it was fixed in stone?

"You want to talk, let's talk." He has knitted his eyebrows together in concern, which makes him look like he has a mono-brow. She struggles to take him seriously. "How are you feeling?"

She groans, contemplates banging her head on the shiny new dashboard. No one ever asks that question expecting an honest answer. Of all the questions she can think of, *how are you feeling?* is the least sincere. *I'm shit, but thanks for asking.* Or, *I feel like I want to slap your face, in fact I feel like I should have slapped it a long time ago.* What does he want her to say? And come to think of it, why does he get to set the parameters of their conversation?

A group of mums tumble out of Mama Rosa's pulling kids with balloons tethered to strings behind them. Please God, don't let Siobhan be one of them. I'm not up to faking happiness right now.

How is she feeling? Like a bag of cats, her dad would have said. She is feeling that something is bothering her and for once she is going to say what is on her mind.

"You didn't seem very surprised," she says, because his reaction has been bugging her for hours.

"By what?"

"When DI Rutter told us that Eve Elliot had been trying to help him." She still can't bring herself to say his full name. "You didn't seem shocked by it."

"Didn't I? Well I was . . . God, what is this? What was I supposed to say?"

"So you didn't know?"

"You think I knew? Is that what you're suggesting?" Sam does this regularly, answers a question with a question.

"If you're investigating a case, you interview witnesses, don't you?"

"I wasn't a witness, was I?"

"Friends or relatives, anyone. You . . . you would speak to people, wouldn't you? How else are you going to investigate?" She's beginning to flounder, can feel the fire going out of her argument. Does she sound paranoid, like the madwoman she suspects Sam believes her to be? This is why she doesn't speak her mind, because the result is rarely coherent. She gazes out across the car park and watches a mother kick a buggy after trying and failing to collapse it.

"Honey," he says, "it's been a tough day, a shitty couple of days in fact. I know that. But I'm on your side, whether you like it or not." He raises a smile, which makes her feel dirty with guilt. He's the closest to her so she takes it out on him every time.

She sighs, puffs air out of her cheeks. "I know, I know. I'm sorry . . ." He puts his finger to her lips to silence her then brushes his hand through her hair, following the contour of her face to her chin. He squeezes it affectionately. Mel lifts her gaze upward toward him. Her body gives an involuntary shiver. She has seen that look in his eyes before, can pinpoint exactly where and when.

"You're tired. Come on, let's go home." He pulls out of the car park. He must still be looking at her as he does, because he appears not to see the little girl in a purple party dress, head obscured by a pink balloon, saved only by her mother's quick reflexes.

The look.

It's late August 2007. She sees everything through a mist, thinks for a moment that she is dead and that this is heaven. The momentary delusion is dispelled by a voice that doesn't sound like God's, unless God happens to be female and speaks with a familiar Dorset accent. "She's opened her eyes." The words perforate the membrane of silence that has surrounded Mel's world for . . . how long? Years? A lifetime?

"Someone tell the nurses, quickly." A door opens and slams, footsteps running. Voices distant, then louder, deafening. Every noise is amplified, throbs through her eardrums, echoes through her brain. She'd like to turn down the volume. She could ask, couldn't she? But her throat is raw, swollen, like someone's been feeding her splinters of glass.

Her eyes move toward the voice. Just a few degrees, that does it. The woman's outline is fuzzy, a sweep of dark hair falls from her head. As she leans in closer, Mel feels the hair feather across her arm, like a breeze it's so light.

"Can you hear me? It's me, Honor."

At first she thinks that Honor is her own name, because it carries such a strong ring of familiarity. But the woman keeps repeating Melody, Melody, like a tune to stir her, and she knows that must be her name.

She'd like to keep her eyes open, but her lids are weighted, and the effort of staying awake is too much.

The cycle of time: dark evaporates into light which dissolves into night again. Curtains open, curtains drawn. Routine is important, the voices say, though to whom they are talking she doesn't know. "She's coming round."

Then her eyes open, the muscles in her lids stronger; she can keep them open for oh, at least ten minutes, half an hour, a whole morning.

"I'm very happy with her progress," the doctor says to the woman in the armchair, her mother, but not to her. No one seems to address themselves to Melody any more.

Except the police.

Her progress is being noted. They arrive after she's had a whole morning of eyes open.

They have questions for her, if she doesn't mind.

"Five minutes, that's all," a voice in the room says. Mel could have sworn she hasn't moved her lips.

She was attacked, what does she remember?

She was found next to Richmond Park six days ago. By a dog walker.

Can she remember being in that area? Richmond Park, or Richmond town center on the evening of August 17. Or in Ham Village? It was a Friday.

Can she give them a description of her attacker?

Does she remember his face?

What did he look like?

Was he white or black or Asian?

Something. Whatever she can remember.

Was he known to her?

Can she . . . does she . . . remember . . . anything at all?

Why did she leave the pub and walk past her house?

Was she meeting someone?

They've checked her phone records: there were no calls, no texts, no e-mails in the hours before she left the pub. How did she make the arrangement? Was there an arrangement at all?

Her head is filled with slurry, thick and viscous. No, she can't give them a description. No, she can't say whether he was black, white or Asian. She doesn't remember seeing his face. Just a car pulling up and footsteps, she says. She waits for their reaction. *Footsteps and a car she can't describe, this will get them nowhere.* They need her memories to be sharp and defined. But how can she explain to them that they are not easily liberated. She closes her eyes. Lets the questions linger, waits for them to stir something in her subconscious. A name surfaces and forms on her lips. She catches it in time, remembers it is a secret, although not the reason why it is a secret. But she is aware that it carries consequences were it to get out.

Her lids are heavy again, too heavy to stay open. Sleep beckons.

Sometimes she wakes and will find her mother fussing around the bed covers, talking to her dad, telling him off for not taking the bins out or still not having fixed the bathroom door handle. "I got stuck in there this morning," she hears her say. It makes her smile, although whether the smile reaches her face she can't say. She must be getting better if her parents are squabbling.

Honor visits again, this time accompanied by Sam. Later she finds out a rota was devised so she was never alone at visiting time, which meant she was rarely alone at all. If anyone had asked her she would have said she'd like to have more time to herself, to find some peace to search her memory, peel back the layers that are obscuring it to reveal . . . what? She doesn't know. But no one did ask her. They assumed she would want company. Now she thinks about it, the assuming has been a defining characteristic of her life since then.

Back to the visit. Honor and Sam. She wakes up to find two figures by her bedside, a gentle murmur of chatter. It takes a moment for her eyes to clear the dust of sleep, pull them into focus. Between them is a bunch of grapes encased in plastic, sweating under cellophane. Her eyes lock with Sam's.

"She's awake." He nudges Honor, who is leafing through a magazine.

"Hey," she says. "What time do you call this?"

They talk about hospital food and her mother's insistence on planning a recovery menu "because no one is going to get well on the stodge they serve here." About Patrick, who plans to visit tomorrow. He was the one who reported her missing. "I never thought I'd say this, but thank God he's so anal," Honor chirps. They remind her that they are both doctors (she hasn't forgotten this fact) and that if there is anything she wants to know about her injuries (which aren't extensive) she should ask them.

Honor, she realizes, is talking very quickly.

She is talking so quickly Mel has stopped processing the information and lets the words swim around the room without trying to catch them.

She stares at each of them in turn. The scene jars with her though she can't say why. Like a spot-the-difference picture. She knows something is wrong but can't put her finger on it. There is also something she'd like to do to satisfy a deep need stirring inside her, but she can't make the connection as to what it is.

At last Honor takes a breath, pauses. "We thought we'd lost you, Mel, I shouldn't have let you walk home alone." There's a noise in the room like a chair scraping along the floor. "I'm so sorry." The noise is coming from Honor. Mel has known her since they were eleven. Never before has she heard her cry like this.

Sam puts his hand on her knee. "Come on, Honor." He passes her a tissue. Mel doesn't hear him say "pull yourself together," but the tone of his voice conveys the sentiment. "Why don't you go and get us all a cup of tea?"

They exchange a look she can't decipher.

"I'm sorry, would you look at me? I'm supposed to be here to cheer you up." Honor rises from the chair and disappears through the door before Mel has time to tell her she's gone off the idea of tea.

Sam draws his chair in toward the bed. His eyes are wet and glassy. His head dips. It's quiet between them, just the beep of the monitor and the occasional click of the drip feeding drugs into her bloodstream. She feels him take her hand, carefully so as not to disturb the cannula. With his finger he strokes it. Just a touch, an electrifying touch that rewires the loose connection in her brain.

Now she knows what it was she wanted to do when she opened her eyes and saw him.

"Can you remember anything, Mel?" The same question the police asked her. Shadows rising to the surface again.

"Very little," she says. "They want to know why I had walked
past my house, why I was out so late. They asked me if I was meeting anyone." She waits, wants to scrutinize his face, but he is looking down at her hand, his finger gently circling the purple bruising
around the cannula. "I must have been, right? Why else would I
have gone there? But it's all hazy." He looks up now; she has his
attention. What is it she's hoping to find in his face? She can't read
the look.

"What did you tell them?"

"I keep thinking back to the pub. I was there with Patrick and
Honor, then I went to the toilet and I left afterward. I thought someone must have called me or texted me." She stops. The dredging
of memories is hurting her head; a tight band of pressure surrounds
it. "They've checked my phone, I didn't receive any texts or messages that night."

"You've suffered severe trauma. Don't underestimate the impact
it will have. It'll take time for everything to settle. You're bound
to be confused."

She nods, no idea if this is true or not, if it's simply a stock phrase
doctors use to reassure patients.

He lifts her hand, kisses it. What is it that she can't access? She
needs to join the dots in her head to make a complete picture, but
this is beyond her.

"Let's not talk about it now, let's wait until you're better. I thought
I had lost you . . . I don't know what I would have done."

"Why would I have had two phones?"

"Two phones?" His face is scrunched up into a question.

"It's just that I remember one being in a black cover and the
other in a white one."

"Maybe you're remembering your old phone. You shouldn't worry
about these things, Mel. You need to concentrate on getting well."
He reaches his hand out toward her face, touches her hair and runs

his finger down her cheek. "It's understandable that things are a bit mixed up."

The look.

Moments later Honor returns with a tray of teas, the happy mask back in place. They sit and talk some more, Honor playing with a thin thread in her hands, twisting it around her fingers so the flesh bulges through it, cutting off the blood supply. She doesn't touch her tea.

Only when her mother comes in to take over the reins does Mel realize why the air between them has been so charged.

Tess is in the corridor talking to Honor, the door ajar. "Thanks for coming," she says. "You've been great really, with so much on your plate, work and planning for your big day."

Honor gives a nervous laugh. "Oh that," she says, "that can wait."

Mel looks at Sam but he is squeezing her hand too tightly, pressing on the bruise.

At home, he makes her a cup of tea, offers to cook dinner, but she's not hungry. "A sandwich will do me," she tells him, cutting a slice of cheese and wedging it in a bread bun. It's barely seven o'clock, but tiredness is heavy on her body, her eyes sting, her bones ache. All she wants to do is put on her pajamas, lie in bed and cocoon herself in the duvet. Sam is sitting in front of the TV watching *The One Show*, although technically he's not watching it. He has his iPhone in his hand, scrolling down. On Twitter probably, a medium made for a man who can say everything he wants in one hundred characters, never mind one hundred and forty. She once read an article that said that if you check your e-mails before you get out of bed or take your phone to the loo you should consider yourself addicted. On this basis she considers Sam addicted. She's seen him on the loo, tweeting and crapping. "Multitasking," he laughed, when he realized he'd left the door ajar and saw the look of disgust on her face.

Shame the Japanese haven't invented a toilet that washes and blow-dries your phone as well as your arse.

She looked at Sam's timeline once to see what was so fascinating and couldn't get her head around it: the incessant noise of it, the hashtags, the inane one-way conversations. What was the point of it? If she was honest, she interpreted it as a slight on her, because their time together was finite, allocated in evenings and the weekends which weren't taken up with work. She viewed this as a meaningless distraction that encroached upon it.

"I'm off to bed," she tells him, hanging her head around the door.

"Already? It's only . . ."

"I know, I'm knackered."

"I thought you wanted to talk."

"Tomorrow," she says, "when I've had some sleep."

Tomorrow he'll be back at work.

She has brought her coat upstairs to the bedroom, her phone too. Once she is undressed and has crawled into bed, she opens her Facebook app, scrolls down. There is one entry today from Honor, two photographs that were posted this morning but actually taken on a night out yesterday. A picture of her grinning in front of cocktails, with two other women Mel has never seen.

Just like the old days, except it isn't her who Honor is having fun with.

There's a familiar clenching in her stomach. She has no right to be jealous. *This is your fault. How else did you think it was going to pan out?*

Mel tries to pinpoint the moment when their friendship disintegrated. It's not the first time she has tried. The conclusion she reaches is always the same. There wasn't a single, definable point in time when the fissure occurred, more a gradual separation that happened over months, almost imperceptible at first. The space between visits and phone calls grew longer with each week until there was no contact at all, only space between them.

There was so much she wanted to say to Honor, to ask her. And yet she never found the courage. Was it too late now?

She places her coat on the bed next to her, feels in her pocket for the hard edges of the card and pulls it out.

Nathaniel Jenkins. 07954 735123

What did Eve discover? Did she find the answers to the questions Mel hasn't asked?

Will Nathaniel be able to tell her anything?

Curiosity burns through her. Her mind fills with thoughts and questions of her own. She doesn't want to sleep tonight for fear that her dreams will erase them and come morning everything will be blank again.

Much later, when Sam comes to bed, she listens to him stretching. You're about to go to sleep, not run a ten-fucking-kilometer race, she thinks. She feels the covers being pulled back on his side, him slipping into bed, careful not to disturb her.

Tomorrow, she thinks, when she's not talking to him, she's going to talk to someone else.

Fourteen

Everyone has a computer; even her granny has one, and she's ninety-four. She plays bingo on it, "only when it's pouring down and I can't make it to the Mecca," she claims. Victoria suspects it's more of a habit than she cares to admit. And why not? If you get to that age, you can be excused a few vices.

But Eve was thirty and there is no way she didn't have a computer. They've found a warranty for a MacBook Air in a drawer in her flat, a spare charger too. But the actual laptop has not been located.

Did she leave it at work? This is unlikely. She was a freelance producer who filled in on different programs, rarely in the same place for more than a few days at a time.

So far they know that Eve worked on a money show with the annoying guy who's always telling everyone to switch their gas and broadband providers for a better deal—Who has time for that, Victoria wonders—*Watchdog, The One Show*, and a few radio programs. The point being you wouldn't leave your laptop somewhere if you weren't returning the next morning.

If she doesn't have the laptop, Victoria can't read what Eve was working on for the last six months. And what she wants to know is whether Eve discovered something she wasn't meant to.

"Be careful you don't get bogged down," DCI Stirling warned her yesterday when she mentioned it. "For all you know there might not be anything *to* read. Don't get sidetracked." He shot her a look: *trust me, I know best.*

Victoria has a lot of respect for Stirling, and not only because his clear-up rate is one of the best in the Met. He's been a mentor to her, encouraged her to go for successive promotions. Who knows, without his support she could still be a detective constable trawling CCTV. Is it a blessing or a curse that her first big case as DI happens to be connected to one of his? Alden was Stirling's first time round. A quick result, the kind that cemented his reputation. He expects no less from her. "This one's hardly going to test you, is it, Rutter?" he said when they brought Alden in for questioning. "Don't fuck it up," he joked.

David Alden was the last known person to see Eve Elliot. He has no alibi for the night she disappeared. He has a conviction for an attack that is strikingly similar, almost identical, to this one. Eve's fingerprints have been found in his flat. Then there's the gold caged bird chain found in Melody Pieterson's hand, placed in Eve Elliot's hand too. It's all pointing in one direction. Stirling hasn't asked why Victoria hasn't charged him yet, but she's seen the question twitching on his lips a few times.

So why hasn't she charged him?

She tells herself that none of Alden's DNA was found on Eve's body. No fibers matching her hair or clothing have been found in his car. There is another niggle too. More than a niggle. Why would you kill a woman who's trying to clear your name?

"She'd obviously come to the same conclusion as us," DCI Stirling said last night. Victoria wasn't aware she had actually voiced her thoughts. It was eight o'clock in the evening. Did the man not have a home to go to? His retirement is two months away. How is he going to fill his time? He's single, twice divorced. The flip side of his professional success. She thinks he might have children, a son at least. He used to keep a picture of a boy in an argyle sweater and a bowl cut on his desk, but she hasn't seen it in years. She peered up from her desk, his bulky frame filling the doorway. "You should go home, Rutter, those kids of yours might want to see you now and again. You can't get the time back, take it from me."

"But why would he kill her? Why repeat the crime when he was already free?"

"Because he's an evil bastard. Now piss off."

That's the other thing she has a problem with: black and white, good and evil. As far as she can tell, the boundaries are never that clearly defined.

Fifteen

N at hadn't gone to my mum's house alone before. His body pushed against a force field that thrust him backward. Every step hurt. The task of walking onward required superhuman effort and he wasn't up to it. He was half way through the estate of 1960s detached houses and already spent, empty. The last time he was here we had remarked on the manicured lawns and hanging baskets and shiny cars on driveways.

"The closest we'll get to a garden is one of those herb pots that you sit on your windowsill," he'd said. No one built homes like this close to London anymore. Just flats, blocks and blocks of apartment buildings. No one our age could afford a house, detached or otherwise. Not unless they were bankers or drug dealers. Neither profession had ever inspired us.

"You might get lucky," I said. "Who knows, in ten years' time you could have a balcony, with enough space for a deckchair to peer down at the roundabout below."

Nat hated the hanging baskets at number 32 today. He wanted to rip each brightly colored pansy from the rockery at number 28. Smash up the Renault Megane in the driveway of 25. *Eve should be here*. It was wrong, all wrong. *She should be here*. He paused for a second, drowning in thought. What was he doing here anyway? Would my mum really want to see him, he wondered.

I heard myself shouting at him. "She *would* want to see you, don't you dare turn around." Couldn't he remember me telling him that when my dad died, hardly any of my mum's friends called around? "People are so worried of doing the wrong thing they don't do anything at all," I'd said. "They don't know what to say so they stay silent." For weeks the phone barely rang. We'd have killed for a distraction, an intrusion. We would have clung on to the person who was brave enough to ring the doorbell and not let them go. We were desperate for anyone or anything to stand between us and the total desolation of grief. Instead we got cottages pies and lasagnes steaming on the doorstep with polite notes: *Thinking of you.*

When he started to move again, I wanted to dive down and kiss him. He approached my mum's door with trepidation. He noticed its color, light powder blue. I had chosen it a few months ago. Nat remembered the discussion vividly, in the back garden of my mum's house. He had a beer in his hand. I had a glass of Pimm's, sipping it as I pored over the color charts.

"You can't have bottle-green gloss," I'd told my mum.

"But it's what we've always had."

I rolled my eyes. "It's not exactly current," I said, pointing her to Farrow and Ball's Blue Gray.

"I don't need my front door to be *current.*" She looked down at the chart, then up at Nat to exchange conspiratorial smiles. "I might have known you'd choose one of those colors too. You might be stupid enough to pay those prices, but I'm not."

We came to a compromise over Dulux First Frost.

Had he called me a color fascist? He smiled when he thought of this. "You need to be careful, Eve, or you'll turn into one of those people."

"Meaning?"

"One of those people we've always taken the piss out of." He laughed. I opened my fingers in a V and drew them down my face.

He rang the doorbell expecting no one to answer, or for Steve to tell him my mum wasn't up to visitors.

It was my mum who came to the door.

She stopped for a moment, gazed at his face as if she couldn't quite remember who he was and why he might be there. Then a flare of recognition lit up her eyes.

"Oh Nat," she said, coming out on to the path to embrace him. "Oh Nat . . ." but she couldn't say anything else. All the words were choked off in her throat.

My mum loved Nat, right from the first time I introduced them. He's gay, so he didn't suffer any of the awkwardness a new boy-friend might have on meeting the parents. He just bowled in and won her over. He laughed at her jokes, and not politely, but rau-cously, like they were the funniest thing he had heard. I love my mum, but she's no comic. Nat, though, always did have a strange sense of humor. On subsequent meetings he'd say, "Nice haircut, Mrs. R," or, "New top? That color suits you." For her part she was always trying to find him a girlfriend, in the same way she would try to convert vegetarians to meat: *but you'll eat a bit of chicken, won't you?*

Now her small bony frame clung to him. He was the first of my friends she had seen in the flesh since she'd heard, and now she held him with a desperation that broke me, as if the touch, the associa-tion could itself bring me back.

They were both crying, a cry that ran so deep it was barely audible. Thin, stretched noises carried on the air around them. Neither of them understood what had happened; the enormity of it toppled their minds. How could they make it real? In the right circumstances, at the right time, death could be a blessing, a re-lease. But not like this. Not snatched and stolen. That sort of death leaves little parcels of guilt with your friends and family that op-press them and taunt them during the night when they hunt sleep. They should have, they could have, what did they miss? What could they have done? Why didn't they see?

They weigh me down too.

If anyone should have seen it coming, it was me.

You couldn't have done anything, I wanted to scream.

Nothing at all.

———

After her initial reaction upon seeing Nat, my mum didn't behave how you might have expected her to behave; you know, the way you see people in the immediate aftermath of death, staring out of the window, popping tranquilizers to dull the pain, wading through days unable to speak. Firstly, there was no way she was going to start popping pills to knock herself out. Why should she be spared the agony when her baby had been murdered? However much it hurt, she needed to feel. Secondly, as I mentioned before, my mum had turned talking into an art form. She drew on it heavily now for its defensive qualities.

"They've arrested him. D'you know that, Nat? Did they tell you?" She dipped her voice. "Paula in there has told me all about it." The Paula she was referring to was a family liaison officer, now hanging back in the kitchen talking to Steve. My mum leaned in to take her mug of tea from the coffee table then gave a small shake of her head. She had always loved tea, couldn't get out of bed without two cups of it in the morning. Now that it was thrust upon her for want of anything better to do or say, its appeal had gone.

I watched the pair of them sitting in a room that was achingly familiar. I knew if you moved the leather armchair just an inch you'd see a stain where I'd spilled red wine last Christmas. "You are drunk, Eve!" my mum had claimed. "S'Christmas," I'd replied with a smile and hugged her.

The cushions were brown and cream geometric prints that I'd bought her last year when she had the house decorated. Now, every time she puffed and rearranged them—which she did regularly—she would be reminded of me. When she looked in her wardrobe to get dressed in the morning, she'd see the items I had picked out for her and she'd wonder, *who the hell is going to steer me away from the comfy slacks now?* Who was going to buy her cushions and laugh at her burned roast dinners? From the most banal and mundane to the bigger picture—never seeing me again or hearing my laugh or holding me tight—every single part of her was saturated with loss.

"She was helping him, Nat, this David character. Well I'm sure I don't need to tell you, no doubt you'll know more about it than I do. But tell me this, why would you do that to someone who was helping you?"

Nat shook his head slowly, absorbing the information. He had suspected the police were interested in David Alden from the interview with DC Chiverton yesterday.

Snippets of my last conversation came back to him.

My mum, as though reading his mind, said: "What was the last thing she said to you about the case, Nat?"

"She thought she had got somewhere, with evidence; she thought she could prove he was innocent."

"Right." My mum looked wired, sleepless eyes glinting, clenching her jaw when she wasn't talking. "And how often have you known Eve to be wrong? Hmmm? I mean, even when you thought she was out left field, it always worked, didn't it? She was a good judge of character. She'd been working on this for what . . . six months, seven months? And she gets to the point where she thinks there's a breakthrough, and she's killed. By the man whose conviction she's trying to overturn?

"You know, when I first heard who it was they had arrested, well, if you had let him near me I would have torn him apart with my bare hands. But since it's the only thing I can think of, I've been going over it, over and over. And I just can't believe she got it so wrong. I won't believe it. I want to know where all her information is, because she must have left something. And what if she was right and this man didn't do it, what if he's convicted again? You're telling me Eve's death will be for nothing?"

I had taken a look at my mum and thought she was beaten. I'd seen a woman of sixty, five foot three inches (and a quarter) who hadn't slept in days, red veins threading her eyes, a woman whose skin was papery, almost translucent. I had underestimated her.

Stubborn? That was me. But if I wanted to know where I got it from, all I needed to do was look at my mum at that moment and feel the determination radiating from her. It rendered Nat speechless. He hadn't expected this madness, the raw fury. She believed me and wouldn't be persuaded otherwise until she saw some hard evidence.

Until that moment I had always thought we were different. But the silk scarves, the court shoes, the domestic perfection had just disguised the truth. At our core my mum and I were the same people.

"And another thing," she leaned in and dipped her voice, "they can't find her computer, which is where I imagine she kept all the information. What if she'd discovered something that someone wanted to keep hidden? If the file is lost, it's unlikely we're going to find out."

Nat felt he was waking up from an extended sleep in that disorientated way when you're unsure if it's day or night. How could he have forgotten? Or not forgotten, just not made the connection? His brain must have gone into crisis mode where he could only deal with the information in front of him.

He took a swig of his tea, pulled a face when he realized it was stone cold.

"I have it," he said slowly. "She e-mailed it all to me as a backup."

My mum regarded him for a moment as if he wasn't quite right in the head. "You have it? You have the file? When did she last send it to you?"

"I'll have to check. But it was recently, probably close to when . . ."

"Well you had better tell them." She pointed in the direction of the kitchen before lowering her voice to a whisper. "But make sure you take a copy first, just in case."

Sixteen

Y ou know those people who are always losing things: keys, phones, a fob for the office, a boarding pass at the airport? That was me. I used to think how much easier my life would have been if I had been more like my friend Kira, who was OCD when it came to organization. Sometimes, as I was chucking my keys down on the nearest surface, I'd catch myself and say, *what would Kira do?* And then place them somewhere easily locatable like in the door. But invariably it didn't last. So yes, I should have had a memory stick as a backup for the file, but honestly, I would have lost it within days.

When Mark was around we had a cloud where we (or he) would store documents, but when Mark went the cloud went too. Or maybe it didn't. Either way I had no knowledge of how to access it. The safest way for me was to e-mail documents to myself and to someone else. Old-school, yes, but effective all the same.

At first I did this sporadically, mainly when I remembered, which wasn't all that often. It was during summer that I upped my game, around the time I began to wonder if someone was trying to scare me off.

One of the disadvantages of being prone to mislaying objects is that I can't say definitively when it started. Sometimes a belt or a pair of jeans or an important letter would go missing for weeks and then turn up in the very place I had been searching. I do remember Glastonbury, though, the last weekend of June, Kira's farewell before she took off on a six-month trip to Southeast Asia (not the Middle East). It rained on the first night but the next morning, to everyone's delight, blue sky appeared and brought with it a glorious three-day stretch of sunshine. I remember gazing at the makeshift city (the size of Sunderland, apparently) spreading out as far as the eye could see, throbbing to the bass under a haze of heat. Food stalls, smells, cider in the sun, Mumford & Sons thunderous on the Pyramid stage closing it down. A long journey home, caked with mud and happiness. Opening the door to my flat, flinging my bags down, three things on my mind: tea, shower and sleep. I went into the kitchen on automatic, opened the cupboard to find a mug, but the mugs weren't there. They were in the next cupboard along. Perhaps I had drunk too much cider over the weekend. I thought no more of it. Until I went to the cupboard to get a fresh towel for the shower. The towels were folded and neatly stacked, alternating white and gray (the only two colors I owned). Magda my cleaner must have been. But Magda came on a Tuesday and wasn't the type of person to seek out extra work. She did her hours, minus fifteen minutes, had a cup of tea and a biscuit, took her money and left. No, this, I thought, had my mum's hallmarks all over it. Anger surged inside me. How dare she come into my flat and rearrange my cupboards. Ok, so my standards might occasionally dip below her minimum levels, but this? I called her number.

"Eve . . . oh hang on a minute. Steve, watch out, that car's reversing. Hello, love, how was Glastonbury?"

"Where are you?"

"We're just setting off from Cheshire."

"Cheshire?"

"Yes, I told you, remember our old neighbors Derek and Liz, we've been to see them this weekend. Lovely part of the world, really, you should see their house. Beautiful . . . and the garden they've got. Harriet said to say hello."

"Harriet?"

"Harriet, who you sat next to in school for three years, you know, your old best friend. You feeling a bit delicate from the weekend then?"

"Mum, have you been in my flat?"

"When?"

"Over the weekend? Any time from Friday?"

"Eve, I just told you we've been in Cheshire, don't you listen to a word I say?"

I tried calling Kira but remembered her battery had died on the way home, so I spoke to Nat instead.

"You sound rough."

"A few hours of sleep won't go amiss."

"Worth it though?" he asked.

"Yeah, I suppose it was."

"Are you OK?"

"Hmmm."

"What's the matter?"

"This is going to sound mad, but the mugs in my kitchen have been moved and the towels are all neatly arranged in the cupboard. White then gray, white then gray."

"Are you serious?"

"Yup, that's weird, isn't it? You don't think . . . ?"

He laughed. I held my breath again.

"Jesus, Eve," he said, "what were you two taking over the weekend?"

I showered quickly, scrubbed at my body to remove the mud, watched brown water trickle off my legs. Drying myself, I felt revived, like I had been given a new layer of skin. Lack of sleep can mess with your head, I told myself. I made a sandwich and ate it in bed reading a book. I mustn't have read more than a page before sleep pulled at my eyes and dragged me away. It was only when I woke hours later with a pain in my neck that I realized my favorite pillow had gone. It was a week later before I found it in the same cupboard as the towels, hidden behind the once symmetrical arrangement.

That was the first time I registered the intrusion. There were others, countless occasions and moments when I noticed something was missing, askew, but not once were they accompanied by any proof that someone had been in my flat. A dress missing from the washing line, tulips in a vase on my return that hadn't been there when I left. The worst one was the disappearance of my Obi-Wan Kenobi Russian nest doll, given to me by my dad on my fourteenth birthday, the last birthday I shared with him. It had pride of place on my bedside table. When that went I knew something was either seriously wrong or I was losing my marbles, each turn of the screw tipping me more toward paranoia. "I wish someone would break into my flat with flowers and organize my towels," Nat joked. He'd come round after Obi-Wan Kenobi went missing. He checked the locks, windows, doors. "I think you've been watching too much *CSI*," he concluded when he couldn't find any sign of a break-in.

So I shut up, kept it to myself and tried to put it out of my mind. But one thing changed: I became strict about sending Nat my files, extracting a promise from him not to hit delete as soon as they landed in his in-box.

"I'm like the online equivalent of one of those containers where you put all the shit you'll never need," he moaned.

But he kept his promise, and on that everything else pivoted. If he hadn't, Melody wouldn't have read it and she wouldn't have got to the truth.

But there I go hypothesizing again.

Seventeen

M el has punched in his number four times so far only for the courage to desert her before she hits the call button. What is she going to say? What exactly does she expect *him* to say? Why did he give her his number in the first place?

Each time she aborts her mission she follows the same routine: makes a cup of coffee, wipes the work surface clean, chops a few more vegetables in preparation for supper in eight hours' time. Then she walks to the huge windows and stares out. Directly off the kitchen is a patio paved with the same light gray tiles as the kitchen floor. When the doors are open you have the sense that there is no delineation between outside and in, so Sam says. *The two spaces effectively merge together*—this from the architect. It is all bollocks, of course. Mel looks out. The wind must be up: white clouds scud across the sky, the bare branches of the cherry tree lean to the right. When she's indoors she has a ceiling above her head, walls that enclose her, the temperature remains a constant 22°C thanks to the thermostat. If she was outdoors she would feel the wind snatch the breath from her, the temperature would dip by at least five degrees, yet at the same time she would feel her insides broiling. Matching tiles or not, any fool can tell the difference between the two.

She paces back to the counter where she pours another cup of coffee in a fresh mug just for the hell of it. She imagines the tarry black liquid flushing through her system. Does she drink too much coffee? If she swapped it for say fennel tea as Erin has suggested would it silence the noise in her head? Could it be one of those rare switches where the reward is proportionally greater than the effort involved?

Would it stop the thoughts exploding like bang snaps in her head? She puts the mug down.

It's curiosity that's driving her, she decides. No. It's not that. Curiosity is too gentle a word to convey the urge that has gripped her, which is raw and visceral. She needs to know what Eve Elliot discovered—if she discovered anything at all; she has to find out why Eve was targeted and killed. Given time, the police will come up with a version of events just like they did in Mel's own case. She suspects that version is already being written. They've arrested him, haven't they? But it's not enough. She wants to work it out herself, get it straight in her own head. She wants to feel it and believe it, not have an outside party impose their truth on her. Until then her imagination will run riot, producing ever more wild and vivid scenarios that she struggles to discount. It's as if she is surrounded by a swarm of wasps; every time she swats one away, ten more buzz around her face.

If there is the slimmest chance that Nathaniel Jenkins might be able to help her get some answers, she has to take it.

"Is that Nathaniel Jenkins?" she asks unnecessarily. Who else would be answering his mobile?

"Uh-huh." He sounds wary, like she might be about to launch into a spiel to sell him life insurance or double glazing.

"This is Melody Pieterson." Once she has dispensed with this statement of fact she is at a loss.

"Oh . . ." he says. She hears him chew and gulp as if he's quickly swallowing whatever was in his mouth so he can talk. "I . . . I didn't expect you to call."

"Me neither."

"But I'm pleased you did."

"You are?"

"I think so."

She emits a nervous laugh. "That's not convincing me."

"Sorry . . . I am really."

"Now you're going to ask me *why* I've called and . . ." She feels the words slip away from her, words that only a few seconds ago were all loaded up in her mind and ready to fire. "I don't have a clue what to say."

"You want to know how far she'd got with David Alden . . . with the investigation, I'm assuming."

She heaves a sigh of relief on hearing him summarize it so succinctly. "How did you know?" It's not really a question, more a quip, but he answers it.

"Because I want to know the same thing."

"Oh," she says. His admission has dashed whatever hopes she had pinned on Nathaniel. What did she expect from him? Some kind of magic, a golden key that would unlock the mystery? He's just as stumped as she is.

"I have it all in front of me," he says.

"What . . . what do you have in front of you?"

"All her work. Well, everything she noted down, and knowing Eve, that would be everything. She's a bit anal like that, you know. There's tons of it . . . runs to more than a hundred pages." He tries to laugh but she hears it break. He's still talking about her in the present tense.

"You have it?" Her pulse is up, her breaths come shallow and fast. A second ago Mel was despairing; now she's flying again. Her stomach feels like it's come away from her, suspended in midair. "*Why* would you have it?" She tries to sound relaxed but her mind is already leaping ahead.

"Because Eve loses everything and I'm very careful." He has an accent she's trying to place, one that makes his sentences rise at the end. Welsh? Geordie? "Because she wanted me to have it in case . . ." Geordie, she thinks, definitely from the north. *In case any-thing happened.* She completes his sentence in her head.

She hears him sigh, and when he speaks next his voice is a note higher. "She was worried someone was . . . I don't know. There was never anything concrete, just weird shit happening, like mugs moved around, or her washing taken from the line, if you know what I mean."

She does.

Mel feels like someone has just kicked dust up in her eyes. Blinded her.

She knows very well.

"Phone calls you answer only to find there's no one on the line. Knocks on your door."

"Yeah, something like that."

"Nathaniel," she says gently. "It wasn't a question. I was telling you what has happened to me."

"Oh . . . right."

"Everyone thinks I've been going out of my mind."

"No one believes you?"

"There's never any proof, just my word."

"I didn't believe Eve, not really. I thought it was . . ."

"In her mind?"

"Yes," he says quietly. "I hate myself."

"Shame we never met, Eve and I . . . I mean, that would have been weird . . . but you know, maybe we would have understood each other . . . then again, I probably would have told her to get lost and stop interfering."

"You're convinced David Alden is guilty?"

Am I? Am I a hundred percent convinced?

She had believed David Alden attacked her. It was a truth, an absolute handed to her in a neat package. Not one she had wanted to accept at first, but she had no choice. And over time she came to see that it gave her a narrative to explain what had happened, offered her a full stop at the end of the story. A chance to move on, rebuild her life: wasn't that what the DI had said to the press. And she *had* built something—the house, a relationship with Sam—but she couldn't shake the feeling it wasn't *her* life she had built, but someone else's, someone who looked like her, talked like her, but was nothing like the person she had left behind.

"I thought I was."

"And now?"

"I'm not sure I'm convinced of anything any more. Do *you* think he did it?"

"I thought Eve was under pressure, a bit paranoid. But I still trust her judgment. Her instincts were almost always right. I think she might have found out too much."

Mel considers this. Her own instincts are telling her what she needs to do now. If she thinks about the consequences for too long she won't act on them. "Would you send it to me?" she asks.

She counts the seconds before he answers.

"You're sure you want it?"

"I am," she says with certainty.

She recites her e-mail address, spells out her name so Nat takes it down correctly.

"OK," he says. "I should warn you there's a lot of it. If you need anything . . . or you want a chat . . . give me a call."

"Thanks," she says.

Two minutes later, Eve's file lands in her in-box.

Part Two

One

D id David Alden attack Melody Pieterson? The question bugged me from the moment I watched him walk out of the pub in Notting Hill. I caught myself wishing, as I always did on *APPEAL*, for special powers that would transport me back to the moment of the attack so I could see for myself the face of the person who tried to kill her.

Six months later I got to look him in the eye because the same person wanted to kill me too. The only difference was this time he succeeded.

Why, you might ask, couldn't I have speculated on David Alden's innocence or guilt for a few moments, hours even, discussed it with a mate and then moved on? Certainly among my circle of friends that would have been the normal response. Why did I have to take it further and start meddling in something that frankly was none of my business?

Ideally I'd say my interest was piqued at the sniff of injustice. I'd wave my CV in your face as proof of my experience and expertise in this area of work. I could point to the fact I sponsored a child called Frank in the Democratic Republic of Congo as evidence of my bleeding-heart liberalism. I could say that basically I was just a very nice person.

I'd be lying.

My motives were far more selfish than I cared to admit.

My job on *APPEAL* was part of my identity. Sad, yes, but true. I had been part of a team, my work mattered. We'd overturned three wrongful convictions in my time there. Three lives changed. When they pulled the plug on it, it wasn't a case of picking up a job at a rival program. *APPEAL* was the last program of its kind. (Don't get me started on that: not sexy enough, no celeb value, etc.) So I found myself picking up shifts on consumer programs investigating dodgy TV repair men, or holiday villages with shit and urine on the bedding and cockroaches in the shower. Then I'd be booking the spokesman from said holiday village to come on the show and either deny everything or apologize profusely depending on what they'd been advised to do in their media training session. I'm not knocking the work, but it didn't speak to me like my old job. I wasn't changing lives, just the quality of holiday accommodation. It wasn't enough.

Then David came along with his story and his claim of innocence and I felt the old rush of curiosity and intrigue, too intoxicating to resist.

After our encounter on the Friday night, I stayed home for the rest of the weekend. Snow had fallen overnight and settled thick on the ground. To my relief the plumber friend of David and Annie's came to fix the boiler on Saturday afternoon. Sludge in the system apparently; all he needed to do was flush it out. "I'll charge you for the chemicals, nothing else," he said, "since you're a friend of David's."

I didn't have the heart, or the cash, to correct him.

I spent my time replaying our conversation from every angle. David seemed like a nice guy, if a little damaged, which could be excused if he was telling the truth. Did I believe that he was? He had been out . . . what . . . a few weeks, and it seemed his sole focus was clearing his name. If you were guilty, would you do that, after you had served your time? Would you be looking for another solicitor to take up your case?

I searched the Internet for newspaper stories from the time of the attack. I typed in *Melody Pieterson* and saw her image appear before me.

She was blond, hair a similar shade and length to mine. In the photograph she wore it half up, half down, held back by an ornate clip adorned with crystals. The neckline of her dress was low, gathered in a cowl neck. It was cerise pink, silk perhaps, a shiny material that caught the light. She had the gloss of a big occasion about her, perfect hair and makeup. Was she at a wedding? In an attempt to study her face I made the image full screen. Her eyes were the palest green, pupils circled by rings of orange.

There was a picture of David too. THE FACE OF EVIL: DJ ADMITS VICIOUS ATTACK ON FRIEND AND NEIGHBOR. And a photograph of a police officer, DI Stuart Stirling. His quote embedded in the body of the story. "David Alden attacked his neighbor *and then left her for dead*, a woman who trusted him, classed him as friend, all because she spurned his advances. He lied about his involvement *again* and *again*. Today the jury returned the right verdict and we hope this sentence will allow Ms. Pieterson and her family to move on and rebuild their lives."

Most people age a bit in six years. New lines appear, existing ones grow deeper, hair might start to show a few flecks of gray. David Alden's face had changed more profoundly. He was still recognizable from the old online photographs but he seemed to have jumped a decade, more. Gone was the healthy, ruddy complexion, the roundness of his face. His cheeks had been hollowed out, his features sharpened and his eyes had lost their brightness. All that was left were dark pools of despair.

Had prison done that to him? Or was it the injustice that had eaten away at him until there was nothing left?

I phoned Annie on Monday. She wasn't the kind of friend I called up, more of a recent acquaintance, a friend of Kira's from university who'd moved back to London after a few years abroad.

"Your brother . . ." I began after we got the preemptive chat out of the way.

"He said you'd met the other night. Life and soul, was he? Look, I'm sorry if it freaked you out, but he's not dangerous . . ." She gave a nervous hollow laugh. "I sound like one of those dog owners who tells you their Rottweiler isn't going to bite."

"Annie, I . . ."

"He didn't do it. You'd expect me to say that, I know, but he didn't. He's trying to find himself a decent solicitor this time to help him clear his name. Actually, I remember Kira saying you worked on that program . . . Do you know of any good ones you could recommend?"

"I do . . . but most of the time you need to go to them with something. Well, it helps anyway if you have new evidence . . . a clear argument for taking it on."

"You mean him saying he didn't do it isn't enough?" She laughed. "Sorry, he has all this information and files he's collected and copies of letters, but he's lost, he doesn't know where to go with it. He can't look at it subjectively."

"That's actually why I was calling." I paused for a moment. "I wondered if you wanted me to have a look."

"Really?" I heard her voice rise in excitement.

"I can't promise anything. I'm sure you know that. The odds are stacked against you, heavily. But I wouldn't mind looking at the case, reading the judge's summing-up . . ."

"I'll bring it all over to you tonight," she said.

She appeared just as the credits for *Panorama* were rolling, carrying a bag. Next to her on the doorsteps were two legs and boxes obscuring a face.

"I hope you don't mind." She nodded and her eyes were stretched wide to tell me what she couldn't say in words. "He wanted to come."

"S'fine," I said, glad that he couldn't see my surprise.

I invited them in and offered them tea, which Annie declined for both of them. "Don't want to keep you," she said. I hadn't given the impression I was in any kind of hurry, so I assumed it was simply a cover and she wanted to leave. "Thanks for this. I've been telling David about the convictions you got overturned on the program." She turned to glare at David, who had now placed the boxes on the kitchen floor and stood like a surly kid scowling. What was going on between them?

I smiled, aware of the awkward silence that both Annie and I wanted David to fill. *Thank you. I appreciate what you are doing. I am grateful.* Something.

"We had the Colin Yates case, that went to a retrial and then he was acquitted. Then there was Maria Baczewski, her conviction for murder . . ." I was aware that I was babbling to fill the space. The more I spoke, the harder he stared.

It struck me that there might be a good reason for his apathy. It's easy to protest your innocence; what else are you going to say to your family and friends? But allowing someone to go over the evidence in detail was a different proposition. Was he worried I would expose his lies all over again?

What was I doing?

"Maybe we can talk again when you know I'm telling the truth," he interrupted. I stopped mid flow. A wave of anger quickly gave way to shame. He'd seen right through me.

It's about me, not you.

Not once had I said I believed him.

Annie texted later that evening to apologize. *No need*, I replied. As uncomfortable as it was to admit it, he was right. My motivations were selfish. Christ, I had even thought of which newspapers to pitch the story to when I was done.

I opened up a new file in my laptop. There had to be something tangible to go on. A reason to drive me on. He needed to know I

believed him but I needed to be convinced too. I copied the old stories I had found from Web sites about the attack and his conviction and pasted them into the file.

If I was going to do this I would be rigorous, adopt the same
approach I always had on APPEAL. Every phone call, chat, every
document and scrap of evidence would be noted and saved.

I stared at Melody's image. Beneath the makeup and the styled
hair I could see we were startlingly similar. If it had been me, I
would want to know the truth.

How was I to know how much it would cost us?

Two

Mel stares at the woman wearing a cerise dress and a pink rose in her hair. It takes a few beats for her brain to pin the outfit to a precise time and location. It was her brother Stephen's wedding. They were posing for photographs in the gardens of a hotel in Sussex. A five-star spa hotel in Turner's Hill, near Crawley, if her memory serves her correctly, although there was no mention of Crawley on the invitations, not even on the directions. She supposed this was a deliberate omission on the part of her sister-in-law, who wanted her wedding to be elegant and stylish, and found the town itself lacking in that respect. Louisa considered herself an arbiter of good taste, although this had not extended to her choice of bridesmaids' dresses. Mel had looked like an overgrown fairy. There was no other way of describing it. And no, she couldn't *get over herself*, as her mother had suggested. She had waited until the main course was finished to deliberately pour wine down her front. Then she went off to change into the dress *she* wanted to wear. Only her mother knew she had done it on purpose. "I'm disappointed in you, Melody. What a day to do a thing like that." She'd opened her mouth to protest but Tess had held her hand up to silence her and walked away to chat to Auntie Sheila.

Was it her mother's idea of karmic revenge to release that image to the press?

"Of all the photographs," Mel had complained when she came

round in hospital and saw the image of herself in the *Evening Standard.*

"I gave it to the police," her mother said. "How was I to know it was going to end up in the papers? Besides, it's a lovely photograph, and even if it wasn't, I had other things on my mind when I picked it out."

Mel is in the living room, slouched on the modular sofa, which isn't really designed for slouching, her laptop resting on her legs. Whatever she had hoped for, it wasn't this. The volume of Eve's file is daunting. She wasn't prepared for pages and pages of text, documents scanned and saved, maps plotted with points of movement, CCTV cameras, test results that appear to be written in a language she can't decipher, and this is only at a glance. She hasn't even begun to read it properly.

She had hoped it would be easily digestible, one gulp and the information would be sent directly to her brain for processing. Now she wonders if she will be able to read it at all. She hasn't read a book in four years, doubts she still has the ability to sit down and concentrate on rows and rows of words and infuse them with meaning. It's not for want of trying either. She used to devour books, the way she's seen people devour cakes, savoring each sentence, revelling in the pictures they painted in her mind, before racing on to the next bite. After the attack, when spare time oppressed her and she would have loved nothing more than a retreat to a fictional world, she suddenly found she couldn't get further than a few paragraphs before the words started to skip and jump in front of her. She persisted at first but the effort of trying to pin them down created a pressure that bored through her temples, drilled down into her teeth. She admitted defeat.

Next to her own pathetic attempts at reading (never mind writing anything more than a shopping list or an e-mail), the scale of Eve's effort intimidates her. It's a sensation not dissimilar to the one she experienced after her fall on the South Bank, looking up to the sky, everyone and everything looming so large, towering above her, and her too insubstantial next to them. She drags the cursor down through the pages. There is no end to them. A large throbbing part of her wishes she hadn't asked to see the file. *Stop now, delete it before it's too late*, a voice tells her. But it is already too late. Having given it the briefest glance, she knows she can't go back. It has changed irrevocably her view of what Eve was doing. It wasn't a whim, the meddling of a woman who fell for a lie. There is method here, detail, analysis of the evidence.

She was attacked. David Alden was convicted. These are points A and B on the map, the only places Mel has ever visited. But Eve's investigation, she knows, covers a world of nuances, theories and suppositions that fall in between those two points. It's uncharted territory.

She leaves the laptop on the sofa, conscious that Sam warns her never to do this. "It'll overheat, ruin the computer." Sam isn't here, though, and she'll do what she wants.

Why has she been so hard on him since her interview at the police station? He let her struggle, allowed her mind to fry while he sipped his shit coffee, that's why. It's for this reason that she can't look him in the eye anymore or listen to what he says, because all she is wondering is if he is telling the truth or if he is hiding from her. Not that she can voice her concerns, not unless she wants to be carted off to the loony bin or prescribed more tranquilizers.

It isn't true what they said, the headlines in the papers, her friends, her parents. She didn't survive. She can trace Melody Pieterson back to that night of August 17, to the moment she turned off the Uxbridge Road, hearing footsteps behind her. At that point the darkness came. And Melody, she admits for the first time, never emerged from it.

She checks her watch. It's half past eleven. Too early to make lunch even if she was hungry, which she isn't. A coffee will do. Yes, another one. Fuck fennel tea. Her footsteps are loud on concrete as she walks through to the kitchen. No matter what she buys to fill the rooms, whatever pieces of furniture she carefully selects (before seeking Sam's approval), nothing seems to deaden the sound. A footstep, a teaspoon falling to the floor, the bang of a door all reverberate around the house. Even when she's alone she has the impression that there are two of her here. Herself and her echo, another person who follows in her shadow.

She goes to make the coffee, deciding that she would like to use the cafetière this time. She spends five minutes searching for it. Sam will have hidden it somewhere, viewing its ongoing use as an affront to the expensive built-in coffee machine he had installed. But she prefers to do it this way, likes scooping out the spoonfuls, boiling the kettle, filling the cafetière, lingering over it, waiting for the final flourish of pushing the plunger down.

Eventually she locates it at the back of the cupboard where she keeps the plastic food containers. While she waits for the coffee to brew, she checks her phone. Sam hasn't called. This is no surprise. It's the weekend. He's gone to his place in Camber for kite-surfing. He'll have been up watching the sun rise, launching himself into the sea to catch the gusts and squalls. What does that feel like, to sit under the sky, taste the salt on your lips and not have your insides curdle with fear? She can't remember. But she knows she is jealous of him, of his ability to live. She calls him just to hear his voice on the answerphone: *It's Sam, leave a message and I'll call back.* It's the same message as always, unnecessarily brusque in her opinion. She hangs up, glances back at the kitchen clock. The coffee will be brewed. She pours it and takes her mug into the living room, to the window, where she stands and looks out. There was a view here once before they erected the fence. When they moved in she could see beyond the drive to the field ahead. She could sit in the living room, not having slept, and wait for the sun to emerge from behind the hills. It was always a relief, catching the first glimpse of it arcing on the horizon. To be pulled out of the endless nighttime hours where she chased sleep but only ever found it in short, fitful bursts. She'd draw back the curtains to see the sun dapple the room. Now the fence obscures the view. If she looks up, only a thin strip of sky is visible.

The image of Eve springs into her mind. Rosy-cheeked, exhilarated, beaming. What would she do if she was here? Mel pictures her gulping in the fresh air, lifting her face to the sun and marveling at the clouds racing across the sky. Would she throw her arms wide open and spin around until she's dizzy to revel in the miracle that has granted her an extra, glorious moment of life? Would she stretch out that second, squeeze every shred of pleasure from it, knowing as she does that time is finite, that it slips past so quickly and when it's gone it can't be repeated?

Would she look at Mel, a lab rat caged by her own neuroses, and think: what a waste. What a terrible waste of life.

Would she think: why me? Why not her?

Mel slams the coffee cup down on the table. She moves at speed, reluctant to allow her thoughts time to sabotage her instincts. Just run, she tells herself. And she does, out into the corridor, to the front door, where she turns the key in the lock. A wave of fresh air hits her face, but she won't let this stop her. Her feet crunch on the gravel driveway. Keep walking, she tells herself. With this one thought she maintains the forward momentum. Her legs are light, she feels them buckling under the weight of her body, but she won't stop. She is at the gate, refusing to cast a look back to gauge the distance between her and the front door. She presses the button, watches it slide open to reveal the green of the fields rolling out in front on her. She draws her eyes back to the road. On either side are trees, leaves spilling from them and collecting on the ground in piles of orange, gold and red. One of them in front of her, a rich scarlet color, eddying in the wind. It falls at her feet. A door bangs close by. The sound shoots through her. She looks up to see the woman from the next house down, one hundred meters or so away, come out on to her driveway. Catching sight of Mel, she smiles, waves. "Beautiful day, isn't it?"

Mel raises her hand tentatively and forces herself to wave back. Is it a beautiful day? She supposes it is. The thought causes her to laugh out loud. She can't quite believe she has done it. It is a beautiful day and she is standing out under the sky breathing it in.

The first time she has been out alone in four years.

Is this what she has been scared of? Part of her wants to cry for everything she has lost to fear.

Her baby.

She never could explain to Sam why she was so apprehensive about it growing inside her. How could she tell him she was frightened of going out on her own? That with a baby there would be doctor's appointments and invitations to baby massage classes and trips to the park, and that it was this, not the pain of the birth or the weight of parenthood or the sleepless nights (she didn't sleep anyway) that terrified her. Was God listening in on her thoughts? She has always assumed the miscarriage was a test he set for her, one she failed. She could have stopped it, couldn't she, if only . . .

No, God must have thought her so ungrateful, so undeserving that he decided to take it away from her and give the life to someone who really wanted it.

Did Sam know that mixed up with the grief, the deep empty ache inside her, there was too a small sliver of relief that she could never admit to?

Mel bends down, picks up the leaf at her feet and walks quickly back to the house, trying to keep her breaths regular, calm. She can run miles with Erin, go for a drive with Sam in the car, a day out walking or for lunch, but she hasn't been able to stand out in their garden alone. Taking giant strides, she watches as the door gets bigger, closer and closer. She feels like she's swimming underwater, her lungs screaming for air. All she wants to do is reach the end, know she is safe again so she can breathe. She touches the door, pushes it open and closes it behind it. Her body sinks down against it, cold against her back. Relief flushes through her but there is something else too. An unfamiliar determination. She can do this.

She will read every word that Eve has written in the file. There's a whole world mapped out between A and B that she hasn't explored, and somewhere between those points she lost herself.

Three

t's been ten minutes, fifteen at a stretch, of family time. Would you class it good quality? How do you define good quality? What would that child psychologist who's always on TV say? Dr. Tanya Byron, that's her name. Victoria gives this a moment's thought. She has no idea what Dr. Tanya Byron would say. What does it matter anyway? They haven't argued, so that's a start, unusual to say the least. Doug and Bella—both Chelsea fans—have been ribbing Oliver about Man U's lack of form, or *the complete and utter disintegration of the team,* as Bella put it somewhat precociously. They've eaten breakfast together around the kitchen table, which is supposed to be a good thing to do because you can talk to your kids, engage with them (and also be reminded of their appalling table manners). They've eaten pancakes cooked by Doug (hers always stick to the pan) and the air is still thick with the pleasant fug of them. Surely she can draw bonus points from this. Isn't that what those glossy women in magazines do? The ones with troops of kids, highflying jobs and—magically—no childcare. *Sundays are sacrosanct. We all sit down to eat breakfast together. It's a bit of a ritual in our house, good-quality family time.*

"How was school this week, any gossip from the badlands of St. Raphael's Primary?" she asks.

Her kids shoot her the same look they always do when she asks this question. *Stop trying to be cool.*

"Jaime got suspended for bringing a baseball bat into the playground and threatening to smash it over Samuel's head."

"Really?" She is genuinely shocked.

"Ha ha, yeah right." Oliver rolls his eyes to the ceiling. "You're so gullible, Mum. But he did get caught putting two Mars Bar cakes into his bag at the cake bake when he'd only paid for one. That's about as bad as this week got." He shovels the last bit of pancake doused in maple syrup into his mouth then licks each of his fingers noisily.

Since when did he use words like "gullible?"

"Can I play on the Wii?" He's pushing himself out from the table.

"I thought we were talking."

"We have talked and it was . . . er . . . interesting. Now can I play on the Wii?"

It's Bella's turn to pipe up. "Can I go round to Antonio's? He's got an amazing new Nerf gun, it's called a Vulcan Blaster. Can I get one?"

"You already have one," Doug says.

"Er, no I don't. I have a Nerf N-Strike, which is totally different to the Vulcan Blaster."

Victoria looks at her daughter. She's wearing jeans that have a hole at the knee and a white T-shirt emblazoned with a Lego Darth Vader. Her thick hair falls about her face. She hasn't brushed it, reserves that treat for the once-a-week wash, and even then it's a battle. Still, she thinks, better than having a house dripping in pink tat and princesses.

"You can go to Antonio's . . ." she starts to say and watches Bella's face break into a smile.

"They have homework, Vic," Doug says, giving them both a playful clip over the head. "Nice try."

"Well I'm playing on the Wii for ten minutes," Oliver says.

"No, it's my turn," Bella shouts and they push each other in a bid to get to the living room first.

Victoria pours herself another cup of tea and tries to avoid looking at the pile of letters on the shelf. She shifts her focus slightly so she can see out to the garden. There she catches sight of her underwear flapping on the clothesline next to a duvet cover, the end of which is trailing on the dirty path. How long has that been out there? At least three days, a week maybe. It's been wet, dry and wet again.

Doug starts clearing away the plates. "Don't let the bastards grind you down," he says and kisses the top of her head.

"The kids aren't that bad, Doug," she jokes.

"Work?"

"Stirling's not happy."

"Because you released Alden on bail? Well it's not his case, Vic, it's yours and you have your reasons."

"It's not that straightforward. It's linked to one of his cases; you can't look at one without the other. In Stirling's mind I'm dragging my heels . . . I'm obsessing over Eve's investigation when I have enough to charge Alden with murder. He thinks I'm undermining his authority."

Doug analyzes her face, the way he often does when he senses his wife is not telling him the whole story.

"And that's it? That's what's bothering you?"

She sighs, rubs her temples. Doug knows her better than she knows herself. Victoria can stand her ground. Challenging authority is not a new one on her and she doesn't bow to pressure easily. If it was simply a case of taking her time in order to be thorough, she'd brush off Stirling's barbed comments. "Big mistake. Huge," he told her yesterday when she informed him she was releasing Alden, unaware no doubt that he'd just pinched a line from Julia Roberts in *Pretty Woman*. No, it's not his disapprobation that's eating away at her. It's Eve's file. Nathaniel Jenkins called yesterday to tell them he had it, *if it was any use*. A conversation with Eve's mum had miraculously reminded him that Eve had been e-mailing it to him as a backup. What is it about people and their memories? Were they all getting high and smoking dope at college while she was at police training college? Is that why everyone she speaks to seems to have irreversibly damaged their powers of recall?

Victoria has the file now. This is the chief source of her anxiety. She's eager to read it but she's also dreading what she might find.

If Eve Elliot was right and David Alden didn't attack Melody Pieterson, Stirling nailed the wrong man. Not only that, but it would mean he was accountable for Eve's murder. Victoria can handle undermining authority, but ruining the reputation of the man who helped shape her career is an altogether more terrifying prospect.

She smiles at Doug. "I'm not convinced Alden killed Eve, it doesn't stack up, and I'd rather not be the person to find out Stirling messed up."

"It doesn't look like you have a choice." He gets up from the table and hands her the car keys from the side. "As much as we'll miss your sparkling conversation, we can live without you for a few hours," he says.

She kisses him. "Thanks, it would give me a chance to . . ."

"Go." He waves her away.

Within minutes her coat is on, she's heading out of the door shouting, "Love you, see you later" to the kids, pretending not to hear Oliver joke to his sister, "Who did she say she was?" or the sniggers that follow.

It's Saturday. The station will be free of Stuart Stirling's presence. She wants to make a good start on the file. Before she settles down at her desk, she walks to the coffee machine, inserts thirty pence and waits as the plastic cup fills with a black liquid tar. It's disgusting, chemical, barely palatable, so they tell her. "How can you drink that, ma'am?" It's something of a joke, extended, in her view, beyond its natural life by the bags of Nicaraguan arabica or Venezuelan Mérida she opens to applause at Christmas. Even DCI Stirling entered into the spirit of it one year by giving her a cafetière. It's found its way into the kitchen now, where its presence is better appreciated. What she doesn't tell them is that at home she enjoys a decent roast but here in the station she prefers to drink this stuff;

the association it has with work centers her in the task. To borrow a phrase from a glossy women's magazine, drinking crap coffee is her ritual.

It comes as no surprise that the file is dense. Eve's background on *APPEAL* must have taught her to be thorough. Victoria scans down through the first few pages of press cuttings detailing Melody's attack and David Alden's subsequent conviction. She is trying to work out how Eve has organized the file, what system she has used, if there is a system at all. Six pages in she finds a list, numbering in order of priority the evidence against Alden: the CCTV, the mobile phone masts that picked up his signal in the area, the last known sighting of Melody, his whereabouts that evening. The e-mail that he sent suggesting she come to the club. The rest of the file deals with each of these points individually with what at a glance looks like supporting evidence. A later section is given over to interviews with witnesses and Melody's friends.

She hears the clock tick-tock above her head. How long did she tell Doug she would be gone? She can't remember if she did. Taking a sip from her plastic cup, feeling the familiar burned taste hit the back of her throat, she starts reading the first section, entitled "CCTV."

Four

H ere's a funny thing. My friend Kira and her brother Rex did a little video for their dad's seventieth birthday reminiscing about what he was like when they were growing up. Kira said he was soft, like a cuddly teddy bear, compared with her mother, who was by far the stricter parent. Her brother said the opposite. He recalled his dad shouting, flying off the handle (they edited that out for the video). Kira couldn't remember one instance when he so much as raised his voice. They lived in the same house, were eighteen months apart in age and according to their parents they had been treated in exactly the same way.

Neither Kira nor Rex were deliberately lying so you ask the question: how could their memories throw up such different experiences?

It boils down to perception. Ask two people what they made of a party, a book or a film and they won't give you the same answer.

In that sense there can be many different stories describing the same event.

In David Alden's case there were two.

The window of time was limited, definite. At the beginning and the end were absolutes. At 10:35 P.M. on August 17, 2007, the clock started. This was when David Alden walked out of the Orb club in Hammersmith. His figure, casually clothed in jeans and a short-sleeved shirt, could be seen descending the stairs from the bar, opening the door on to the street and fading out of shot. It was all recorded on the club's in-house CCTV. In the minutes that followed he walked to his car, a vintage Porsche 911 in racing green, parked around the corner. He waited, allowed the engine to turn over before driving up Shepherd's Bush Road, skirting the roundabout to turn left on to the Uxbridge Road.

Roughly half a mile from there he stopped at a garage to buy a packet of Malboro Lights and chewing gum. This too was recorded on the CCTV, so he could be seen both inside the shop and outside on the forecourt. According to the timer on the recording it was 10:51 P.M. when his car pulled out of the garage back on to the Uxbridge Road heading west. Between nine o'clock and midnight twenty-three cars made the same maneuver. The police logged their registrations as a matter of procedure but it was the green Porsche 911 that particularly interested them. It placed their suspect in the right area at the right time.

Until this juncture there had been one unified narrative, undisputed by Alden and the officers questioning him. But this was the moment it forked into two conflicting stories.

Story A: the case against David Alden

David Alden drove out of the Texaco garage on Uxbridge Road to meet Melody Pieterson at a predetermined location. Ostensibly he was going to take her back to the club, but in fact he had other things on his mind. He wanted to have sex with her, thought she wanted the same; hadn't she led him on after all? They went out together regularly, exchanged e-mails, texts, chats over the garden fence. They shared music. He knew the signals. It had been building for months, this thing, so he made a move, in the car. Why not? Except when he tried to kiss her she pushed him away and he realized, his head filling with shame, that he had got it all wrong. She didn't want him after all. Had she laughed? Shouted? Was that why he flew into a violent rage? Was it why his hands reached out to her throat and found they could clasp around it so easily? Too easily. She was only slight, a thin slip of a woman. A few minutes earlier he had wanted to kiss the sloping curve of her neck; now it was where he applied pressure to squeeze the breath out of her.

It was over so quickly. A few minutes, five at the most. Minutes in which he lost himself in the act. It was only when he stopped, released his hands from the grasp, that the enormity of what he had done washed over him. He was a different person to the one who had bought cigarettes and chewing gum ten minutes before. He was a murderer now. At least he thought so. He couldn't wake her, didn't know she had slipped into a coma. He panicked. What should he do? What would a killer do? He would get rid of the body as quickly as possible.

So he drove out to Ham, a place familiar to him since it was near where he had grown up. His car was seen close to Ham Woods Common on CCTV. This was where he dumped Melody Pieterson. After that he got back in his car and drove back to the club in Hammersmith. The CCTV recorded him walking through the doors again at 11.52 P.M. This was the end of the window of time. Perhaps he wasn't in the mood to play to a crowd that night. Who could have blamed him? But he had to, out of necessity, because as alibis go, playing in front of a crowd of two hundred was as good as it got. When he was finished, he invited a friend back to his flat, a man by the name of Jack Wilton, who stayed until the next morning.

The next day Alden took his car to be valeted on Goldhawk Road in Shepherd's Bush. The receipt was found in his wallet. It was the prosecution's case that this was intended to destroy evidence of what he had done the night before. But he forgot to clean his coat. When that was analyzed, strands of Melody Pieterson's hair and clothing were present.

Story B: the case for the defense
David Alden claimed he had been driving to meet a friend in Brentford (it didn't help his case that the friend turned out to

be an acquaintance made through occasional and small-scale drug deals.) It was the fifth time they had met outside the same pub, the Seven Stars. On each occasion the transaction lasted no more than a few minutes. David Alden had not felt the need to ask questions of Ritchie, such as his surname, his address. He didn't even know whether his supplier was a regular at the pub or simply used it as a convenient place to do business. Of course by the time he found himself in a police interview room he wished he had asked a few questions, gleaned pertinent information that would have made Ritchie seem less imaginary construct, more real person. While he wasn't naturally inclined to disclose the identity of a drug dealer, it was preferable to being charged with the attempted murder of a friend.

He didn't drive beyond Brentford that night. Indeed it was hard to determine the make or model of the car seen close to Ham Common Woods. The CCTV was of such poor quality, it was difficult to see more than headlights in the dark.

He cleaned his car regularly, always on a Saturday. There was nothing unusual about this.

He had given Melody Pieterson a lift two days before the attack and this was the reason, he suggested, why her hair and fibers from her clothes were found on his coat. It must have been sitting on the passenger seat when she got in.

On April 29, 2008, a jury of five women and seven men convicted David Alden of grievous bodily harm with intent. Story A had got their vote.

*Melody Pieterson was not a witness in the trial. Melody does not remember anything about the night of the attack?

I spent three evenings going through the judge's summing-up and case notes in order to make my own. It wasn't fun, let me tell you, but it was important to boil it down into proper English because judges and barristers and even police officers tend not to talk like anyone else you know. On the third evening, at half past ten, I wrapped up warm with gloves, a scarf and a hat and headed out to my car. The snow had crusted on the windscreen. I considered abandoning the plan or postponing it at least. But I wasn't in the mood to wait. Patience and I had never been the best of friends.

I gave the car a cursory glance. A can of deicer would have been a helpful if surprising find but in its absence I resorted to scraping at the windscreen with a credit card. When I'd cleared a patch of frost large enough to see through, I headed out of my street. The wheels skidded on ice. Of all the nights, I thought. But I wasn't going back and to my relief the Uxbridge Road had been gritted. Half a mile up it, I pulled in to the Texaco garage, bought some crisps and a hot chocolate and waited in the car until my watch said 10:51 P.M. Then I pulled out, turning left on to the road. A quarter of a mile from there I turned left again at Emlyn Road and parked for two minutes before continuing my journey. The traffic flowed easily all the way to Ham, a small suburban town bordering the Thames. I located Ham Gate Avenue and drove to the top, to the gates of Richmond Park. Again I pulled over and waited a few minutes before turning round and retracing my route. I tried to keep my speed steady, hovering around the limit all the way. Eyes on the road, not daring to look at the dashboard clock because it held the answer and I didn't want to know the answer until I had stopped. I passed my own street and headed to the Orb in Hammersmith instead. Parking was easy at that time of night. I found a spot around the corner, got out of my car and walked to the entrance of the club, where I finally allowed myself to look at my watch. It was 12:01 A.M.

If David Alden had attacked Melody, he must have moved quickly.

I was a good sleeper, bordering on the professional in the sense that if I put my mind to it I could sleep anywhere, at any time. I even fell asleep standing up once, although there was a certain amount of wine involved in that feat. The night I returned from Ham I couldn't sleep at all; loud thoughts and adrenalin wouldn't allow it.

By the time the gray morning light crept into my room I was stale. I craved air and space. It was early, around seven, and I was on a later production shift that day so I threw on my trainers, joggers and a coat and headed out. *If you have a problem, take it for a walk*, my dad used to say. He was a firm believer that the motion, the rhythm of the steps could help you find a way out of any quandary. He always walked down by the river and I followed his example.

I parked by the banks of the Thames at Hammersmith. The sun was up, the dreary sky of an hour ago was now a golden haze. The river greeted me, winking and gleaming in the light. Out toward the middle of the river a team of rowers sliced through the water spurred on by their cox shouting instructions through a loudspeaker. Cold air streamed through my lungs and made my nose run.

What was I going to do?

Should I go back to David and Annie and offer to help, or let it pass? Was I up to doing it alone?

I reached for my phone and called Nat.

"Why are you ringing me at half past seven?"

"I need to talk to you."

"Can't it wait?"

"No."

"What you mean is it can wait but you're too impatient."

"Something like that. Have you got time?"

"I'm actually on the toilet having a dump, but if you're happy with that situation then go ahead."

"OK, I'm going to put that mental picture out of my mind and I won't ask why you have your phone with you on the loo. Now listen . . ."

I started to tell him David Alden's story in detail, the files I'd looked at, the trip to Ham Gate.

"Bullet points please, darling," he said. "I haven't got all morning."

"All right, I hear you. I can't see how he would have had time to attack her and dump her body."

"You don't think the police would have worked that out?"

"Come on . . ." We'd both covered enough stories to know the police made mistakes, accidental or otherwise. "And Annie said his legal team were all over the place at the trial."

"So what are you going to do?"

"I don't know. It's a lot to take on. What do *you* think I should do?"

"Run a mile."

"Seriously?"

"I think you already know what you should do, otherwise you wouldn't be bothering me at seven in the morning when I am trying to empty my bowels."

"Thanks. That's why I love you."

"Pleasure's all mine, Eve."

"The window of time was so slim it would have been almost impossible for you to have picked Melody Pieterson up in your car, strangled her, dumped her body and then returned to the club by midnight." I tried to drain my voice of excitement. I'm not altogether sure I was successful.

"On top of that, there's no clear image of your car in Richmond. Just one grainy CCTV shot that an expert witness claimed *could* have been your car. But if you look at it, it's impossible to tell even what kind of car it is."

Annie was staring at David but his head was down, hands clasped in front of him as if he was meditating. On the table were the remnants of three full English breakfasts and three mugs of tea. I was learning fast that David was a complex character. He gave off so many different signals at once—happy, nervous, sulky, pensive, each one layered over the other—that it was impossible to determine what mood he was in.

"What are you saying, Eve?" he said finally.

With my fork I prodded an uneaten sausage before looking up at him. "I'm saying that if you really want to do this then I'm prepared to help."

David turned to Annie. For a few beats there was no one else in the café. Years of strain and setbacks and hurt condensed in that moment.

She reached out with one hand to squeeze his. With her other hand she took a napkin to wipe her eyes. David turned back to me.

"Why would you do this? It's not like you have to."

I stared at his face. The reason for his reticence, the holding back all shot into focus. Hope costs. It's what breaks you. David Alden didn't part with it easily, if you were him you wouldn't either. If he was going to hand it over to me, he needed to be clear on my motives.

"I believe you," I said.

And for the first time I knew that I did.

For a long while after I died, I hated myself for taking David's hope. What arrogance to think I was worthy of being its custodian. Where had it got him? Here was a man, shrunken and huddled in his flat, listening for the knock at the door, a man on bail, waiting for the inevitable murder charge. Any hope I had ignited had burned out, leaving a shell. The substance had been gutted from him. He abandoned any notion of clearing his name, threw Annie out of his flat when she suggested continuing: "Can't you see the damage it's done already?" He considered a range of suicides, pleased to find that in this respect his mind still offered creative solutions. He studied buildings and cliff faces, calculated the scale of the drop, studied terminal velocity. Mainly though he just thought of the end. Of his body hitting a hard surface and being obliterated. It was all his own fault. It was pride, conceit, he told himself, that had pushed him to clear his name. If only he could have settled for the scraps that life had doled out to him I would still be alive.

It broke my heart to see his body crushed by the weight of blame. I wanted to tell him not to give up, how I still held on to a piece of that hope I had taken from him.

Five

*M*elody does not remember anything **about the night of her attack?** *?*

She reads the words in the file, the asterisk by her name, the question mark that suggested doubt. What was it that Eve doubted? That someone could have every last remnant of an attack suctioned from their mind? That not even the smallest shadow of memory, an imprint, a sound or shape, would remain?

Two conflicting statements battle it out in her head: a) Melody remembers; b) Melody can't remember. They are diametrically opposed and yet she knows each of them to be true.

When it comes to the attack itself she draws a blank, like someone has cloaked it in a thick blanket to block out even the thinnest spill of light. She doesn't know who was driving the car or what kind of car it was. If there were words spoken between them, she can't recall them. Statement A is therefore true.

According to the story handed down from the police, the official verified version, she was attacked soon after she got in the car. In fact she recalls it differently, like a dense fog rolling over her, her body drifting apart from her mind. A weightlessness, her eyelids heavy. Sleep—she remembers it like the deepest of sleeps, lasting hours, days. The motion of the car. The sound of wheels on gravel. Statement B is also true.

She remembers more, too, much more. And it's not true to say she has kept this all to herself. She tried at first to explain, to the police, to Sam, to her parents. But here's the thing. Her memories didn't fit into the boxes provided for them, they were awkward in shape. Circles in square holes. Within days of her waking up, Detective Inspector Stirling arrived to tell her they had arrested someone.

"I'm afraid you know him," he said. "I assume you are familiar with the name David Alden?"

She was sipping from a glass of water when he told her. She thought she was choking on it. Sprayed it everywhere. The coughing hurt her throat, her muscles still tender from the attack.

"Take your time," he said, fetching her paper towels. Each time she tried to speak, she coughed some more.

"No," she said eventually. Her breaths were rasping. "No, you've made a mistake." She knew David, he was a great friend. She knew he wouldn't do that to her, or to anyone for that matter. The thought of it was grotesque, absurd. You don't spend nights getting drunk on shots of Jägermeister and having dance-offs to Run-DMC with a man who then tries to kill you.

The DI smiled, an unpleasant, patronizing smile. "I'm afraid the case against him is compelling," he said. "His car was in the vicinity at the exact time you were last seen. It was picked up on CCTV near Ham Gate."

Mel was shaking her head so furiously she thought it might come loose from her neck. Did she have to listen to this nonsense? She felt dizzied, hypnotized by the intensity of his pale, lightless eyes. She could feel him wresting her experience from her, taking it into his ownership.

She wanted to shout, "Back off, you've got half of it arse over tit." But instead she remained polite. "You are making a terrible error of judgment," she said, surprised by how calm she sounded. DI Stirling raised his hand to hush her, the way her teachers used to when she got too excitable.

"We have found matches for your hair and fibers from your clothing on his coat. A coat he bought four days before you were attacked.

You've already told my officers you didn't see him in the days leading up to the attack."

She turned her head away from DI Stirling. She had nothing more to say to him.

It was this moment, more than the attack itself, that changed her. She could recover from her physical injuries but the knowledge that it was someone she'd trusted corroded her insides like acid. When she picked over their friendship, searched for a damning clue or a sign that would have pointed her toward this, she couldn't find a single one. But the police had shown her the evidence and it was compelling. Her monumental failure of judgment undermined everything that had gone before. Everything she had taken for granted, all the absolutes in her life disintegrated. She couldn't trust her own thoughts. When forced to make even the smallest decision—*fruit salad or crumble? walk or a swim?*—she found herself paralyzed. "You choose," she would say to whoever happened to be with her, because this one single thing, the knowledge that David Alden had attacked her, almost killed her, had overridden every natural instinct and reflex she had.

Mel sits back in her chair, surveys the scene around her. She is alone. Sam left for work hours ago, before she got up. She has been reading the file for a good hour; her eyes are beginning to sting from concentration. She glances over to an empty cereal bowl on the counter that has been there for as long as she has been reading. She knows this because she is daring herself to leave it *in situ* along with the cereal box. The effort of doing it is making her limbs twitch. She is fighting the impulse to clean every trace of herself away. She sits still, reads Eve's description of David Alden in the café again and for once allows her own memories of him to break out and tumble into view.

They flare up with surprising ease, except that she struggles to remember what he looked like, the exact arrangement of his features. When she was told he'd pleaded guilty, she began the process of superimposing his mug shot over every image she had of his face, obliterating the laughing, happy friend she knew. Instead she remembers him in smells and sounds, a barbecue in the first instance, its association with summer. First impressions? She thought he was trying a bit hard to be cool. But subsequent encounters reset her opinion. She found out he was a DJ, a semifamous one in clubbing circles (she'd googled him of course). A DJ who played to hundreds, sometimes thousands of people and grew marrows and courgettes and peas in his vegetable patch. Vegetables he delivered to her when there was a surplus, and there was always a surplus. A chain smoker who ran five miles every day and juiced vegetables for breakfast. A man with the biggest record collection she'd ever seen who admitted to having a soft spot for Wham!. He made her playlists, had a knack of knowing which records she'd love before she heard them herself. Whenever there was a leaking tap or a picture that needed hanging she'd ask him, providing Patrick wasn't around. She was fond of both of them but they weren't keen on each other. They clashed over loud music, the fact that David routinely put his rubbish out on the wrong day. *The foxes must love him*, Patrick would say in disgust. Equally his habit of repairing his car on the pavement so no one could get past aroused Patrick's ire. They were minor transgressions, all of them, but their combined effect meant the two men barely passed the time of day.

He wanted to have sex with her, thought she wanted the same; hadn't she led him on after all?

Her eyes scan the words in the file again, the words that Eve wrote as part of her summary of the case against David Alden. The prosecution must have argued this was David's motive during the trial, not that she had been there to hear it. Mel had only spent one morning at the Old Bailey giving evidence. There wasn't a whole lot you could ask a woman whose memory had failed her.

Only now, five and a half years on, is she acquainting herself with the full argument that was used to convict him. It doesn't ring true.

As proof, she digs out her memories of the weekend they spent together in Barcelona. It was 2005, early summer if she's not mistaken. He was playing at a big music festival, Primavera, just outside the city. "Fancy coming?" he'd asked three days before he was due to fly out. "New Order are playing and I know how much you love them." He gave her a cheeky wink. She hated New Order.

Still, she didn't have anything planned. "Why not," she said. An hour later she'd booked her flight.

Mel wasn't prepared for the scale of the festival. There must have been fifty thousand people massed in a giant leisure complex. She remembers the hairs on her arms standing up in excitement as she looked out at the music tents and stages and the crowds of people, and the sea beyond, dazzling in the sun. It sure beat staying in Shepherd's Bush on a Saturday night. The day, she recalls, was pleasantly hot. Warm enough for her shorts and the floaty white top she'd chosen so as not to look out of place. She'd accessorized with a straw cowboy hat and big glasses. They spent the afternoon wandering around the site, catching bands here and there, the silver bracelets on her wrist chinking against the cold bottles of San Miguel David plied her with. It was gone eleven by the time his set came around and the relaxed daytime atmosphere had shifted up a gear into a more hedonistic party vibe. As he started playing, Mel, who sat close to him in the booth staring out at the sea of faces, felt her stomach clench with nerves. It was a huge crowd to please and while his taste in music was impeccable, quirky and eclectic, she hadn't seen him perform in public before, never mind to this many people. What if he fucked it up? What if he played Wham! by mistake?

"And there was me thinking you were out of your depth," she laughed to him later. She couldn't take the smile from her face. Was it really David, her next-door neighbor, provider of homegrown marrows, who had just performed that feat, playing to the crowd, reading their mood and translating it into tunes, finding the exact mix to lift them and stir them, to bring it down when it was getting too frenzied. The layering of softer tracks with big bold anthems, the casual mastery of it all was intoxicating. She had been entranced, utterly lost in the experience.

"Glad to hear you had confidence," David said. He was beaming, the energy drawn from the crowd snapping through him and sparking in his eyes.

They found a bar just off the Placa del Sol in Gracia, the hip barrio where they were staying, and settled down with G&Ts.

"I hadn't realized how bored I was at home until you dragged me away," Mel said.

"I didn't realize I had dragged you anywhere."

"Willingly. If you can drag someone willingly. It's made me think that I need to get away, traveling or something. I always wanted to do it, I just didn't get around to it."

"You mean you don't want to sell breakfast cereals and live in Shepherd's Bush for the rest of your life?"

"I do not sell breakfast cereals. I do PR. Once, only once did I have a client who sold breakfast bars, not cereals. There is a difference."

He held his hands up. "My mistake. So why don't you do it, then? Go traveling, take off, what's holding you back?"

She thought about it for a second. "Nothing really, I guess I've just got caught up in the day-to-day and forgotten to see the bigger picture. What about you? What does the future hold? A mobile disco? I can just picture you doing requests at weddings and bar mitzvahs."

"Very funny. If you want to know, I'm salting my money away to buy a place out of London, a hotel, and hold gigs and small festivals there."

"You just want a bigger vegetable patch," she said.

"There's that too. I'm all out of space for courgettes."

"Well we should hold each other to it, make sure we don't let life get in the way of dreams."

"Deal." He tipped his glass toward hers. If he'd kissed her then she wouldn't have hesitated. The truth is the reverse of what everyone believed. It wasn't David who fancied Mel, it was the other way around. Surely if he was going to make a move he would have done it then?

Mel springs up from the chair, crosses the kitchen to grab the cereal bowl from the counter. She puts it in the dishwasher, then takes the cereal box and returns it to its rightful place in the cupboard. There is nothing else to do in the kitchen so she runs up to her room taking the stairs two at a time. She has to keep moving, but even in this cavernous barn there is not enough square footage to cover. She could go out in the garden, but she wants to see the day in its entirety; she's sick of having her view interrupted by the huge fence that circles their land. For once she wants to shrink under the immense sky and not stop until she has outrun the thoughts that are chasing her down.

There's no need to change; her loungewear is nothing if not versatile. She pulls on her trainers, locates her keys, her phone and finds a ten-pound note in Sam's wardrobe, just in case. In case of what, she has no idea, but she's not stopping to think. Pacing to the front door, she unlocks it, slips out and hears the heavy weight of it crash behind her.

It is Erin who plans the routes normally. Mel follows. Mel follows in such a way that she doesn't pay a huge amount of attention to where they go. They moved here more than four years ago and the roads and paths still have the ability to disorientate her, as if she is just passing through for the day.

The village, she thinks. Head down toward it and then to the river. She knows the path along the river and knows she can turn back when she's had enough. She looks up to check for traffic as she crosses the road, and feels her heart flap in her chest, her stomach spasm. There is no one next to her. There will be no one next to her all the way. The prospect both exhilarates and terrifies her. She used to seek out situations that scared her: public speaking, snow-boarding down a black run, a new job that she thought was beyond her abilities, a relationship that should have been off limits. She'd go for them all, because if she was never scared, she wasn't push-ing herself, she wasn't growing and learning and experiencing life. She was standing still. And if there was one thing Melody Pieter-son hated, it was standing still.

The thought propels her forward. At first she keeps her gaze low, eyes fixed on her feet kicking out in front of her. It's a good way to avoid the puddles and dog shit but after a while it makes her dizzy and she is forced to look ahead. There are three people on the pave-ment, all walking toward her though not together. Of course she sees people when she's running with Erin, but this is different. To-day she views them as enemies in the field of combat. The closest is a man, in his fifties at a guess, carrying a jute shopping bag with a leek poking out from it. She holds her breath, picks up her speed and passes him without making eye contact. The next is coming at her quickly, a mother pushing a buggy with a toddler slumped asleep inside. Thank God Mel doesn't recognize her. Every time she passes someone, more people keep emerging. Faster and faster she runs, sprinting through town. Shops and buildings cram her at either side, people gather in groups, marauding, laughing. Car doors slamming, people shouting. She is under attack. It was a mistake to come out, a huge miscalculation to allow herself to be so exposed. Space. Quiet. That is what she needs, although not so quiet she will be completely alone. Picking up the pace, she runs at full pelt. The sudden increase in speed makes her head spin. She begins to see flecks of light dancing in front of her eyes, as if someone has just released ticker tape over her head. *Don't faint, whatever you do don't faint.* She has a sense that she is drifting outside of herself, no lon-ger contained by her body. She is considering a good spot to pass out when she turns a corner and the road opens ahead of her to reveal the river. A familiar sight. If she carries on for a few more minutes there is a patch of grass, a bench. She can rest.

Finally she stops, feeling like her lungs are raw and bloodied.

Bending over, her hands on her hips, she heaves up the cereal she had for breakfast.

It doesn't ring true.

However fast she runs, she cannot escape from it. The possibility has already invaded her mind. All this time she has believed that David Alden took her dreams and stamped all over them. Her own pain and suffering, her survival has been her sole focus. But what if David is innocent? Then he'd be as much a victim as her, a victim who has had his own dreams crushed.

She looks around. If he is innocent, it would mean that whoever attacked her is still out there, probably the same person who murdered Eve. If it is not David then she has no face to pin to the crime. He could be anyone, anywhere. He could be close by. He could be getting out of that blue Ford S-Max just across the road right now.

But if it wasn't David it would mean she could look at that blue Ford S-Max and believe it was blue, not silver or red. Her gaze extends across the river; a flock of geese have grouped on the bank opposite. She counts seven of them. If David Alden was innocent she would trust herself that there were seven and not ten or five. Being told that David attacked her was like looking at a blue sky and having everyone tell her it was yellow. And somehow she had to train her mind to believe it was yellow even if every part of her screamed that it was blue. It is the reason she doesn't go out alone, because she can no longer trust what she sees. She needs others to direct her and instruct her, she allows them to interpret the world for her because she was proved to be so inept at doing it herself.

Her heart rate slows. By degrees her body pulls her back in. Taking deep breaths she smells the mossy scent of the riverbank. The same smell you get just after it has rained. Petrichor, that's what it's called. She searched for the term on the Internet years ago. Tilting her head up toward the sun, she closes her eyes and feels its gentle heat stroke her cheeks, a light breeze that dusts her skin. Her whole body relaxes as if it has been defused. Even her mind allows her to remain in the moment without turning over its next move.

When she opens her eyes, she takes in the sight. Running through a village, along a river or sitting in a restaurant with your boyfriend isn't necessarily the best way to get to know a place. It strikes her that she could be seeing all this for the first time. Why has she not noticed the narrow boats that line the river's edge before? Each one is painted in bright, distinctive colors. She can make out the names on those closest to her. *Iona*, *Aubrey*, and her favorite, *Marge the Barge*.

When she looks up to the sky, she sees ribbons of sun escaping the clouds only to be swallowed up again. The changing light has a transformative effect. Under the sun the river glints and sparkles before changing back to a murky brown when it slips behind the clouds once more.

Gradually her ears become attuned to the chatter of others, the sound of kids shrieking and giggling, the faint hum of aircraft overhead. She doesn't want to run home. For the first time in years she would like to stay where there is life and noise and bustle. Feeling her back pocket, she remembers the tenner she brought out, just in case.

The village is more like a town, a town that smells of percolating coffee. It seems to Mel that people around here either work like dogs or spend all day exchanging gossip in cafés; there is little in between. She chooses one that is housed in an elegant double-fronted villa with tables and chairs on a small patio at the front. Mercifully it is free of mothers and children, presumably because the tables are too tightly packed to allow for buggies. Once inside, she realizes there is another reason. The place is piled high with antiques and ceramics, vintage chandeliers hang from the ceiling, sweet-smelling candles are arranged on tables around chunky silver and gold jewelry. Mel thinks she must have read the word *Café* by mistake and is about to turn and leave when she sees a pile of pastries stacked up on old wooden table and hears the sound of milk being frothed.

She smiles to herself. She wasn't imagining it after all.

Her juice—fennel, orange and carrot—is offset by the pain aux abricots. She takes both and finds a table facing the door, next to the window. The café is on the main square around which village life seems to revolve. Opposite, on one of the narrow lanes that flow off the square, a delivery driver appears to have got his van stuck. She's watching the small gesticulating crowd that's gathered around when her phone rings.

It's Nathaniel Jenkins.

It's his turn to sound nervous.

"Mel, it's Nat . . . Nathaniel, although no one calls me that except for my mum, but you don't really need to know that, do you . . ." His babble raises a smile. It's the kind of waffle she would come out with to fill silence. "I hope you don't mind me calling."

Mel thinks about this. Does she mind? The fact that she's not trying to close down the call immediately tells her she doesn't. She could go further and say she is actually pleased to hear from him. "Not at all."

"I've been worried that I cocked up . . . sending you that file. I didn't really think it through, you know, how hard it might be for you."

"I'm glad you didn't." She's had enough of people thinking about her, tailoring their conversation and actions to what they believe might upset her.

"Have you read it?"

"Have you seen how much there is? I've made a start, that's all. It's a bit weird to be honest, it's all about what happened to me but some of it I'm reading for the first time."

"Such as?"

"Well I didn't go to the trial, I couldn't face it, and now seeing it all written down in black and white . . ." She can't finish her sentence, doesn't think she's ready to release the words from her head just yet.

"He was a mate, wasn't he, David?"

"He was."

"Did you ever have any doubts . . ." he pauses, sensing the delicate territory he is walking, "that he did it?"

She presses her finger down on to her plate, collects a few remaining flakes of her pastry and exhales. "Yes. Yes, I did."

They could meet, he says, quickly qualifying his suggestion with "Only if you wanted to . . . if you weren't too busy."

Her reflex is to say thanks but that won't be possible. She wouldn't invite him to the house and she can't go out. Then she reminds herself where she is, looks across the square and sees the van emerging from the tight spot, another man slapping the back of the vehicle to let the driver know he has cleared the lane.

She is out. Alone. It is physically possible. Does she want to meet Nat? Yes, she does, and instinctively, before she has thought about it, she knows why. Beyond a photograph, some basic details, she knows nothing about Eve. Who was she? What motivated her? Would Melody have liked her? The questions aren't necessarily logical, she is aware of this. But she's followed logic for six years and it's left her empty and unsatisfied.

"Tomorrow?" she says quickly before she can change her mind.

"Tomorrow works for me."

"I don't have a car. I live in Surrey, would you mind . . ."

"I can come to you," he says. "Where shall we meet?"

"I live in Rockside. There's a coffee shop just off the square." She glances down at the menu. "It's called Nest," she says, tickled with her newly acquired local knowledge.

"Eleven?"

"Perfect."

Six

He's shorter than she remembers, like those actors who appear tall on the screen only for you to realize they're walking around in Cuban heels. She sees him seeking her out across the café, which is busier than yesterday with a large table of what looks like the local WI, green wellies and Barbours slung on the back of chairs and pearl earrings and ever so yah. One of the women with particularly big hair is taking notes, occasionally tapping her pen on the side of her cup in an attempt to steer the conversation back to the matter of the *fair* and away from gossip and tittle-tattle. She isn't having much luck.

Nat spots her immediately. Mel is reminded of their first encounter in the police station and feels her anticipation turn to dread. There is no escaping the circumstances that have brought them together. A large part of her longs to be talking jam and cakes too.

She smiles self-consciously and drops her gaze, watches his feet, two desert boots negotiating their way around the display tables. He looks more rested, healthier than when she saw him last, wearing a fresh checked shirt. His hair is combed into a small quiff. On his wrist a chunky watch glints in the light.

He reaches out to shake her hand.

What the hell are we going to say? she panics, feeling her palms grow clammy.

He waits for his coffee to arrive before promptly knocking it over. It spills across the table, drips down to his jeans.

"Great, now it looks like I've pissed myself, or maybe I have pissed myself and this was just an attempt to cover it." He winks at her. "Sorry, I've been bricking it all morning that this is going to be really awkward."

Mel breaks into a laugh. She is relieved to find she likes him, an instant gut reaction born from his tendency to say exactly what is on his mind. Who else in her life does that? She relaxes into her chair.

"Don't take this the wrong way, but you look like Eve. Not exactly, but similar. That's why I came across all strange in the police station."

"You thought I was her?"

"Yeah." He nods. "Until I heard the copper say your name. Is it Melody or Mel?"

It was always Melody. She insisted upon the long form because she liked to hear the full three syllables of her name sounded out like a song.

When did it become Mel?

"Either really," she says.

"Melody then," he says without hesitation. "It is the superior name of the two." He smiles but it doesn't reach his eyes.

"It must be a tough time for you. Were you two together?"

He stares at her for a moment before the question registers. "Oh no, not like that. Although we always said it was a shame I was gay because it would have been much easier if we could have got together. Actually no . . ." he laughs, "we would have driven each other up the wall." He pauses, closes his eyes for a moment. "It still hasn't really sunk in. It's not like we saw each other every day anyway. But I catch myself thinking, oh Eve would love that, or I must call Eve and tell her about this, and it slams into me that she isn't here and she isn't coming back."

"I'm sorry."

"The police think he did it . . ." He sighs. "Now it's my turn to apologize. Just tell me if you don't want to talk about it . . ."

"I'm fine, go ahead."

"Eve was sure David was innocent. She thought she was getting somewhere with the investigation. She was a good judge of character, you know, smart, too smart sometimes because she wouldn't back down when she thought something was right or true even if it meant getting up people's noses. It was why she was so good at her job; well she was when she still had it. You know that's what she did, don't you? She worked on *APPEAL*, the investigations program."

Mel shakes her head. "I hadn't known." It made sense though. No wonder it had seemed so professional. Eve wasn't just anyone blindly heading in to an investigation. She knew exactly what she was doing. Nat catches the waitress' attention and orders a replacement coffee. "She had looked at loads of cases like David Alden's, she knew what she was doing and I'm not convinced she would have got it so wrong."

"Some people are good liars."

He considers this. "Yeah, I know they are, but what if Eve was right? What if she got too close and she was killed because someone wanted to shut her up?"

"If they get it wrong again and charge David Alden, Eve's work counts for nothing, you mean?"

"Exactly." Mel sees the tears swell in his eyes. "I would hate that to happen."

"But the police have her file too. Surely they're going to read it and find out exactly what Eve discovered."

"Yeah, and the police are great at admitting their own mistakes . . ." The sarcasm in Nat's voice pierces her. "Sorry . . . they have a vested interest in pinning it on David Alden, that's what worries me. I guess I don't trust them."

Mel feels the doubts infest the air. She scratches at her skin. Her house might be empty and soulless but it's also clean and sterile and safe.

"You said you had your own questions about the conviction." Nat's tone is gently coaxing.

"He was a friend of mine," Mel says. "I thought I was a good judge of character too . . . until it happened. I didn't believe he could do that and then they told me my hair was found on his jacket and fibers from my clothes too. It's hard to argue with science."

"And now?"

She sucks air in. "I don't know what to think. Reading Eve's file about what was said in court is odd."

"In what way?"

"They said he tried to come on to me. But he had never tried to do that, not once, it wasn't that sort of friendship. It was easy and cool. We had a laugh."

Nat regards her intensely. "Eve said that if she were you she'd want to know the truth. Do you?"

The question grabs Mel by the throat; she feels herself trying to squirm away from it. Before she answers, she'd like to know what the truth will cost her. She'd like a crystal ball to see where it will lead her. She doesn't like walking in the dark with no sense of what lies ahead. Maybe it's not a matter of whether she wants the truth but if she is strong enough to handle it. A wave of panic crashes over her. She looks at Nat, his eyes burning with loss. He can't sit still. His whole body is restless with the need to make sense of Eve's death. Mel's mind produces a picture of Eve, working alone, determined to get to the truth because she trusts her instincts over scientific evidence and police theories and legal process; not stopping to consider the cost because whatever it was, the truth is always worth it.

"Yes," she tells Nat finally. "I honestly think I do."

His face breaks into a smile. "Eve was right after all."

They ask the waitress for the bill. The WI women have gone now. Apart from Nat and Mel there's only one other older couple who've finished their coffees and are now browsing the ceramics. "I'll be reading it at the same time as you. Let's keep in touch, shall we," Nat says.

"I'd like that."

"And Melody . . ."

"Yes?"

"It might be a good idea not to tell anyone you have it . . . I'm probably just being overcautious, but . . . well, after what's happened, it just seems like we should be careful."

"Understood."

He glances at his watch. "I've got five minutes to make my train." They kiss each other good-bye and Mel watches him dart across the square toward the station. Once he's out of sight, she leaves and jogs all the way home without stopping.

Twenty minutes later she is back in the safety of the house, her breath ragged. She gives herself a moment to recover before she opens her laptop and starts writing.

For once she will air her own memories of August 17, 2007, the ones that were discounted and undermined and locked away because they didn't fit with what everyone else told her. She looks out to the garden, to a patch of sky. It is blue. It is not yellow or purple.

She received a text that night arranging a time and a meeting place.

She writes the name of the person she was going to meet.

She writes the word CHAIN in capitals, followed by a question mark.

Why does it seem so familiar?

Seven

T he chain bothers Victoria. No one has given her anything close to an adequate explanation for it. Certainly not David Alden, but then it wouldn't be in his interests to do so. She can't remember it featuring highly in the investigation into Melody's Pieterson's attack. Stirling liked to direct his resources where he was most likely to get a quick result. So far all she knows is that the chain was produced by a wholesaler in Kent, a family-run business that stopped making them three years ago.

If all else fails, she knows what she'll have to do. It's her least favorite option, but if need be she'll slap on a bit of makeup, sweat under the camera flashes and ask for the public's help through the press.

She's not there yet, though.

In recent days she's been avoiding DCI Stirling. However bad it gets, she can always console herself that he is two months away from retirement. Technically he is still in charge but his influence is ebbing. His authority has gone into terminal decline. Not that anyone is upfront about it. Stirling pretends he's still got it, everyone pretends he has. But they all know. In eight weeks' time he won't matter. Victoria's reluctance to charge Alden is salt in the wounds.

She's no closer to doing it either. If anything, she's further away. After reading the CCTV section in Eve's file, she traced Alden's route from Shepherd's Bush to Ham herself before turning around and going back to Hammersmith. Did he have enough time to dump his friend and return to the club? Her heart pounded as she looked at the dashboard clock when the journey was over. She wanted Eve Elliot to be wrong. She needed her to be wrong in the same way she needs to kiss her kids when she comes home late at night, to know that they are alive and breathing and that her world is still stable.

Eve had to be wrong because it was DC Victoria Rutter who searched the CCTV in Melody Pieterson's case. And it was her, in her youthful exuberance, who found the blurred image of a green car close to Ham Gate and presented it to Stirling. Had she believed it was David Alden's Porsche 911? Was it discernible through the glow of headlights? It wasn't for her to say. She was simply giving her boss a potential lead. Someone else had been tasked with finding the expert who testified in court that it was Alden's car. What she does know is that the subsequent praise from Stirling made her feel sick, like she'd gorged on too many sweets. It could have been any green car and she knew it.

And no one, not Victoria or her colleagues, had taken it upon themselves to plot out each sighting on CCTV and work out the timings, determine whether it was possible for David Alden to get from Hammersmith to Ham and back again in the window of time available.

Victoria needed Eve to be wrong.

But Eve was right.

"Brought you a coffee." DCI Stirling lumbers into her office brandishing a takeaway cup.

She hesitates before taking it from him. "Thanks, but it's not my birthday."

"You should stop drinking that crap from the machine, it's toxic."

"And that from a man who has a Greggs pasty for breakfast every day." She tastes the coffee, has to admit it's a good one. It's not even from Greggs but the posh deli round the corner. She should stop being so cynical, accept the gift without thinking he's only bought it to give him a reason to come into her office, stalk her.

She feels a stab of sympathy for him. What the hell is he going to do with himself when he leaves work? As far as she knows he doesn't even play golf. His face is pallid, he wears a beard, yellowed around his upper lip from the fags he claims he has given up. Eighteen holes would be too much for him anyway; he struggles to make it to Greggs and back without being out of breath. When her dad had a heart attack he changed his lifestyle completely, started jogging and took up t'ai chi at sixty-seven. DCI Stirling on the other hand seems to be playing a game of chicken with life.

"I've been wondering about the significance of the chain," she says, turning away from him to tidy papers on her desk. "It's bugging me. Did you have any theories?"

"I didn't need to, the case was as clear-cut as I've ever seen. And we never released the details of the chain to the press so he can hardly claim it's a copycat."

"Uh-huh." She slurps the coffee. "And David Alden never gave you a reason?"

He gives a cynical laugh. "Come on you're better than that. "Why would he? It's all about the power. He holds out, gets a kick from keeping us in the dark. You've never watched *Cracker*?"

"Before my time, sir."

His laughter quickly produces a phlegmy cough. "You need to rein back on the hours then, you're not aging well."

"I'll bear it in mind."

"Look, I know you, Rutter, you're clever. But let me tell you something: don't go looking for complications when there aren't any. Sometimes cases practically solve themselves. It doesn't happen very often, once or twice in a career, but when it does, you embrace it. The worst thing you can do is make it harder for yourself." He picks up the photo of Oliver and Bella that sits on her desk. They're smiling in their school uniform. Only she notices the patch of Weetabix on Oliver's collar. She'd sent them out without brushing their hair, without clean jumpers, having ignored the reminders from school that they were having their photograph taken that day. She always has the same reaction when she looks at it. Their toothy grins, the way they lean in to each other laughing makes her burst with pride. And then she sees the Weetabix stain and her mood deflates. It's like a symbol of all the missed sports days and concerts and cinema Sundays. "You could have this case wrapped up if you stopped making life difficult for yourself, reacquainted yourself with your family." He places the frame back on her desk.

"Enjoy the coffee," he says as he walks out.

The camera flashes glint off the gold. You're on camera, don't blink, Victoria tells herself. She's holding it up, not the exact chain found in Eve Elliot's hand but a replica sourced from Meopham and Sons in Maidstone, Kent, who made the original.

When the photographers and cameramen have taken their shots, DI Rutter starts talking. Her statement is short, to the point. "This is an identical chain to the one found on Eve Elliot's person when she was discovered," she tells the assembled press. "We believe it is of significance to the killer. If anyone has seen a chain like this either recently or in the past we would ask them to get in touch. Perhaps they might have sold one to someone in a secondhand shop or online; again we would like to hear from them."

She doesn't tell them they found one on Melody too. She's not giving everything away so easily.

Back in her office, she is removing her makeup with a face wipe when she hears the familiar wheeze in the doorway.

"Opened a can of worms there, Rutter." He's carrying a takeaway coffee. He doesn't offer it to her.

Eight

From my investigations I had gathered an abstract mental picture of Melody. Part collage of images, part word cloud formed from the descriptions people gave of her. *Funny. Joy. Laughter. Wine. Busy. Energy. Summer.* I saw a woman with shoulder-length blond hair and a full-beam smile that rarely slipped. She took risks, she pushed it. She liked proof that life was pumping inside her. Occasionally she wore leopard-skin trousers and fake fur and always red lipstick, and when her friends asked her when she was going to grow up and get respectable, she'd say, "I don't understand the question." I liked her style. I could have pictured myself whiling away a weekend with her under the big fat sun that followed her around.

Only this was Melody before the attack. The way people described her afterward suggested that Melody had vanished. Her world had shrunk, she was delicate, in need of protection. The word *worry* cropped up a lot. No one mentioned red lipstick and leopard prints.

After I died I had a chance to see Melody for myself which sounds weird and creepy, I know, but if you were in my shoes you'd have done the same. First impressions? Ok. And OK, there was no evidence of sartorial flare, no sign of a honking laugh, but then most of the time she was alone and I wouldn't have expected her to laugh at herself. The woman I saw looked a little drab but she didn't seem shrunken or delicate. In fact I thought, there's a woman who's done well for herself, who has taken adversity and given it a kick up the arse. I had to blink when I looked into her house because it was so sparkly, it dazzled from every angle. I thought, my God, is *that* her kitchen? Then slowly it grew on me that something wasn't quite right, though I couldn't say what exactly. The cleaning was way over the top for starters; she was always checking parcels and delivery times and ordering crap from Lakeland . If I was alive there was no way I'd spend a nanosecond ordering Mary Berry cake lifters from Lakeland. I'd be out there skipping under the sun. I'd be bear-hugging my mum. But this was how Melody chose to run her days. The atmosphere around her was jagged and sharp, and on closer inspection it was as if her whole body was clenched, braced for attack. It hit me that she hadn't laughed in the face of adversity, she had put up a front, and the effort of maintaining it had made her brittle. So brittle I worried that one single, tiny thing could break her.

And then I worried some more, because she was reading my file and there wasn't one single thing in it to break her, but pages of them, truths that would explode in her face. And yes, I wanted her to uncover them but I thought, wouldn't it be kinder if only I could tell her myself, break it to her gently? But when I looked at her again I saw a woman who had been told too many different truths. She had to work this one out for herself. Cruel as it was, Melody had to fall apart before she had any hope of putting herself back together again.

The file took months to compile. By week five I had created a huge table detailing every piece of evidence against David Alden, every lead in the case. Photographs of the crime scene, the surrounding area. What was followed up, what wasn't. Where were the holes? Where had they made a mistake?

I applied for documents and statements to be released; every telephone call, conversation and scrap of paper relating to the case was noted, collected, retained. I went back to the beginning, to the time when Melody was found on the edge of the park, looking not for what had been found, but what had been missed.

It was then that my first breakthrough came.

Two people had called the police to say they had found a woman, presumed dead, in the undergrowth at Ham Common Woods.

According to the log, the calls came in at roughly the same time: 7:32 A.M. and 7:34 A.M. on Sunday, August 19, 2007. Both were men; one a jogger, the other a man walking his dog. Both gave statements to the police, depicting the same scene.

Only the jogger, Mr. Colin Regus, was called as a prosecution witness at trial.

Why wasn't the other witness called? Why choose one over the other? Was there a reason?

There was always a reason.

Eddie Morgan's house smelt of dogs, or one dog in particular, a collie Labrador cross called Jessie who jumped up and licked my face as Eddie welcomed me in. He lived in a flat not far from the common, a cozy throwback to the seventies, patterned carpets and a brown three-piece suite.

"Such a long time ago," he said. He spoke with a West Indian accent, had a face that made you happy. "I thought it was all done and dusted."

"I appreciate you might not be able to remember much . . ."

"Remember it? You don't forget something like that no matter how much time passes. Poor girl. I can see her face now. We thought she was dead, she looked about as dead as you can get."

"We?"

"Me and the other man, Colin was his name. He was out for a run, training for a half-marathon. The first time he'd run that way, he told me. I bet it was the last time he tried it too."

Eddie offered to make tea, told me to sit down and make myself comfortable. At a guess he was in his mid seventies, happy for the chance to talk. On the mantelpiece was a photograph of him and a woman, faded by the years, taken before his hair had gone gray.

He emerged from the kitchen carrying two mugs of tea. "Sorry I don't have any cake." He pointed to the photograph, "She used to make the best ginger cake, wouldn't ever part with the recipe, not even to me, she said it was all in her head, and now it's gone with her." He cackled. "She's probably laughing at me up there, buying all the no-good ones from the supermarket." He settled down in his armchair. "So you gonna tell me what this is all about?"

I was straight with Eddie, he deserved it. He'd invited me into his house without suspicion. I knew it would rarely be this easy.

"Ah well, the police, it's not like they never make a mistake now, is it?" he said when I had finished. "Just tell me how I can help."

"Colin Regus was called as a witness at the trial."

"That's right."

"Did they ask you?"

"They didn't, my suits weren't as good apparently." He laughed. "They said my services wouldn't be needed. Poor Mr. Regus, he takes that route once and ends up going to court, and there's me and Jessie walking there every morning and night and no one bothers us."

I took a sip from my mug. "You make a good cup of tea."

"A man has to have a skill in life."

"Every morning and night, you say?"

"That's what I said. We're less regular now. Jessie has arthritis and my knees are no good." He reached down and patted the dog.

"But back then you took exactly the same route twice a day?"

"That's correct. Jessie always leads the way, knows where she wants to go, this one."

"But you didn't see Melody Pieterson on the Saturday?"

"No."

I thought of the photographs of the scene, the undergrowth, how well her body might have been hidden. "She would have been easy to miss, I guess."

He shook his head. "No, dear. We didn't see her because she wasn't there. Jessie has got a nose like a bloodhound when it comes to sniffing things out."

"And you told the police this?"

"I told them how often we walked there. I told them Jessie had a talent for sniffing thing out."

"Thanks," I said. "That's very interesting."

He looked puzzled. "Well, like I say, happy to help."

To get a conviction, the police needed David Alden to have dumped Melody on the Friday night. He had an alibi for the rest of the weekend, which made me think there was a good reason why Colin Regus was called as a witness and Eddie Morgan wasn't. And it wasn't one that had anything to do with his suits. Eddie's testimony alone wouldn't have destroyed the prosecution's case, but it might have introduced an element of doubt.

It also got me thinking: there was almost thirty-two hours between the last sighting of Melody and the time when she was found in Ham Common Woods. Everyone had assumed she was driven there and dumped directly after she was picked up. But what if she had been taken somewhere first? Where would we find evidence that could prove she was dumped in the woods outside David Alden's window of opportunity?

Together with David's solicitor we requested the archive samples of Melody's clothing from the Metropolitan Police. The excuses varied so much you knew they had to be making them up. *They've been misplaced/lost/destroyed*, and when they tired of those, they went for the more traditional route, ignoring our e-mails entirely. The thing to do is never give up. For every e-mail ignored I sent another two, always aggressively polite in tone. I had time. David had time. He'd waited long enough. Some police forces take the same approach as the customer services at a budget airline. They make it so hard for you to extract anything from them that only the persistent will ever get a refund for ending up in the arse end of Italy when you were supposed to land in Florence. Most people don't have the patience; life's too short, they think. Me, I didn't mind the wait. Part of me even enjoyed it because I knew I was tormenting them far more than they could ever annoy me.

I was right. After four months we took receipt of two slides containing tiny pieces of the blue shirt Melody had worn the evening she was attacked. My hope was that hidden within the fibers of the fabric was a residue of soil that might tell us a different story to the one that led to David Alden's conviction.

It was late August by the time the samples eventually arrived, but the summer hadn't been wasted. I'd spent much of it gathering witness statements, interviewing Melody's friends who were with her on the night she was attacked and a few who weren't.

What became apparent was that more than one of them had something to hide.

Nine

In their bedroom, it's dark save for a thin strip of light that beats its way through the curtains and another that slips in under the door. It's the way they always do it. Not always, she corrects herself, not at the beginning, when the seeing was part of the discovery, the thrill. Watching his face, the need and want in it, knowing that she was doing that to him. His eyes open, never closed. He didn't want to miss a bit of her.

He doesn't look at her now. Not with his eyes shut he can't. She wonders who she is tonight: a woman at work who's caught his eye? A face and a body plucked from a magazine? A fellow surfer he's seen on the beach? There are times when she could swear she smells someone else on him. She mentioned it once; he pushed her away. "Well if that's what you think of me," he said and ignored her for days afterward. Although to be fair she hadn't realized he had fallen out with her until three days later when she asked him which charlotte royales he thought would win the *Great British Bake Off* semifinal and he'd refused to answer.

Now she can picture all the cakes lined up waiting for the judges to taste them. *Stop thinking about cakes. Remove the image of perfect Swiss rolls and delicate bavarois from your head. Think of sex.* What *does* she think of sex? Occasionally it can be a bit hit and miss, like an episode of *Homeland*, but on the whole it delivers. It's good sex, above average she would say, although she lacks the evidence to support this claim. It's just separate. Before, it was about a mutual connection. A coming together, if you can excuse the pun. These days they don't make love to each other, they assume roles, body doubles for their fantasy of the moment. She knows this because she does it too. Except tonight, when finally having put charlotte royales from her mind, she dares herself to look at him.

His features shift and distort as he rocks back and forth, his face changes as it catches the light.

When they're done, there is a perfunctory kiss, an "I love you" said with little trace of sentiment and each of them turns to face away from the other. Mel listens for his breath growing heavy. She's waiting for the twitch in his leg that she knows is the tipping point, the transition between wakefulness and sleep. "A hypnic jerk is the proper term," he told her once. "A twitch," she repeated. She refuses to call it a hypnic jerk. From here he slides deeper and deeper into sleep. She waits until she is certain he has gone before pulling back the covers and heading downstairs.

She was reading the file most of the day, with the exception of a few screen breaks when her eyes began to burn in their sockets. Typical then that just as she heard Sam arrive she saw a name that caught her attention.

Patrick.

His statement to the police after she was attacked.

And an interview with Eve.

Any attempt at sleep is pointless until she reads what he said.

Original statement from Patrick Carling to police
This statement consisting of two page(s) signed by me is true to the best of my knowledge and belief and I make it knowing that if it is tendered in evidence, I shall be liable to prosecution if I have willfully stated in it anything which I know to be false or do not believe to be true.
(Signature) Dr. P. Carling Date: August 21, 2007

I live at 25 Percy Road, Shepherd's Bush. I am a doctor at Chelsea and Westminster Hospital specializing in gynecology.

For the past year and a half Melody Pieterson has been my lodger. We have been close friends since we met at university in 1998. On the night of August 17, 2007, Melody met me and a group of friends after work at the Horse and Hound pub in Shepherd's Bush. She was the last to arrive, around 8 P.M., and came and sat with us. She shared a bottle of wine with our mutual friend Honor Flannigan. She had not been drinking excessively.

I think she left the pub around 10.30 P.M.. She lost her footing and almost fell down the steps into the beer garden but I didn't think she was drunk. I assumed she was going home and offered to walk her back. She declined.

I returned home at around 11 P.M. A colleague, Dr. Sonny Ferguson, had been working late and had arranged to stay at my flat. He slept on the sofa. We were traveling to the coast the next morning to go surfing.

I returned home late on Saturday night. Melody was not there. I called her mobile and when I got no answer I called Honor Flannigan and Sam Chapman, our friends. Neither of them had heard from her. I waited until Sunday morning when I reported her missing.

Mel reads on to the notes Eve wrote up after her own meeting with Patrick, which took place at a café in Hammersmith just over three months before she died.

Exchange between Patrick Carling and Eve Elliot transcribed from May 26, 2013
Patrick Carling: I'll help you as far as I can but I hope you know what you're doing. This might just be another story for you but it has destroyed Mel. She never took life seriously before, always saw the good in people, you know, she was the life and soul. She's gone from that to being a recluse practically. She thinks people are following her, says they ring her phone late at night. She's called the police because she thought there was someone in her

garden, looking in her window. None of it happens when anyone else is around. Do you understand what I'm saying?

Mel pauses, runs her eyes back over the words and picks out the one that stings.

Recluse.

Is that what Patrick thinks she is? How could he have known? Hadn't she kept it expertly disguised? Had she not fooled everyone around her that she left the house like a normal person every day?

Mel pushes the chair away from the table and moves across the kitchen to the huge glass doors. Her body feels light, without substance to ground it. When she reaches the back of the room, she rests the tips of her fingers on the cold glass before peeling them off. If she looks closely, she can see the whorls and ridges of her fingerprints. A pattern of arches and loops that is unique to her. Her identity, all that is left of it.

If Patrick knew her secret, Sam did too. Who else? Her parents? Siobhan? Did they all know she was too scared to go out alone?

She balls her hand into a fist, pounds it against the glass. If she had the strength, she would smash it, watch it shatter into a million little pieces. Then she would let the shards splice into the soles of her feet, watch the blood trickle out. Only then would she be sure that what she was seeing was real.

She thought her act had convinced them. She believed she could present them with a shell of her former self and they wouldn't know the difference.

She has been fooling herself.

They think she is paranoid. Delusional. Reclusive. A woman who sees danger where there isn't any, threats where there are none.

Only she has ever heard the phone ring and stop and ring again and stop so many times until she didn't know whether the ring was real or in her head. No one but her has seen the shadow in their garden at night, the one that kept returning. Every time something happened she'd have to gather herself together again, force herself to carry on as the doubt chipped away at her. She would do it. She wouldn't be beaten. She still had a job and a life. These things were imaginings, Sam told her, Patrick told her. Dust yourself down, carry on. So she kept on getting up again, though each time it was a little harder, she was a bit more unsure of herself. Until she couldn't do it anymore.

It was November 2009, more than two years after the attack. They'd moved into the new house a few months earlier. She had arrived at the station from work to find there were no taxis. It was Friday, Sam was working a night shift. Patrick was coming round later for a drink. I'll walk, she thought. The night air would clear her head of work, set her up for the weekend. What could go wrong? It was a main road, lit all the way and busy too, so she reckoned. It was important she started to set and achieve goals, build her confidence, establish her independence again; wasn't that what her therapist was always telling her? So she walked up the hill to the junction, where she turned right on the road that led to their house. She was a couple of hundred meters down when she realized that most of the traffic had carried straight on at the junction. She was alone. She started to count the seconds between cars: one . . . two . . . three . . . four . . . She needed her body to work with her, move fast, take her home to safety . . . five . . . six . . . car headlights behind her, casting a misty light on the path ahead. She breathed relief. There were other people around her. Safety in numbers. She waited for the car to flash past her, disappear into the road ahead. Instead its speed dipped to a crawl, lights switched to full beam. The brightness dazzled her. She was caught in the glare, unable to see the path ahead. A connection in her head fused, a million thoughts and images streamed through her mind at the same time. There wasn't one David Alden. There were hundreds of him, thousands, wearing different masks and guises. She was going to die. She had cheated death before. And no one likes a cheat.

She closed her eyes and screamed, carried on screaming until she had no breath left. And when she opened her eyes again the car had gone, swallowed up by the night as if it had never existed at all. She scrambled for her phone, dialed the most recent number on her display. Patrick. He eventually found her huddled by the side of the road, shivering uncontrollably. He took her home, sat her down, shrouded her in a blanket and poured her a glass of wine.

"You're OK, Mel," he told her. "You are OK. You're just shaken up, that's all." He had his arm around her and pulled her in close. "You're going to get a bit freaked out now and again after everything that's happened."

"It was . . . there . . . it slowed down . . . on purpose." Patrick had put the fire on. She watched the flames curl around the logs, felt the heat from it filter out into the room, but her teeth wouldn't stop chattering.

"I'm sure there was a reason . . ." Patrick started to say, but she tuned out. He hadn't seen what she had seen, he didn't believe her. If no one believed her, did that mean it wasn't real? If no one saw her, would she not exist?

"You need some sleep," Patrick said.

"I don't think I can . . ."

"Fine," he said, "We'll stay up until you fall asleep. Just like old times only with better wine."

"And no burned toast."

"Deal."

In the end she was asleep on the sofa within half an hour, but it had helped just knowing he was there.

When she next saw Patrick, they didn't mention the incident. Mel could trust him to keep quiet. He knew instinctively she wouldn't want Sam to hear about it. What Mel didn't tell Patrick was that she hadn't set foot across the door for the whole weekend after he had left. Nor was she inclined to admit that on the following Monday she had called in sick to work and had followed the same pattern again on Tuesday, Wednesday and Thursday. On Friday she rang her boss to resign, "it's time for a new challenge," she said nebulously. It took her two weeks before she could pluck up the courage to share her news with Sam or Patrick, "I need a change," she'd explained, figuring that change was something people could empathize with and far more socially acceptable than admitting she was scared to leave the house alone.

Yet still the phone rang with phantom callers and the shadows still stalked her. Once she heard someone knocking at the door. Sam found her curled into a ball crying and shaking. "Make it go away," she told him.

He called the police but there were no signs anyone had been on their property.

So Sam built the huge perimeter fence, installed the electronic security gates to make her feel safe. To reassure her. He did all this for her but he could not bring himself to believe her fears had a physical foundation.

Melody walks back across the kitchen, the concrete cold on her bare feet. The room is dark, save from the glow of the laptop. She sits back down at the table, types the name EVE ELLIOT into the search box and sees her face appear on the screen before her.

Her hand reaches out to touch it, follow the contours of Eve's face. She wishes she could breathe life back into her, draw her out from the screen so Eve could sit next to her and guide her through the mess of her life, help her make sense of it. She would recount to Eve everything that has happened to her, all the things that no one else believes to be real. And Eve would smile and hold her hand and tell her it *is* real because it happened to her too.

What else would she tell her, she wonders.

Sam.

If Eve has spoken to Patrick wouldn't she have contacted Sam as well?

Mel does a word search for his name in Eve's file, and in a matter of seconds Sam's interview appears on the screen before her.

Ten

M elody had agreed to marry him, a fact I had gleaned from his repeated use of the word "fiancée." It had always struck me as an antiquated term, like "courting" or "betrothed."

Sam Chapman used the term possessively. It set my teeth on edge. "My fiancée has had a terrible time . . ." he said in his public school estuary mash-up of an accent that posh boys favored.

"Melody, you mean?" I itched to correct him.

I couldn't help but wonder: what was she doing with him?

It was the middle of June. We were in the Harris + Hoole coffee shop not far from the hospital—his suggestion not mine, being unfamiliar with Guildford as I was. It was mid afternoon, post-lunchtime rush, and the selection of sandwiches on display had dwindled to a handful of mozzarella and tomato baguettes and a few cheese and pickle subs. I had arrived intentionally early in order to secure a table, disappointed to see no quiet corner but rather a stretch of tables running the length of the back wall of the café. The side nearest to the wall was fitted out with orange leather banquettes. I sat down there to allow myself a view of the door and the counter, pulling up his photograph from the hospital Web site on my phone so I would be sure to recognize him. He was clean-cut, like a model in a John Lewis catalog. Someone your mum might choose for you. Too overtly handsome to be my type (no man can be too handsome, Kira would have said), but I could appreciate that some women would have found him devastatingly attractive.

By 2:40 P.M. I had begun to doubt he was coming at all when I saw a head of blond hair breeze through the door with another woman. They stopped at the counter, engrossed in conversation. Now and again he'd touch her arm lightly or nod in agreement with whatever she was saying. She had his full attention; not once did he turn around to see if I was waiting for him. He smiled a lot, I noted, appeared genuinely interested in what his companion—a striking woman with long dark hair, tight red trousers and gold ballet pumps—was saying. The scene was completely at odds with the impression I had garnered of him during repeated and terse e-mail exchanges. I thought he would be arrogant, cold, difficult to handle. Basically a bit of a wanker. I felt my shoulders loosen as I heard the woman, who was now clutching one of the remaining mozzarella and tomato baguettes, say good-bye.

Once he had watched her go, he took his coffee from the woman serving and proceeded to quibble over the change. "I gave you ten, not five," he said. I watched her blush, check the till before apologizing and giving him the correct change. He took it from her with a shake of his head. Only then did he turn and scan the room. I lifted a hand to wave and smiled, waiting for him to feed one back to me. But the warmth of a moment ago had disappeared from his face as if someone had flicked the off switch.

"Eve Elliot," I said. We shook hands, or rather he shook mine, for too long, too hard, an orthopedic surgeon trying to crush my bones in a handshake.

"I don't have long," he said before he had even sat down. "I have to be back in surgery in an hour."

He looked irked, drummed his fingers on the table impatiently. "I have no idea what you think you are going to achieve with this," he said.

"I appreciate that you're short of time, so I won't mess around. I have been gathering new evidence and testing the credibility of

THE LIFE I LEFT BEHIND 215

the original evidence in David Alden's case. It's my opinion that he was wrongly convicted."

"Is that so?" He pushed back his chair, crossed his arms. "You are aware that he is already out of prison, aren't you? Aren't you a few years too late with this one? I thought the point was to over-turn a conviction while someone was actually serving a sentence. Although from my point of view I'm very glad you didn't."

Words flashed up in my head. Pompous. Twat.

"How important is your reputation to you, Mr. Chapman?"

"He wasn't a doctor."

"No, you're right, he was a DJ, but even so, no one wants to be convicted of trying to kill a woman if they didn't do it. It doesn't do much for your prospects."

"If you're expecting me to feel sorry for him, I should tell you it ain't gonna work." His accent slipped into estuary again to em-phasize his point.

"I have no intention of trying to make you feel sorry for him. I simply want to go over your statement, what you were doing on the night it happened. What your relationship with Melody was."

"It's all there in the original statement."

"I have it here. Do you mind if I go through it?" I took it from a plastic file on the table and started reading.

"'I live with my fiancée Honor Flannigan at 31 Cowper Road, Acton. I am a doctor at University College Hospital, London, spe-cializing in orthopedics. Melody Pieterson is a childhood friend of my fiancée. That is how I met her. I have known her for four years. The last time I saw her was Saturday, August 9, 2007, at a barbe-cue in our garden . . .'

"That's all correct?"

"You expect me to say it isn't?"

I ignored his question. "Forgive me," I said. "Can I ask if you are still with your fiancée, Honor Flannigan. I've traced her to a surgery in Dorset."

He shifted in his chair, ran his hands through his hair and

glanced down at his watch, a Rolex if I wasn't mistaken. "We're not together anymore. I don't see why that comes into any of this."

"Do you still see Melody?"

His cheeks colored and he drained his cup of coffee before fixing me with the first smile I'd seen from him during our conversation. It made me long for his scowl again. "I live with her. She is my fiancée," he said, like a threat.

I ignored his tone. "Congratulations. Have you set the date yet?" As I'd hoped, my feigned interest wrong-footed him. Even Sam Chapman struggled to be rude in the face of such aggressive enthusiasm.

"December this year," he said.

"I think I'm in the wedding phase right now; you know, the time of life when you get about five invitations a year. I need a separate salary just to support my wedding attendances. Then again, at least you get to see all your old friends. When else do you have the chance to get everyone together?"

Boredom crept over his face. In general men have a tolerance of about thirty seconds for wedding talk. I had exhausted Sam's.

"Is yours going to be a big affair?"

"Relatively." He raised his wrist to look at his watch again. I knew my time was almost up. Time to throw in the grenade.

"Will Honor be there? Does she still keep in touch with Melody or is it a bit awkward? These things can be, can't they?" I held my smile in place, gave nothing away. His features reset into a frown.

"Look," he said, leaning across the table. "Since you didn't seem to get the message in my e-mails, I agreed to meet you to make my position clear. They got the right man. Have you, in all your investigations, found a reason why her hair was on his jacket? Huh?" His raised eyebrows demanded an answer. "No, I thought as much. This might be a little diversion for you, but it's someone's life you are playing with. Have you considered what effect this would have on Mel?"

"I think she is entitled to the truth."

"The truth?" he shouted too loudly, immediately dipping his

voice to a hiss to compensate. "You don't know the truth. You're just sniffing around to see if you can make something of it. What are your credentials anyway? What gives you the right, what makes you . . ." he stabbed the air with his index finger, "think you are better qualified than the police to uncover the truth?"

"I do have experience in this field."

"Do you? Oh yes, on *APPEAL*, of course, a program that was pulled a year ago." He glared at me. "Don't look so surprised, you're not the only one who can do research, you know."

He puffed air out through his teeth, making a *pfft* sound. "The thing is, I don't really care what you do, or what you did. But if you go anywhere near my fiancée, let me tell you . . . I . . . Let's just say she is still very fragile. She can't even go out on her own. I don't want anything to happen to upset her. Now I really do have to go."

He got up and, without saying good-bye, marched to the door. I watched him leave, his gelled hair lifting like a flap as the wind caught it outside.

In many respects Sam was like his house, good-looking on the outside, toxic inside. Sure, he could turn on the charm, channel it at the people who had something he wanted. Like the woman in the red trousers. They would get the full dazzle of his smile. But the rest—the barista, an irritating patient, a woman asking questions about an attack six years ago—they were just shit on his shoes. What did Melody see in him? Fragile, he'd called her. Did he stay with her out of love, or sympathy, or something else entirely? I feared for Melody because I knew that if I was fragile I wouldn't want to be anywhere near him. I'd worry that his ego would destroy me altogether.

Eleven

Her eyes are fixed on one word.

Fragile.

Her head provides her with an accurate definition: *easily broken or damaged, flimsy, weak.*

This is how Sam sees her.

It takes a minute to climb the stairs, less time to switch on the light and jump on to the bed. She cannot bear to be under the same roof as him for a moment more without having her questions answered.

"How long have you known?"

He blinks, repeatedly. His eyes are having trouble adjusting to the brightness.

"What's going on? What time is it . . . ?" He glances at the bed-side clock. "Jesus, Mel, what the hell are you doing?"

"Just tell me how long you've known."

The answer comes ten minutes later, after an initial attempt to feign ignorance and then another one suggesting they talk about it in the morning.

"It is the morning," Mel says.

"It's three o'clock in the morning."

"So let's talk."

"A few years," he says eventually. "It was something Siobhan said about you always inviting her here and never going out that got me thinking. And then . . . it just fell into place. You had given up work but you didn't seem keen on finding anything else. You only ever shop online."

"Why the hell didn't you say anything?" She spits the words out.

"Me? I'm not the only one who was holding things back here."

They're sitting opposite each other on the bed. His face is so close to hers she has no choice but to stare at it. She sees him almost every day, has done for the past four years. She can feel the texture of his hair without touching it: thick, wiry, rendered dry, like straw, from the time he spends in the sea. Its color changes with the seasons: white blond in the summer, darker roots emerging over the winter months. His frown creates furrows, two lines down between his eyebrows, and the wrinkles around his eyes are now more pronounced, carved into his skin. On the bridge of his nose there's a bump where it was broken once in a rugby game, at school or university, she can't remember which. All those hours spent chasing waves have left his skin leathery, weather-beaten. She can see the landscape of it, every freckle and mark, without looking. She is fighting the urge to slap it.

He has a point, of course. She wasn't honest with him. Funny, that. She didn't fancy telling him she spent her days locked in the house. Therefore, the argument goes, she can't blame *him* for lying. Except she can. This is his fault. Just because she can't explain the logic behind her argument at this precise moment doesn't mean it isn't true. She knows it in the same way she knows the sky is blue. It is not yellow. Never has been.

"I didn't want to push you, darling." He strokes her arm. It's like an insect crawling on her. She flicks it away. "Think about it, Mel, I wanted you to work it out for yourself. Why do you think I found Julia, drove you there every week? I thought she would help. I kept on hoping it was working."

He's using that plaintive voice of his, dipping his eyes dolefully as if he is Princess fucking Diana at the Taj Mahal. *You have to believe me because it's the truth.*

"Do you know what I think, Sam?"

"I do."

Did he just say that? Pressure builds in her head. She can hear whistling in her ears. "No you don't. You do not know what I am thinking. I think you are a coward. See, I know *I* am a coward, I've known for a long time now, but you, you're just as bad and you don't even see it. You're like one of those enablers, you know, the people who live with alcoholics and think they're helping but really they're just allowing them to carry on their destructive behavior, pussyfooting around them, too scared to stand up and say what's really happening."

He's shaking his head. "No, no, no," he says, as if the truth is simply a matter of repetition. "All I wanted was to make you feel secure. I thought all this would help, the house, the wedding, the baby."

The baby.

How did he think that would help?

She had made Sam promise not to tell anyone at first. Twelve weeks, she'd said, not before. *We don't want to jinx it.* Then, after the scan, when they walked away with a grainy image of a fetus the size of a pea pod, she'd begged him to wait a little longer. There was no bump to speak of and it wasn't as if her social diary was crammed. He'd agreed. At eighteen weeks he'd gone to Stockholm on a week-long conference. It coincided with David Alden's release but she assured him she would be fine, plus there was Patrick, who had insisted on coming round for dinner that evening to keep her company. He was working in Guildford the next day and it wasn't unusual for him to stay overnight if he had an early start.

Over dinner he remarked that she looked peaky, off color. Sometimes she hated doctors and their unsolicited diagnoses.

"He's not going to hurt you, if that's what you're worrying about," he said, though quite how he could promise this she had no idea. He insisted she sit down while he tidied up, made them both a cup of the special Night Time tea. It was as good as useless at getting her to sleep but she decided to drink it anyway to keep Patrick happy and ward off any more unwanted questions about her welfare. He might be right this time, she thought; she felt like she was coming down with something. Her head was light, a wave of tiredness crashed over her. "I think I might go to bed after all."

For once there was no need to coax herself to sleep. It was already waiting to welcome her. She couldn't even remember undressing and getting into bed.

It was the pain that woke her the next morning. White hot. Like someone was clawing deep into her belly, gouging out her insides. She stumbled out of bed into the hallway. The house was silent. Patrick had already gone, must have left before she got up. She went to walk downstairs to make a cup of tea but a cramp doubled her over. She cried out, not that anyone could hear her. *The baby.* She knew it. She hadn't believed she could create another life. Now she was being proved right.

She called the hospital. "Are you bleeding?" the woman asked.

"Not yet," she said, as if it was inevitable.

"You need to come to the ward so we can assess you."

"My boyfriend isn't here to bring me."

"Well get a taxi then," she said, as if it was the easiest thing in the world to get in a car with someone you'd never met before and travel five miles to the hospital. Mel hung up, called Sam's mobile and listened as his phone went straight to voice mail. Quite how she thought he could be of assistance when he was in Sweden she didn't know. *Water will help*, she remembered reading that in one of those pregnancy books Sam had bought. She ran herself a bath, eased herself down into it as another band of pressure clenched around her stomach. She screamed. Fuck the water. The water was no help. She got out of the bath again, struggling to move, and then saw the blood. Drip, drip on the white tiles. The brightest red pooling at her feet. She knew what she had to do and she knew she couldn't do it. She was failing the test. *Get yourself to hospital and save your baby, give it a chance at least.* All those stories she'd heard about women who would do anything for their children, lay down their lives, and here she was unwilling even to walk out of the front door and get into a taxi because she was pitiful and weak and feeble. She didn't deserve to be entrusted with another life. And the fact that she couldn't hold on to it told her what she had long suspected. There wasn't enough life inside her to sustain another.

Reaching for her mobile, she called Patrick. There was nothing else for it. She would have to tell him. Three calls, two messages. Third time lucky, he picked up.

"I'll be there as soon as I can."

She wipes her eyes but it's useless. The tears won't stop coming. Sam has rarely seen her cry since the day of the ladybirds. She thought she could stop the flow of her emotions but this was just another deceit. They have collected in a dam that has now been breached by one single truth. They come at her with such force she can't find the air to breathe. She lied to Sam, to herself. He lied to her. Nothing is fixed or anchored in reality; *say what you want people to hear, see what you want to believe.* None of this should come as a surprise. The deceit can be traced all the way back to the beginning. They've built their relationship on lies.

"I could have saved it."

Sam has his arm around her, his eyes fixed on hers. "It would have happened anyway, Mel. It was a miscarriage."

What would he know? It wasn't his responsibility to carry that baby around. It was a girl; she didn't even give her a name. The only task entrusted to her in years and she wasn't up to it. She hadn't been feeling well the night before, she could have done something then, and those lost hours in the morning, the window of time before Patrick arrived and took her to hospital, if she had acted then, the outcome could have been different. No one will persuade her otherwise.

Eventually she speaks. "Why didn't you tell me you had met

her?" Her eyes are intense on him. She wants to gauge his reaction, draw it out of him.

"Met who? Who are you talking about?"

"Eve," she says. "Eve Elliot."

Panic forces his eyes wide open. She can see him making the calculation. *Should he feign ignorance? How much does she know?*

Don't lie. Her eyes are drilling into him. *Don't dare lie.*

"How do you know?"

"It doesn't matter how I know."

He exhales, a deep, weary sigh. "So you're thinking I've lied to you again. I can see how it looks but . . . Oh God," he throws up his arms in surrender, "I've cocked up. Right. I get it. But I wasn't trying to deceive you. She approached me. I told her I didn't want to go over old ground, I knew the evidence against David Alden was convincing. And I didn't see how telling you would help."

"Have you told the police?"

"Of course I've told them."

"So it was only me who you didn't think to tell."

"I'm sorry, I'm really sorry."

She's not listening. What does sorry mean anyway. Does it mean he will never lie to her again?

"We can't get married," she says.

He takes hold of her, a hand on each of her arms. "Don't talk like that, you're just upset . . ."

"Why would you want to marry me? Why would you want to marry someone who can't go out alone, who needs you to take her out? Surely there are plenty of women out there you could have. They'd be impressed by all of this, you know, the house . . . they might appreciate the architectural fucking integrity of it. Why stick with me? What is it I can offer that they can't? It's not my conversation, that's for sure. I haven't had an interesting thought in years. Is it the sex? The blow jobs? I mean, I'm not good at much but I play to my strengths. It's not a reason to marry me, though."

"Mel, stop it. Stop it. I want to marry you because I love you. I know that now and I knew it when I first met you and you were wearing that ridiculous beanie hat."

"It was a ushanka hat," she cries, "a Russian trapper hat. I have never worn a beanie in my life. You can't even remember the hat correctly."

"A trapper hat, a beanie, a fucking fedora." He's shouting now. His eyes spark. "Listen to me, would you? I don't care what hat it was. The hat is not the point, Mel. The point is that I remember you looking ridiculous and beautiful and intriguing all at once and I couldn't stop looking at you." He takes her hand, holds it tight in between both palms. "I want to marry you because I still love you and I want to make this better."

"It's not your job to fix everything. You didn't do this, you don't have to punish yourself by trying to make it better."

"You think I don't feel guilty? You think you are the only one who's been shattered by this? Do you have any idea how many times I've run it over in my head." His eyes water, a tear spills out, cuts down his face. "I don't know what to do anymore, I don't have the answers." She's close to his body, feels it shake in an attempt to contain his emotion, but it's too much. He can't. "It was my fault and I'm sorry." He wipes his eyes with the back of his hand. "Just tell me what I can do to make it better." He starts to sob, bawls in a way that makes his body judder. She can't stand to see him like this; she feels her anger dissipate.

She draws him in toward her, holds him tight. Inhales. It is Sam, she thinks. The same Sam she fell for; it's always been him but they lost each other, themselves. Their defenses are down, the deceit is stripped away. There is such relief in it, the relief of searching and searching and believing something precious is lost to you forever only to find it again. "You don't have to pretend you have the answers," she says. "Maybe the answers will find us." She kisses him where she used to, her favorite spot, on his neck, tracing the line down from his ear, tastes the oil on his skin.

This time they keep the lights on. Eyes open.

The alarm sounds too soon. They're woozy from lack of sleep, but giddy. They've been so removed from each other, the newfound closeness invigorates them. It's not perfect, it'll take time, but she knows there is a foundation now. She gets up with Sam and dresses in her sports clothes, tells him she is going for a run. His face springs into a smile. "Not far," she says, "a little further every day." He kisses her hard on the lips as she leaves the house.

The air is chilled, autumn is settling in. The sky stretches out as far as she can see, the lightest blue bleached by the sun. She searches for a cloud, even the smallest wisp, but she can't find one. Down the hill she runs, slowing her speed so her legs don't buckle underneath her. She breaths deep into her lungs, allows the breaths to power her body. Each morning it gets easier. She passes through town, reaches the river without incident. It's a beautiful morning to be out running. Her eyes feast on the colors, the sharpness of them. It's autumn but she feels a sense of renewal. There's a long way to go, she knows this. But Sam loves her. She loves him. They've allowed themselves to become entangled in lies. Last night, she believes, they started unravelling them, getting back to what brought them together in the first place.

She stops for a few minutes to catch her breath. Close by a toddler throws bread on the path to the geese, and retreats giggling as they flock around her. Mel has turned to head back home, unusually contented, when his words flood her mind.

It was my fault and I'm sorry.

Twelve

I t's her own fault so she can't complain, wouldn't dare to within earshot of Stuart Stirling, or anyone else for that matter. The press appeal for information on the chain has generated the usual response from loonies and crank callers and well-meaning old men reporting that they once gave their wives something similar *but it was just a bird, it wasn't in a cage.* It's why she only ever makes these appeals as a last resort. What she is hoping is that among all the crap something will shine, the sparkle of a proper lead. "He's just playing with us," DCI Stirling told her. He's been cruising the incident room, arms crossed, disapproval seeping out of his skin along with last night's half-bottle of whiskey. "There doesn't have to be a story behind it. You're looking for something that's not there." Maybe she is, but if she doesn't look, she has no hope of finding it.

Ideally she'd ask for more manpower, but that would mean admitting that they are swamped, and she won't do that. In her pep talk this morning she told the team that the next couple of days might be frantic but it would be worth it. She was talking rubbish of course and they knew it. From the looks on their faces, the refusal to smile, Victoria could tell they were tired and overworked and they wanted to believe her but couldn't quite make the required leap of imagination.

Now she sits in her office dissecting a sandwich she bought for lunch two hours ago, attempting to plow through Eve Elliot's file. The more she reads, the more she admires Eve and her single-mindedness. She gets the impression she would have liked Eve, could have happily shared a bottle of wine in her company and talked, among other things, about their mutual suspicion of crushing hand-shakes.

This case is unique in Victoria's experience. Never before has she been able to look back on the last six months of a victim's life in such detail. She wouldn't be so crass as to claim she knows Eve, but the sense of her coming out of the pages is so strong she can almost feel her in the room. So far Eve and her observations have made Victoria smile, laugh out loud even. To keep banging on doors when no one answers, to plug away, alone, when everyone is telling you it's useless; that takes some guts, some spirit.

Eve managed to summarize all of Victoria's reservations about Sam Chapman way more eloquently than she ever could. They interviewed him a few days after Melody had come in, when he called with "a rather delicate matter." He'd met Eve, he said, *only briefly you understand*. In his statement he elaborated, telling DS Ravindra where the meeting had taken place, and when, and recalling with some precision what he had said.

"I offered to help as much as I could but I asked her not to contact Melody. I didn't want her to get upset." He qualified this, somewhat unnecessarily in her view, with an explanation of a miscarriage earlier in the year. "She's still shaky," he said.

Victoria listened to the recording of his interview with some amusement, sitting as she was with Eve's own verbatim notes in front of her.

Funny how two people can interpret the same meeting entirely differently. Every word in this file, every line she reads, serves to strengthen her resolve to find out what really happened.

What a waste. What a terrible shitty waste of a life. If Eve was right—and Victoria has a growing suspicion that she was—and the police got it wrong, then they all have blood on their hands. Yes, they're only human, everyone makes mistakes, blah blah blah. She knows all the excuses, but it doesn't detract from the cold facts that she now sees emerging: they didn't investigate it properly, they didn't follow the leads. Stirling, helped by his officers (she includes her-self in this), went for the easiest option.

This is the reason she hasn't been home before midnight for three days. She might not have seen her kids in that time but she thinks of them all the time. What if it was Bella who was dead and dumped in woodland? All those crazy ambitions and eccentricities and dreams stored up in her string-bean body, gone forever? What if she herself was the mother whose heart had been ripped out and when she looked at the day she didn't understand it anymore, how the sun could shine but she couldn't feel it, not even the faintest touch of heat? Or Oliver even, accused of a crime he didn't commit—who would stand up for her son and fight in his corner when the police were thinking of targets and clear-up rates and pleasing their su-periors to grease their way up the pole?

Eve and David might not be her children but she will investi-gate the case as if they were. They deserve that much at least.

She is extracting a round of tomato from her sandwich when there's a rap on the door. Why do sandwich-makers persist in add-ing tomato? All they do is leak and make the bread soggy. If she had the time, she'd wait in the queue and buy a baguette made to fit her requirements, *no tomato*, but the queues for the bespoke lunches are hideous, snake all the way out on to the pavement, so she always has to make do with one off the shelf.

Taking a bite, she feels the bread wet and spongy and flings it to one side in disgust. "Come in," she says. DC Rollings' face ap-pears from behind the door.

"If it's a day off you want, I'm afraid the answer is no."

He looks bemused. "Nope. I'm still paying the summer holiday off the credit card; trust me, I need the overtime."

"Well what is it, then? Tell me something that's going to make me smile. I've had people coming to me with shit all morning and half of the afternoon."

"I thought you might be interested to know we've just followed up a call from a woman who said her friend wore exactly the same chain."

"Go on."

"She committed suicide—the friend, not the caller, obviously."

Victoria looks across the room at Rollings. He has the same expectant expression that the contestants on *MasterChef* wear—Doug's choice, not hers—when the judges are tasting their food. She feels a spark of interest, only for him to throw water on it in the next sentence.

"She died twenty-six years ago."

Victoria picks a bit of chicken out from the sandwich and shoves it into her mouth. She skipped breakfast again; her stomach moans in protest.

"More than quarter of a century ago," she says. It's a statement that DC Rollings is savvy enough to interpret as a question. *Where the hell is this going to take us?*

"What's interesting is that it was the woman's son found her body. She was wearing the chain at the time; it had been a birthday present from him. Apparently he had been with her alone for hours before anyone found him."

"Do we know what happened to the boy after she died?"

"He was looked after by his father apparently; our caller moved away from the village a few years after it happened. She said he was ten or thereabouts at the time, so he'd be in his late thirties now."

"Have you got names?"

"The woman's name was Rosemary Crighton. Her son was called Charlie."

"Whereabouts did this happen?"

"Sussex. It was a holiday home apparently; they didn't live in the village. Ever heard of a place called Climping?"

"As a matter of fact I have," Victoria said. "I went there on holiday as a kid. Try and locate all the Charles Crightons of that age, will you, and come back to me? And find the address of the house too."

"I'll get on to it."

Oliver is almost ten. What would that do to a boy, coming home and finding his mother's body? Did he sit by her, talking, asking her to wake up, alone in the silence, waiting for help to come?

She slaps herself down. It might not even be true. Even if it is, the chances are there won't be a link to Eve's murder. It appeals to her because she likes to understand the stories behind the cases she solves, to trace the narrative from beginning to end. Usually, though not always, that's where she finds the motivation for the crime. Random murders happen, but in her experience they're rare. She's happier if they have a reason, however warped it might be.

She's still thinking about the boy when she turns back to Eve's file. They've spoken to Sam Chapman, and Melody's friend Patrick Carling has come forward too, but in the absence of a call from Honor Flannigan, they will have to pay her a visit themselves.

Thirteen

had thick skin, like rhinoceros hide, so Nat reminded everyone
at my funeral. Far from provoking an outcry, he had pretty much
the whole room nodding and giggling in agreement. "Nearly all
of us have our own stories about Eve. It was impossible to embar-
rass her, she wasn't big on subtlety. I'd go so far as to say she lacked
a certain amount of social awareness. Like the time we treated ourselves to one night in a posh hotel in France and drank too much
wine. Eve got up in the middle of the night to go to the bathroom,
only she opened the wrong door and went out into the hallway instead, completely nude, and locked herself out. What did she do? She
borrowed two cushions from the armchair in the hall and took the
lift down to reception, where she asked in her loud voice"—cue
laughter—"if someone could kindly let her back into her room.

"The next day when the receptionist remarked that it was lovely
to see her with her clothes on, she planted a kiss on his lips and
handed him a fat tip without so much as a blush.

"Looking back on my friendship with Eve, I see all the things
she made me do: going on to a club because she refused to let the
night end, running a marathon just because she didn't fancy doing it alone. I've climbed the Old Man of Coniston with a hangover, watched her haggle with a man in Egypt, not over the price
of a camel ride but how long we could spend on it—two hours in
the end; I swore I'd never forgive her. I've done all this because Eve
wouldn't take no for an answer. She was a force that made my life

bigger and more exciting . . . and I don't know what I'm supposed to do without her."

Nat was being kind. In truth, friendships are about balance. Yin and yang. He supported me as much in his own inimitable way as I pushed him. Like the time in the summer when I hit a wall with the investigation. I'd spoken to Sam and Patrick and others but Honor Flannigan was blanking me. Three e-mails—no reply. Two voice mails left at her place of work—unreturned. When a hand-written letter failed to elicit a response it was abundantly clear, even to someone with a rhinoceros hide, that she didn't want to talk to me. I would have to go to her.

At least that was what I'd been telling myself for three weeks. The trouble was I couldn't muster the enthusiasm, the courage, the energy, whatever it was that I needed to make me drive to Dorset to use all my powers of persuasion on a woman who had no inten- tion of talking to me. My day job was getting increasingly demand- ing. I had worked three fifteen-hour days in the past week, staking out a takeaway outlet that had been closed down after rat feces were found in a curry only to open again with the same management in the same location. All they had done was paint over the name on the door. Every night I returned to my flat and stared hopelessly at the mountain of paperwork, the chart marked with highlighter about which leads to follow, which pieces of evidence to question. It looked like the workings of an unstable mind. Was it? Was I go- ing round the twist? What had made me so confident I could do this? When was I going to find the time? I doubted myself and my own judgment, hated the way investigating a case made me ques- tion everything, see lies when people may well have been telling the truth. I wanted a break from my head.

I invited Nat around for dinner.

The fact that I invited him was clear evidence that I wasn't think- ing straight. I had plenty of friends who would have consoled me, sympathized and assured me that no, I wasn't ruining their Fri- day night with my endless moaning. Nat was not one of them.

He stood sipping a glass of white wine of his own choosing and plucked an olive from the bowl on the coffee table. He held it up to the light to examine it.

"Where did you buy these?" he asked.

"There's a deli round the corner . . ."

"Liar."

"OK, they're from Sainsbury's but they're good, try them."

He screwed his face up before popping one into his mouth and pretending to gag. Not only was Nat a wine snob, he was an olive snob too.

"I'll sort the music," he said, picking up my iPod. This was another long-standing area of conflict. He would never trust me to choose. "So what have you been listening to this week?" he asked, shuffling through my playlist before turning to me in mock horror. "Fucking hell, Eve, you've been listening to REM? Why didn't you call me? I had no idea it was that bad."

"Get lost." I felt the tears rise in my throat.

"Oh God, don't get upset. You've always had terrible taste in music." He came over to me, put his arm around me. "Come on then, tell me about it."

I spewed it out, everything that had been stewing in my head in one monologue.

"I know I've done it before, but this is different. I always had a team around me, people to bounce ideas off. We'd scoop each other up after a setback. There was support. Do you know what I'm saying? Now there's only me. Me. One person. No one else. There isn't even anyone to come home to. I talk to myself, Nat, honestly, you'd think I was mad. Yes, I know you already think I'm mad. But I argue and reason with myself about this investigation because there is no one to talk to. I've jumped on this train and I have no idea when and where it's going to end and I'm scared I've promised too much and I don't have any hope of delivering it."

He maneuvers me across the room to the sofa and sits down next to me.

"So give up."

"What? Just like that? I'm supposed to call David and Annie and say, sorry, I've changed my mind, it's too much like hard work? You can't mess around with people's lives like that, Nat. You can't give them hope and then tear it away because you can't be arsed any more."

He smiled, amused by my angst. "So what are you moaning about, then?"

"I'm not moaning. I'm just saying it's hard."

"Of course it's hard. He would have done it himself if it was easy. But you knew that, so why moan now?"

"Jesus, Nat, I just want . . ."

"Me to feel sorry for you? Well I don't, because since you lost that job you've been banging on about missing the purpose it gave you. We both know you're made for this kind of stuff. It requires someone who is pigheaded and stubborn, which makes you perfect for it. Anyone else and I would say drop it, you must be out of your mind. But the thing is, Eve, you're not anyone, are you? If one person can do this, it's you. Come here and give me a hug."

I leaned in to him and cried some more. "Please don't snot on my shirt," he said. "It's new."

I pushed him away, fished a tissue out from my pocket and blew my nose.

"Attractive," he laughed.

"Don't," I said. "You'll start me off again."

"Now can we have dinner? Those olives are rank."

Honor lived on a narrow pedestrianized street in Bridport, a market town on the Dorset coast a few hours from London. I circled the town center looking for a space as close to her house as possible. After finding one and cobbling together the change for the meter, I walked back to her address. It was gone midday and the town was a busy hustle of markets and stalls, selling cheeses and breads and chutneys. What would I do if she wasn't in? I couldn't lurk in her street all day. And what would I say if she *was* in? I'd have less than a minute to convince her. I ran through my pitch in my head as I walked anxiously down to number 21, a green door. Taking a deep breath, I rang the bell. Waited. No answer. There was a café a little farther down the street on the opposite side. I'd sit there and wait.

I ordered lunch, a chicken salad, checked my e-mails on my phone for something to do, and when the window seat became free I moved places to get a better view of the street. Someone had left a copy of *Dorset Life* on the table. I read it cover to cover, peering at all the country properties and imagining myself playing on the tennis courts, taking a morning dip in the indoor heated swimming pools. By a quarter to five I was two coffees, a glass of water and a millionaire's shortbread down. My bladder was complaining. The waitress started to clear up around me, spraying and wiping down the tables. I looked out across the street to see a figure walk up to number 21 and let herself in.

"I'm Eve Elliot," I said, trying to make myself sound as friendly as possible. "I wanted . . ."

"I have nothing to say to you." Her smile was fixed, as if someone had drawn it on to her face. She was a few years older than me, brown hair cut in a crop.

"I haven't come here to ask you anything. I have information for you." It was a tactic to wrong-foot her, make myself seem like less of a threat. It had worked for me in the past.

She raised her eyebrows, snickered.

Nice try.

It wasn't going to work with Honor Flannigan.

"I am going to close the door now," she said.

"If you give me five minutes, I will show you why the wrong man was jailed for the attack. I will show you how David Alden couldn't have done it. I don't want to cause trouble, I am simply trying to get to the truth. Five minutes, that's all, and then I'll leave you alone."

"What makes you think I can help you with that?" she asks.

"I don't know that you can, but I was hoping that as her friend you might think it was worth trying."

Honor regarded me for a moment, trying to size up the damage it would do to give me five minutes of her time. I could see she wasn't convinced.

"Look, I've been drinking coffee all day waiting for you and I'm about to pee myself. Even if you don't want to talk to me, could you stretch to letting me use your loo?" I crossed my legs for emphasis.

She shook her head in annoyance before standing aside and allowing me to enter.

We sat in the kitchen. Her hospitality stretched to a glass of water, which I accepted. It's harder to kick someone out of your house when you've offered them refreshment.

As she handed me the glass, I asked if it was OK to put it on the table. It was an old oak number, gnarled and worn but homely. "It's seen worse than water," she said.

The house was bigger inside than its exterior suggested. The wall between the kitchen and dining room had been knocked down to create a large but cozy space. Crammed bookshelves, photographs in an assortment of frames. A cat jumped up onto my chair. "Just bat her away, she's a nosy creature, she wants to know what you're doing here."

I took that as a cue, reached down to my bag and pulled out a map, which I unfolded.

"All the points marked in highlighter are where David Alden was picked up on CCTV on the night Melody Pieterson was attacked. I've written the exact time he was recorded too." I laid it out on the table so she could see it.

"Is this supposed to tell me something?"

"It's almost impossible to do this route in the window of time he had. I have driven it myself, four times, and only once did I make it, with three minutes to spare. And that was without attacking someone and lifting their body out of a car to dump in a secluded spot. It just isn't feasible."

Honor stroked the cat, which had now settled on her lap.

"And this is what the police said proved his car was near Richmond Park late that night." I handed her an image grabbed from CCTV. She peered at it, held it at arm's length to bring it into focus. "What do you see? Can you tell me what car that is?" The glare of the headlights had burned everything else out of the picture.

"I can only see headlights," she said, "but surely the police have experts who deal with this kind of thing?"

"They do, but even experts can't reveal something within a picture that isn't there. This was the image shown to the jury. It could be any car."

I waited as she distilled the information. It proved nothing, of course, but it introduced the smallest seed of doubt into Honor's mind. Once I was satisfied it was there, I posed the question I had wanted to ask since my meeting with Sam.

"Are you still in touch with Melody?"

She shook her head. "Not for a while now." She glanced down to the table, focusing on her finger as it moved in a small figure of eight. "It's wasn't easy . . . afterward . . ."

"These things must take their toll. I've spoken to a few others . . . Patrick Carling says Melody hasn't worked for years. He says she's scared to leave the house alone."

Honor lifted her eyes from the table and locked them on to mine. "Really? Patrick said that?"

"Uh-huh."

"Oh . . ." she said, expelling breath. A sadness pulled at her face. "I knew it wasn't easy for her . . . more than anything I think she struggled accepting that it was David who did it. I know that sounds stupid but she couldn't remember the attack itself, very little before it. Being told that her friend had done it, that really knocked her, but the last I heard she had gone back to work."

"She's getting married, did you know?"

Honor shook her head, dipped her eyes away from mine. "That's all she needs," she said, her words barely audible.

"You two were together?"

"Six years. You're probably wondering why I was such a crap friend, deserting her when she needed me most."

"I imagine you had your reasons."

At this she feigned a laugh. "It was difficult."

"Sam said they got together months after the attack," I said, watching her closely to see if her reaction gave anything away.

"Of course he did," she said bitterly. "I did try. I visited her in hospital, at her parents' house. I planned a trip to London, just the two of us, like old times. But it was a disaster. We were pretending we could just go back, but there's a line and when it's crossed there's no going back, no matter how much you want to. It's complicated. There was all this guilt mixed up with it. I tried. She tried. Sometimes you have to accept that what was there has gone."

She stared at me for a second as if unpicking the significance of what she had told me. Sam had lied, Melody had lied, and so too had Honor. None of them had mentioned the affair in their statements.

She stood up to shake herself out of the reverie.

"I think your five minutes are up."

On the way out I noticed a framed photograph of two young women, tanned faces squashed together, grinning into the camera, the line of the sea and the horizon drawn behind them.

"Tarifa, 2004. We learned how to windsurf."

"You both look so happy."

"We were," she said. "We were."

Fourteen

Tarifa, 2004; the salt. She can taste it on her lips, feels it cracking on her hot sandy skin as they walk the path from the beach back to their apartment. Flip-flops click on the gravel, stones work their way between her toes. The wind, always wind, whipping up from the sea. Mel casts a look back. Foamy waves rise like meringue peaks from the ocean. Tomorrow, she thinks, they'll master it tomorrow. Tonight is about bathing her aching body, a beer, then food. "An early night." Honor winks knowingly. They said that last night, and the night before too. But a cold bottle of San Miguel from the fridge always works the tiredness away. Two bottles and they'll be heading into town, through the cobbled streets where the scent of jasmine hangs heavy, to their favorite tapas bar, loading up on *boquerones* and *berenjenas con miel*, clams and chorizo. Afterward they will saunter back to the beach, where they'll find others, surfers, smoking, drinking, strumming guitars as late night tumbles into early morning. Burrowing hot toes in cold, damp sand. Drinking more. No wonder they don't have the head for windsurfing when ten o'clock comes around.

They've been here three weeks and they still can't windsurf. It's become a joke. Neither of them has been able to stand on the board for more than a few minutes, but each time they fall in, they haul themselves back up again. Mel aches in places she didn't know she had muscles, sees the lines of her veins through her arms now. "It's not beating me," Honor declares, twisting the top off her second bottle of beer. "I refuse to go home until I can do it." If it was down to Mel, they would have given up after day one. But Honor won't let her quit. It's one of the things Mel loves about her. She never gives up. Never has. Her influence has made Mel stronger than she would be alone.

The holiday in Tarifa was nine years ago, yet the memories come hurtling back so clear and sharp they sting. She had Honor to herself; the wild, funny Honor of her childhood before coupledom planed her rough edges and turned her into someone else.

Mel has no right to own these memories now. It is a legacy she has destroyed. What she did afterward undercut everything, their friendship, their trust, their shared history. Yes, it hadn't been the same between them for a good while. Honor had seemed diminished somehow, quiet where before Mel struggled to get a word in edgeways. Was this Mel's way of punishing her friend for changing? Whatever, there were no excuses. She knew what she was doing even in the heat of it. She knew she was throwing it all away and still she didn't stop.

The photo in Honor's hallway, Mel has it too. Their last day in Tarifa. They cracked it, stayed on their boards, glided back and forth in the water for hours. Why had it been so difficult, they wondered, when it came so instinctively now? Honor has kept the photograph, must see it every day. In this Mel finds the smallest sliver of hope.

This is how it happened.

Another holiday. Ibiza this time. Honor and Sam, Patrick and Melody together in a villa near Portinatx at the northernmost tip of the island.

She couldn't sleep. Above her the fan rotated to no discernible effect. She rose from the bed, naked, pulling on a vest, knickers, as little clothing as possible, took her book from the bedside table and went outside.

The whistle of crickets, the hum of the refrigerator, the distant lapping of waves; it reminded her of the sound she heard when she put a shell to her ear as a child. She read a page of her book, shuffled on the chair. She was restless. Tonight the plan had been to skip booze, give their livers a rest. She sighed. *Sod it, I'm on holiday.* The indulgence appealed to her: reading and drinking, semi-naked, alone.

With her wine, she settled back down to read. One glass, followed by another.

"How many books is that? Your fourth?" The voice came at her through the darkness.

"Shit." She jumped. Red wine spilled down her vest. Across the terrace she could make out his shape.

"How long have you been there?"

"Long enough," he said, "to know that you're on to your second glass of wine."

"I'm on holiday. To hell with abstinence."

"Well since you put it like that . . ." he got up and disappeared into the kitchen, returning with a glass that he filled with wine before sitting down next to her.

"It's a stupid idea."

"That's not what I asked," Sam said.

"The answer is no."

"You disappoint me, Melody, where's your sense of fun, adventure?"

"I'm drunk."

"You've been drinking. There's a difference between that and being drunk. I'll go on my own, then." He hauled himself out of the chair, stretched his arms out wide, flexed his wrists so she could hear the little snapping sounds his bones made.

"You could drown and no one would know."

"Not if you were watching I couldn't."

The beach, all to themselves, sunbeds stacked, chained together.

Straw shades rustled as they caught the wind. Black shadows of waves shifted in the distance. Stars jeweled the sky.

Sam stripped off.

"I'm going in, what are you . . . waiting for?" The last two words faded out as he crashed into the foam.

When she looked, she could only see his head now. "It's lovely, come on. I dare you, what are you scared of?" he shouted. His voice distant and echoing.

What *was* she scared of?

She removed her vest, kept her knickers on, a semblance of propriety. She ran down toward the water's edge, arms crossed to cover her chest and hold her boobs in place. A semicircle of moon illuminated the sand, its light dancing off the water. She crept in, prepared for the cold to slap her skin. Instead she found it tepid, like a cooling bath. One . . . two . . . three, she counted. Then under.

Her arms pushed through the water, lightness filled her limbs. As she swam she was aware of the thermal changes; swimming through warm water only to be encircled by pockets of cold. Moving through the black sea under the dark sky pierced with stars, she felt herself become fluid, in tune with her environment. Down and down she swam, conscious of the tightening in her chest. When she could bear it no longer, she put her hands by her sides and allowed the water to propel her upward, bursting through the surface and gasping for breath. Then she turned over on to her back and gazed at the sky, allowing her body to be carried by the current. She'd never known a feeling like it before—the magical liberation of being reduced to her simplest instincts.

Afterward, on the beach, they huddled close, towels pulled around their shoulders. There was an effervescence about her, the energy of the sea still fizzing through her body.

With her finger she carved out an M in the sand.

"We should be getting back," she said, but her voice carried no conviction. She wasn't ready to abandon the night just yet, to go back to the villa and lie wide awake in bed catching the intermittent drafts of the fan.

She wanted to remain stripped back, with only her instincts, a while longer.

A fly landed on her cheek. Sam leaned in to swat it away. He stayed there, close to her face, a current sparking between them.

"Dare you," she swore he said, but his lips were already on hers.

Mel had been fucking her best friend's boyfriend behind her back. And Honor knew. It's all there, written down in words on the screen in front of her.

There's a line and when it's crossed there's no going back, no matter how much you want to.

Once they'd started, they couldn't stop. Or wouldn't stop? Not that it mattered now. The consequences were the same. And Honor had found out. How?

It made sense now, the awkwardness that characterized their meetings toward the end. Honor had put her own feelings to one side when Mel had been in hospital and even in the months after when she was recuperating. Doing what was expected of her. But friendships are predicated on trust. If you lose it, there is nowhere left to go. Maybe if Mel had had the decency to own up, say sorry, she could have changed the course of things. But Sam counseled against it.

"She doesn't know, why tell her now? What good would that do?"

"She's not stupid, I'm sure she knows," Mel told him, thinking of their aborted trip to London, the excruciating silences on the train journey.

"No she doesn't. You're just projecting your paranoia on to her."

It's all in your head.

Sam wanted to keep their story neat and tidy, with no messy overlaps.

In his head it went something like this: Honor told him she was leaving shortly after the attack. Sam and Mel got together six months afterward, which was an entirely respectable amount of time to have elapsed between two relationships.

He could say it as many times as he wanted, but Mel knew Honor didn't see it that way.

She snaps the laptop shut. She feels both vindicated and ashamed. The more she reads Eve's file, the more she realizes how delusional she has been, swaddled in layers of lies.

Her mobile is on the table next to her. There is still a number for Honor in there, obsolete now, she imagines. How many times has her finger hovered over that number, willing herself to call?

No, she thinks, calling her is not good enough. She imagines the distance between them on the line would be too great. It would allow for words to be misconstrued and distorted. What she wants is to see her, to stand next to her and hear the tone of her voice, to face up to her friend and what she did to her. To say sorry.

It is long overdue.

Sam's car is too precious to be squeezed in to a space in the hospital car park, at least Mel assumes this is why he always bikes to the station and takes the train to work. His keys will be hanging on a hook in the cupboard underneath the stairs. Everything in their house has a place. Even me, she thinks. Opening the cupboard door she switches on the light and sees them glinting at her, next to a row of other keys. Above every hook is a label. SHED, FRONT DOOR, WINDOWS, KITCHEN DOORS. Beneath them the shoe storage, each pair with its own cubbyhole. She thumbs the metal logo on the key ring. The circular blue and white roundel. It's his new car. Would he mind? She laughs. Who's she kidding? The last time she drove alone was three years ago, when she mounted the curb and hit a bollard as she was turning the corner. The impact left a little dimple in the side of the car. He didn't shout. It would have been better if he had. Instead she got the silent treatment, swore she could almost hear the anger whistling out of him, like a pressure cooker blowing off steam.

"If you want a little runaround, we can get one," he said eventually, but she wasn't to drive his car anymore. Still, he'd kept her on the insurance. There were always exceptions to the rule. Like when they were out and he wanted to drink, he was prepared to overlook her lack of spatial awareness then.

She pictures his face when he realizes it's missing. The thought makes her smile.

She unhooks the key, slips it in her pocket and runs upstairs to gather a few bits of clothing: a jumper, trousers, a toothbrush, clean underwear as a contingency. She will take her laptop too. The prospect of driving the distance alone daunts her, but it's not like she'll be surrounded by people. She'll be confined within £30,000 worth of German engineering. She locks the front door behind her, and holding the key fob out in front of her presses the button to open the garage. The door rises slowly to reveal Sam's car. Beetle black, shining.

After the first twenty miles or so, when she allowed her grip to relax on the steering wheel and brought her breathing under control, she began to relax into the drive. Now, two hours in, she'd go so far as to say that watching the world flicker by in her peripheral vision is giving her an absurd amount of pleasure. She's opted for the longer, scenic route that follows the curves of the coast. Cruising at sixty with her window down, she hears that strange juddering sound caused by the wind, feels its vibrations in her chest. It makes her giddy, along with the briny air that rolls in from the sea. She's forgotten how glorious the light is here, the way it constantly changes and shifts; the same scene painted in a different palette every time you look. Today it is warm and golden and the cliff faces are the color of honeycomb, like a Cadbury's Crunchie.

It gives her an idea.

She recognizes the turning and indicates right, driving down a narrow road. There's a small car park at the end. It's only half full, so she has her choice of spaces. Once she has parked, she gets out and without pause starts walking downhill. She focuses on her trainers kicking out in front of her. She's counting in her head, conscious of the undulating path, the uneven clumps of grass, the way the earth is soft and waterlogged in parts, the stretches where it is hard and solid underfoot. Occasionally she jumps to dodge a pile of dog shit but for the most part she keeps her stride steady, enjoying the way it shuttles her back to an earlier time. This is what they used to do. Her and Honor. The closest to a natural high you could get. On the count of four hundred, Mel knows she has reached the point closest to the cliff edge that juts out proud over the sea. Finally she allows herself to look.

The sensation slams into her. Simultaneously her feet scramble backward as her body sways forward. A surge of fear and exhilaration charges through her. She feels it in her limbs, her muscles. It ripples through her bloodstream.

She holds her arms open wide and lifts her head up. Clouds score the sky above, gold-edged where the sun shoots through them. A gust of wind could take her and propel her forward. That is the allure, skirting so close to the edge. She peers down the sheer drop of the cliff face before gazing out at the stretch of water, a blurred line where it hits the horizon. Down below the sand has been scooped out from the cliffs. She hears the distant bark of a dog, the pull and suck of the sea.

This.

Her body hasn't let her down; the visceral reaction to step back from danger is as raw and powerful as ever. She may have spent years ignoring her instincts but they have not deserted her. Nothing is lost. Casting a final glance down to the beach, she turns and walks back up the path to the car.

They sit on the sofa. It is soft gray wool. Next to Mel is a cushion in purple velvet; she watches the shade of it change from lighter to darker as she brushes her finger up and down the fabric. Honor always had good taste, seemed to amass pictures and odd bits of furniture and fabrics that Mel would think looked hideous only to see them *in situ* a month later and marvel at Honor's vision. Her

house is everything that Mel's isn't. There are layers of personality
to it, the trinkets from her travels, the photographs, the rugs. It has
color and life. It's grown and evolved over the years Honor has lived
here. Mel thinks of her own home, chosen from magazines and bro-
chures, delivered and installed. There's no love in that.

Being here is like settling into an old chair again. The comfort
and smell of it. For a moment Mel sinks back and lets it cushion
her. Then she turns and locks eyes with Honor and immediately
corrects her position. It's not for her to feel comfortable here anymore.

Words, she'd love to find the right ones. Sentences that would
mean something and have the power to rewind her life all the way
back to that night in Ibiza when she said to Sam, "We should be
getting back." Words that would allow her to get up from the beach
at that precise moment and walk back to the villa and lie in bed
under the fan. She wouldn't have kissed Sam. They wouldn't have
fucked each other. She didn't appreciate the fact that one reckless,
selfish decision could destroy so much.

Her sliding-doors moment.

She'd change it if she could.

She stares at the teapot. It's the same old china one Honor bought
in Alfie's Antique Market years ago. Butterfly Bloom; she even remembers the name of the collection. Mel listened in amusement
to the sales patter from the assistant, knowing full well Honor was
already sold. She was like a magpie, and Mel was familiar with the
sparkle in her eyes when she happened upon something special.

Honor has served Mel tea from this pot countless times before—
hungover Sunday mornings, late nights, afternoons sharing a slab
of cake —but not once have her hands trembled like they do now.

"You look well . . ." Mel says. These are not the words she had
in mind but they are spoken with conviction nevertheless. Honor
does look good, different to how Mel remembers her in London. She
was always at the gym, her face gaunt, losing too much weight, losing herself. "Come back," Mel wanted to shout. But she didn't. Why
not? Isn't that what friends are supposed to do? Stage an intervention?

Tell the truth when no one else is brave enough to confront it? Now her face is fuller and flushed with color, her hair cut in a crop that accentuates her perfectly chiseled cheekbones. She seems to have returned to the Honor Mel knew. It is she who has changed and shrunk since they last saw each other.

"I should have called . . . to warn you . . ." she says eventually. "It's just . . ."

"I wasn't doing anything special." Honor hands her a teacup and saucer. They match the pot. Mel imagines her scouring eBay and markets to source them. Everything about this house reminds her of how well she once knew her friend, and yet here they are unable to find more than a sentence of conversation.

She can't do it. She puts her cup down on the table. "This is really weird . . . You're making me tea and I expected you to shout at me. I wouldn't blame you if you hated me. It'd probably make me feel better if you screamed at me."

"I don't hate you," Honor says slowly. "So don't expect me to scream."

"I'm sorry . . . that came out wrong. What I meant was . . . well I just didn't expect to be sitting here drinking tea with you."

"That makes two of us. It's been a long time . . . why now?"

"I wanted to say sorry. I know it won't change anything, but I wanted you to know. I've wanted to say it for years I was just too scared."

"Of me?" Honor raises an eyebrow incredulously.

Mel shakes her head. "Of facing up to what I had done. Admitting that it was my fault I had lost you." She glances around at Honor's photographs. There are no obvious signs she has a partner, no evidence of a child in the house. "He said you didn't know, that I shouldn't tell you. Not that it excuses anything . . ."

"That sounds about right. I don't see why he would bother to tell you after all this time, though."

"It wasn't Sam who told me. It was Eve Elliot. Well, not directly, I mean. But that's how I found out you knew."

Honor's eyes slide over to Mel's. "I might have known she'd go nosying around you too," she says bitterly. "I suppose you know that she's trying to help David Alden clear his name. But I don't see how going over all this stuff . . ." she flings her hands out in front of her, "about who knew what and when can help. What does it matter?"

Mel is surprised that her old friend can see it so clinically after everything that's happened. She feels a sudden need to defend Eve. "It matters to me. It matters because I felt like I had to bury all the questions I had. It matters because she's dead and I'm not convinced a man would murder a woman who was trying to clear his name." She stops, aware of a shift in Honor's expression, as if the muscles in her face have collapsed. The thought deposits itself in her head.

"You didn't know, did you?"

Honor's eyes shine with horror.

"Oh Honor," Mel says, "I'm sorry."

Honor extracts the details from Mel: the connections between the two cases, where Eve's body was found, David Alden's arrest and release on bail.

She listens with mounting shock and in silence until she breaks. She screws her eyes tight shut and lets out a sob so raw and fierce it disturbs Mel. It's like something has physically broken inside her. Mel tries to console her, to no avail. She cannot coax her out of the hole she has tumbled into. It jars. It jars because Mel can't shake the sense that Honor is reacting to something more than Eve's death. She would have expected her to be shocked and saddened. Who wouldn't be? But what Mel is witnessing doesn't tally. Honor only met Eve once, briefly. There is more to it.

"Tell me," Mel says.

Honor gulps and stares at Mel. Eventually, after an age, the crying subsides.

"It's not you who should be sorry," she says, wiping her smudged face with the back of her hand.

———

Dominoes lined up around the room. It was Mel's dad's idea of a wet weekend's entertainment. He'd spend hours constructing the display and when he was finished he'd count her down: three, two, one. Mel would flick the first one and listen as they all fell down. Clickety-clack.

It's the sound that fills the room now.

"I knew," Honor says. "At least I thought I did. Something about his air, it was more pompous than usual, and the sex was better than it had been for years. Like he was imagining doing it with someone else."

Mel flinches. *A face and a body plucked from a magazine? A fellow surfer he's seen on the beach?* She knows that feeling.

"It was just a hunch but I asked him anyway. That was a mistake. He said I was mad: *how could you even think it?*" Mel can picture Sam's injured expression. "So I dropped it but I took note of the late nights, the new clothes, the whole cliché of it, and then I brought it up again. He called me a paranoid bitch." Honor laughs at the memory now. "Why did I let him talk to me like that? I always thought that happened to other women, weaker women. I'd never let it happen to me, so I thought. It was only then that I realized what had happened to me. He took up so much room in my head there was nothing left for me. Nothing I did was ever quite right. I had stopped going out as much, my confidence had gone. Maybe I *was* a paranoid bitch. I stopped sleeping, spent all my spare time in the gym, running on the machine, the belt turning, never taking me anywhere.

"But even people like Sam make mistakes eventually. He was out playing football one evening when I heard a message buzz. It wasn't my phone so it had to be his. I found it in his jacket, this cheap little handset with a text that read, *"Where are you? I'm still wearing clothes, I thought you would have them off me by now."*

Mel's eyes widen. Heat pricks her face. Her head is firing out messages and images and words that overtake everything else. She can see her fingers composing sleazy texts on a white phone, a phone given to her by Sam after one of their illicit hotel meetings. He'd handed it to her with a smile; *just to be on the safe side.* Mel was right. Each of them had two phones to avoid being caught out. Only Sam had denied it when she had questioned him in the hospital. What was it he had said? *"It's understandable things are a bit mixed up."*

Mel's eyes are closed but Honor continues her story at pace. "It all fell into place. He must have bought another phone especially. A private line between him and his lover. He was good like that, well organized."

Honor tells Mel that the idea came to her the following night, sitting opposite Sam in a restaurant, watching him chew on a steak. A bit of fiber caught between his teeth, suspended, flapping when it caught his breath as he spoke.

"I couldn't take my eyes off it. It made me feel sick and thankful at the same time. I knew I didn't want to be with him. He'd made me feel special once. When had that stopped? When had the compliments become veiled criticisms? 'Are you having another slice of cake?' 'Haven't you drunk enough wine?' 'Is that what you're wearing?' "

She said she had conceded every time until concessions were no longer necessary. Her instincts were attuned to give him what he wanted.

"I had to leave him. But first I wanted to know who his next victim was."

It was Friday evening. If she was going to catch Sam out she needed to give him some space. "I decided to come to the pub to meet you and Patrick but before I left I found his phone in his briefcase and I sent a text. *Can you meet me? 11pm at the junction of Emlyn Road and Uxbridge Road? I'll pick you up.* I can remember the exact words, they're drilled in my mind. My plan was to drive to the pub then leave around ten thirty and drive back to Emlyn Road to see who it was Sam was seeing, if they turned up that is. I knew it was a long shot."

A thought explodes in Mel's mind. *It can't be, can it?* She goes to stand up but the floor lurches beneath her. She detects Honor's hand on her arm, its tight grip. "It was you." The words burn as she utters them. She can't look at her, doesn't dare. What will she see if she does? The walls of the living room are closing in on her. She needs to get out of this house. She has to. Run. But she is immobilized. All these years she wanted to find the reason why she was wandering the streets alone at night. And now she finally has it she wants to strip it from her mind again. "You." She says again. "I . . . I need to leave."

"Look at me Mel. Look. At. Me." Honor reaches over and with her hand tilts Mel's face upward. She flinches at her touch.

"No, don't do that. Tell me that's not what you're thinking. You can't. Not even for a moment. I would never hurt you. Never. You must know that."

Mel can't speak. She doesn't know anything anymore. Deceit has corroded everything. She has no way of telling the truth from the lies.

"You have to hear me out. Just let me finish." It sounds like an order. Mel sits upright, nails digging into the skin on her thighs.

"Go on," she says.

"I left the pub about twenty minutes after you. I drove down to Emlyn Road. I remember regretting it even then. What was I doing? What had I been reduced to? Lurking around late at night trying to catch Sam out. Why should I care anyway, I was leaving him, he would be free to do what he pleased.

"Then I turned the corner and saw you" Honor says, her voice dipped to a whisper. "You were swaying, blowing in the wind. The funny thing is, I was about to pull down my window and ask what you were doing there. I almost beeped my horn and offered you a lift." She gives a crazy person's laugh, which chills Mel. "That's how stupid I was. And then suddenly it smashed into me. It was you."

I hated you. I'm not going to deny it. You of all people . . . how could you do that to me? You'd have thought I would have wanted to slap you and scratch your eyes out, but when I saw you there, late at night, waiting for him, I just pitied you. I knew what you were letting yourself in for. I turned around and drove away.

"I got back and I told Sam you were waiting for him. I showed him the text and told him I was leaving him. He called me a bitch then he went out to find you. I threw some things into a bag and drove through the night to Dorset."

Bars of sunlight fall through the window on to her face. She keeps her eyes open and stares directly into the light in the hope that it will burn away the images that parade in her mind. Honor, in the right place at the right time, with motive. Lying to the police to cover her tracks.

"When Sam called to tell me you had been found unconscious, I . . . I can't explain what went through my mind. One stupid text . . . if I hadn't sent it, you wouldn't have been out there that night. I couldn't think straight. How the fuck was I going to live with myself?

"They would have thought it was me, wouldn't they? I was the only one who saw you there. I had just found out you were having an affair with my fiancé." Honor stops and stares intently at Mel. "Or they would have thought it was Sam. I wasn't his greatest fan but I knew him. He wasn't capable of that. So we agreed that we'd say we were together all night."

Honor gave Sam an alibi and in return he provided one for her.

The room swims. Nothing is fixed down anymore. The collectibles, the knickknacks, the essence of Honor are all spinning around Mel's head. The air in the room is thick and fat. It bears down on her chest. She needs space, oxygen. There isn't any to breathe in here.

"I have to go," she says again. This time her limbs work for her.

"Stay, please," she hears Honor say. She has jumped up, pulling on Mel's arm to stop her leaving but she pushes her away and stumbles into the hallway. Her hand reaches for the door handle, pulls on it hard and she runs out on to the pavement.

The wind is up. Mel drunk and woozy lifts her face to catch the gusts in the hope they will bring her round. Honor's words ring in her head. *I would never hurt you.* Just words without any meaning tacked to them. Didn't she say in the same breath that when she saw Mel standing waiting for Sam she hated her, wanted to scratch her eyes out? Mel can understand that kind of razor sharp betrayal that buries itself under your skin. She knows the extremes to which it could push you. She knows because she had to run out of Honor's house not just for her own safety but Honor's too. Rage has possessed her. Given the chance she could have happily torn Honor apart. And Sam? Did he really go out to look for her on the night of her attack? Did he find her? What then? It's pointless asking him for the truth, she's done that already, extracted a promise of honesty, even fucked with the lights on afterward as a sign of renewed trust and now she finds out he was lying all along. There are hundreds of different ways she would like to hurt him. She'd start slowly, sink her nails in to his face and gouge out his skin. She'd ratchet up the pain with each act of violence and she'd savor it. That's what betrayal can do to you.

Wading through the streets she locates the black BMW. For now she contents herself with running a key along the perfect paintwork of his car to carve out a sizeable zig zig of silver on each side. She stands back to survey her work. It's nothing really, not compared with what he's put her though.

Soon Mel is following the road out of Bridport along the familiar route to her parents' house. The clouds have closed in. A spot of rain snaps on to the windscreen, followed by another. She casts a look up to the bruised sky covered by a dark sheet of cloud. Could Honor have attacked her? Or Sam? They were both there at the time she went missing. Was it Sam and his twisted mind that orchestrated the campaign against her, the shadows in the garden, the repeated phone calls that went dead when she answered? The knock on the door? Who else would have known she was home alone? That is the ultimate power, worse than murder. If she had died in the attack she would have died once, but she has been dying every day since then, a slow, painful disintegration of her mind.

She can trace the lies all the way back to one instance in her hospital room a few days after she emerged from the coma. Taking a sip of water to wet her mouth before speaking, she came out with it. "It was you I was supposed to be meeting, wasn't it?"

He laughed, gazed at her like a child who had said something faintly amusing. "Honey," he said, "I was with Honor all night."

A single lie to protect themselves. But lies breed lies, complications consequences

Mel stares at the road ahead. It's pouring now, rain dancing off the windscreen. It reminds her of something else, she thinks, stilling her thoughts to allow her mind to reel back in time.

It's the sound that comes first, the lashing of the rain against her coat. Wet feet. Pools of water amassed at the side of the road, cars whooshing past. She feels spray against her face and her coat, looks down and sees filthy puddle water pouring off her. Her hands ache, the plastic handles of the shopping bags dig into her palms. A calculation: four more streets, then home; and a thought, too: she's not going to netball tonight. She's not going out in this again. Then, a horn beeping. She ignores it; there are always horns sounding on Uxbridge Road. But when it beeps again, she looks and sees the green Porsche pulling over. "Nice day for it," he shouts, opening the passenger door. She jumps in. "I was about to get washed away. I think you have just saved my life."

She moves a garment from the seat and sits with it in her lap and she runs her hands through her hair. They drive back home, say good-bye, go their separate ways.

Netball, she thinks. Wednesday-night netball.

The last time she saw David Alden. Two days before the attack.

It was his jacket she had in her lap.

A perfectly good reason why strands of her hair and fibers from her yellow coat were found on it.

She drives on through the gloom. She feels the car buffeted by wind as she travels along the coast road. It reminds her of family walks along the beach in winter, the ones her mother forced upon them to blow the cobwebs away: squally showers, black waves breaking on the shore, sand kicking up in her face. Instinctively she blinks to clear her vision.

Fifteen

A grain of sand magnified two hundred and fifty times is a thing of surprising beauty. Under the microscope it can easily be mistaken for a gem, a semiprecious stone translucent in color with unique patterns and markings.

It can also tell you a story if you look close enough.

Dr. John Beer knew how to look for stories from grains of soil. He took the samples we'd obtained of Melody Pieterson's clothing and analyzed them. He was an academic at Oxford University who specialized in forensic sedimentology—the use of geologic materials as evidence in criminal cases to you and me. We'd used him once or twice on *APPEAL* because he was exactly the person you wanted on your side. His evidence had been featured in a series of high-profile murder cases and he always cut to the chase. Conveniently he'd also offered to run the tests free of charge, being less than impressed to hear that the samples had not been tested in the first instance. On the few occasions I'd met him, I got the distinct impression he'd still be looking at soil and sand under a microscope even if he wasn't paid to do it.

His results arrived on the first Friday of September, sandwiched in between an e-mail from Groupon for laser hair removal and one from Kira with her weekly travel missive.

From: Drjohnbeer@ox.cu.uk
To: eelliot83@gmail.com

Eve,

The samples tested show the presence of two quite distinctive soil types. One can be excluded as having derived from the Ham Common area as a result of their different overall grain size, acidity (pH), quartz grain surface analysis of individual sand grains, chemical composition, distinctive mineralogy and micro fossil assemblages.

There is the presence of a mixture of light-colored sand/ silt soil of alkali pH (8.5). The soils contained much quartz sand material of characteristic beach and river provenance. Interestingly the sand also contained modern-day micro- sized (50–150 micron) foraminifera characteristic of English Channel beach environments. Pollen from winter brassicas and summer cereal grains are evidently grown nearby to the sample site. An important provenance indicator in the soil is grains of pyrite (fool's gold) and more specifically marcasite, known as white iron pyrite. Both minerals, but particularly marcasite, are renowned in and about areas of coastal Sussex.

The second soil type is consistent with that found in Ham Common Wood. It contains fine-grained sand, silt and predominantly clay of high organic content. The quartz grains in these samples are classic River Thames terrace materials with distinctive grain smoothing typical of the proto-Thames sediments. Pollen taken from the soil showed many grasses, thistle, poplar and horse chestnut tree. Soil acidity was neutral and chemical assay of the soil showed high levels of phosphate and nitrate (commercial fertilizer).

If you need clarification, do give me a call.

John

I called him.

I was no scientist but I could understand the gist of what he was telling me. I just needed to hear it in plain English before I could allow it to sink in.

"Does it mean what I think it means?" I asked.

"The samples would indicate that she was taken to a near coast environment. I'd say the south coast of England. Sussex if I was to be more exact." My head was erupting in song. I paced up and down the room and then I heard the real music in his next sentence. "There are no areas like it close to London."

"Not within half an hour's drive?"

"Not within an hour's drive."

"I love you." Because at that time there was no one in the world I loved more than Dr. John Beer.

"It'll pass," he said. "There's more, too, but I wanted to get you those results as soon as I could."

"Now you *are* spoiling me."

"There's the presence of a pollen too. Ever heard of *Hibiscus syriacus*?"

"Nope."

"Look it up. It's a common plant, bright pink in color. It's found in many residential gardens. I bet you won't find it in Ham Common Woods. I'll send you something over when I get back from holiday. I'm just tying up a few things before I go."

"Anywhere nice?"

"India, for three weeks."

"I'm jealous. Let's speak when you get back . . . and John, I owe you one. You have made me a very happy woman."

"If only my wife found soil so interesting."

I could have told her: a grain of sand is a thing of beauty indeed.

It was a search for the *Hibiscus syriacus* that brought me to Ham Common Woods first thing that Saturday morning. Even though

Dr. Beer had said I wouldn't find it there, I figured there was no harm in checking before I broke the news to David Alden.

In contrast with the wide sweep of Richmond Park, the common was a strip of densely packed woodland. It was like stepping from day into night, dark and dank, thanks to the thick canopy of trees that blocked the sunlight. I walked the length of it and back noting the palette of colors, the range of greens from olive to sage, the brown of the earth. Not so much as a flash of pink.

I hurried out, glad to see sunlight again and the blue sky that promised another scorcher. The place gave me the heebie-jeebies. I imagined Melody lying half dead among the bushes waiting to be found. On reflection, it could have been foresight. A week later, my own body was found in the same place by a red setter and a man called Jim.

Sixteen

The samples from Eve's clothing and Melody's are almost identical. Both of them, Victoria has been informed, contained traces of pollen derived from the same plant, and the samples of soil indicate they were taken to an identical coastal location before they were eventually dumped. David Alden wasn't the man who attacked Melody and left her in the woods.

It was someone else who took her, and Eve, to the coast. Forensics haven't pinpointed the exact location yet.

She reads their analysis again: *a south coast environment, on chalk, near fields, flattish land, definitely not urban.* It's like playing a game of Guess Who? with locations rather than people. They've warned her it could take time to match the sample with a physical place. But they're confident they will get there. Eventually. Why does everyone assume they have time when Victoria has the unsettling feeling in her bones that it's running out?

Perhaps it is because this was as far as Eve got. Her investigation ended with the results of the soil samples. The e-mail she received from Dr. John Beer is the last entry in her file. It came the day before she was killed. Victoria imagines the elation she must have felt, the sense of vindication. She met David Alden to tell him the good news, celebrated in the pub and then vanished. No sighting of her afterward, no image detectable on any of the CCTV in the area. *Where did you go, Eve?* Victoria has to work it out before . . . what? She can't say, but she feels the sense of urgency roll off the screen in front of her.

The scale of what she is dealing with is now piercingly clear. David Alden spent five and a half years in prison because the samples from Melody Pieterson's hair and clothes were stored and locked away, never analyzed. Because the prosecution, with the help of a CCTV image Victoria herself had found, argued that he was in the Ham area on the night Melody disappeared. Because no one had bothered to do a simple calculation to show he didn't have time to drive all that way and back to Hammersmith. A series of oversights and blunders and a man's life is ruined. A young woman murdered. Victoria can't change the past, but she needs to atone, work out what really happened. But still the truth is dangling just out of her reach.

She shakes her head. A pain throbs between her temples. It's gone nine at night and she's sitting at her desk in the station. Pulling out a bottle of wine, she opens it and pours herself a glass. The kids will be asleep now. She spoke to them half an hour ago, asked them about their day: "How was school?" "Fine." It's always the same answer. She once read that you had to be more specific with your questions to your children, and she tried it for a while. "Good game of cricket?" Or "What did you do in maths?" "We did maths in maths, what do you think we did?" Oliver answered. She reverted to her old style of questioning after that.

She takes a swig of wine. One glass, two at the max, that's all she'll have to loosen her head so she can think. Overindulgence is not her thing. DCI Stirling on the other hand is a high-functioning alcoholic. She's known as much for some time. Although the more she looks into the case of Melody Pieterson, the more inclined she is to drop the high-functioning.

Victoria stares at her screen and compares the results from her own forensics with the analysis from Dr. Beer once again. They're almost identical, except Dr. Beer has gone one step further in narrowing down the geography: *Both minerals, but particularly marcasite, are renowned in and about areas of coastal Sussex.*

She takes another sip of wine and closes her eyes. Sussex. Sand and shells. She can recall the crunch they made underfoot, the exact red jelly shoes she wore, bought especially for the holiday. They gave her blisters for the first two days but she refused to swap them for her trainers. It was warm, gently so, at least that's how she remembers it. Blue skies and sunny, enough to leave her cheeks and shoulders red and hot around the straps of her sun top at the end of the day. These were the days before suncream and UV suits, when people still fried themselves in cooking oil to get a tan. At lunchtime they'd huddle behind a stripy nylon windbreak to eat their sandwiches, but still the sand found its way in. Like eating eggshells. "Take your time," her mother would say as she watched Victoria inhale her food. "If you don't chew properly you'll be farting all afternoon," that piece of advice from her dad. But she was ten and she didn't have time to eat, not when there was a sea to swim in, and giant icy waves to leap over, when there were towers to build out of sand and decorate with shells and shingle.

Her mum and dad took it slowly. They were laid-back, chilled types. Never hassled or rushed. There was never anything to worry about, always plenty of time.

Until there was none left.

The holiday in Climping was their last together. Her parents died in a car crash six months later. Victoria has been in a hurry ever since.

She knows what losing a parent when you're ten years old can do to you. You want to make sense of it, extract some meaning from it. All her fury and anger, her unfathomable sadness has driven her to this job, but she knows full well it could have taken her in a different direction altogether.

It's why she wants to know who the ten-year-old Charlie Crighton has become.

It might be a long shot, but she has already ordered samples to be taken of soil around the village of Climping to see if they match those found on Eve and Melody.

Near fields, flattish land, definitely not urban. It fits the description at least.

Seventeen

Friday September 7th 2013
Phone call with Dr. John Beer
According to Dr. Beer the soil samples strongly suggest Melody
was taken to another location before she was left for dead in
Ham Common Woods.

  Dr. Beer states this location was more than an hour's drive
from London in a coastal zone, most likely Sussex due to the
properties of the soil he found on the sample of her clothing.

Mel sits in her childhood bedroom, the laptop balanced on her knees. She said goodnight to her parents an hour ago feigning tiredness although it's not tiredness that's afflicting her, more a form of delirium that won't permit sleep. The day keeps coming at her. First Honor revealing herself, now this. In the last sixty minutes she's raced through chunks of Eve's file, gulped down information and here she is reading Eve's last entry, written the weekend she died. David Alden didn't attack Mel. It's not just a hunch anymore. It is supported by scientific evidence. She was taken to the coast and David didn't have time to drive all that way and back in an hour. The information shames and terrifies her in equal measure.

  It also opens up a new realm of horror. Mel pictures her body limp in someone's possession, dirty eyes feasting on her, lingering, hands touching her; she can see the smile on her captor's face though not the face itself, imagines a warm fuzz of satisfaction spreading through their veins.

Just thinking about it makes her skin feel raw and exposed as if she is being unpeeled. But she will not allow herself to indulge in self-pity. Not this time. Not now that she knows the price David has paid. Five and a half years in prison and now a life tainted by a criminal record. She has to put it right. She will go to the police tomorrow. What will she tell them? That Honor and Sam lied, that neither had an alibi, that she suspects her childhood friend could have attacked her? Or worse, her fiancé?

She draws the duvet tight around her shoulders and buries her head in it. The softness, the scent of it comforts her. It smells of home. Peaches and Jasmine washing powder, distinctive and reassuring. She is sitting on the old sofa bed with shot springs that dig into her bum and squeak every time she moves. Her eyes cast around the room. It's hard to reconcile the neat order with the chaos that once reigned here. Her parents use it as an office and a spare bedroom now. The walls are bare apart from two shelves stacked with box files marked LIFE INSURANCE and ISAs and ANNUITIES and CAR!—though what the car file has done to merit an exclamation mark is not clear. A National Trust calendar hangs to the side of her old desk where a large laptop sits. The room, she notes, is painted the same pale green shade as the living room and the downstairs loo. Knowing her mother Mel suspects the color was on special offer. Once there would have been piles of clothes on the floor; Blur and Oasis posters tacked to the wall, much to her mother's annoyance: *Look at the greasy marks the Blu-Tack leaves.* She remembers the arguments they'd have: *You're not going out until you tidy that room,* and Mel would kick the clothes under her bed. There was too much fun to be had to spend precious time tidying up.

Across the hallway in the bathroom she hears her dad brushing his teeth, the distinctive circular motion he favors that sounds like he's scouring pans. She prays he doesn't knock on her door, poke his head around it to say *good night love* and blow her a kiss like he used to. She doesn't want to explain why she is crying.

The very moment she walked through the door of her parent's home she felt herself being transported back to her past, struck by the discombobulating sensation of being somewhere so familiar and yet seeing it for the first time in years. Three years to be exact. Sam hated the journey and she was too scared to travel alone, so her parents have always visited them in Surrey instead. Mel gazed at the family photographs in the hallway of her and her brother as toddlers, on holiday in France when it pissed down the whole time, with their wonky fringes that her mother swore blind were straight; the jars in the kitchen that announce their contents, TEA and COFFEE and PASTA. It's all part of who she is and it is exactly what she has tried to avoid for years. Seeing it again however she found she wanted to mine every detail of it and store it deep in her consciousness. It was like walking into an old sweet shop that sells cough candy and aniseed twists and cola bottles by the quarter. She wanted to savor it all. Unusually she drank a few glasses of wine over dinner, hoping it might defuse the tension in her body, remove Honor from her thoughts for a moment. It had the adverse affect of course, but she realized that too late and resigned herself to finishing the bottle with her dad. After leaving Honor's she had stopped off on the way to buy him a decent red, an apology of sorts.

Her dad was always easy to win over.

"I knew there was something I missed about you," he had joked after releasing her from a hug and taking the wine from her hand.

"Is she still buying the paint stripper then?" Mel asked, nodding in the direction of her mother, trying to keep her voice light.

"What do you think?" He smiled, then turning to Tess he held the bottle aloft. "Look, someone thinks I'm worth it."

"That's because she doesn't live with you," her mother replied.

After they finished dinner. Mel and her dad were instructed by Tess to move to the living room. Mel chose the armchair and tucked her feet under. Her dad topped up her glass and handed it to her. "I wish I could drink this every night," he said, admiring the label, then, "We thought you had gotten too used to the high life to come here anymore."

"Is that really what you thought?" From the kitchen she could hear her mother loading the dishwasher, the crackle of the kettle as it started to heat. She rubbed her temples, the first waves of a headache were hitting her.

"Not me, no, but your mother . . . well you know what she's like."

She sighed wearily, leaned forward and placed her glass on a coaster printed with the image of a black cat.

"I thought she hated cats?"

"They were free . . . obviously."

"Look, I'm sorry . . . I know I've been rubbish. It's been difficult . . . I . . ." The pitch of her voice rose. *Don't cry. Don't cry.* She stopped, didn't trust herself to continue. Her dad's eyes burned into her.

"I'd be going mad stuck in that big house on the edge of nowhere," he said.

"It's six miles from Guildford . . ."

"Same difference." He chuckled and shook his head. "How's Sam?" he asked, his tone instantly more serious.

"He's at work."

"Tea, anyone?" Her mum's voice came from the kitchen.

"We'll stick to wine, thanks." He gave Mel a conspiratorial wink. He cleared his throat. "Listen love, what you don't want is to get to my age and be full of regret for all the opportunities you missed."

She went to say something but found the words tangled in her throat. Her mother dished out advice like tea and Mel had learned to tune out long ago. But her dad was economical with his emotions, when he showed them they came at her with force.

"Are you?" she said.

He shook his head. "God, no." They listened as her mother's footsteps trundled through the hallway toward them. "Hard as that might be to believe."

Tess placed a tray of biscuits on the coffee table. "I've no pudding I'm afraid. I didn't know you were coming. You're lucky I've salvaged a few bourbons, your father can eat a packet in one sitting, isn't that right?" Mel watched her dad to see if he would rise to the bait, surprised when he didn't. Old age must be mellowing them, she thought.

"Are you still running?" He said.

"Why do you ask?"

"Do you know what I used to love about watching you in those races?" Her dad always loved reminiscing about her athletic triumphs.

"Go on."

"The worse the conditions, the better you ran. When it was torrential rain and you were knee deep in mud, that's when you came into your own. You always started at the back and one by one you'd overtake everyone. No one could write you off." She stared at him, the way his eyes burned in to hers. "You were a fighter Melody. Don't you ever forget it."

Tears and tiredness sting her eyes but there is one more paragraph left in Eve's file and she has no intention of stopping until she's done. The wine has made her head light, sapped her concentration. Her pulse is up, her breath shallow. She's realizes she's doesn't want to let Eve go. As long as she's reading her words she is still alive in Mel's head. When it ends she will lose her.

Mel reads a Latin name on the screen, one she has never come across before, stutters as she tries to pronounce it.

Hybiscus Syriacus.

Its pollen found on the shirt she was wearing on the night of the attack.

Hybiscus Syriacus is a hardy deciduous shrub with large trumpet-shaped rich violet flowers. It flowers in late summer and autumn. The species has been naturalized well in suburban areas and may be seen as invasive so frequently does it seed around.

When Mel searches for pictures of the flower her screen fills with images of purple and pink blooms, each with a single stamen protruding from the open flower. She's no gardener, but she's seen them before. Perhaps there is an innocent explanation why her shirt was covered in their pollen. Did she brush against one that day? Surely not on the way to work, Uxbridge Road is not known for its foliage. Not even in the Horse and Hounds, with its patioed beer garden. So where?

These are not questions Eve can answer for her. She has found everything there is to discover in the file. There is only one line remaining.

*Arranged meeting with David Alden and Annie tomorrow Sat September 8 to explain the development. Finally, a breakthrough!

Mel snaps the laptop shut. She curls up into a ball. Grief and rage stab her. She can see Eve, all too real in her mind. She can picture the smile on her face as she typed her last words. Beautiful, jubilant, vindicated Eve on the cusp of death.

It's late by the time she calls the only person she wants to speak to.

"Hiya, Mel," he says in his familiar Geordie accent.

"Can we meet, tomorrow? I have a lot to tell you."

"Since you put it like that, yes. I start work at eleven, though, and it would have to be in London. Southbank is good for me."

"I can do that."

"Nine?"

"Perfect."

After she's hung up, she types a text.

I had to go away. I have your car. Don't worry, it's safe.

Mel sets the alarm on her phone. She has an early rise in the morning in order to get to London for nine. The next thought catches her unaware, as if her subconscious has already settled on a course of action she has yet to register. Tomorrow, before she goes to the police station she will go back home to pack her things. Sam will be at work. With any luck she'll never have to see him again.

The morning is bright with promise. Not a single cloud stains the sky. Only a vapor trail from a plane breaks up the blue but even that fades quickly, like breath on a mirror. Mel is early, remarkably so given the long drive and then the train journey from Guildford to Waterloo. She stands on Queen's walk, outside the Royal Festival Hall, and looks out at the city, the spires and towers that shine and glimmer in the sun, the river buses ferrying commuters and tourists up and down the Thames. She feels drunk, a once familiar energy snapping through her. It could be lack of sleep but she prefers to think it's the buzz of the city feeding into her the way it used to.

"Melody." She hears Nat's voice call out to her, turns to find him waving. He's wearing turned-up jeans and desert boots, Ray-Ban Wayfarers over his eyes, a leather satchel slung across his body.

He links his arm into hers. "Come on, let's get breakfast. I could eat a scabby horse," he says and they head toward the Royal Festival Hall.

"Jeez," he says when Mel has finished telling him about Sam and Honor and their lies. "When you said you had news, I didn't expect *that* kind of news." They're in Canteen, in a window seat, waiting for their breakfast to arrive. Nat tilts his face up to the ceiling and strokes what looks like the beginnings of a beard. "So what happens now?"

"I'm going home to pack after I leave you. I can't stay with him. And then I'm going to contact the police. Beyond that, I haven't got a clue."

"You think they could have . . . ?"

"I don't know what to think anymore but I don't trust either of them. How can I when they've been lying to me and the police all along?"

"Does Sam know you went to see Honor?"

Mel shakes her head. "Not unless Honor contacted him after I'd left, but that's unlikely. He'll be more worried about his precious car."

"His car?

"I took it yesterday without his permission."

"You twocked his car? Nice work." Mel screws her eyes up in confusion. "Taking without owner's consent," Nat says, "or twocking as it was known where I grew up. There was a lot of it about. Where is it now?"

"At Guildford station without a ticket. With any luck it'll be clamped by the time he finds it. It was the least I could do."

His eyes assess her, the beginning of a smile appearing on his face.

"What?" she says. "You look like you need to pass wind."

"Just you, I underestimated you. I was worried I'd done the wrong thing giving you Eve's file. When we first met I thought . . . well I thought you were a bit feeble. I worried reading it would be the end of you. But you seem different . . . sparkier. If anything, it's woken you up."

"You're kidding, it's ruined my life," she says, mocking him before her face softens. "It's just made me realize I didn't want that life anyway. It wasn't really mine. I feel a huge sense of relief. Is that weird?"

He shakes his head. "I don't think so. Where *is* your life then?" he asks.

"Somewhere out there," she says, pointing out of the window. "Not stuck in an echoey house all day buying tat on the shopping channel. I keep thinking of Eve . . . about how none of us know how long we've got left. What would she have done if she'd had a second chance at life? I've wasted mine so far. I don't want to waste it anymore."

The waitress arrives and places two English breakfasts in front of them. "Thank God for that," Nat say. "I'm welling up."

Eighteen

H e was crying. Fat tears he made no attempt to hide. "I don't
know what to say, Eve . . ."

The three of us were together in his garden, Annie and I
tucked under the shade of the apple tree, ducking when we heard
the rustle of an apple falling to the ground. Soft, overripe fruit oozed
on to the patio attracting a haze of fruit flies. Summer hadn't been
this loyal in years. It was September now and still its heat clung.
We were getting cocky, imagining it would never end.

The table was laid with fresh bread, ham, cheese, a bowl of salad,
lettuce rescued from his vegetable patch, to make us feel virtuous.
None of us was eating. None of us wanted to do anything other than
bask in the moment, terrified that if we let it pass it would cease
to be real.

I pulled at the fabric of my T-shirt to let the air circulate. I'd
run to David's from my flat, partly out of a desire to keep up my
training, partly because I couldn't wait to tell him the news. Parking was a nightmare on his street.

"You don't have to say anything. It's a start, it doesn't mean . . ."
but I stopped. Why detract from the achievement? Allow him this
without caveats and warnings, I thought.

"I know it's not the end, Eve . . . but I've not even come close to
seeing the end before. This . . ." he waved the e-mail I had printed
out, "you are sure about all this?"

I smiled. "Don't worry, I thought I'd get my facts straight before I told you. I spoke to Dr. Beer to check. It's all there. The nearest beach is over an hour away. There is no way you could have got there and back. And you have an alibi for the rest of the weekend."

"You are a fucking marvel, Eve. I honestly don't know how to thank you."

Annie, who had been unusually quiet, grabbed me and hugged me. "And there was me thinking it was all too much for you . . ." she joked.

"Glad I inspired so much confidence," I said.

David's head fell into his hands. Annie knelt down beside him, her long brown hair forming a cloak of privacy. His shoulders shook gently.

I had spent months pulling apart individual statements, pieces of evidence, analyzing them in microscopic detail to the point where I thought my head would explode. Out of necessity I had become obsessed with the tiny minutiae of the case and forgotten the narrative that arced around it.

Six years of suspicion is a heavy load to carry. I sat in the heat of the day watching it lift from his shoulders.

"I do all this and no one has even offered me a beer yet?" I said.

David got up, dipped into the kitchen and fetched them from the fridge, handing one to each of us.

"To the future," Annie said, chinking her bottle against David's then mine.

"To Eve," David said. "Where would we be without you?"

After I died, I honestly thought he'd have been better off if he'd never set eyes on me. When the police were gunning for him I wished we hadn't met. I cursed the spilled strawberry daiquiri and Kira for dragging me out that night. I blamed the boiler, my laziness for not having it serviced. But slowly, to my considerable delight, I realized I was wrong. DI Rutter was a pedant like me. She liked to be thorough. She wanted to understand the case where her predecessor had just wanted it off his hands. She'd come round to my way of thinking; she wanted to find my killer and she knew it wasn't David. For the first time I felt the tide turning.

Now when I conjured David and Annie from my memories of that late summer day, the precise moment in his garden when I told them about the evidence, it was no longer infested with regret. The nauseating sense of *what if...* had passed. All I saw were their megawatt smiles beaming out relief and elation.

Then there was Melody, defying all my expectations. When I first saw her cleaning and cooking and behaving all *Stepford Wives*, I thought there wasn't a chance in hell she'd delve into her past and unpick the scabs to get to the truth. Turns out I was wrong on that one too. That manic, crazy woman who seemed so brittle I thought she might break wasn't Melody at all. That was only a front. She was strong, ironclad. Once she remembered who she was, deep down at her core, the truth didn't scare her. She was charging head first toward it, gaining speed all the time, and I couldn't shake the feeling that she was edging closer to me. That was when the revelation hit, vivid, intense, terrifying. I knew exactly why I had been left behind.

Nineteen

Mel tells herself that Eve is standing next to her. She'd rather not be alone in the house, so she deduces that Eve's imaginary presence might help to still her nerves. She is in their bedroom. His bedroom now. It won't be hers anymore. Gathering up clothes and shoving them into the suitcase. It's not her normal packing style; she has dispensed with her folding and rolling crease-prevention technique. There is no room in her head to accommodate the micro-details that usually preoccupy her. For once they have been eclipsed by the bigger picture: grabbing what she can, getting out as soon as she can.

Her body has gone into survival mode. It is straining to flee the house. Her heart rate is up, the beats reverberating in her throat. She has to be disciplined, concentrate, and then she will leave. Easier said than done. A few weeks ago her panic was induced by going out alone. Now it is the reverse. Being here, with the prospect of Sam returning, threatens to overwhelm her.

She has already called Patrick, preempted his interrogation with an "I'll explain later." He has been sworn to secrecy: no sneaky calls to Sam to alert him. She has already worked out where the division of friendship lies. Patrick, she concluded, was her friend first, Sam's by association.

She can stay with him; it's "cool," apparently. Predictably Lottie is already off the scene, another blond fading into his past, so there will be no problem on that front. Nor did he ask her how long she needed to stay, not in the course of their hurried phone conversation. Maybe he will tonight. What will she tell him? She has money. Not a lot, but a decent sum from the compensation from her attack. She could rent a flat, get a job. Her mind whirs with the possibilities and logistics. Then it stops.

It stops to consider the footfall on the stairs.

The air in the room thins. In her hand is a pair of knickers in cream silk with black lace trim. She stares at them, expensive ones she doesn't care for. On the rare occasions she's worn them, they've ridden up her bum, cut her in two. There's a bra to match buried at the back of her drawer, which is where she would return the knickers if it didn't mean she'd have to turn around. And she can't do that because she knows he is standing there, waiting for her to face him. She looks down to her chest, heaving in and out. Blood rushes to her head.

His words, when they come, cause an involuntary twitch in her body, like an electric shock. "You're leaving, then?" he asks. His tone is even but she knows it has required a monumental effort for him to stay calm. She remains still, her gaze fixed on the knickers as if they are some kind of wonder. She eyes the label. They're an eight, a size too small for her. A present from Sam. Now she sees hidden messages everywhere she looks. *Lose weight and they won't ride up your arse, bitch.*

"So that's it, six years and you were going to piss off without even telling me? Were you going to leave a note? Or just send me a text? Maybe you wanted me to figure it out by myself." She hears his footsteps walk across the room. He's close to her now. She hears the flow of his breath, fast like he's been running. When she slides her eyes to her right she can see the hairs on his muscular arms, the veins that ripple as he clenches his hand into a fist.

"What the fuck is going on, Mel? We're supposed to be getting married in two months . . . Do I not deserve a fucking explanation?"

Deserve. Even in her heightened state the word amuses her. She can think of a lot of things Sam deserves but an explanation is not one of them. With the knickers still in her hand, she turns to go back to the wardrobe, takes one step before she feels his grip on her arm.

"Do you have anything to say?" She drops her gaze to his hand, which is still gripping her arm. It's too tight, like a Chinese burn pinching the skin. She stares at it and feels him loosen his hold. She has lots to say, which is ironic given that she has struggled with conversation for years. What should they talk about? She'd rehearse topics before he came home. It wasn't like her days were filled with excitement, incidents and outrages that could be embellished and relayed over dinner. Her days were filled with nothing. She didn't watch the news. Nor did she have any knowledge of Sam's job. She had no interests of her own beyond cooking and running. Where was she supposed to harvest the anecdotes to pepper her conversation? She wanted to talk but had nothing to say. And now she has so much to say but won't talk. She's fucked if she's going to put him out of his misery just like that, not when he's spent years smothering her in lies.

"Take your hand off me," she says. She would try to remove it herself but he's stronger than her and she'd rather not highlight her weaknesses.

"Tell me what's going on." With his free hand he tilts her chin upward so she has no choice but to look at his face. It's red and blotchy. His eyes black like ink. Were they always this dark? She thought they were brown. Couldn't she see every curve and line, from the scar above his lip where he burst it open as a kid trying to shave to the bump on his nose sustained in a rugby game? Hadn't she prided herself on seeing him without even looking? Why didn't she look at him, scrutinize that face? Maybe she would have seen its slow transformation into this person in front of her. Because she knows that the figure towering over her now is not the man who persuaded her to swim at night, whose touch she couldn't resist on the cold sand. He is not the person for whom she betrayed her friend. Not just any friend, her best friend. That man was worth crossing lines for. She would have done anything for him. She did. Though for the life of her she can't remember why.

Was it the sex?

Is that it? Was theirs simply a passion that flared and burned out? A chemical attraction, the indulgence of two people who weren't strong enough to say no? And all the while they've been kidding themselves that this thing was deeper, that it had grown roots deep enough to sustain and support a relationship, a marriage even. No wonder she's felt untethered, as if her world has been floating around her. There was nothing to hold her down.

Who is this man? Where do his lies end? She looks at him and thinks he would be capable of anything. Of course it was him. He went out to find her and she disappeared. And all this time she has trusted him. She deserves to die for being so stupid.

A minute ago her body was warm. Ripping around, gathering what she needed, she'd removed her cardigan to cool herself down. Now she stands in a sleeveless top and a skirt. The heat has been sucked from the room, from her. A draft brushes her skin. She shivers. Her vision is disturbed; Sam's features shift and change in front of her eyes. He is her boyfriend, was soon to be her husband, he is a hospital consultant who people trust with their limbs if not their lives.

She hears his breath hiss. "I'm asking you to tell me, Mel." He tugs on her arm for emphasis.

No, she thinks, this is not true. He is not asking. He hasn't said please. She's willing to bet he won't thank her when she tells him. He has his hand on her arm and is wrenching it so hard she fears it will slip out of joint. He is trying to extract information under duress.

She is trapped with him in this house with its impenetrable walls. They were supposed to keep the world at bay, stop danger intruding into her life. How was she to know the danger was inside them all the time?

Fear makes her light, like her body is blurring at the edges.

"Sit down. Mel." She feels herself pushed on to the bed. "I'm going to ask you one more time what the fuck is going on."

Her eyes lock on to his. "It was you," she says. "It was always you." She speaks with the abandon of someone with nothing to lose. "I went to see Honor yesterday," she continues, annoyed by the weakness in her voice, the way it betrays her fear. "She told me about the night I was attacked." Confusion fills his face, replaced quickly by surprise then horror. "So it's out now, your secret . . . shame, since you've gone to such lengths to conceal it."

"Mel, I . . ." He tries to cut across her, releases her arm from his grasp.

"There is nothing you can say . . . nothing. I knew, that's the thing that gets me most. I knew but I didn't trust myself and you took advantage of it. I was going to meet you that night and I didn't come back. That's what I remember and it is the truth. You left Honor to find me and you didn't come back. Where did you go, Sam . . . I deserve to know that at least . . . was it you? You and Honor were the only people who knew where I was that night and you've both lied about it ever since."

She is still sitting on the bed; he has crouched down next to her, searching for eye contact. "You think I did it?" He prods his chest with his finger for emphasis. "Me? Are you completely insane?" He laughs, nervously. "Mel, why would I do that?"

"You tell me."

"Well I can't because I didn't . . . I didn't attack you . . . I'd never touch you." Her eyes shift down to her arm, red where he held her only a minute before. "Don't," he says. "Don't do that. You think because I stopped you leaving I'm capable of trying to kill you?" He paces up and down the bedroom in front of her. She watches his feet, black socks marching three steps to her right then turning to come back toward her.

"I love you. You can't think like that. I won't let you." His hands are on his head, tugging at his hair as he walks. "All right, I lied. I'm sorry. But . . . we had no choice. You must see that . . . Mel . . . please . . . we were having an affair, my fiancée didn't know, she was your best friend. I went out to find you and you'd gone. I mean come on . . . who's going to believe that?"

He says this without a trace of irony.

"I would have been arrested. Honor would have been arrested, is that what you wanted?" He stops pacing and has knelt down close to her again, taking her by the shoulders. "I couldn't tell you, not in the hospital. You weren't with it, there were police swarming about the place waiting to question you. How was I to know you wouldn't blurt it out? It was one lie, Mel. One lie . . . and it didn't seem to . . ."

She pushes him off her. She knows what's coming next.

"Matter? That's what you were going to say, isn't it?" Rage surges through her, white hot, whirls and spins her around the room. He might be twice the size of her but right now the force that surges through her is limitless. It would be no match for him. "MATTER. Have you any idea . . ." She stops herself. At that precise moment she can't tell which is the greater crime: a) he attacked her, or b) he didn't attack her but is arrogant enough to believe his lie has had no lasting effects. Has he paid her so little attention that he hasn't seen the consequences unfolding? The lie has flourished and grown, gained a pulse that has emasculated her own. It has consumed her.

Whatever she does wouldn't be enough. She could claw at his eyes, scratch his cornea—painful, so she's heard—push him to the ground and kick him in the head, watch the blood leak on to the cream carpet and she wouldn't be able to stop. Mel knows all about crossing lines of decency but right now she can't see any lines. The fury has made them disappear. She hurls herself at him.

"Mel . . . for fuck's sake, Mel . . ."

"You bastard, you fucking bastard." He tries to prise her off him but she's quick, draws a line down his face with her nails. He pushes her on to the floor, where she sits watching the blood bubble to the surface.

Sam traces the line of the cut with his fingers, holds them out in front of him to examine the blood.

"You are off your head," he says. He peers down at her as if he is studying a specimen in a lab. She scrambles to her feet, feels the room swim around her.

Her hand is on the zip of the case. It doesn't matter what she has now, whether she takes anything at all. All that matters is that she gets away from Sam while she can.

His hand comes to rest on hers. It's cold and clammy like putty. "I'm afraid," he says, "I can't let you do that."

This is what is going to happen.

Mel will stay until she believes him. He will repeat his story. She will repeat it. The repetition will breed belief.

How will he know when she believes him?

That's easy. He knows everything.

Just do what he says and everything will be fine.

Simple. OK?

OK.

First they must eat. Has she eaten? Of course she hasn't. She needs to eat. He will see to that. He swings into action like he's dealing with a major incident. He's known as Dr. Earth for a reason. Nobody panic. He's going to the kitchen to cook, OK? OK. A healthy supper. That will help, won't it? Kale and carrots and spinach and brown rice. An oily fish, mackerel perhaps. Have we got any mackerel? Not sure? He'll check. Omega three, fish oils. Just what the doctor ordered.

They go downstairs together, him holding her hand on the descent the same way she used to hold her granny's. He's talking in a raised tone, speaking slowly as if she is not quite right in the head. "LAST STEP. THERE WE GO."

Mel acquiesces. It's not real. Not this. She feels like a puppet only Sam knows how to operate; she no longer has control over herself. Has she slipped into a dream without remembering falling asleep? Everything around her is normal yet it is so completely askew. Like she's walking down the high street to find everyone is speaking a language she doesn't understand. Her surroundings, her routine, so familiar, have turned on her. Terror lies in the crushing normality of it.

She'll wake up soon and Sam will tell her to leave, don't come back. Or kill her. One or the other. Her expectations oscillate between the two.

When they reach the kitchen, he pulls a chair out for her. "Sit down." She sits down.

Before he begins the search for oily fish, he uncorks a bottle of wine, pours two glasses. He downs his in two gulps, pours another before giving one to Mel. "Drink. You need a drink."

He starts chopping.

Onions. Garlic. She listens to the rap of the knife on the board. He could stab her with that. It's sharp enough and she should know, she bought it two months ago from the shopping channel. Chop the onions and garlic first then start on his girlfriend. Make it look like self-defense. *If I was going to kill her with a knife, I wouldn't have used it to slice vegetables first, now would I?*

It's an image of domestic perfection: the couple converging on the kitchen in the early evening to cook, chat, share a bottle of wine. If anyone looked in right now (which they can't, given the perimeter fence), they would gaze at the size of the space, the quality of the cabinetry, the layers of lighting (ambient, task and mood), and deduce that the couple had the kind of success early in life most will never attain. They might experience a pang of envy, the way people do when they're flicking through glossy lifestyle magazines: *why can't I have that? Why do I have to put up with my crappy kitchen from B&Q, my knackered oven, when these people have everything?*

They might not know, as Melody does, that everything is not a goal worth striving for. That even when it looks like you have it, there will always be something missing.

To stress her point she would instruct these imaginary voyeurs to move from the wide shot to the zoom. Closer scrutiny, she would hint, may reveal a different kind of truth. Look at Sam preparing dinner. He's standing on the far side of the island, a position that affords him a view of his girlfriend. Touching, you say? Look again. Chop, chop, chop, then he raises his eyes from the counter, shoots a look at her. He repeats this on a three-second cycle. Now watch her reaction. When she feels the heat of his stare, her eyes dart away. What does her expression tell you? Nothing? Precisely. It's a mask, drawn on to conceal her fear. Look at her body, perched on the edge of the chair. Her left leg is turned to the door because that's where she would like to go, only he has her in his sights and three seconds isn't enough time to run without him noticing. There are clues everywhere if you look. The wine glass on the table in front of her is full. She hasn't taken more than a sip. She needs a clear head. It's important that she's alert when he tries to kill her.

He sets a plate down in front of her. The mackerel stares at her with its glassy, dead eye. She hears the scrape of Sam's chair as he drags it across the concrete, tucking himself in to the table.

"Eat," he says. "Or it will get cold."

Mel keeps her eyes down, takes the lemon on the side of her plate and squeezes it over the fish. Its silver skin glistens, iridescent under the light of the pendant that hangs low over the table. She can't focus on anything except the intermittent clacking sound of Sam chewing, the unfortunate clicking of his jaw. She imagines the white flesh of the fish being shredded through his teeth, his moist mouth salivating as he shovels in the next forkful.

"Eat something, will you." A speck of unidentifiable matter from his mouth lands on the table not far from her plate. With her knife she slices the mackerel down the middle. It's translucent, barely cooked. He's watching; she feels his eyes burn into her. She loads a tiny morsel of fish on to her fork and slips it into her mouth. It's wet and cold, stuck to her tongue without any saliva to swallow it.

"I want you to listen, OK. Carefully. This is what happened." He rests his cutlery on the table, draws a deep breath and begins his monologue.

"Honor told me she knew it was you, she had worked out that you and I were . . ." his fingers are raised in commas in the air, "fucking. Then . . . are you following? . . . then she told me she had just driven by Emlyn Road and had seen you standing there, that's how she knew it was you. She was screaming at me, 'How the hell could you do that with my best friend?' I tried your phone . . . yes, your other phone . . . but you didn't pick up so I went out to find you and by the time I got there you had gone. I thought you'd got bored of waiting and walked home. I was in the car. I drove around for a bit to see if I could spot you, and when I didn't, I just kept driving. Why would I have gone back home? I just drove and before I knew it I was heading out on to the M20 to Camber Sands. I parked up beside the beach and slept. The next morning I swam in the sea, bought myself breakfast and then turned around and headed back. I tried to call you again, but you didn't answer. It was only when Patrick called later that day and told me you hadn't come home that I started to worry. When I found out what had happened I destroyed the phone. Yours was never found.

"That is what happened. You have to believe me. I didn't see you. I didn't touch you. I didn't try to kill you. Do you understand, Mel?" He has the satisfied air of someone who has tackled a dirty job and won. *Done and dusted.*

He's watching her, waiting for a reaction. Keep up, she thinks, say something. But she's lagging behind, caught in the complicated weave of his explanation, the circuitous routes and stop-offs, swims in the sea and breakfasts and phone calls that no one witnessed.

"MEL." She jumps, sucks in air and propels the piece of fish to the back of her throat, where it sticks. She coughs, rises from the chair, unable to breathe. "SIT DOWN."

She wants to tell him she needs water because she's choking. She staggers to the cupboard, grabs a glass and thrusts it under the tap, gulps the water down to dislodge the fish. Sam is next to her, his fish breath on her. "Get away from me . . ." She attempts to push him away but her hand comes up against the solid mass of his chest. Tensed, unyielding.

"I needed a glass of water."

He escorts her back to the table. When they're seated again he continues. "Did you hear what I said?"

She nods.

"Good, because that is what happened. Now I want you to forget it all." He pushes his plate to one side. All that's left of the fish is the head and eyes and its skeleton. The skin, in slimy gray lumps, sits next to a few remnants of kale.

For the first time since they've been in the kitchen she has the courage to study his face. Her eyes are pinched, trying to drill through the surface, work out what lies underneath. She's familiar with the look he wears, the one he uses when administering diagnosis—*you have a virus, you need rest*—or expounding theories or arguments. It's a face you put your trust in. Solemn, in control, knowing.

There's nothing in his demeanor, not a twitch or a glint in his eyes, that betrays the madness of this situation.

She feels like she's falling through a crack, slipping downward into a parallel universe where her perceptions of truth and lies no longer hold tight.

Who is insane? Is it her or Sam? The smart money would go on Melody. No question. But . . . what if it's Sam? Mel has only had him to compare herself with all these years. Trying to meet his expectations, follow his thinking, understand his world view. And now sitting here in front of him she no longer knows whose grip on reality has become lost, whose behavior is reasonable and whose is unsound.

His tongue emerges snake-like to wet his lips. "The only story you have to remember is that Honor and I were together all night. OK?"

"No."

"What?"

"You just told me you weren't together."

"I also told you to forget I said that."

"Well why did you tell me in the first place?"

"So you'd know that I didn't attack you."

"And these two stories are just supposed to sit alongside each other, are they? Despite the fact that they blatantly contradict each other?"

THE LIFE I LEFT BEHIND   285

"That's why I said forget it. Why are you making this so hard? You have to believe me . . ."

"Why?"

"Because if you don't, you'll leave here and go to the police and it will all be over."

The clarity comes at her with force. It's only ever been about him. Sam is at the very core of everything, conducting, manipulating. She knows how persuasive he is. The lie would have been his idea. Honor has always had a much more faithful relationship with the truth than him. God, she has been thick. Even their affair, its origins that night, she can see how he must have plotted it. The swim under the stars, the kiss. What perfect stage management. He must have thought she was weak, knew she wouldn't resist. And then later, he didn't confront her fear of going out alone because what did it matter to him? They went out together, Mel was always there when he returned, all the better when she learned to cook. Sam is the sun around which everything else orbits. And Melody is in possession of a newly discovered truth that threatens to upset the planetary alignment.

It is that knowledge that sends fear slicing through her. It is piercingly clear. Sam is insane.

Daylight has faded completely. Beyond the glass, in the world outside, a sea of dark. He is still talking, there is no let-up, although his words have become slurred with booze. "Youhavetopromiseme youwon't . . ." The noise assails her. She closes her eyes hoping he won't notice, and allows herself to drift out in the shadowy blackness of the night. It holds no fear anymore. This encounter has freed her of that. If she could turn a key in the door, she would wander down their driveway and out to the fields through the long grass and bracken and listen as the trees shifted and rustled around her. She'd look up and see the constellations of stars studding the sky winking down at her. And she wouldn't startle at the cry of a fox or the sound of a snake weaving its way through the field. She'd just walk, go wherever her instincts led her. Make up for lost time.

"MEL!" His voice snaps her out of the reverie. There's a stench in the room as if something is rotting. She looks down and eyes the fish. "You're falling asleep, you should get some rest."

He leads her back upstairs, passing her handbag on the way. Her phone is in it. She longs to reach out, feel its cold round edges in her hand, hear a voice on the end of the line. Has Nat called? She promised she'd ring him to tell him she was OK. Is he worried? She wants to grab the phone and call him, but it's pointless. Wait until Sam's asleep, sneak down, out of the house, that is her plan.

Sam undresses, waits for her to do the same. Instead she removes her skirt and slips into bed, positions herself on the outermost edge of it and draws her knees tight to her chest. She waits.

It's the rhythm of his breathing, the wave-like push and suck that interferes with her plans. She is focusing on it too keenly. Without her noticing, sleep creeps up on her.

The bed is empty and cold on his side by the time she wakes. It's ten past nine. Shit, shit, shit. How could that have happened? How could she sleep longer than she has in recent history on the very night it was imperative she stay awake?

Silence cloaks the house. Her head scrambles to remember the day. It's Friday. He should be at work but that means nothing. She thought he would be at work yesterday and look where that got her. Her phone. She can creep downstairs and get her phone if he is in the kitchen. She reels off a Hail Mary under her breath at lightning speed, surprised she still knows the words. Please let it have battery. I'll start going to church every week, I'll clean the floors, do the offertory, flower-arrange . . . just let it have battery.

Her skirt is on the floor; she pulls it on quickly. There are only two squeaky floorboards in the whole house and she knows exactly where they are, on the threshold of the door and on the first step on the stairs. She avoids both, floats downstairs. Her bag is where she left it. Relief flushes through her. Silence still. Do not be fooled. Her hand dips into her bag, craving the feel of her phone, the comfort of it in her hand.

It's not there.

Not in the pocket. Not in the main compartment. She stops. The door is three meters away. What is she thinking? Just get out. Away from him and this house.

She is at the door, turning the Yale. It won't open. It won't open because the door is locked. Scream, she'd like to scream or cry, she could easily cry. *Don't you dare, don't you fucking dare. Go to the cupboard and find the key.*

She's in the cupboard.

SHED, FRONT DOOR, WINDOWS, KITCHEN DOORS, the labels are still there, to taunt her she supposes, because the line of hooks, drilled like question marks into the wall, is empty. No answers to be found there. He's taken them all, right down to the one for the shed. He's thorough like that. She turns, half expecting him to be smiling over her shoulder, chalking up another victory over her. He is not there. "SAM!" she screams. "SAM!" She repeats the call in every room she searches before concluding that he has gone.

He has gone to work and locked her in. Taken her phone. Her laptop too. In the living room she scans the sideboard where the handsets for the landline sit. They are gone. Rage ignites in her. She's felt anger before but not like this; nothing has come close to the white-hot fury that burns through her now, so pure and raw. She could do anything. If he was standing in front of her she could tear him apart, take pleasure in ripping his skin off. Running into the kitchen, she opens the cupboards. Her eyes come to rest on the wine glasses. Without thinking, she hurls them one by one across the room until the floor is carpeted with shards of glass that look like diamonds in the light morning sun.

The crackle of bare feet crunching over them pleases her. She could be walking on feathers for all she knows. Against her anger it is impossible to feel anything. When she reaches the glass doors, as far as she can go, Mel peers at the thin, shady image of the woman staring back at her. The shadow of a ghost that burns out when the sun bursts through only to return when it slips back behind the clouds. Her blond hair tumbles down; strands of it curl around her face. She wears a smile, warm and reassuring.

It is not Mel.

It is Eve.

Mel reaches out to touch the glass with her fingertips but the image of Eve vanishes. She sinks down onto the floor and lets out a wail from deep inside her. The tears come, fat and hot to sting her cheeks. She cries not out of fear but for what she has lost and squandered, for the years she has been buried in this house. She cries for Eve who has shown her so much, who is afforded no second chances.

Wiping the snot and tears away, she glances out to the garden. Blades of grass glisten with morning dew, leaves of gold, russet and red spin and dance on the wind. Up above she spies a murmuration of starlings like a dark cloud of iron shavings wheeling, turning and swooping in the sky. The sun cracks through the clouds, bathing everything in a golden light.

It looks like a beautiful day.

Later, hours later, the sound of a key turning in the door. A voice calling her name.

A voice that is not Sam's.

"Patrick." She runs through to the hall to see him standing there.

Minutes later she is in his car, pulling out of the driveway. She doesn't look back but focuses instead on the road ahead, the line of fierce blue sky. She was right. It is a beautiful day.

Twenty

T he day was still alive. The midday heat had lingered through the afternoon and toward evening. Swirls of smoke from barbecues drifted over us, a steady hum of lawnmowers; occasionally we caught the sound of bass, emitted from a passing car, rising and falling.

Going on to the pub was not part of the plan, but like all the best days this one had a mind of its own. Besides, we had exhausted the food and alcohol supply at David's. Strolling down Goldhawk Road, woozy from afternoon beers, we wore smiles that no amount of beeping horns or swearing drunks or dog shit on the pavement could lift from our faces. We were buzzing off each other, with the help of three bottles of Kronenbourg and a gin and tonic apiece.

We chose a pub off Goldhawk Road in Brackenbury Village, an affluent pocket of delis and gastropubs wedged in between Shepherd's Bush and Hammersmith, and ordered a bottle of champagne. David's ordeal wasn't over. But we thought we had arrived at the beginning of the end. That was reason enough to celebrate.

It fell to David to bring me back to earth. "Let's not forget Melody in this. I lost a good friend and no one knows who tried to kill her." He shook his head and took a gulp of his champagne.

Over dinner we made a few aborted attempts to discuss a plan of action—we would need to apply to the Criminal Cases Review Commission for the conviction to be looked at—but no one wanted to be bogged down in detail. Today was about enjoying a small achievement.

"I'm done," David announced. "I'm not made for drinking the posh stuff, I haven't been this drunk in ages. My bed is calling me." He leaned over and kissed me again, on the cheek. "Thank God for spilled strawberry daiquiris" were his parting words.

Annie left shortly afterward. "I'd invite you back," she said slowly, her focus sliding from my face, "but I'm not quite sure I can talk. You are very special, do you know that?"

"I've been trying to tell people that for a long time."

She laughed. "You'll call a cab, right?"

"Of course," and I waved her off.

I got up to go; my legs swayed underneath me. I knew when I was beaten. I needed a taxi and fast. I called the number on my phone and a guy with barely passable English told me it would be half an hour. The barman came round, clearing drinks from the tables. "Come on, time to finish up," he said loudly as he approached. I looked around. There were a few people still standing at the bar. I was peering, trying to keep my vision straight, but was listing. A man turned around and gave me a wave, hesitant, as if he was uncertain I would recognize him.

I waved back, but it was only as I walked past him out the door that I realized who it was.

On the street I clung to the hope that I'd be able to flag a taxi. My flat was only a mile or so away, but it was too far at that time of night with six hours' worth of wine and beer sloshing around inside me. I watched a few taxis streak past; never any when you want one. Reluctantly I had started to walk when I heard a voice call my name.

I turned around to see him.

To be honest, I wasn't up for conversation. Keep it short, I told myself.

"I thought that was you." He was taller than I remembered, tanned too, cropped dark hair and piercing eyes.

Get a grip.

"Sod's law."

"What?" he said.

"Never any taxis when you want one." I was aware of the slight slur in my words and tried to overcompensate by speaking very slowly. "Anyway . . ." I raised a hand to wave good-bye and turned to walk up the street, only to realize he was going in the same direction. For a moment I was caught in a dilemma. Do I run, pretend I've remembered something urgent? Do I hang about waiting for a free taxi that is patently not going to come? Or do I just act like an adult, walk at the same pace as him and resign myself to conversation.

"How are you doing?" he asked, and we started walking.

Twenty-one

H er stomach lurches as her mobile skitters across her desk.
What now? It'll be Doug, she's sure of it, filling her in on the
latest calamity to befall the kids. Her immediate thought is
for herself. *Selfish cow.* Another evening lost, bleached out under
the halogen lights of Kingston Hospital's accident and emergency
department. She's embarrassed going there now, worried the doctors might suspect her of some form of Munchausen by proxy given
the frequency of her visits: pen top lodged up the nose (Bella), a
broken nose (Oliver playing rugby), a chipped wrist (Bella in the
playground), suspected meningitis (Oliver), a fractured arm (Bella
at ballet!). She's no good at the enforced idleness the waiting demands, the endless hours spent leafing through sticky, dog-eared
copies of *Hello!.* Free time to sit and think and audit her to-do list
is something she avoids if possible. Doing nothing when a million
things need her attention produces a strange curdling stress inside
her.

And it's her who the kids want. Without fail. Doug runs the
house, arranges the online shop, packs the lunches in the morning,
cooks at suppertime, manages their growing timetable of extracur-
ricular activities, but none of it counts when the chips are down.
Bella and Oliver want their mum, and galling as that may be for
her husband, a part of her loves it. For all her maternal shortcom-
ings, it's good to be reminded she is still wanted and needed.

So Victoria is thinking of her children, hospitals and plastic chairs and stained lino and the smell of bleach mixed with vomit, as she looks at the phone dancing across the desk. She is not, for once, thinking of the investigation that has been monopolizing her time.

A quick glance at the screen, however, and she knows it's not Doug, or the school. It's a mobile number. She answers and hears a woman's voice on the end of the line.

Words race out. Not sentences, just words, a dump of them through which she hears gulps of air as if the caller, who has yet to identify herself, is out of breath. It's the urgency in her tone, the sense that whatever she is recounting is happening right now, that makes Victoria's pulse quicken. She reaches for a notepad and pen on her desk, ready to scribble down whatever details she can extract.

"Can you tell me your name?" she says.

The words come to a halt. "It's Melody. Melody Pieterson," she says, as if it should have been obvious all along.

Less than an hour later, Melody Pieterson sits in front of her in the interview room. Having declined coffee and tea, she has accepted a plastic cup of water from the filter. Victoria hasn't seen her drink any. Instead she cradles it in her hand, running her finger back and forth around the rim.

"Are you sure you are OK to do this now?" she asks.

Melody nods. "I'm fine, fine." Clearly this is not true. Her sun top is smeared with reddish-brown stains. Gashes pattern the palms of her hands. Melody administers to them with balled tissues soaked with blood. Her blond hair is scraped back into a loose ponytail, a halo of frizz surrounding her head. She is a different woman to the one who sat here only a few weeks ago, manicured, polished. And the manner in which she speaks, freely, withholding nothing, is in direct contrast to that careful, clipped performance. It's like she's been uncorked.

"Did he do that?"

Mel opens her palms and studies them as if she has only realized now the state they are in.

"No." She shakes her head slowly. "I smashed some glass. I couldn't get out, you see. He locked me in. I'd still be there if it wasn't for Patrick."

"Patrick?"

"Patrick Carling, my friend who brought me here. He came round to check on me. I'd called him to ask him to meet me at the station, and when I didn't turn up, he was worried."

"I see," DI Rutter says, her mind beginning to whir with the information. "Shall we start at the beginning?"

"I have Eve Elliot's file . . . she'd spoken to all of them, all my friends, Sam . . ."

Victoria smiles. How the hell did Melody get hold of that? Then she remembers how it came into her own possession. She'll be having words with Nathaniel Jenkins later. "This would be the file detailing Eve's investigation of David Alden's conviction?"

Either Melody doesn't hear the question or she chooses to ignore it, refusing to allow anything to derail her story. "Honor had found out we were having an affair, it was totally obvious to me when I read it. You know, Sam and me were . . . well, we were . . . behind her back."

Victoria raises an eyebrow more to remind Melody of her previous lie than anything else. Hadn't she asked her only a few weeks ago if she had been seeing anyone at the time of her attack? "No," she'd said. The answer couldn't have been more emphatic.

Melody picks up on her irritation. "I know. I know." She raises her hands in the air. "I'm sorry I didn't mention that before. I was ashamed of myself, some friend I was. After I read Eve's file, I went to see Honor. We haven't spoken in years, drifted apart after the attack. You're probably wondering how I didn't guess she had rumbled us. I mean, it would be obvious. Except Sam kept telling me she hadn't. That's why I went to see her . . . because of what she said to Eve. She didn't know Eve was dead. You should have seen her face when I told her, it was awful. I guess that's why she told me everything . . . you know, because a woman had died and she didn't want to lie anymore."

"Lie?"

"They weren't together on the night I was attacked. Sam doesn't have an alibi. It was him I thought I was meeting. He says by the time he came out to find me, I was gone."

"So you confronted him?" Victoria is increasingly confused.

"Not intentionally. I went home to get my stuff—I don't want to be anywhere near him—but he came home. He said he wouldn't let me go until I believed him."

When Melody starts talking about fish, how Sam served her uncooked mackerel and demanded she eat, Victoria ends the interview. She's not a fan of fish at the best of times and she can spot a superfluous fact when it hits her. Besides, Melody clearly needs some rest.

"What are you going to do with him?" Melody demands.

"Don't worry," Victoria says. "Someone is already on their way to Mr. Chapman's house. You will be the first to know of any developments."

Sometimes she catches herself and hates the way she sounds. Officious, uncaring, procedural. But she can't tell Melody that Sam Chapman is already on her radar. She's read the file too. And the fact that it's now alleged that at least two of Melody's friends have had something to hide makes them all the more interesting to her. She feels her face color, a charge of excitement whips through her. You wait long enough and it comes. It always does. This is the bit she likes, when what has been stagnant starts springing to life.

She thinks of the man who accompanied Melody when she came here a few weeks ago. The imposing stature, the supreme confidence, the crushing handshake. She never trusts a man whose grip is that hard. It makes her suspicious of what they are trying to prove.

"Do you have someone you can stay with?"

"Patrick . . . He's waiting in reception."

"We'll need a number for you, and an address." She pushes a blank piece of paper across the table to Melody and hands her a pen. "If you can write his full name and address down. And we'll need a contact number for you, since you don't have your phone."

"You can reach me on Patrick's . . . the one I called you on before.

He won't mind." Her hands shake as she scrawls the address. "Here," she says, scraping the chair along the floor as she pushes it out.

They walk to reception together. "We have people you can talk to if you need to, trained and sensitive," Victoria says gently before handing her a card. Melody puts it straight into her pocket without looking at it.

Ahead a man dressed in jeans, a white shirt and a blazer rises to his feet as he sees them approach. Patrick Carling. His face is etched with concern. Melody walks straight to him, lets his chest support her head. He puts a protective arm around her back.

"I'll be in touch tomorrow," Victoria says and watches them disappear through the doors into the evening.

It's a shame, she thinks, what this job does to her. Anyone else would look at that scene and see the kindness in it, whereas all she does is search for ulterior motives.

She turns and heads back to the matter that was occupying her before Melody called. The results from the samples of soil she ordered from Climping. She's had them compared with the grains of soil found on Melody and Eve.

The properties are so similar it would lead us to the conclusion that they are taken from the same geographical location.

Tomorrow she is sending DS Cook and DC Rollings down to Climping with one of her more unusual instructions. To locate the cottage that once belonged to Rosemary Crighton and look for any sign of *Hibiscus syriacus.* She's told it is in bloom at this time of year.

Twenty-two

They're still in Richmond, edging around the one-way system. Stop. Start. If it was her dad driving he'd turn the engine off every time they came to a halt to save petrol. To her left is a bar, its exterior painted an elegant dusty gray, baskets of purple and white flowers spilling from the windows. Not a pink one in sight, she notes gratefully. She watches a group of women disappear through the door under a red awning. They're dressed up, the working week behind them. What will they drink? Cocktails? A bottle of wine to share? Tears bubble up. They are only a few meters away from her, tucked inside the bar now, but she is a thousand times removed from them.

She stares at the palms of her hands. They're grubby and bloodied. She needs a shower to wash away all the filth of yesterday and today, and the stench of fish that still clings to her hair. She needs to brush the fur from her teeth and tongue.

The car moves ten meters or so and the bar slips away behind her. Ahead the road glows red with brake lights, a throbbing vein that twists its way through town.

"You don't honestly believe Sam did it, do you?" Patrick asks.

It was only a few weeks ago that she was in Sam's car picking their way out of the town back to Surrey. How could she have sat next to him and not suspected him? All she was focused on was the newness of the car, the cloying smell of new upholstery and sealers. Is that why he changed his car, because he had carried Eve's body in the old one? Were her senses more alert than her brain, ahead of the game, trying to show her something she wasn't willing to see?

"I don't know," she says. "I don't know anything really. I don't know what to think. It's out of my hands, the police will have arrested him by now."

They approach the roundabout, join the snarl of traffic waiting for the lights to change. Patrick turns to her as if to say something, but shakes his head.

"What?" she asks. "What is it?"

"Will they tell you if they don't arrest him, tonight I mean? If he's not at home or work?"

The thought hasn't occurred to her. She accepted without question that he would be taken into custody tonight. The stupidity of the assumption slaps her in the face. Why would he be at home waiting? The moment he realized she was missing, surely he would come looking for her.

"You don't think he would come . . . ?"

"I don't know . . . It's the obvious place to look for you, but . . ."

"Where else can we go? She needs the security of knowing Sam can't find her. Now that they have acknowledged the possibility that he might turn up at Patrick's, she can't go there. Not until she receives a call from DI Rutter to tell her he is in custody.

Patrick pauses, screws up his face as if deep in thought. "I have an idea," he says, and takes a sharp right instead of going straight ahead.

Twenty-three

S am Chapman has not shaken her hand this time. Even if he had, she suspects it would have had none of the crunching strength of before. Funny, she thinks, how different situations can completely change a person's demeanor and how you perceive them. Last week it was Sam's physique that had grabbed her attention. He must be six foot four at least, towering and muscular. He had that sheen of success and wealth, all white teeth and bright eyes. When he spoke, his tone was measured, in command, if a little pompous. Now when she looks at him she doesn't notice his height, not when he's hunched into the seat at any rate. Without the careful styling of before, his hair is wild, rising up in vertical shoots like one of those cress heads her kids grow out of yogurt pots.

She has to award him a few points for effort. His opening gambit went like this: "I was with Honor on the night Melody was attacked so that in itself wasn't a lie; it was just that I wasn't there all night. It was a simple oversight."

On hearing this she laughed, deep and throaty, threw her head back and stared up to the cork ceiling tiles for a moment to make her point. Everything in the station is a shade of brown; it's like working in a tea bag.

When she came back to face him, she smiled one her best dazzlers and winked.

"Shall we start again?"

———

"Melody went crazy, I mean you should have seen her." He points to the gouge on his cheek. "She did this . . ." He pauses, as if waiting for her to agree that the scratch is indeed evidence of Melody's insanity. When she doesn't, he continues. "I wanted her to calm down before she left. Of course I wasn't going to keep her there against her will."

"But you took her phone, her laptop, locked her in."

"Alright, I know how that looks . . . I wasn't thinking. I just wanted her to calm down so I could talk to her properly."

"You thought locking her in would calm her down?"

He sighs, like a weight is crushing him. "She was in a state. Accusing me," he taps his chest with his index finger, "of hurting her."

"You can see how she might draw that conclusion since you were the one she was supposed to be meeting on the night she was attacked. And you went out to find her. Not only that, but you had lied to her."

"Hmm . . ." He mulls this over for a moment before shaking his head. "Well no, actually I can't. Mel knows me, for God's sake. Why would I hurt her and then live with her? You do know we are getting married, don't you?"

This time it's her DS who sniggers. One third of all female murder victims are killed by their partner; ten percent of emergency calls are domestic violence related. Statistics like these lodge themselves in your head. And here is Sam Chapman suggesting that his desire to marry Mel is proof he wouldn't harm her.

She ignores the question, wants him to know that these arguments will not gain purchase here. There are already two offenses she can and will charge him with: perverting the course of justice and false imprisonment. What else did he do? And there's Honor to speak to. She was the one who saw Melody just before she disappeared, the only person who has now admitted to it. Could she have attacked Melody? Could she have done it with Sam?

Honor Flannigan is on her way here from Dorset. She'll speak to her tomorrow.

It doesn't take long before Sam starts to cry. Victoria could have predicted this. She's seen it all before: the realization that his normal methods of persuasion and manipulation are not going to get him anywhere; the mask of confidence that's a millimeter thick, easy to shatter, and when it goes, everything underneath collapses. Like a tearful schoolboy rumbled for a misdemeanor, his speech is faltering and shaky, heavy with contrition. His eyes keep darting to the door; he'd love to be anywhere but here in this room with its recycled air, with her. But he's not going anywhere. See how you like it now, she thinks. He is not pompous today, just pathetic.

"I freaked out, that's what happened. We were having an affair, my girlfriend found out, and Mel goes missing at the same time that I'm trawling the streets looking for her. I was scared. I knew I would be a suspect, and if I was, you wouldn't have caught the person who did do it." She can barely keep up with him. In comparison to his previous slow and measured speech, his words come out fast, like he has one speed for the truth and another for everything else.

Victoria sits back, arms folded across her chest, allowing the new version of his story to buffer the old one. She's not convinced that either one takes her any closer to the truth.

Twenty-four

He won't tell her where they are going, except to say he planned to take her once before, when they had organized a weekend away: "But something better came along and you ditched me," he says, deadpanning.

They're on the M3 now and Mel is grateful he is giving the road his full attention. That way he can't see the color rise in her cheeks. She remembers the weekend in point, years back, and the reason why she canceled on him. Honor had decided to go to Dorset at the last minute. She had Sam all to herself.

Patrick switches on the radio. They're just far enough out of town that the London stations slip out of signal. He tries Radio 2. "Folksy shite," he announces before fumbling for a CD and inserting it. He turns it to track four and waits for the first few bars of the song to play. "Remember this?" he asks, one hand tapping the steering wheel in time to the music.

"Oh God, no . . . I thought we had agreed all copies of that would be destroyed."

"I lied," he laughs.

It's not a bad song; it was one of her favorites at the time, which was the reason it was in her car on their camping trip to the Lakes in 2006. Patrick had forgotten to pack his music so they listened to it for three days solid. She could sing the lyrics in her sleep, even now. Paolo Nutini.

"Let's see how good your memory is; can you guess the track?"

She doesn't even have to think. " 'Rewind.' " The sound of it takes her back to boggy fields and the smell of damp air trapped in polyester; wet feet, the sky, a uniform sheet of gray that stubbornly refused to lift. Only once in three days did she spy the sun, one horizontal strip where light burst through, as if someone had ripped the fabric of the cloud. Vodka, she remembers that too, notable by the volume they consumed.

"I'm surprised we can actually remember anything about it. Thankfully the vodka helped blot it out."

"It wasn't all bad."

"No, you're right, the bit where we left and came home, that was OK."

He shoots her a look; something burns in his eyes. Sadness, anger? Her assessment of the trip can't have upset him, surely?

"Oh come on, Patrick, it was awful. The tent leaked, it didn't stop raining, not for a single moment. I actually worried we would never see the sun again. We packed up at six in the morning because there was rain running down my neck."

She waits for him to surrender and agree. His hand has stopped beating in time to the music and is firmly clenched around the wheel. His brows are knitted together, straining in concentration at the road. He's a looker, she's always thought that, thick dark hair that he wears cropped now, and startling light blue eyes. He's never been short of suitors; even back at university there was always a steady stream of blonds of varying shades: strawberry, bleached, golden. He's got the patter, the charm he turns on, she's seen him in action. But the few that he hasn't dumped have tired of him. Mel suspects they found his petulance every bit as irritating as she does.

"So are you going to tell me where it is?" she asks to break the mood.

"We'll be there in an hour," he says and turns the music up.

Sod him, she thinks, and closing her eyes she reclines the seat and pretends to sleep.

———

At some undefined point the pretending ceases and becomes the real thing. Occasionally she opens her eyes only for her lids to droop again. The strain of the past few days has caught up with her and she is carried off, relieved of her thoughts for however long her dreams last. They are rich and vivid. She is walking through tight, once familiar streets, assaulted by food smells and colors: the pink of bougainvillea, white of jasmine, the deep blue of morning glory. She hears the distant rush of the sea, feels its breeze catch her face. She follows her senses and walks toward it, down the path where the sound of the waves grows stronger and the salt air thicker. When she feels her toes sink into the soft sand she opens her eyes. Ahead the azure sea ripples and winks in the sunlight. She turns and sees her friend by her side. It could be Tarifa, it could be anywhere, all the places she can go. There is nothing to stop her now.

She wakes. Jolts. The car has slowed, down a gear and then another. She doesn't understand it at first, the sensation she has woken to, sprung from the heat of her dreams to a chill, the slow slide of an ice cube falling down her back. It takes a few beats to hear the crackle of wheels on the driveway. And even then she hasn't grasped it. Only when they finally come to a stop and the engine falls silent does it make sense.

Twenty-five

Heading up the road, the pleasantries were quickly exhausted. *How are you doing? Fine, quite pissed actually. How are you? Fine, stone-cold sober and on call.* We carried on for a few moments in an uneasy silence, which he broke with the obvious question. "How's it going then?"

"*It* is going very well," I told him.

"Really? I thought you would have thrown in the towel by now; not the easiest case to disprove."

"I didn't say it was easy." My tone was mocking. I shot him a look: *it's all about skill and persistence.* At least that was the sentiment I wanted it to convey. In reality I probably looked a bit bog-eyed and drunk.

I waited because I knew he wanted me to tell him more but I was quite enjoying being the keeper of information for once. If he wanted to know, he could ask. I wasn't going to offer.

I wasn't expecting what came next. "Look, Mel's a good friend, one of my best, and for all my reservations, which . . ." and he laughed, "I think I made clear to you a few months ago, if it wasn't David Alden, we'd all be better off knowing."

The glow of the street lamp bounced off his face. I could see his blue eyes burning into me. Waiting.

"Well it wasn't David Alden. I'm sure of that now, but I haven't found out who it was. I'm not that good, not yet anyway," I said.

He stopped. "This is my house, you're welcome to call a cab and wait here. I can make you a coffee to sober you up. Not that I'm suggesting you need to."

I thought about walking the distance home. "Black, two sugars," I stumbled up the steps to his house.

Twenty-six

W e're here," he says. Her eyes remain closed. She can't open them. Won't. "Come on, Mel." He gives her a gentle prod. "Let's get inside, I'll show you around."

She prises them open. He's smiling at her with the same light blue eyes, the same face she's picked out in crowds and concerts, in bars and airport arrivals for eighteen years, always there, solid, dependable. He looks at her quizzically. "Sorry, did I give you a fright?" This is Sam's legacy, this fear: doubt everyone, trust no one. *Fuck Sam.*

"Where the hell are we?" She's disorientated. When she last looked there were cars and lights all around them. Now she can't see more than five feet in front of her: a few trees, a small stretch of path illuminated by the yellow glow of the car's headlights.

"Remember the place I told you about, the one I wanted to bring you to. Well this is it. Don't expect too much inside. It's basic, and that's being kind."

"It's yours?" He's talked about it once or twice before, a sanctuary where he used to escape with his mum when he was a child and fly kites on the hill behind the house. It had been her mother's before. Mel had no idea it was here he had planned to take her. The weekend she'd spent screwing Sam instead. *Some friend.*

"I'd hardly bring you here if it wasn't. I got it after my dad died. But that shower you're after . . ."

"A shower is not a luxury, it's an essential."

"It was in 1975 when this place was last updated."

"Is this your way of telling me I'm going to have to bathe in a tub?"

He shook his head and grinned playfully. "Don't be stupid, there's a bath. You'll just have to boil the water to fill it."

There's a torch, somewhere, either lost in the footwell of the car or left behind in the cottage last time, so he leaves the headlights on and they stumble up the path. "Don't they have streetlights around these parts?" Mel asks, and she trips and rights herself just before she tumbles facedown onto the gravel.

"They don't even have streets," he jokes.

It's brisk, at least ten degrees colder than when they left London. She listens . . . to what? Nothing, apart from the gentle sound of the wind singing through the bushes. She should be used to this, the intense quiet, having lived in the depths of Surrey. But being here, the air so empty of sirens or dogs or the distant rumbling of trains, she realizes that the house was only remote in her mind. They were six miles from Guildford, a mile and a half from the village, where there were cafés and cake shops, a Tesco Metro for God's sake.

She looks up, sees the black sky pierced with throbbing stars. Vast, uninterrupted.

They reach the front door, shrouded in darkness. Close up she can see it is warped. Deep crevices run down the wood. What little paint remains is bubbled and peeling. She braces herself for her first view of the interior, can't imagine it will be the refuge she had in mind. "I hope you've got wine," she says, trying to sound upbeat, "because I plan on drinking heavily."

"Wine I can do."

"Just no vodka, and no Paolo Nutini."

Patrick flicks on the light and she gets her first glimpse. He was right about it being basic. It is authentically old as opposed to cutesy vintage old. She feels like she's stepped onto the set of one of those

TV docudramas: *A 1980s Family.* Off a dark hallway is a large living room with a moss-green velvet sofa and two matching armchairs. A teak coffee table sits in the middle of the room, which is dominated by an oversized stone fireplace. There are a few empty wine bottles on the mantelpiece with candles stuck in them, tears of wax dried down the sides. A bare bulb hangs from the ceiling. Its glare is brutal and unforgiving. The air is misted with dust particles. She coughs. It's damp and musty. She feels like a child who hasn't been given what they want.

He must read her thoughts. "Wait till I get the fire started and it warms up, it'll be transformed."

She smiles and nods. "I'll take your word for it." She heads out to the hallway to retrieve a fleece from her case. The bath can wait. It's too cold to remove any layers yet.

He must have been here recently: the basket next to the fire is piled with logs and kindling. There's a newspaper on the coffee table, a *Times* from a few weeks earlier which she starts to leaf through for want of anything else to do, only to have him snatch it from her grasp. "For the fire," he says. "Old news anyway."

He rips the sheets out from the paper and balls them up in the grate, piling the kindling on in layers before striking a match. Within seconds the paper is alight, flames surging up toward the wood. She hears the kindling snap and hiss as the fire takes hold, watches as flecks of orange spiral and twist in the air above. When he's satisfied with the fire, Patrick lights candles, turns on a lamp and switches off the ceiling bulb. He was right. The room pulls them into its warm glow, like a cuddle. The air too is revived by the earthy smell of wood burning, which drives away the dampness. Mel feels her body relax as the heat reaches her to thaw her bones.

Patrick disappears, returning a good ten minutes later. "I've run you a bath. I even removed the spiders and the cobwebs. Not everyone gets this kind of service." He hands her a towel—it's stiff and smells clean—and points her in the direction of the bathroom.

———

Cold air bites as she undresses. Tentatively she dips her toe in the water. It's hot, almost scalding. Within seconds she has submerged her whole body. Emptying her mind of everything else, she concentrates on the heat searing through her. Just when she thinks she can't take it anymore and will have to get out, the pain abates. She always marvels at this, her body's unfailing ability to adapt and acclimatize.

She gulps in air, exhales before sucking in another breath, then sinks her face under the water. Her hair fans out around her, gently brushing her shoulders. How long can you hold your breath under water? It was a game she used to play with her brother Stephen when she was little. She always won, much to his annoyance. He never seemed to understand that the key was to empty your mind, think of nothing, remain as still as possible. You use less oxygen that way. She counts all the way to one hundred before her lungs sing for air. Lifting her face out of the water, she inhales.

She emerges ten minutes later scrubbed, renewed.

There is a glass of wine waiting for her in the living room. She sips it. It's cold for red, having been stored in the cottage, but the alcohol heats her as it trickles down. For tonight at least she will put everything else from her mind.

"We have pizza," Patrick says.

"They have takeaways around here?"

"Yeah right." He laughs. "From the freezer. You're either organized or you starve."

Mel accepts the plate from him; she is ravenous. "So, do you come here often?" she laughs, blowing on a slice of pizza to cool it. "You don't talk about it much."

He stares into the fire before his eyes flick over to Mel. "There's a lot we haven't talked about these past few years."

They sit eating and drinking in silence, watching the flames consume each new log he throws on, gradually turning it to white-hot embers. Although she was inclined to disagree at first, Patrick is right. There is a lot they haven't said. Sure, they've seen each other regularly for lunch or dinner, or when he comes to stay, but that's different, skirting the surface with niceties and small talk. Mel has turned this into an art form, talking but not saying anything of import or meaning. Has there been one occasion in the last six years when they have dived beneath the surface of their friendship? If there is, she can't think of it. Even when she lost the baby she's not even sure she thanked him properly for his help and support. Then there's this place. She casts her eyes around. He must have been coming here regularly and she had no inkling. And why has he left it exactly as it was thirty years ago, practically untouched? It's not like he doesn't have the money to do it up. The Patrick she knows, or thinks she knows, would have had it ripped out in a weekend, come in armed with mood boards (she has seen this in action), sourced tasteful pieces of mid century furniture from markets and fairs and paired them with photographs and pictures from his collection. She wouldn't be sitting on this moss-green velvet sofa. The fact that he hasn't touched the place bothers her because it reveals a side to him she didn't know existed. And she wonders what else has been going on in his life that she is not aware of.

To think how they used to sit up all night together at university with a bottle of vodka, making endless rounds of toast, talking about anything, everything. Bad sex, good sex, desired but rebuffed sex, workload, stresses, bitchy friends. Tiny, inconsequential problems they seem now, but at the time they threatened to destabilize their fragile self-esteem. Or maybe it was just hers, because thinking about it, it was she who did most of the talking. "I'm a good listener," Patrick would always say.

Can they go back there, after everything that's happened? Probably not. But they could salvage something, reestablish trust. She should have nurtured her friendships more carefully, that much is obvious to her now. Instead she's let them go to seed.

"Thanks," she says, breaking the silence, "for all this . . . You didn't have to really." For a moment she thinks she's going to cry. She coughs to disguise the emotion in her voice. "Did you know too?"

"Know what?"

"That Sam and I had been seeing each other while he was still with Honor?" She stares at him hard. *Don't dare lie.* She can't handle lies today.

"Yeah. Sorry."

"Were we that obvious?"

"Not especially."

"So how?"

"I came back one weekend and saw his car parked outside the flat."

"Why didn't you say anything?"

He smiles wryly. "What could I have said? Melody don't do it, you're making a mistake? Don't fuck your friend over, he's not worth it?"

"All right . . ." She raises her hands in the air in surrender. "All right. I hear you." The sharpness of his tone startles her. She takes a breath, goes back to unpick his words. "You didn't think he was worth it?"

"Look, as a friend I like the guy. I was never going to be the one whose life he screwed. I just credited you with a bit more . . . I dunno," he takes a hefty glug of wine, "intelligence, self-respect. I didn't think you would have gone there."

His criticism nettles her. Heat rises up her back and neck. *You wanted honesty.* She just hadn't expected it to be so brutal. Glancing up, she catches his eyes reflecting the orange flames of the fire.

"You sound like my dad," she says in an attempt to defuse the atmosphere. He doesn't play along.

"When was he there for you, Mel? I mean *really* there, I don't mean just a presence in the house? How many times did you call me because you couldn't get through to him? Did it ever occur to you what he was doing when he was absent? Yeah . . . consultants work hard, but not *that* hard. He didn't have to go to that conference and leave you when you were pregnant."

"He thought I'd be fine, I was pregnant not ill."

"And that's why he asked me to keep an eye on you, was it?"

Mel curls her knees tight, locks them in to her chest with her arms. "He told you? We hadn't told anyone . . ."

"*You* hadn't told anyone."

The room swims around her. When she turns her gaze away from the fire, light trails linger in her vision. Patrick comes into focus then slips back out again, his edges fuzzy and blurred. She can't deal with this today, can't face any more conflict. She's been sitting too close to the flames, allowing her brain to broil, and now she wants to lie down, press her hot cheeks against cold sheets and close her eyes. From experience she knows she needs to move quickly to beat the waves of nausea rising inside her. If she's not asleep within five minutes, she'll throw up.

"I need to go to bed," she says, hauling her body from the chair.

"Yours is the room at the front. And Mel . . . ?"

"Yes."

"I'm sorry . . . about the baby . . ."

She raises her hand and rakes it through the air. *What has happened has happened.* She knocks her leg on the arm of the chair on the way out. He says something, words that she catches but needs time to process. Right now she is focused on sleep, achieving it as quickly as possible.

It's like stepping into a fridge, icy, blissful. The nausea subsides. She peels the covers back—at least they had duvets in the 1980s—burrows her head into the cool pillow and screws her eyes shut against the world. As she teeters on the precipice of sleep, her mind organizes his last words into a sentence. *It was for the best.* She hears her own breath, the sharp intake of it, and tries to hold down the thought. But it crumbles away. Sleep fills her.

Twenty-seven

H is flat reminded me of some of the city's cooler eateries, with that industrial retro look they favored: a large open-plan living and kitchen area with stainless-steel finishes and bare lightbulb pendants hanging down over the table. A few oversized frames hung on the wall adding splashes of color, a carefully curated selection of sculptures and *objets* placed around the room to add interest.

"Nice," I said. There was a built-in coffee maker, semi hidden from view, "Very nice." I immediately regretted the repetition, the way it sounded so fangirly. "Weird, though, are you always this tidy?"

It was true, there was not one thing out of place. I would have liked to set my mum loose in here, challenge her to find fault. It would have been her first fail.

"You mean am I sad?" He looked at me, eyes twinkling, face arranged in mock indignation. Oh Jeez, I thought, he is really quite attractive, which was the strangest thing, because in the whole six months since Mark's departure, I hadn't even thought of myself as vaguely sexual, as someone who might fancy again and be fancied. *This is what happens when you get pissed.* I reminded myself that David had told me he was a prick, though I couldn't remember exactly why he was supposed to be a prick. I realized I was thinking all this while staring at him and quickly snapped my eyes away from his, feigning interest in an old film poster hanging on the wall next to me. The idea that he would even be interested in me was laughable. *Look at this place and then look at yourself.* My gaze fell to my trainers. God, I was still in my running gear, wearing an old T-shirt.

"Well, yes . . . I was just trying to be polite."

"The cleaner comes on a Saturday."

"You must be her favorite job." I laughed nervously, unsure of how far to push my sarcasm on someone I didn't know.

He handed me a mug. "Thanks."

He moved toward the sofa, picked up a remote and the room was filled with music. "I have a few minutes to inflict my musical taste on you."

He peered over the top of his mug, gave me the full force of his attention. "So what do you do when you're not fighting injustice, Eve?"

Fuck, I thought. The taxi better hurry up.

His phone vibrating announced its arrival ten minutes later. I was simultaneously relieved and disappointed. He stood over me waiting for me to grab my bag, then walked me through to the hallway. His hand pulled the latch open but not the door. He lingered. "Well," he said, "maybe we'll bump into each other again . . ."

I was standing by the entrance to what I assumed was his bedroom. The door was ajar so I had a clear view inside. Two small lights overhanging each side of the bed cast a cool light on the room. White wooden floorboards shone, the perfectly made bed without so much as a crease. At the side of his bed a book and something else. It took a second for my eyes to adjust and bring it into focus. An Obi-Wan Kenobi nesting doll. The words were on my lips, "I have one of those," like it was proof we were soul mates, when I remembered I didn't have it anymore. It had gone missing from my flat. The doll my dad gave me for my fourteenth birthday. Stillness settled in my head. An eerie calm. My eyes saucered wide. Then BOOM. The bomb exploded inside me. My face contorted in horror, my gaze wouldn't leave his room. I heard his sentence drift unfinished into the air between us. *Pull your eyes away from that doll. Smile. Get out. leave the flat. Now.* Lying eyes, I wished I had them. It could have been different. Everything could have been different if he hadn't looked at me and understood what I had seen burning in them.

Twenty-eight

H
e pounces on her as she swipes herself through the doors. Has he been standing there all morning?

"Morning, DS Ravindra," she says.

"I've been trying to call you on your mobile."

"I was driving."

"There's something you need to see."

He hands her a photocopy of a newspaper story from the *Sussex Times* dated October 19, 1987.

BOY, 10, FOUND NEXT TO MOTHER'S BODY.

A boy aged 10 was found cradling the body of his dead mother more than 24 hours after police believe she committed suicide. The pair were holidaying at their cottage in Climping, West Sussex, when Rosemary Crighton is believed to have taken an overdose. Police say the boy had been playing with friends and returned home to find his mother dead. The boy's father, who had been working in London, arrived the next morning to find his son asleep next to his dead wife.

Mrs. Crighton's father, Patrick Carling, described his daughter as a wonderful mother who doted on her son. "We are devastated by her loss."

"Patrick Carling, Melody's friend . . . he changed his name to his grandfather's. She left the station with him yesterday. Get a team to his address in Hammersmith." She runs through to her office, finds the address Melody wrote down for her. Dalling Road, Hammersmith. The same street as the pub Eve left on the night she disappeared.

"Alert our colleagues in Sussex. DS Cook and DC Rollings should be almost in Climping by now. Tell me we've got an address for Rosemary Crighton's old house." She glares at him. She can't let it happen again, for Eve, for Melody, for herself.

"We do, ma'am."

"Well get Cook and Rollings there immediately."

Twenty-nine

The car slowed. From my position lying in the back seat, tiny vibrations shot through me. The sound of wheels ripping through gravel filled my ears. I was awake, although not entirely; drifting between two states of consciousness. Each time I scrabbled to regain control over my brain, the effort felled me and I slipped back into my fractured reality. I was hurtling through the sky, and down where the world spread out below, everyone was going about their lives. They didn't see me falling, a black dot on the horizon. And that was the single most terrifying thing. No one knew I needed help.

Footsteps on the gravel crunched toward me. I heard the click of a door opening. A cool breeze brushed my cheeks. I felt the pressure of a hand on my arm pulling me upright. Once my body was at ninety degrees, the light of a torch beamed into my face. I closed my eyes against the brightness that sent sparks dancing on my eyelids. But also so I wouldn't see the man behind it. How long was it since I'd watched him fix us a coffee in his flat, homing in on his eyes, the sparkle of them, the angular cut of his features anchored in his strong jaw. Whatever I saw in his face now, I knew I wouldn't see this.

He had administered something—a drug, though what I couldn't be sure—to induce the drowsiness. Even if he hadn't, I think I would still have pissed myself. My first thought when he hauled me out of the car was this. Embarrassment that my trousers were soaked, that he would know I had lost control of my bodily functions. Until I remembered he was probably going to kill me, and if there was ever an excuse to let my standards slip, then staring death in the eye was one of them.

My feet touched the ground for the first time in hours. I was upright, or as close to upright as I could get, dizzied from the motion of the car and the drugs racing round my system. He dragged me forward. The torch projected a circle of white light immediately in front of us but everything else was steeped in black. Unlike the darkness that descended on London, pierced by office lights and street lamps and the glow of neon takeaway signs, this was comprehensive, complete. We were alone. That much couldn't have been clearer.

He hadn't spoken yet, which was both eerie and reassuring. I recall these moments as a transition, a kind of phoney war. From a certain angle I could almost convince myself that everything would be OK, that my world had not yet been shunted so far off its axis as to make realignment impossible.

I clung to my mum's words: *It's never too late.*

There's nothing that can't be fixed.

I knew they weren't true.

I was still dressed for a late summer's day, in shorts and a T-shirt, but we had driven into a changed season. A squally wind beat through invisible trees, branches creaked and groaned; somewhere behind us a tin can was lifted up from the ground and blown back onto the path. A dog barked, distant, echoing.

I heard the jangle of keys, we stepped up toward a door, and to my left the brush of a plant on my skin. I turned, pink flowers leaning in the wind. *Hibiscus syriacus.* I knew we were here.

My breaths came rasped and quick. My poor battered heart was beating out of its cage.

I screamed but the sound was lost in the rush of the trees and wind.

The terror. Nothing had come close.

Thirty

I n the few moments it takes her to assimilate her surroundings, she is a child again, at her grandparents' house. It's 1986. The duvet cover is thin, patterned with blue cornflowers, infused with a smell that is both roasted food and mustiness. Not altogether unpleasant, but distinct. Beyond the door the scent of frying bacon drifts down the corridor into her room.

Clues begin to undermine her initial perception. The dryness of her mouth, the acrid taste. She pulls back the covers, hot and sweating, to find she has slept in yesterday's clothes. Her legs are too long to belong to her nine-year-old self, the evidence of breasts is another giveaway. She looks again. The spare room at her grandparents' house was permanently dim, positioned at the back of the house to duck any natural light. This room is filled with it, bleached out under its rays. She forgot to close the curtains last night. And at the window, pressed against the pane, a mass of color. Large pink funnels of flower. They could be beautiful, in another life.

She knows exactly where she is.

Absurdly, her first thought is for water. She is gripped by a furious thirst that blinds her to everything else. Her bones, her throat, her body are so dry she imagines every atom of moisture has been sucked out of them overnight. She craves water. The knowledge that the bathroom is next door drags her creeping out from her room. She freezes, a foot suspended mid step as she hears voices from the kitchen. Her brain is slow to dispel the threat; the tinny sound, the familiar Irish accent: it takes a few beats for her to be satisfied it is Graham Norton's voice. Radio 2, Saturday morning. They used to listen to it together, coffee and croissants, and she'd take the piss out of him that he was old before his time. "My mum listens to this," she'd laugh. Not so funny now. She moves quickly, on tiptoes, figuring the smaller the surface area to come into contact with the floorboards the better. The old cottage is her enemy now; every creak and groan and unoiled hinge works against her.

The squeak of the tap, the water spitting out unevenly, traitors all of them. She thrusts her mouth under the tap. Gulps. When she is satisfied, she takes one hand, cups it and throws cold water into her face.

Patrick.

There is the Patrick she has known half her life and now there is the other Patrick, the one revealed to her in sounds and sights: gravel, flowers, a throwaway comment as she headed for bed last night. His inverse. Positive and negative. He deserves more than this, doesn't he? Surely eighteen years of friendship, a previously unblemished track record, would buy him a bit of slack. *Not Patrick, no, no, no!* Wasn't that the way she reacted when police told her that David Alden had attacked her? Disbelief. So why not extend the same courtesy to Patrick?

There is a reason. Among all the whys that are screaming through her head there is something else. A million tiny incidents that have punctuated their history examined from a different perspective.

"Come on, don't tell me you don't see it," Sam would say.

The conveyor belt of blonds, small and slim. "He's still trying to find you," Sam teased. "Shame that you're mine," and he'd lock his arms around her waist proprietorially.

It's not the kind of conceit you admit to. "We're friends, get over yourself," she'd tell Sam. But when they were together in a room, no matter how many others were there she'd catch Patrick watching her, his burning eyes lingering too long. There were times when he didn't look her way at all, didn't call her for weeks. Often when she assumed that his infatuation had extinguished, she would fan the flames again only to back off. It was good to feel wanted. Sam wasn't the only one who played games.

Fear balloons in her chest. It has driven the residue of last night's hangover from her mind. She is startlingly alert, more than she has been in six years. Time matters. Every microsecond counts. Edging out of the bathroom, she listens again. A song playing, happy, melodic. Saturday morning listening. Patrick's coat has been discarded, thrown over the banister. She slips down the hallway, dips her hand into the left-hand pocket, where she feels a packet of gum. In the right-hand pocket there is nothing. *Think*. She gropes around once more, her last hope. He is not stupid. He is not going to leave his phone lying around. Her only hope is to get out.

Three steps and she's at the door. Every thought that is unrelated to her escape is wiped from her mind. The moment is too huge, too terrifying to accommodate anything else. It is all she can do to propel her body forward, force herself to live it.

The air around is so stretched she doesn't dare breathe it for fear it may snap and bring all manner of horrors cascading down upon her. She tries to still her shaking hand, allow it to pull on the latch. Make no noise. Her heart soars when it opens.

Once outside, wind brushing her skin, she runs, like a cartoon character whose legs are ahead of their body. Distance, ground between them, that is what she craves. Only then can she stop. Stones scratch at her feet, bushes scour her ankles and arms. When she reaches the end of the drive, she stops for a second. Which way? Right or left? What is it to the left that lures her? The distant roar of the sea. Of course, she thinks. It had to be.

Thick trees and bushes flank the lane, form a canopy overhead. The sun projects shapes of light on the path. There is no one around and she can't call out yet, not when she's this close to the cottage. She must keep going. As long as she's moving and his footsteps aren't trailing hers, she'll be all right. Casting a look backward, she sees the cottage grow smaller.

She pauses, frozen by the familiar sound of wheels on gravel. About one hundred meters ahead, where the lane curves around the bend, a car is approaching. She starts to wave, flag it down for help. Relief surges through her only to dissipate, replaced by terror. The car edges closer to her. It is Patrick's. He is behind the wheel.

Thirty-one

W here were you going?"

Past tense, she thinks. Wherever it was, I'm not going there any more. In the split second she was deliberating which way to run, whether to run at all, he had caught her up. The car kicking up a gritty cloud of dust on the lane, Patrick's face emerging through it, waving an arm in front of him to clear the fog. "I only went to get some milk," he smiles, a look she's seen a thousand times before but no longer recognizes. He has his arm around her shoulder, pulls her in toward him. She recoils but he holds her tight. "Come on, bacon sandwiches, tea. Saturday mornings don't come better than this."

Her chest heaves from the exertion of running but her breaths are shallow, wheezing. "I'll walk," she says, attempting to keep her voice even. "I need a bit of fresh air."

He pushes her forward and with his hand on her head forces her down into the car. "Fresh air is overrated."

Pretending, it's what I'm good at, she tells herself. What she needs is to pull off the performance of her life. Right here and now, in this kitchen. At this old oak table ringed with cup marks. Where Patrick would have sat as a baby, as a boy, drinking juice. Happy families. What went wrong?

Drink the tea, eat the sandwich. Smile. Smile like you know the person sitting in front of you, because he is reading every flicker and twitch in your face. Every time your eyes dart to the door. He sees it all. Pretend, for fuck's sake.

Her eyes drift to the window. It is pocked with dirt and grime, sticky with sap from the trees. A weak light filters in but the room is cold, her breath mists in front of her.

"Not hungry?" His voice makes her start. Tea sloshes out from the mug she is holding. She shakes her head. She feels the panic press down on her, sending shoots of pain deep into her chest. Tears surge. She needs to suppress them. Once they come, she will be powerless to control them.

Her gaze falls back to him. He regards her with faint amusement, smirking when their eyes lock. He is enjoying it, this spectacle, watching her fry like an ant under his magnifying glass.

"Why?" she says. Fuck pretending. If she's going to die, she wants some answers.

He rocks back in the chair, locks his hands behind his head, yawns as he stretches out. He's going to keep her hanging for a bit longer, eke it out. Isn't that what she's been doing to him?

The silence splinters when his fist smashes down on the table like a gavel.

"Why do you always have to ruin it?"

He can recount, with alarming precision, each occasion when she has ruined it. The night in the club in Ibiza, drunk on shots, when they danced so close their bodies moulded together. They lasted until five in the morning, when they got a taxi back and she rested her head on his lap. He stroked her hair, bright blond from the sun. He thought she understood then that what they had was special and should be nurtured (if only he knew that two nights later she was swimming naked with Sam). Why, when she turned to him with a broken heart, did she not see as clearly as daylight that all she needed was right in front of her?

"I could have spared you all that shit if only you'd listened. But you're just like her."

"Her?"

"My mother. You can't even remember, can you?" He waits for an answer. "I told you all about her when we were camping that night. I hadn't told anyone before. I told you what happened. She didn't die, she committed suicide. She killed herself because my dad destroyed her with his affairs. Every time it happened she'd tell me we were leaving and then he'd win her back. Words, that's all they were, just hollow empty words. Because he'd go and do the same again. She was beautiful . . ." he pauses, his voice grows shaky, "like you."

A memory rises to the surface, faded, blurred. A photograph of a woman, blond hair, jewel-green eyes. A chain around her neck. "You showed me a picture of her that night with the chain?"

He nods. "It was the school holidays. My dad was supposed to be coming down that morning. She told me to go out and play so I went to my den in the garden. I could spend hours there, getting lost in games I'd dream up. I only came in because I was hungry. She hadn't called me for lunch so I went inside. She was in the living room lying on the floor. I thought she was asleep, so I tried to shake her but she wouldn't wake up. I just lay next to her, talking to her all afternoon, telling her what I had been doing. She looked so peaceful, so calm. Just the two of us there in the room. She was wearing the chain I had given her for her birthday. They buried her in it. I imagined there was always part of me with her.

"I told you everything and we kissed. You can remember that much, can't you? And the next morning you laughed as if it had been a joke. You laughed and said I had tried to kiss you and you didn't mention anything else."

She doesn't think this is true. Not all of it. They kissed, that much she recalls, and he told her something about his mother, but surely she would have remembered this, the manner in which she died, Patrick finding her and lying next to her body, chatting about football teams and dens as the heat faded from her? That information would have wedged itself deep in her brain, sprung up again the next morning the moment she looked at his face. She wouldn't have laughed, not even about the kiss. She would have shown more consideration.

"I don't . . ." She stops. Rage clouds his face. She shuffles in her chair, hears it scrape along the flagstones. A pulse throbs through her body.

"It happened. I remember everything. The smell of you, the birthmark above your hip. All of it. Don't tell me it didn't happen, don't try to make excuses for yourself. I'd bought you the same chain as a present. I was waiting for the right time to give it to you. But there wasn't a right time, was there?

"Tell me, was I too nice, too dependable, did you want someone who was more of a bastard?" He laughs, a throaty cackle. "Obviously that's why you started fucking Sam."

Her mind whirs. "That weekend I canceled on you. You came back and saw us in the flat, didn't you?"

"Everything." His laugh is vicious. "He was all over you." He sees her shudder. "Don't worry, you weren't naked, you were in too much of a hurry for that, evidently. Too immersed in each other to see someone watching." His eyes spark and dance. "That hurt, let me tell you, seeing the weight of him on you, the look on your face.

"Did he tell you he was going to leave her? Or did you not mind sharing him with your friend? Well?" His voice is sharp, deafening. "Or was it just about the sex?"

Words stick in her throat, choke her.

"Yeah, I thought as much."

He heard her phone buzz that Friday night in the pub. He read the message. He knew where she was going. Another clandestine meeting with Sam. For ages he'd wanted to stop her, warn her about what she was getting into, but the chance hadn't arisen. She was always out, with Sam, at work, too busy. The time they spent just the two of them was nonexistent. When he saw the text, he knew he had to do something. The plan formed in his head. He could bring her here. "You'd promised to come after all. A promise is a promise," he says smiling. "But I doubted you'd agree to it so I slipped a little something into your glass of rosé. You were so intent on getting plastered I knew you wouldn't notice it."

"You drugged me?

"Flunitrazepam is the medical term, though it's often referred to as the date rape drug. Not that I would ever have raped you." His eyes grow wide in horror. "That wasn't why I did it."

If she survives this, at least she'll know she can have more than one glass of wine before she falls over. *If she survives.*

"It's not that easy to detect in the bloodstream. By the time you were tested it would have gone." His tone is so matter-of-fact she finds herself losing her grasp on reality.

"Well that's a relief," she says, her voice thick with forced sarcasm. "That you weren't going to rape . . ." She meant to stand up to him but by the end of the sentence her words have lost their bite.

"I wanted to talk to you, that's all. Make you see what he was like and what you were doing. It took you ages to wake up, you were out for the whole night, half of the next morning. I was watching you, looking after you the whole time. You looked so peaceful, your lips so red against your skin. And then you woke up and you looked around and freaked out. I couldn't calm you down. I didn't want to hurt you. Honestly. You left me with no choice."

I ruined everything once again.

"You play dead very well; you even convinced me, a doctor, that you were dead. Mind you, I was panicking, thinking the worst anyway. I drove back to London that night. I remembered walking past the stretch of common with you in the summer, just through the gate, and I decided to leave you there."

"And Eve?"

"That was unfortunate, a sloppy mistake on my part, but once she knew it was me I had no choice. Still, it was risky doing it a second time. Lucky for me that David Alden had been released. I knew if I left Eve in the same place with the chain they'd think it was him again. It caused a delay, mind you, I had to search for an identical one first on the Internet. They stopped making them."

"You kept her here while you shopped for a chain? You are sick."

He shakes his head. "That's just a convenient, lazy argument to convince yourself you're better than me. I'm not sick, Mel, I'm perfectly sane. You hurt me; you have no idea of all the different ways you twisted the knife into me over the years. I couldn't go on any more without telling you how I felt. I didn't want to hurt you." He peers at her intently. "It. Was. A. Mistake. Understand? You freaked out and I panicked and since then all I've been doing is trying to protect myself. It's not evil that made me kill Eve, just self-preservation. You'd be surprised at what you can do when you're pushed."

He's wrong. Mel wouldn't be surprised at all. She could have killed Sam the other day, and if someone magically handed her a knife now she would drive it into Patrick's chest without a second's hesitation.

"It's actually something of a relief to tell you. I've carried it around for so long, the guilt. Because I do feel guilty. Especially when you went back to him. I kept on trying to show you it wouldn't work. When was he ever there when you needed him?"

The phone calls, the shadows in the garden, the car tailing her.

"I was always there, Mel."

She can't look at him. She feels her insides slip away, dissolving. She sinks down into the chair as if there is no substance left to her. David, Sam, all the people he has placed under suspicion. And it was him all along. Sam was a shit, arrogant and conceited, a bully, too, but next to this . . .

Still he continues. He has to stop, she has to do something to make him stop . . . "And then you went and got pregnant. That would never have worked, would it?"

The baby.

Oh God, no, no . . .

"You gave me something that night when you came to the house . . . ?"

"It doesn't always work . . . I guess you were lucky."

Rage engulfs her, a tidal wave that swallows her up. There are tears now, she is sure of it, too many to stop. Screams that aren't his so must be her own.

"Nobody can hear you," he says.

Thirty-two

N obody can hear you," he said.

I stopped screaming, stumbled inside, heard him click a switch. A naked lightbulb hanging from the ceiling flickered into life. The glow was harsh and dazzling and made my head spin. I reached one hand out to the wall to steady myself, closed my eyes against the brightness, against everything.

"You OK?" The stale coffee scent from his breath mixed with the smell of the place, wet, damp, like clothes that had been left too long to dry. The walls were the color of cream from gold-top milk, open wounds in the paintwork, bubbles that looked like spots and warts.

What do you think?

Gently he nudged me toward a door to our right. The living room, I presumed, with a huge fire taking center stage. It looked like a throwback to a different era: my mum's taste in decor circa 1988, the greens and pinks dulled and washed out under a layer of dirt and dust. My whole body shook. Cold penetrated my bones. Icy drafts scoured my bare skin. I tried to swallow but my throat constricted with fear. I coughed.

"Do you want a drink?"

I nodded.

"Sit down. I'll get some water."

His tone wasn't harsh, not in the way I would have expected, more accommodating and obliging, which disconcerted me all the more. I gazed over to the window. Nothing but blackness outside.

Helplessness and panic swelled in my head, rooting me to the chair while my mind bawled at me to move. I should be doing something, thinking my way out of this hole. Where were my will and guts and determination? Why was I sitting in a green velvet armchair waiting for a glass of water? For death? My eyes darted around searching for a way out, a poker from the fire, a heavy ornament, something that I could launch at him when he returned.

I looked up and saw his face appear through the door.

"Here." He handed me an old plastic cup, a child's one with a faded image of Winnie-the-Pooh on it. Of course he wasn't going to give me a glass. Not for me to smash it in his face. I drank greedily in noisy gulps, placing the cup at my feet when I had finished.

With my throat lubricated, the words came untangled: "Why have you brought me here?"

"Oh Eve," he said, shaking his head slowly, eyes stabbing me. "Let's cut the crap."

"I don't know . . ."

"Yes you do know. You saw it. I'm annoyed with myself. So careless really . . . one lapse of concentration and here we are." He raised his palms in the air. "I'm sorry about that, I hope you believe me. I was fond of you, right from the very first time we met. You reminded me of Mel. I mean, you look like her, you do know that, don't you? Of course you do, you've seen the photographs. The similarity is striking. I was quite taken with you, those green eyes of yours. Hers aren't so bright anymore, lost their luster, which is a shame. But you had that spark too that she used to have. Plucky . . . I think is the word they use. You are very similar. Don't look so horrified, it's meant to be a compliment."

"So what now?" I was sitting on my hands so he wouldn't see them shaking.

"You ask a lot of questions, don't you? So tell me, Nancy Drew, did you think it was me?" His eyes locked on to mine. I dropped my gaze to avoid him. "Look at me, Eve." I refused. I stared at his feet, gray New Balance trainers with a red N. They were crossing the beige carpet between us now, each step causing the floorboards to creak. I was aware of my breaths, shallow and rasping, and the deafening pulse that drummed through me. The feet had almost reached me. But still I wouldn't look up. A small, final act of defiance.

His arm stretched out. I closed my eyes, braced for a crack against my face, my head. His fingers came under my chin, gently titling my head up. "Open your eyes, Eve. Look at me."

I opened them. His face filled my vision. I watched his mouth move. "Look at me." I stared at the patchwork of lines on his lips, dry and cracked like the walls of the cottage. His jaw was covered with stubble, except for a small scar on his chin where no hair grew at all.

I watched his mouth form more words: "Did you know it was me?"

I looked up at him, pupils huge and black. "Yes," I said. "I knew it was you."

He moved in, right up to my face, so there was only a few centimeters between his eyes and mine. He didn't blink. Sucked in air. Air that was meant for two of us. He was so close there was none left for me to breathe.

"Liar," he said. Spit landed on my cheek. "I'll ask you again. Did you know it was me?"

"Yes," I said. "It's all documented. Everyone will know it's you."

He smiled. "I don't believe you." His lips were almost on mine now; the question reverberated off them, sent a charge of panic through me. I pushed him to get him out of my face but he grabbed my arms, shook me so hard I felt my head loosen from my neck. I opened my mouth to scream but there was pressure around my throat. His hands locked around my neck, pulsing and tightening, pressing deep into my arteries. I pictured the indents his thumbs would leave on my skin, which in turn made me think of plasticine and how I used to love sinking my fingers into it to leave their mark. What mark would I leave behind? I considered this too, albeit fleetingly, before I remembered. Melody still didn't know. I had come so far but I hadn't warned her. It was my last thought, pushed out the next second by a swelling in my head. Pressure rose behind my eyeballs. I had the sensation that my body was being filled with foam that expanded inside me, crushing my lungs, blocking my arteries.

Lightness flooded me.

Thirty-three

She pleads with her eyes. There is no other way to ask him to stop. His hands are pressing into her neck, "Compressing your carotid arteries," Sam would correct her. He is not here. Mel thought she never wanted to look at his face again. What she would give for it now, to have him unclasp Patrick's hands from around her, to allow her to draw in one breath and then another.

It's unlikely she'll see him again, or anyone else. She closes her eyes, tries to conjure up a congregation of all the people with whom she'd like to see before she dies. Her dad, her mother. David. She needs another minute with David because how else can she say sorry for not believing him, or herself? For destroying his life when deep down she knew, always did, that he wasn't capable of hurting her.

She feels another pulse on her neck. The pressure forces her eyes open. Patrick is too close to her, stealing her, eyeball to eyeball. Dilated black pupils swallow up the blue of his irises. He steps back so she can see his face now. No glee just sadness, twisted fucked up emotions. "There is nothing to be scared of Mel." Perhaps he will let her go after all. She believes this for no more than a second as she watches his breath wisp in the air between them. His. Not hers. She has none left. She forces her eyes closed again and stills herself before going under. She imagines her brother Stephen. They're children, still young enough to take a bath together. Mel submerges her face. Stephen's voice reaches her through the water. He starts the count. One . . . two . . . three . . .

Remember, she instructs herself, you can last longer than anyone you know.

Twenty-one . . . twenty-two . . .

Pressure rises inside her skull. Her stomach bloats, fills up with air she can't breathe.

Forty-five . . . forty-six . . .

She has gone deeper now, deeper than she has before. Stephen's voice is barely audible through the water. The temptation is to move but she knows this would be a mistake. She remains still. Her limbs are light, as if they are detaching themselves from her body.

Sixty-four . . . sixty-five . . .

There's a thudding noise. She has no idea where it is coming from. Muffled sounds. She's gone too deep to make them out.

Shafts of light pierce her vision. Her body begins to move through the water, propelled forward by a current. Her hands are outstretched. The light dazzles now as she picks up speed. Her body weightless.

She is almost there, by Eve's side.

Part Three

t is happening again. Everything Melody is experiencing is channeling through me: the paralyzing fear that crashes over you, the fading hope that help will arrive, the first squeeze of his fingers around your neck. You think: it can't, it won't end like this. You think someone will come to save you. Because that's what always happens. Except it doesn't. Not always.

Initially I thought I'd been left in this limbo as a punishment. But the truth slammed into me just as the girl had promised it would.

You just know.

And I did.

This is why I haven't left her side in days. Why I was with her in the house when Sam confronted her, and later when he locked her in. Why yesterday I watched her leave the police station and wade through a sea of commuters, the spill of her blond hair, her translucent pallor, like a ghost cut out of the lilac evening sky. She was oblivious to the moment that was passing, blind to its significance.

I wasn't. I knew exactly where she was going—the sliding-doors moment on which her life pivoted.

I was left behind for her, and for second chances.

———

By the time she reaches me, she is already traveling at speed. I feel the rush in the air, a trace of heat that doesn't belong here. A muscular current propels her onward. But I won't let her go. Not yet. This is the reason I am here. I tell her she has a choice, and only a few beats in which to make it before life slips away altogether.

I say it would be easier to allow the lightness to consume her body, to surrender to the intoxicating, dizzying pull of it. To allow him to win.

But then everything would be lost.

We share a single moment, warm in the knowledge that each of us has allowed the other to move on.

And then we say good-bye.

MELODY

She sees everything through a mist, thinks for a moment that she is dead and that this is heaven. The momentary delusion is dispelled by a voice that doesn't sound like God's, unless God happens to be male and speaks with a familiar Geordie accent. "She's opened her eyes." The words perforate the membrane of silence that has surrounded Mel's world for . . . how long? Years? A lifetime?

"Someone get a doctor, quickly." A door opens and slams, footsteps running. Voices distant, then louder, deafening. Every noise is amplified, throbs through her eardrums, echoes through her brain. She'd like to turn down the volume. She could ask, couldn't she? But her throat is raw, swollen, like someone's been feeding her splinters of glass.

Her eyes move toward the voice. Just a few degrees, that does it. It's a man's outline. His hair is combed into a small quiff. Strands of light filter into the room. The metal of his watch glints and blinds her.

"Can you hear me, Melody? It's Nat."

It takes her a moment to adjust, to place herself in her surroundings. She has the sense that she has been here before, living the same event over again. The room, the tightness in her throat, the face smiling at her from the chair, they are all so familiar.

And yet it is different too. The slow but steady trickle of memories that surface tell her exactly why she is here. There's no struggle to recollect, no dark shadows to obscure her view. There will be no need to rely on what others tell her. She knows.

"They got to you in the nick of time, Melody," the voice says. He brushes his hand against hers. She sees the beginning of a smile creep across his face. "It's going to be OK."

It is her turn to smile.